A Heart Racing Thrill
"This futuristic thriller ̶ ̶ ̶ ̶ ̶ ̶ ̶ ̶ ̶ ̶ ̶ take you on an emotional, spiritual, and political ride that you won't forget. I loved it!"

An Eerie Thought of What is to Come
"This sci-fi, futuristic Tek world is an eerie thought of what is to come. Surveillance drones hovering overhead 24/7. A.I. in our homes, our ears, everywhere we look. No more pets, how about a robo-dog?...I'm definitely looking forward to book two of this series!"

Captivating
"Austin Dragon has created a book that will not only captivate its reader from the very first sentence, it will not let go until the very last word and leave you eagerly awaiting more. Thy Kingdom Fall has all the elements to make a perfect story that includes so many aspects all over the spectrum of genres that includes thriller, science fiction, religion, politics, and so much more...Dragon's writing style will go under my classification as one of the top 10 authors I've read."

World of Tomorrow Today!
"When I read the description of this book I had to give it a read. What's not to like politics, thriller, action adventure, intrigue, and imminent war on the horizon...The author has made the technology believable as it will probably be in the future. The author has put together a very amazing world with vividly portrayed characters."

Overflowing with Intrigue
"Deft political maneuvers, abolishment of religion as we know it, and a growing dependency on technology fuse together to create a sprawling plot that completely sucked me in from page one. Political leaders are so well-written that I was able to actually see them and hear their speeches. The reference to the Three Towers was especially lifelike and chilling. The book handles religion so wildly that I'm not sure it's ever been done quite like this. It feels very current as you move through the book, even though it's futuristic...A page-turner for certain - you won't be disappointed. I will be purchasing the complete series as quickly as the author completes them."

THY KINGDOM FALL

THE AFTER EDEN SERIES: BOOK ONE

Austin Dragon

WELL-TAILORED BOOKS

This is a work of fiction. Names, characters, places, and incidents are the product of the author's imagination or are used fictitiously. Any resemblance to actual persons, living or dead, events, or locales is entirely coincidental.

Copyright © 2012 by Austin Dragon

All rights reserved.

Published by Well-Tailored Books, California

ISBN 978-0-9887235-0-4 (paperback)
ISBN 978-0-9887235-1-1 (hardcover)
ISBN 978-0-9887235-2-8 (ebook)

Boook cover design by Luna Oliveira

Printed in the United States of America

ACKNOWLEDGEMENTS

A special thank-you to my editor Stephanie Mitchell who, to use a Doylean phrase, may not be luminous but is a conductor of light, and whose one simple question elevated the book from the stratosphere into space; Luna Oliveira, my book cover designer and all around digital Jedi, because people do judge a book by its cover; and to all my beta readers through the process, especially Lawrence Phillips, Erica Diamond, and Veronica Olofsson.

Special shout out to Mom and Dad—no good son would forget such a thing.

And a final thanks to Him. Inexplicable talent in anyone—myself aside—is truly an amazing testament. What will the lightning strike of inspiration bring next?

"After Eden, Thy Kingdom Fall. All Kingdoms Fall, New Kingdoms Rise."

World War III. It was inevitably going to be one of religion, this great, grim, evil war of humans, machines, and *other things* in the shadows that have never existed before. Unfortunately, neither the cause nor the outcome was within our perception, though the former should have been. No one could ever have imagined that it would not just be the third of the world wars, as that is unremarkable, but the explosion of the first global war of the Technological Age, the Tek Age—a hell we had never seen before.

Net-Dictionary: '**Wolf 359**'

1. A red dwarf star located in the Leo constellation, approximately 7.8 light-years from Earth, making it one of the stars nearest to our solar system.

2. A fictional space battle in the Star Trek Universe between the United Federation of Planets and the Borg Collective in the year 2367.

3. The opening battle of World War III in New York City on September 11, 2125. Over sixty percent of United States of America Atlantic Oceanic Battle Fleet was destroyed by the Supreme Islamic Caliphate Battle Group on the first day.

Other terms:

Pagan: (American usage) a non-believer of god or gods; one that doesn't believe in religion, often negative to, hostile to or hateful of religion.

Jew-Christian: (American usage) a religious person, other than Muslim.

TABLE OF CONTENTS

A BRAVE TEK WORLD 1
   1: Wolf 359 3
   2: Tek World! 8
   3: The Devil I Know 15
   4: The Lords of Earth 19
   5: Preach, Baby, Preach 32
   6: The Butterfly Demonicus Effect 53
   7: Stillborn 75
   8: I Could Kiss Arafat on the Mouth 89
   9: Weird People 100
   10: The Math That Lost America 117
   11: Scare(y) Decisis 122
   12: Trog-Land 140
   13: The Man Made Out of String 158

THE PROTESTANT ORDER 193
   14: It's Always Sunny in Hell 195
   15: Faith World! 218
   16: Good Blood 244
   17: A "Free," "Safe," and "Civilized" Society 250
   18: Locking the Gates 265
   19: The Last Christians 291
   20: Resistance Rising 311
   21: Guess Who's Coming to Passover Seder Dinner 335
   22: Objects Are Closer Than They Appear 348
   23: Teeth 372
   24: The Magi 377
   25: Slow Boil 386
   26: The Continuum 400

A BRAVE TEK WORLD

(Supremacy of the Pagans)

America

Wolf 359

"A date which will live in infamy." – Franklin D. Roosevelt, 32nd President of the United States of America

America would have three dates of infamy. One of which was December 7, 1941, when the Imperial Navy of the Empire of Japan attacked the United States Naval Base at Pearl Harbor, Hawaii. Four US Navy battleships were sunk, four others damaged; eight other sea-craft were sunk or destroyed; 188 aircraft were destroyed; and 2,402 Americans were killed, with another 1,282 wounded.

Another had been 127 years earlier, in the War of 1812 against the United Kingdom of Great Britain and Ireland. On August 24, 1814, British forces invaded and occupied Washington DC, burning public buildings including the White House and the US Capitol, which were both mostly destroyed. It was the only time a foreign nation captured and occupied the nation's capital.

The third was September 11, 2001, known universally as "9/11," when nineteen Muslim terrorists hijacked four commercial airliners and crashed two into the World Trade Center's Twin Towers and one into the Pentagon. The other was headed for the White House or the US Capitol building before brave passengers seized the plane and it crashed in the fields of Pennsylvania. Over three thousand people were killed that day, and the 110-story Twin Towers collapsed and were destroyed.

**Top of the World Restaurant, The Three Towers, New York City
8:02 a.m., 11 September, 2125**

The New York City police commissioner gazes out the massive, slightly blue-tinted bow windows. He stands in the same spot as he always does at this time and day of the year. The Three Towers that Kanien built.

The breakfast meeting of senior New York brass, male and female, some in office-suits, others in dress blues, has ended. They mill around talking to one another, drinking their beverages, eating more food, and checking their mobile devices for messages.

President Cree Kanien had all the right credentials: longtime party activist and loyalist; the right "religion": Pagan, with the requisite number of public anti-religious comments over his career; the right universities: Harvard and Yale; the right family: partner (hetero), two sons (unverified), two dogs and a cat; mayor of Buffalo; governor of New York; vice president and then president. There was nothing in his background that suggested he would go Jew-Christian crazy one day while in office, but it was a unique craziness. He said he awoke one day and heard a voice which told him that he had to build it "so they will come and your army can destroy them." Days later, he directed federal troops to seize the site of the One World Trade Center and its surrounding areas and by executive order commissioned its total demolishment and the subsequent construction of the new Three Towers.

He would be only the third American president impeached by the US House of Representatives in America's 349-year history. But unlike Andrew Johnson in 1868 and William Clinton in 1999, who were acquitted by the US Senate, he was convicted. Everyone still wrongly says Richard Nixon was impeached over Watergate (most people have no clue as to what Watergate was). Nixon was the only other president who *would* have been impeached and convicted, but he resigned the office in 1974—the only American president ever to do so.

President Kanien had the sole distinction of being the only American president to be impeached, convicted, and removed from office by the legislative branch, for gross abuse of power over the Three Towers. But the ex-president was a marketing genius. The nation's power elite hated the buildings, but Kanien made the people of New York love them. And when New Yorkers call something theirs, whether a person, place or thing, heaven help the person who messes with it. No one, not even another president, would be removing the Three Towers to rebuild the Old World Trade Center—*One World Trade Center? What's that?*

At the opening ceremony for the building, Kanien stood shoulder-to-shoulder with his invited attendees as he gave his remarks. These *special guests* were descendants of the victims of the original 9/11 event. Kanien had some thirty-thousand present. He revealed in his speech that he too was a descendant of a victim—though Homeland Security personal background files still refute his claim to this day. It was reported that Kanien's list of the "Children of the Three Towers," as he had named his special guests, had over a million names; after all, nearly sixty countries aside from America lost people in the attack, Old Britain, the Dominican Republic, and Japan being the countries with the next-highest losses in human lives. No one would touch these buildings; they were the new international symbol of 22nd-century New York.

All a moot point now; the Three Towers have been standing for fifty-three years.

"Maybe Kanien wasn't so crazy after all," he whispers to himself as he stares off into the sky. From his vantage point inside the restaurant, 170 stories up, he can see almost eye-level into the clouds, the very curvature of the planet, and at night it seems to him as if one could literally step out into space itself. The view of the Atlantic Ocean is breathtaking; seeming so close that he could stretch out his arm and touch its blue surface.

He smiles. To think that the man-made-global-warming "Flat-Earthers" over a century ago said that massive flood barriers would need to be built all along the East Coast, including New York, because of flooding from melting polar ice caps and rising global sea levels. Now the experts are back to "we're heading for the next Ice Age" again.

As far as New Yorkers and most Americans are concerned, the Three Towers are the tallest buildings in the world. The actual distinction goes to towers within Caliphate and CHIN countries, but they only built taller buildings to spite America.

The opinion of the American security and intelligence community, however, is that the buildings are a security nightmare. More money is expended to protect these three buildings than even the White House, and every year on this date, New York Homeland personnel wake up in a cold sweat wondering if this is the year the Muslims will "try for it"—some attack reminiscent of 9/11. Or maybe even the CHINs.

The police commissioner's predecessor had actually resigned his post because he couldn't handle the stress anymore. The commissioner has already had one stomach transplant, from one of the best body farms, because he developed chronic ulcers. He pops a pill in his mouth—his daily medicine for life to ensure he doesn't develop any problems with his new stomach.

Nine-Eleven Holiday ceremonies will take up most of his day, and despite the elevated threat level, everyone will pretend to have a good time.

"Commissioner, Kanien's limo caravan is here. Fifth Avenue." The voice of his chief of staff sounds in both his ears through his flesh-colored ear-set device.

He touches the reply button on his wrist-band. "Keep him back until I get there."

"Yes, Commissioner." The line disconnects.

This is truly intolerable. Kanien is an ex-president of the United States of America who still draws a federal retirement stipend and has a Secret Service detail, but has been designated as a potential terrorist by the current president. Technically, Kanien should not even be allowed to enter New York City Metro, but everyone from the local beat cop to the New York Homeland Defense and Intelligence Agency regional director ignores the terrorist threat directive on him. Kanien is an insane old man, not a terrorist, and, more significantly, he's one of the biggest private donors to the New York sports culture community—the Yankees, the Giants, the Nicks. What one sports writer called the "real three towers" in New York. It's the kind of charity that buys *a lot* of good will, loyalty, and friends in this town.

The commissioner shakes his head. Most likely he'll have to fly to the Capitol *again* to talk about it. But then, the president is an old man too. If this were even twenty years ago, no one, himself included, would ever have *ignored* a presidential directive. However, the president strangely isn't pushing the issue at all. It's as if he is allowing Kanien to be protected for some reason. Everyone expects the president to be gone after the next election; his life-long reason for political existence and the focus of political hatred—the Jew-Christians—are gone. Nothing in the world has been the same.

"Commissioner! The east side!" The voice yells so loud in his ears that the commissioner leaps straight up in the air. He bolts from his spot and runs to the east-side observation-window-wall of the restaurant, pushing tables, chairs, and people out of his way. The room is in a panic as police officers follow him.

For an American elite society that so hates religion, it is curious how many of the words and phrases are just that—religious. He is at the east side: "My God!"

This is not possible! Nothing can breach our Atlantic Seaboard Defense!

Over the Atlantic Ocean, they can see them in the distance. *The sky is filled with approaching sky-ships, an air armada of what seem to be ancient 767s.*

People yell out in shock, run for the elevators, or faint and fall to the floor. The commissioner grabs his chest at his heart as his face contorts from a sharp pain.

Thirty-seven years earlier…

Tek World!

"Behold this Brave Tek World of the new quasi-cyber-human lording over the new tek metropolises of New Earth. Eden, Babylon, Paradise are all one; created in our own image of perfection, in our own likeness of excitement. I must extend beyond even my own atheistic DNA, for the appropriate word does not exist in our Pagan vocabulary, so we must commandeer their word constructs—we are Gods!" – author Ahn Droid, *We Are Borg: On the Evolution of Species by Means of Technological Transcendent Assimilation, or the Elevation of the Favored Race in the Pleasurable Pursuit of Life*, 2070

"The first requisite for the happiness of the people is the abolition of religion." – Karl Marx, Old Germany revolutionary socialist and author of *The Communist Manifesto*, 1848

Shopping District, Baltimore, Maryland
7:05 p.m., 25 December 2088

Busy times, busy days and the New Year rock-and-rolls in next week.

Some say there's nothing like winter on the East Coast, with the slight chill in the air and the increasing frequency of evil-wicked parties (celebrations for the more timid, orgies for the more adventurous) as the year nears its end. In the typical tek-city, none of the uncomfortable qualities of a season can ever fully impact the population: harsh cold, burning heat, and high winds are all kept at bay. Only heavy rains are allowed to invade, but that is more for urban-management reasons: let's give the city a quick shower.

Logan wanders down the city streets to finish his shopping list. He is forty, average height and build, nicely groomed straight black hair, clean-shaven, a fair complexion. He wears a paper-thin black overcoat over an untucked white shirt and charcoal blue skin-jeans. His glow-boots radiate a steady white light for no purpose at all other than fashion.

Winter Solstice is that last explosion of unrestrained consumerism before the year ends, and the streets do seem to be packed with literally everyone in the city. He stands at a corner for a moment staring at his e-pad. The device is auto-synced for commercial roaming, so at every store he walks to, the four-inch-by-six-inch screen shows the items on sale, pictures of salespeople, and mini-commercial vids of products. He steps a bit closer to the wall of the store to avoid the crowds.

The ever-flashing, ever-changing digital billboards on top of every commercial building lining either side of the street catch his attention next. Music, movies, clothes, the latest devices, latest cars, restaurants, vacation trips, virtual reality dens, drug parlors, massage services; the advertisements are everywhere. These advids are either rapid stop-motion live-def static photos or full-fledged vids. The colors are as bold and vibrant as the sounds are loud and frenetic. Both rapidly pulsate to create an atmosphere that completely engulfs the sight and hearing of anyone within range.

Above the buildings, he barely notices a drone fly by. It's a globe surveillance model, a twenty-inch-diameter flying sphere in a muted silver color. Law enforcement use the drones to keep an ever-watchful vigil on the tek-city. In the past, these sophisticated flying vid-cams were twice their current size and more plane-shaped, with short wings, but hover-tek has advanced so much, they can zip around more than a hundred feet in the air. People see them flying or hovering about so often that they forget about them, making the drones invisible in plain sight. With drones and Eyes—the common term for the government's ever-watching, ever-recording stationary vid-surveillance camera network—literally everywhere, government monitors the tek-cities to instantly alert ground police of any disturbance, crime, or act of terrorism.

He walks under the low hum of an environmental systems unit. The massive air-regulator machines are constructed right into almost every building and are centrally coordinated to either heat or cool the entire tek-city using advanced air-flow dynamics. The air has a nice, warm feeling. One would never know that outside the tek-city it's freezing at twenty degrees Fahrenheit. Solar and wind power still account for only a fraction of urban power consumption, as the Grid sucks unimaginable amounts of energy by the nano-second. Primary energy is all fission, since nothing else can match the insatiable public demand.

He walks a few steps up the sidewalk and stops again to engage in his favorite pastime: people watching. The streets are packed and brimming with life, energy, and excitement. There is nothing like the hustle and bustle of a tek-city, both the automation and the people. The obsolete adjective is *technological* and the obsolete noun is *technology*, but no one under the age of eighty uses those words anymore—the word is tek. It isn't just slang that, after a few decades of common use, has replaced its original reference; it's an attitude.

For tek-city dwellers, the styles of dress are endless. On one end of the scale, there are the traditional business types in their office-suits, shirts, maybe vests, maybe ties, maybe not, in a variety of colors from simple blacks and whites to earth tones to natural rainbow colors to synthetic, techno colors, or even the so-called futuristic shiny silver everything; then the traditional faux-leather, plastic, cloth, or hemp dress shoes or the trendy glow-boots or -shoes. On the other end of the spectrum would be the nudist or quasi-nudist, but there aren't many in major tek-cities anymore; they stay mostly in the outer tek-cites and Trog-land. From time to time, you see one of them, totally nude or wearing a single piece of clothing. There is even a hard-core group called Streakers who run around naked, yelling at everyone wherever they go, wearing only five-toe slip-on sandals.

In between, you had casuals like Logan. The style is never an office-suit of any kind but skin-jeans, skinny jeans, straight-cut jeans, bell-bottom jeans or bucket jeans; any solid color or a variety of colored stripes. Casual shirts, tee shirts, sleeve-less tops, half-tops; any color, any pattern, with words or symbols or not; also, a wide variety of glow clothes. And hats galore: from simple to outrageous. If it were sunny, there would be people with day umbrellas.

Devices are carried by everyone: e-pads, each around the size of a large playing card; or the larger tablets, usually eight-by-eleven inches with a handle or case. There are collapsible e-pads and tablets, and even wearable tek, the merging of device and clothing.

Despite the loud advids from the digital billboards, almost everyone in the streets is actively engaged in conversations on their devices of choice through ear-sets, a combination of phone, head-set and ear bud, worn in one ear or both ears or attached to a pair of glasses so one can answer an incoming call, make a call, or voice interface—all these people talking aloud just adds to the daily urban craziness.

Logan laughs at the sight of a man with a phone-only. Only in Africa, the Spanish Americas or very rural parts of the Asian Consortium do you see people with them, devices one can only use to talk to a person and nothing else. They're tek from so far in the past that they don't even deserve to be classified as tek.

Most of the people wear clear glasses, glowing with some type of light. No one has bad eyesight in this time; those who need corrective eye surgery receive it during the neo-natal or natal stage. People wear clear glasses to attach their ear-sets, to avoid the in-ear versions or to use a visual optical interface—text floating at the sides of your field of view: the current time, the name of a caller, the number of voice messages or emails, a dot indicating breaking news stories, etcetera—it can be programmed to display anything.

Most clothes are chosen for their unisex appeal, but then most women, and maybe ten percent of men, dress feminine all the time: lipstick, nail polish, eye shadow, eye liner; any color at all, though shades of red remain the most popular; and some kind of high-heeled shoe. There really isn't any dress that is considered masculine except for the traditional tuxedo; clothes are classified as unisex or female.

Then there are pets, animal or mechanical. What little creatures do they take everywhere with them? Dogs, cats, ferrets, lizards, birds—those are the most common and legal ones. Logan has seen people with snakes, monkeys, and once a twelve-foot mantis. Mechanical animals were far more popular in the past.

One does see an occasional humanoid, personal robot. The biggest hype with no pay-off ever in history was the launch of personal robots. They looked impressive but couldn't do a damn thing—talking and walking are not the hallmarks of impressiveness. It is another example of the negative consequences of two hundred years of science fiction movies without the science fact being able to deliver to a picky, hedonistic consumer population. They were good for some things: jogging or work-out partners, toys for kids or the mentally retarded, and in Japan they were even the star celebrities of *Domu! (kaminari no domu)*, their televised, robots-only mixed martial arts competitions. Or is the problem that the public is simply subconsciously afraid of the robots-going-berserk-and-killing-people scenario?

Logan notices maybe a few dozen people wearing masks over their noses and mouths, a common sight in the Asian Consortium countries and CHIN territories, but one that has never caught on in America. They are most likely tourists from those areas and not used to the residual drugs in the air. But you have to be careful, because obscuring your face too much in any way is illegal. Eyes must be able to see your face at all times, otherwise authorities are alerted and you could be arrested. However, facial-recog tek is so sophisticated nowadays it can actually see through any soft mask. Even the Muslims are smart enough not to have their women in any kind of full body cloak or face veils. They only allow their married women to walk in public, always with a male; unmarried women almost never leave the house or community.

People on motorized bicycles, skates, or segways zoom by every so often as Logan notices two patrol cops walk up the street casually. "Bobbies," as his British employer would say, but called storm troopers by the general public. They are dressed in black armored uniforms, silver helmets, dark eye shades, and clear face guards over the bottom halves of their faces. He always likes to see them walking the beat. Most likely they were alerted by a drone or Eyes to check out something or someone.

He feels his ear-set vibrate in his ear and touches the ear lobe button.

"What are you doing?" the voice says.

"Well, hello to you too, Edison," Logan says.

"You're not on some bloody walk-about wasting your hard-earned money on things you don't need again, are you?"

Logan smiles to himself. "I believe it's called being an American."

"Well, I can't relate to that."

On the line is his primary employer of sorts, Edison Blair. Originally from pre-Islamic England, he fled to America over twenty years ago with millions of his fellow Western Europeans when the Muslim majority seized control of the region to form the Supreme Islamic Caliphate. He is officially an American citizen now, but still refers to himself as British or English and is always put off by being called an American, even after two decades. It seems to be a common quirk of all the "refugees," as Logan calls these former Western Europeans.

They can joke about it now, and the former-British are the best at humor of all kinds, especially the self-deprecating kind. But there was nothing funny about the fall of secular Western Europe to the Muslims. Though he never speaks of it and has created a wildly successful life here in America, Edison lost everything there, including close friends and family—people on a very long list of those killed or missing. While "native" Americans have an almost genetic loathing of anything religious, including the new religions like Vampirism, Warlockism, Vulcanism, and Jedi-ism, these solidly Pagan new-Americans' hatred is off the charts when it comes to Islam.

"Well, you *colonists* didn't think we'd forget, did you? This is our chance to re-conquer our rightful subjects and steal America back, especially now that your General George Washington isn't around anymore."

"Why are you calling?" Logan amusingly asks.

"I have a job for you."

"I'm not taking any jobs now, Edison. December is my Solstice shopping time."

"You're a freelancer, so there's no vacation for you."

"Didn't you refugees used to have two-month, three-month, six-month vacations?"

"In Rome, you do as the Romans. No vacations is the American way."

"Edison, call one of your other free-lancers. I'm serious. I gave you three hot stories just a few weeks ago."

"And my bank account made passionate love to your bank account and created an offspring of lots of cash."

Logan laughs and says, "Edison, try me next week."

"Okay. Go waste your money. We'll talk next week. I'll be looking for a great 2089 story. Something to curl people's toes."

Logan laughs again and says, "Good-bye Edison. You have my permission to go play with some beautiful people."

He touches his ear-set again and disconnects the line—time to finish shopping. A digi-sign flashes in multi-colors: Next Year Will a Be Great Year!

Tek World is simply wonderful.

The Devil I Know

"To see and listen to the wicked is already the beginning of wickedness." – Confucius, Chinese philosopher, teacher, and politician, 551-479 BCE

Washington DC
5:30 a.m., 1 January, 2089

The streets of the nation's Capitol are covered in a slush of multi-colored confetti, streamers, balloons, and balloonettes. The coming of the New Year is always a party of parties. New Las Vegas, Miami, Dallas, Neo-Orleans (pronounced Nee-Orleans), San Francisco all claim to be the best party tek-cities in America, but none of them are home to the nation's power elite—elected officials, appointed leaders, policy makers and advisors, and big donors.

The annual New Year's celebrations did not disappoint. The strict street curfews are lifted so that people can celebrate, dance, drink, smoke, drug, and engage in every other vice right outside the gates of the Capitol building, the District monuments and even the White House well into the witching hour, the time after midnight and before sunrise. But then it stops: curfews reinstated, crowd level and noise restrictions reinstated, proximity and speech rules reinstated; everyone goes home.

Mechanized sanitation-bots sweep, spray, and vacuum the streets, and within an hour it will be as if there had never been a million-person street party in one of the most powerful tek-cities in the world.

The line rings. "Meet us in the Garden at five under the tree like before. Bring the stuff. No tricks or your boss crashes and burns today," the voice says. The line disconnects.

Washington DC Metro Park
5 a.m., 1 January, 2089

What a duplicitous snake of a man, an audacity of superiority, a conceit of invincibility.

Lucifer Mestopheles steps into the street lamp's warm light with a wide smile on his weathered face. Many would say he is a strange little man—sixty plus in age, barely over five feet, dark complexioned, his leathery face covered in pockmarks, black hair, and dark penetrating eyes. But strange is all relative these days. His office-suit is black leather, sharp and immaculate, and his red leather fedora that he always wears when outside his own Capitol Hill offices fits firmly on his bald head. He strolls along the path in his trademark silver-pointed, yellow-brown snake-skin shoes.

He is DC royalty. His parents are among the most respectable and influential of the power elite, major donors and social movers in the District for six decades and through twelve different presidential administrations. They were born at the turn of the last century and in their youth were the average Hedonist, Nihilist, neo-Anarchist type, later neo-Satanists, and very much part of the anti-religious fervor that gained steam in the '30s. They chose their son's name deliberately as a poke in the face of Jew-Christians—they meant Mephistopheles, but they felt that was too many syllables for a last name. That was all before they grew up, put on office-suits, got jobs, and started making lots of money in their chosen vocation of politics.

They are so proud of their only son, Lucifer, who has risen to become the most powerful king-maker in politics, even greater than them. Friends and enemies alike in the District's power circles simply call him Lou. Half the elected officials in this town have, at some point in their careers, owed their political existence and success to him.

Lou looks around at the pre-dawn emptiness of the place—

Washington DC Metropolitan Park, commonly called the Garden. He loves everything about gardens—the green, the plants, the flowers, the smells—all except for those flying rats—pigeons! He watches them strut around in disgust, as he waits.

Moments later he quiets his cackling. "The dumbest creations on the planet," he says, but not looking at the pigeons. "All dumb things should be eradicated." He stares at the two of them, grinning.

"The stuff," the male says impatiently. "Or we walk and dump your data worldwide." Lou's audience of two seems unable to stand still for even a second. They wear almost identical white-silver, hooded jackets which practically obscure their faces, and matching pants. Their white shoes, unlike the rest of their clothing, are anything but crisp and clean—blackened, scuffed, and muddied.

Lou smiles. "When I allowed you to hack my device I was actually engaging in an act of murder. That's what I did. Knowledge, at its essence, is such a transformative thing. You were reborn by my knowledge. I re-birthed you in my image, just like a mythical god. And you were stupid, willing accomplices. You thought you were the hunters, clever blackmailers with the mark of a lifetime in your palm. But you were the dupes, the clueless pawns, acting according to my plan. I will always be the creator and destroyer of empires. You are nothing but dust under my feet.

"I alone rule this town. And if you rule here, you rule the world. Even the president is my creation. Did you really think you could threaten me? With all the power I have. With all the people I command. I am a supreme being," he says.

Everyone knows Lou as a real talker, famous for his grandiose and overblown language. He loves the sound of his own voice. But that's fine because in politics it isn't policy or goodness that makes one powerful; it's the stagecraft surrounding the spoken word that is the true power—and, of course, access to disgusting amounts of digital cash.

"You still don't grasp what I'm telling you. You didn't discover the plan. I allowed you to discover it. I revealed this scandal-to-be, to bring down a president, to you. You can't blackmail me to not tell it, because my intention from the beginning was for you to tell it. Off with you, you flying rats. Go tell the world."

"Why?" the male asks. "Why do this?"

With vengeful satisfaction, Lou says, "Because everyone must know that no matter how high you rise, however powerful you may become, I can still utterly destroy you."

"He thought so," the female says. "The message is this: Lou, thanks for the wild ride. I can tolerate anything from my friends, *except* interference in my timetable. I will not tolerate anyone interfering with my plans. Not even once. The closer the friend, the more final my retaliation."

Lou stares at them in astonishment, now realizing everything, realizing who sent them. His fairytale life is over.

It is more than an hour later when the tour guide leads the crowd through the Garden. He is a thin man with silver hair, wearing red, white, and blue clothes. The tourists follow him as he speaks in a baritone voice describing the history of the site.

"My dear visitors, you must now consider yourselves to be members of the initiated. You must never refer to this grand tek-city as Washington DC or even simply DC. That is the language of the unsophisticated. There are forty thousand cities in America, but there is only one District."

Not far away, the violently bloody, lifeless body of Lucifer Mestopheles lies under a tree, his leather fedora beside his bald head. His mouth contorted in rage. His open eyes stare off into space. A group of pigeons flies down to the ground and walk, strutting and head-bobbing, to the body. A fly lands precisely on one open eye. Yummy.

Someone screams. Body found.

The Lords of Earth

"On January 24th, Apple computers will introduce Macintosh. And you'll see why 1984 won't be like 1984." – Old Hollywood film director Sir Ridley Scott's classic "1984" Apple Macintosh commercial, first aired 15 Dec. 1983, Top Ten Commercials of All Time, 2050 edition

"Well, it all did lead to 1984." – Goli, the tek-lord

Washington DC Metro Expressway, Washington DC
10:35 a.m., 2 January 2089

Logan watches two globe-drones fly by just above the tree line. North 4, North 695 expressways. Arlington, Virginia, here I come.

He sits in his car reading the news on his tablet and sipping his coffee from a long, thin silver mug. He glances out at the large digital billboards with the advids of the day: vacation getaways, movie and television premieres, new cars, new devices, alcoholic drinks, drugs, escorts. A political ad for Mount Vernon: some local ex-pat Brit is kicking off his candidacy. They say the Brits have taken over the whole town. Guess they really do mean to "reacquire" their original thirteen colonies.

The ubiquitous Gyrating Elvis commercial. The man's been dead for so long, but here he is on a digital screen doing his wiggle-dance in a silver jumpsuit selling some male sexual enhancement product. Logan laughs. Old Hollywood stars are in a lot of commercials these days and probably violently turning over in their graves, if you believe in that kind of thing. But actors and politicians of today are not having it, which seems odd on reflection, since Pagans don't believe in an afterlife, so what difference would it make? But a whole new niche law has emerged called immortal likeness protection—no image or likeness of said dead person can be used in any visual, audio, or sensory medium, ever, for the duration of the existence of humankind. These contracts have all been legally upheld in the courts.

A fast-track whizzes by on the elevated mono-rail above the expressway in the same direction, a twenty-car bullet train painted in a camouflage design of greens, browns, and off-whites. He likes a good scenic train ride from time to time, but from where he lives in Calvert County, a personal car is the best option, especially in his profession.

The traffic is light for this time of day, not all that bad for a tek-city where it's always rush-hour, but even the District is allowing more tele-working, like the rest of civilized society. However, there is something about physically being in the center of the action rather than working at home. Pagans truly worship this town.

His car is the last in the queue, ten cars almost bumper to bumper in auto-drive mode speeding down the expressway at nearly ninety-five miles an hour. Ahead, another ten-car set, behind yet another, in all lanes the same. The very new tek-cities like Neo-Orleans and New Vegas have expressways of public car pods—personal vehicles not needed and not allowed—that go even faster. However, for older and larger cities it simply isn't practical, as municipalities would have to literally demolish their entire city, interstate highways, and local freeways and then re-build an entire metropolis from scratch—logistically and economically impossible, even with federal dollars. Auto-drive has been the savior. Retro-fitted tek expressways on one hand, newly designed smart-cars on the other. This driverless car tek was a revolution: a network of vid-cams, collision-avoidance laser-sonar, and GPS sat-link allow the tek-city's transportation Grid to manage its entire traffic flow by computer alone. The end of car-driving stress and vehicular fatalities forever as human control no longer exists for most of the general population. There are those hard-core few that insist on being able to manually drive their cars, but most tek-cities, including the District, do not allow manual control of cars at all. It seems insane that there are still a few holdouts against tek progress; after all, it was the manual control of cars that led to some hundred deaths per day at its peak in the stone ages, as the modern past is called. Probably hasn't been a car death in America in over a decade, and accidents with no deaths are so few as to be a statistical nothing in a nation of six hundred million people.

It doesn't take long to get to Edison's place after reaching the 395 expressway. Engaging in his favorite pastime again, Logan relaxes in his car. *How many people can I commit to memory this time?*

Residential Offices of MW2B, Arlington, Virginia
10:50 a.m.

Edison lives in the most upscale part of Arlington, and his three-story mansion is the center of his media empire. The brick-and-mortar mega news organizations, both print and broadcast, went the way of the dinosaurs when net streaming and digital broadcasting, televisions, and computer screens became one and the same at the beginning of the century. News gathering is all solo, cell-based or freelance. Tek advancements weren't the only reason for the extinction of the major newspaper chains like the *New York Times* and *Washington Post* or news media corporations like ABC, NBC, CBS, CNN, and FOX, with newsrooms of bulky cameras and unwieldy equipment and highly compensated union workers were replaced by faster and cheaper devices a child could purchase loaded with tek to make even an idiot novice appear to be an award-winning broadcaster. The transformation or demise (depending on your point of view) coincided with the rise of the blogosphere and the lone gunmen of guerilla journalism. These one-person shops, bloggers and citizen reporters, often broke the major stories of the day before the majors rolled out of bed.

The other common news model is cell-based: small groups of

bloggers and citizen journalists, often working out of someone's home office, or connected via the Net to create a virtual office so the cell could have members spread across a city, a country, or the globe.

Edison started out as a solo operation and then, with success, attracted other hungry, talented journalists to create his own media cell operation. The stories were always centered on the happenings of the District or global politics and were always exciting, unique, and had a solid buzz-life—*everyone* talked about them for months.

That's how he attracted Logan to add to his crew.

His business has now evolved into the freelance model, with a stable of bloggers, citizen journalists, on-the-street investigators, and a vast network of confidential informants in all levels of the government. It is a powerhouse that has made his site, the Source, the first-look Net magazine for hundreds of millions of people around the world, especially in the District.

Arlington falls under historic architectural preservation zoning laws requiring that the exteriors of the buildings retain their original look going back centuries. Edison's mansion is a bright white, three-story structure that looks the same as it did in the 1800s, impressive two-story double columns on each side of the main front entrance ending in a pointed arch, extremely large rectangular windows on all three levels, and a dark red brick roof. In a tek-city obsessed with newness, it is actually refreshing to see authentic ancient buildings in the style of when the nation was founded.

However, inside is quite another matter. Tek-retrofitting is a must for the modern tek-dweller. Logan's bios—his unique biometric identity—are programmed into the smart-house, so the outside gates open automatically when he walks up the driveway. The front door opens as he walks up the steps, and the door bell auto-rings. There is no such thing as keys in a tek-city. Doors and barriers are programmed to let in only the people authorized or, if needed, everyone or no one. Inside, every wall is a holo-wall with three-dimensional panoramic scenes flipping from lush, green fields to sandy beaches with churning oceans to nostalgic street scenes of Old British landmarks which sadly no longer exist.

But one part of the wall has three large full-body static photos—"the Lords of Earth." The world is ruled by three Lords of Earth, the cutesy phrase coined by a reporter some years ago. President of the United States Torrey E.C. Wilson, the center photo, has been in the White House for nine years now, known by the public as President T. Wilson since he is the second president of America to have the last name. The Emperor Al-Siddiq has ruled the Supreme Islamic Caliphate for about the same length of time; during his reign, has expanded their territorial conquests with the Fall of Jewish Israel and into Africa with the Islamic-Christian War. Now everyone knows about his recent destruction of Palestine Israel, the main Muslim antagonists within the Islamic empire. His late father led the Fall of Western Europe—all of Western Europe falling to radical Islam decades ago, with millions of people fleeing, those fortunate enough to escape. President Wen rules the other Pagan-majority empire, the Chinese-Indian Alliance or CHIN. The previous reign of his father, which forced the union with India to create the Alliance, saw the decline of the Russian Bloc and the cessation of Caliphate incursions into CHIN territories.

With three remaining superpowers on the planet, it's so easy to forget the dangerous geo-politics that America faces at all times dealing with threats and crises from behind closed doors and secure situation rooms. But tek-city dwellers are just too busy with their gadgets, celebrities, and recreational activities to care—enter the Source, one of the most read netzines in the world.

While the eye is captivated by the changing scenes of the holo-walls, the rest of the first floor is very sparsely furnished. Edison hates clutter, and he keeps only the bare minimum of furniture to preserve as much as open space as possible.

Logan follows the yellow arrows flashing on the floor. His eyes move from the trance of the holo-walls to the arrows to a circular work area of desks with multiple standing flat-screens and chairs. There sits an Amazon woman tapping away on her desk keyboard at lightning speeds. Edison doesn't believe in voice-tap—the voice-interface that allows the computer to type what you speak. As Edison often says: "It drives me batty. I'm not interested in your damn bloody life. I'm not interested in hearing your damn bloody business. Ssshh!"

She looks up and smiles. "Hey Logan."

"Hey Bouncin' Bodacious Bunny."

BB Bunny is Edison's slave. The word has no negative connotations at all anymore. Only Jew-Christians still despise the word, but in Tek World it's slang for a personal assistant, gal or guy Friday. She's six feet tall, long blond hair braided into a ponytail running in front of her body down her side to her waist, long lashes, shiny lipstick, always wearing some short-sleeve, one-piece, brightly colored dress. The Amazon woman is, as her name implies, very bouncy and readily volunteers the fact that she is surgically enhanced from head to toe. Her left forearm is also covered with a Sleeve, a snuggly wrapped, wearable e-pad.

"What's the latest in Logan Land?" She always walks barefoot inside, but he sees her six-inch heels next to her desk.

"Ask me after I talk to your master."

"So when are you available?"

"For what?"

"Don't play oblivious. You know I'm on the circuit."

She means that she's free for frequent sexual encounters, a common pastime. Bunny has asked him many times before, but not only is he so over that scene; he has a rule not to get involved in a physical relationship of any kind with people he works with.

"You don't need me, then."

"You did hear me? I'm on the circuit."

"You're always on the circuit."

"Exactly, so jump aboard. It's better to be first than fiftieth."

"That sounds *appealing*. Almost as appealing as when I went to this parasite-infested, virus-ridden jungle in Asian Consortium territory for a story and we had to take all kinds of biotics. One of them had a label that read 'May cause rectal leaking.'"

Logan turns and walks past her area as she shoots him a dirty look. He yells out, "Edison, the Americans are coming, the Americans are coming. Where are you?"

Edison's office is near the back of the first floor. He walks down the very long hallway and the mahogany door opens. The holo-walls in this room do not auto-rotate. All the images are of Old Britain: Buckingham Palace, the Palace of Westminster, the Tower of London, Big Ben, Windsor Castle, Blackpool Tower, the London Eye, Number 10 Downing Street. Other than Buckingham Palace, the official residence of the Islamic governor of Greater Britain, all are now gone.

In the center of the room, Edison sits in his work area, a model of typical minimalist interior design—circular desk with several standing vertical flat-screens. He is a tall, thin man with wavy white hair and blue eyes in his late fifties. He only wears tight-fitting white shirts and dark-colored, somewhat baggy pants held up by suspenders, and inside, he typically wears his five-toed slip-ons. He is wearing clear glasses showing him virtual imagery, invisible to anyone else, most likely newsfeeds from all over the globe. If something happens, Edison will know about it in real time.

"So there you are," Edison says. "I'm glad to see you've decided to rejoin MW2B. We only have two of the biggest stories of the decade happening, and you're lollygagging about." He looks at one of his screens. "Oh, here's something for us to digress on for a moment. I was looking at turn-of-the-century prep stories they're working on as if the eleven years can't go by fast enough. Ten things we had at the turn of the last century in 2000 that we won't have when we get to 2100: one, dentists."

"What's a dentist? I know dental transplants."

"Well, if you can believe it, people went to these dentists because of tooth decay, they called it cavities. People spent all kinds of obscene money to replace the decayed parts of their tooth or pull the whole bloody thing out and put in a false one. Now we got enamel bonding and re-bonding. No more bad teeth ever. See how far we've evolved. Number two: physical music discs. This is before digitality. Instead of downloading music and movies and vids, they stored them on and played them from these silver discs. Number three is one you should appreciate. When I called you last week, you were actually celebrating this ancient holiday by shopping. You were doing what was called in the past, *Christmas*."

"Oh, December 25th. Wasn't that religious?"

"Yep, a Jew-Christian religious day dedicated to one of their gods, and consumerism was to celebrate his birth." He reads further. "Here's an especially dumb one—daylight savings time," he laughs. "People would actually change all the clocks in their houses and cars *manually*. Clocks weren't auto-synced like today. They manually—yes, by hand—put all the clocks one hour ahead in spring and one hour behind in the fall."

Logan laughs too. "Why did they do that?"

"A hold-over from the stone ages when this was an agricultural country. You know, fall and winter it gets darker earlier, spring and summer stays light longer."

"People actually manually changed their clocks. That's stupid. Why not leave it?"

"What's another good one for me to share? Oh, forget this crap. You can read it in eleven years like everyone else when we bring in the twenty-second century. Back to the two stories of the decade."

"Yes, I've been monitoring both since I woke up this morning. And you know I get up early."

Logan learned yesterday about the death of Lucifer Mestopheles. Then, this morning, news broke of the total destruction of Palestine Israel by the Islamic Caliphate; possibly millions dead in the space of a few days. The massacre actually happened last month, in December some time. It was leaked by internal sources, but the details were sketchy since Caliphate territory is closed to outsiders.

"So which one: the destruction of Palestine Israel or the death of a favorite son of the District?"

Edison gives him a weird look. "How many years have you known me? Do you honestly think I give a damn about Muslims killing Muslims?"

"Yes, a stupid question."

"In a few days, it will be forgotten by everyone. The Lou story, however, has legs. Fireworks all around. The man who got the *president* into the White House—likely the most powerful president ever in this nation's history; the man who got half the District's power elite into the Senate and the Congress; the man with political tentacles going back forty years to the wealthy and powerful all over the nation and the globe."

"But unfortunately we're late to the dance."

"Late, but not too late. That's why I called you. Do your magic for me. Let's figure out an angle. Did you get a chance to do some homework?"

"As soon as I woke up, I completely immersed myself in this Lou story. And made calls."

Edison shoots him a weird look again. "If you knew I didn't care about the Muslim story, why did you ask the question?"

Logan smiles and says, "I'm doing my American duty to annoy a Brit today."

"Damn Yanks." Edison leans back in his chair. "So do tell. What do you think? Does the story have any exploitable angles?"

"You think like me, and I know you've done the analysis already. Murder, but no arrests, no descriptions, no nothing."

"Yes, he was stabbed dozens of times. Pardon the pun, the crime scene was a bloody mess. In the center of the Garden. The body was found randomly by a tour group."

"Suspects?"

"None." Edison is reading the Net-feed on his glasses. "Only that it must be an off-Grider."

"Is that the consensus already?"

"Well, all Muslims in public are monitored so we know it wasn't them. Anyone living off-Grid isn't so easy to track."

Logan sits quietly for a moment. "It doesn't track."

"Why? What are you thinking?"

"Edison, it doesn't matter if the perpetrators were off-Grid or not. Location matters. This murder didn't happen in some off-Grid, Trog-town. It happened in the middle of the District. How could someone, especially of that caliber, get stabbed a dozen times in a public park without anyone at all being instantly apprehended? There are Eyes everywhere. Drones everywhere. And you and I both know that Eyes are far more than simple vid-surveillance. We're talking mind-reading tek to read your emotional state, facial expressions, body language, perspiration rate. The audio not only analyzes voice intonations for signs of aggression or violence, but also reads your heart-rate for elevated rates indicating extreme nervousness—hello suicide bomber. There is so much security in this town that law enforcement would have been there right after the first stab. Stabbed a dozen times? No one arrested? No vids of the attack? Not possible."

Edison smiles. Logan realizes that his boss of sorts has already thought the very same thing.

"Where does that lead your train of thought now?" Edison asks.

"Only two possibilities, and both are equally disturbing. Either our vaunted, trillion-dollar-plus, see-everything, hear-everything security network of the nation's capital is full of holes, placing every resident in jeopardy of terrorist attacks or even the common street criminal, or…"

"Go on."

"*The government killed him.*"

The two men stare at each other. Secret nefarious plots, grand conspiracies, government run amok against its own people, even in free America, have been the staple of fiction and the imagination of conspiracy theorists for several decades, but the reality is that they do not happen. Such an action could topple an entire administration and reconfigure the entire US government if it were ever to happen. At least, that was what government cheerleaders told everyone, but many journalists—and Edison was honest enough to admit he was one of them—wished for it to be true and for it to be exposed in glorious detail. It would be a media frenzy beyond imagination.

"The story of the decade," Logan says, smiling. "More, even."

"Potentially dangerous, though."

"That's why we make the money we do. What are your District CIs saying?"

"No confidential informants on this one. The Fifth Estate must not be French-kissing the First, Second, Third, and Fourth. We have to be pristine clean. No congressional or executive branch or Supreme Senate sources on this one."

The *Fourth Estate* historically always referred to the media, but since the Old Constitution was abolished for the new Rule of Law, there were now four branches of government, pushing the media to fifth.

"Edison, I know you like the whole Fifth Estate mythos that we're providing an essential public service to the masses by watching the watchers, but..."

"This is not a normal story, especially if our instincts have any semblance of merit. Even without that, we're talking about sniffing about some of the most powerful and politically connected people in the world. These people can be as certifiable about what's said about them as they are about how they look. Not only must the story be bullet-proof, so must we. That is really what killed the old brick-and-mortar media empires of the past. It wasn't just that their business model was completely obsolete. It was them getting in bed butt-naked with the very politicians they were supposed to be watching, acting as de-facto public relations pansies for them, advancing the political agendas for them rather than objectively reporting news. They completely turned their backs to the journalistic oath: inform the public and tell them what they need to know. Even if we have a large segment that doesn't read, doesn't think, and stands around with their left feet in their mouths sucking their own toes and hopping on their right legs with their hands in their pants and long strings of spittle dripping from the corners of their mouths. That's not *our* public. We serve the public. The public that rightly lost all respect and trust in them. So no entanglements whatsoever here. We're going to bypass our usual Capitol informants. Besides, the other vultures, our competition, are picking their brains and mouths clean as we speak. We must go where none of them have even thought of."

Logan smiles for a moment before putting on his poker-face again. "I can't access that caliber of human intel for a potential blockbuster story like this out of thin air."

"You already have. Otherwise, you wouldn't have driven seventy miles, visually groped my BB Bunny, to just tell me in a high-pitched, pathetic voice, 'Edison, I can't do it.'"

Logan smiles again. "You know me too well. It's actually kind of creepy. I'll need an increase of my expenses limit on this one."

"Done."

"And clearly this will not be at my normal rate."

"Clearly."

Logan nods. "I'll get started now. Actually, I'll continue since I've already been working on it since five thirty this morning."

Edison nods. "Listen to me carefully: I want you to play this smart. This may be a possible serious-as-hell security breakdown, possible ageing infrastructure story that cost the life of one of the most prominent political king-makers in the District. But don't even hint at anything else. What our guts are really thinking. Encrypt everything. And you can't use any of your normal, tek-head resources. Besides, all the good ones are already hired by our competition."

"I have a few tricks up my sleeve."

"Be very careful, and I don't mean just watching out for story thieves."

"Edison, I know my job."

"I know you know your job. But pretend you're a lone reporter in Mexico or CHIN territory or even the Caliphate and that at any minute government storm troopers can break down your door in the middle of the night and snatch you off into the darkness. I want you to be that careful. I have a good instinct for danger."

"I have a good instinct for Pulitzers." Logan smiles.

Edison grins. The Source already has dozens of journalism's highest awards.

The official name of Edison's business is MW2B: (Edward) Murrow, (Mike) Wallace, (Bob) Woodward and (Carl) Bernstein. His homage to what he considers the most influential journalists of all time and two reporters that broke a story that shook the very foundation of the nation. Except for the political junkie or media historian, most have no idea who these men were anymore. Most have no idea what Watergate was, especially with all the juicier scandals that have happened in the District since.

"Who knows where this story could lead. Edison, we'll be like the real Woodie-Bernie team."

"Please don't butcher their names. I've never understood why Americans have to truncate every natural word there is. Woodward and Bernstein, please."

Logan stands. "Anything else, boss?"

Edison shakes his head. "Just remember the first and only rule of journalism: ferret out that greatest story in the cosmos without getting jailed or dead so you can collect a good payday and do it all over again. Now go make us rich, Woodie-B."

Preach, Baby, Preach

"The First Amendment has erected a wall between church and state. That wall must be kept high and impregnable. We could not approve the slightest breach." – Justice Hugo Black, majority opinion, firmly incorporated Thomas Jefferson's "wall of separation" language out of context into American jurisprudence in his majority opinion in Everson v. Board of Education, 1947

"We must not make the mistake of thinking that 'secular' means 'neutral.' Secularism is a religious worldview, the most bigoted faith on earth: its goal is to extirpate every other faith."
– Ron Gray, Canada's Christian Heritage Party Leader, 2003

The Blue Country Club, Arlington, Virginia
1:33 p.m., 2 January 2089

Blues is only miles from Edison's place and closer still to Capitol Hill. It's an exclusive, members-only club for the local Washington DC Metro law enforcement community. The building externally is very unimpressive, with its concrete and glass façade, but that is the point with most exclusive clubs—don't attract the attention of outsiders. Logan has been a full-fledged member for eleven years, though he hasn't been on active duty for ten.

In the parking lot are several hover-cars, which are the current rage. It's amazing the number of movies where every citizen has their own flying car and the traffic goes everywhere high, high above the ground. "Balderdash!" as Edison would say. In the world of terrorism, what mayor or chief of police would allow flying cars in their city? Near tall buildings? A complete nightmare from the deepest recesses of urban security hell. A car's place is parked or driving on the ground. Hover-cars were advertised as the next evolution of the car but are still super-expensive and hover only about a foot off the ground—anti-gravity remains science fiction, so they are cars without wheels and no more. They float using the same tek as many decades ago—a high-pressure cushion of air created by fan turbines. With the spread of auto-drive tek and expanding public transportation, they are a luxury item that came to market a few decades too late. But Logan can barely take his eyes off of them: they really do look chic.

The District is littered with exclusive clubs: the Congressional Club (politicians and staff only), the Senators' Club, political staffers only, children of elected politicians only, lobbyists only; men only, women only, heterosexuals only, homosexuals only, gender-bender only, short people only, six-foot and over only, blondes only, foreign-born only, cyborgs only, etc. In the past there would definitely have been race-only clubs, but there is no race anymore.

Most of his journalist competitors track down their police informants at their home police station or the local police bar. The police station is the absolute worst place to conduct an interview—their boss is around, their partner is around, their colleagues are around, it's busy and noisy, and even internally there are vid-cams everywhere. The local police bar is the second-worst place, because the officer is totally checked out from serious work and is focused on drinking, drugging, chatting it up with colleagues, and hooking up with bed-mates. Most officers these days are not interested in meeting with a reporter off-site or on their off-hours, as legally, due to an array of anti-leaking legislation at all government levels, they have to report any contact with media. If they don't, they can leave themselves open for serious trouble with Internal Affairs—suspension, termination, or even criminal prosecution.

Through the main doors, the true elegance of the building is visible. Logan is immediately met by an usher. A kid, most likely the son of some member, dressed in a dark-blue long-sleeved shirt and matching blue pants and shoes.

"Welcome to Blues, sir."

It is the normal behavior of polite District society—use of gender specific terms such as "sir," "ma'am," and "miss." At one time, only "sir" was used, but enough women were put off by being addressed as "sir" that they brought the other words back. Especially in the District, titles are essential, a mark of the civilized, not like the lesser people outside the tek-cities. Honorable, Senator, Congressman, Deputy, Judge, Doctor, Mister, Miss are the common titles for this town—when you know which to use. For everyone else, it's sir or ma'am.

"What's the lunch special today?"

The male usher leads him to the main counter. "Lean syn-steak with choice of sauce and sides, sir, with the house beverage." A similarly dressed young female reaches out her hand.

Logan hands her his digi-card. "I'll order as soon as I find my party." Syn-steak is definitely sinful, sinfully delicious. But then all synthetic meat is, even though it's not real meat at all—lab-grown to tasty perfection. Real meat hasn't been mass-cultivated in the States for decades now, with the notable exception of the segregated communities of Jew-Christians. They, of course, don't share. Special shipments are possible for the meat-purist, but exports from the Spanish Americas, Africa, or Australia are extremely expensive.

The woman scans the card. She sees his profile picture and stats appear on her counter-top angled view-screen. "Welcome back, Mr. Logan." She hands the card back.

Blues is considered an old-fashioned establishment. It still requires members to use physical cards, refusing to upgrade to biometric sensors to mechanically and automatically read the members as they enter to allow them access. About half the exclusive members-only clubs in the District have also refused. The reason is simple: members want the human touch when so much of their world is automated. Especially with the amount of money paid annually in membership dues.

"We'll notify your party, sir," the male usher says. He leads Logan to the lounge area.

Blues is much larger inside than you'd guess from outside. The ground level includes the main lounge area, private conference rooms, public office centers, bar and cafeteria, and smoking rooms. The second floor has the private bedrooms, unisex restrooms, massage parlors, barber/manicure-pedicure shops, garment cleaners, saunas, and hot tubs. The underground levels have the gyms and swimming pools, virtual reality rooms, golf course, pool hall, and gun range.

The male usher leads him to the lounge area. With high, vaulted ceilings, the area seems massive. All throughout the space are single couches with computer interfaces built into the arms; between each single couch are pairs of couches facing each other with a small table in between them. The outer wall area is for larger parties, with couch set-ups for three to seven people.

"Have a good day, sir." The male usher leaves him.

Logan waits in the fairly crowded room. Officer Steev appears, waving to him. The policeman is in civilian clothes and raises his hand to summon an usher.

"Officer Steev," Logan says.

"Officer Logan." Pagans don't shake hands. A female usher arrives. "My usual drinks," he says to her. To Logan, "Let's sit in the back."

Steev is a huge man, muscles and no fat at six feet. Brown hair, tall crew-cut, and a goatee. His eyes are a strange metallic blue—bionic implants. Lots of law enforcement have had the surgery done for enhanced sight. Steev can switch his sight to infrared, night, or ultraviolet by how he blinks his eyes.

Logan prefers wearable tek to having it surgically implanted in his body. After all, tek becomes obsolete. When the optics in your smart-glasses go out of date, take them in and upgrade to the latest version. When your bionic eyes become obsolete, another surgery? A surgery every six months? He had no desire to become like the cybernetically insane Japanese.

The other downside is he could never set foot near a Jew-Christian ghetto. They have advanced tek-jammers which cause all tek to cease working or, in some cases, cause it serious damage. But Steev's seniority grants him the privilege of being able to legally avoid any assignments he doesn't want, and he wants nothing to do with

Jew-Christians of any kind.

They sit facing each other, with their drinks and devices on tiny side tables next to them.

"So how's the most famous, and only, skin-runner-turned-celebrity-reporter doing these days?" Steev asks, before glancing at his device.

"Your former work partner is hardly a celebrity."

"The size of your bank account would say otherwise." He looks at an incoming message on his e-pad as he sips his drink. "Well, you only come to see me when you're hot on a story."

Logan finishes reading a message on his e-pad. "You only call me when the Agency wants to data dump a story for good or evil purposes."

"It's called national security." He texts a message. "Still living in Alexandria?"

"I moved last year. Calvert County now. Still close to the action, but on the outskirts of the tek-city."

"Another upscale community."

"Don't you still live in the penthouse?"

"Government housing."

"A penthouse is a penthouse."

"How's the public transportation there?"

"Spotty, but that's the point."

"You really do like this journalist gig. Do you think you'll ever come back to being a real cop again? After you get bored."

"No." He glances up from his e-pad. "I actually never thought of skin-running as being part of the force. We worked for CDC, infection prevention and control."

"We were police officers."

"Medical officers was the official title."

"When you carry a gun, you're a police officer. And we were under Homeland Defense." He looks at him, thinking. "You're still hung up on that incident."

"You're not a skin-runner anymore either."

"I got promoted. Section chief in the nation's capital. More money, more prestige. But I do miss that action. We were like bounty hunters. Track down the mutants, bag 'em, and transport them to quarantine detention."

"Don't call them mutants."

"Why? Sexually infected, highly contagious, human biological hazards, as designated by the Centers for Disease Control. 'Mutant' is simpler." He smiles. "So do you think 'heaven' is better?"

"Heaven?" Logan looks at him, perplexed.

"Yeah, the District is heaven to you. It and all the other major tek-cities. In the ten years since you left, have you ever set foot outside a major tek-city?"

"Why would I? I cover the District exclusively. My subjects and sources live here, not in Outland or Trog-land."

"You just want to be in heaven—safe and clean, with all the beautiful people. Not like the 'hell' of Outland and Trog-land. One problem, though."

"Please educate me, Officer Teacher."

"The District, Trog-land, and the Outlands in between are all the same hell."

"For a hard-core Pagan, you sure like using the Jew-Christian words. And the major tek-cities are nothing like the outer lands, nothing."

"Don't be fooled by the District's beautiful people or any other main tek-city. We're all the same, heading to the same oblivion. Just take in the randomness of life and enjoy the ride."

"You're very talkative today. What happened to the work partner I knew and loved with the grunts, barks, and howls?"

He smiles looking up from his device. "Maybe I'm a clone or an android."

"Or an extraterrestrial, which I personally always suspected. I never did like the word, actually."

"What word?"

"Skin-runner. Trying to make something sound exalted when it's not. It sounds like slave-runner."

"Same difference. Go after the live bodies. Both related to sex. You're still not past it."

"Why would I be? You left too because of it, despite your cover story of accepting a promotion."

"You got me there." Steev smiles. "Actually I was scared I'd catch some nasty microbe and everything below the waist would shrivel off."

"I didn't want to touch another dirty, diseased human leper ever again, no matter how thick the body suits or the gloves."

"Listen to you. I only call them mutants, but jokingly."

"I'll stay in heaven, thank you."

Ten years ago, a younger-looking Logan and a non-bionic Steev, dressed in black police uniforms and jackets labeled "CDC" on the back, arrive. They run up the stairs of the apartment complex and Steev kicks open a door. Both men are shocked at what they see.

Both policemen put on their plastic face masks and plastic gloves.

"Stay where you are!" *Steev yells as he draws his stun-stick. Three naked men rush him, and he stuns all of them. They fall to the ground.*

Later, the two men are joined by several regular policemen. Steev directs them as they hand-cuff naked and nearly naked men and women of all ages.

"We're all switched off, you fascists. You have no authority over our sexual activity," *says one of them.*

"You can't mess with free love, coppers," *another says.*

"Who cares if I'm communicable. You're just a liar!" *a third one yells.*

Steev yells back at them, "Knowingly infecting people with communicable diseases is bio-terrorism, you mutants!"

The arrestees in the room laugh at him.

"I got a hundred steady partners, so I must be a big-time terrorist."

Logan stares at a three-year-old boy smiling at him, in handcuffs.

"We do only what we want to do, and I like to do anything," *the boy says, laughing.*

Steev takes another drink. "People should be allowed to live how they want."

"You're law enforcement."

"So? People should be allowed to live how they want. And law enforcement should be allowed to sanction those who break the rules set by the beautiful people." He smiles.

"I'm glad you see this as funny. Chaos and anarchy are not funny. I like routine. I'm boring that way. When was the last time *you* were outside the tek-city?"

"I have all I need here too. Ordered chaos and near-anarchy right here for me." He swipes to another screen on his e-pad. "Boredom—the root of all evil. What did they teach us in human behavioral classes at the Academy? Sensations must be steadily intensified if boredom is to be kept at bay. Keeping crime low is directly related to keeping the people close to their tek, drugs, sex and other recreation."

"Radical Anarchists, radical Hedonists, radical Nihilists, radical narcissists. Maybe we should be worried."

"It's called healthy expressionism. So we have a few bad apples. Most people are just into silly behavior: playing, partying, horseplay, drinking, smoking, joking, living on the circuit."

"Violence, vandalism, suicide, drug zombie-ism."

"Drug zombie-ism?" Steev laughs. "It's called chemical emancipation."

"Reading books again? I warned you about that. How about mindless hatred of law and authority?"

"What's next on your list? Toppling the government, destroying the planet, and then the universe. Maybe you've forgotten, but law enforcement does quite a great job protecting its people and the Homeland. And the real degenerative lifestyles are all outside the tek-city, which you never leave, so why worry about it?"

"I remember. Whatever threatens the Homeland: confront, isolate, disrupt..."

"And destroy. Let the people be what they want to be: wholly liberated human beings. I'm all for that. If it threatens the Homeland, we kill it. It's never been any other way. So don't worry. We keep a watchful eye on the mindless violence and, since you seem particularly focused on it, other dangerous recreational activities. We keep the people and the nation safe."

"What if it comes here?"

"No one has the right to say what's right and wrong."

"Then what were we doing, Officer Steev?"

"Don't misunderstand me. Not right and wrong—acceptable and unacceptable. That's what we were doing. Stopping the unacceptable, as determined by the people with the power—the beautiful people. That's how it's always been. Even when the country was run by Jew-Christians that you seem to be sounding a lot like lately." He laughs. "Morality is an archaic, imaginary construct."

"My morality is simple: what happens if everyone does a thing? If it crashes society, then that's my indication that it's bad and shouldn't be done, ever. We had to arrest that entire community of what, three thousand?—children as young as three and adults up to eighty, parent-child pairings, siblings, and there were a bunch of animals too. I view that as unacceptable."

"What brought all this up today? You've been out for ten years."

"January 1st I was released from recall duty."

"Congratulations. The government can't recall you to active police service ever again. You're free and clear now, Officer Civilian for life." He laughs. "You can even read some illegal holy books now."

"I don't read anything that has profanity like 'thou shall not.'"

Steev laughs. "What hot story are you hunting down today?"

"We're finished small-talking?"

"I sure am. You're giving me a headache."

Logan smiles. "Help me understand clearly what happened, the Lou murder."

"It's simple. The System monitoring the Garden was daydreaming," Steev says.

Logan gives him a confused look. "Daydreaming?"

"The System is extremely complex and smart."

"A.I. is that."

"Not A.I. A.H.I. Artificial human intelligence. Not artificial dog intelligence or bird intelligence. Human. The System is designed to protect against terrorism and violence of any kind, and in the Garden, all it's doing is watching people come in and out and doing nothing. So it was daydreaming."

Logan touches his e-pad. "Voice-text record only. How does that work exactly? When it day-dreams. It blocks out all vid and audio recording?"

"Look, we have the best teks around analyzing the problem, and the best architects will rebuild the necessary code. It will be fixed."

"How will you reassure the public that this isn't some catastrophic security vulnerability in the District? Inviting terrorism?"

"That's not going to happen. We've increased foot and drone patrols everywhere. Also, the System has multiple personalities." When it comes to computer tek, multiple-personalities are a good thing—advanced multi-tasking capabilities. "The low-target areas, like the Park, are monitored by one persona and the high-target areas, the Capitol, High Court and White House, are covered by another. Because of this murder, we've put the entire city on the highest level of security."

"I must say I've never heard of AI daydreaming before."

"Not something you advertise when it comes to urban security, but it's been written about in tek journals before. It's funny, we continue to make computers more and more human, and then when they become more human, people are surprised. Even the computer you have at home is like a thousand human brains."

"But it's still a computer," Logan says. "So no live witnesses or sat-recon captures?"

Steev laughs. "We'll find the murderers."

"So that's a 'no' on the witnesses and sat-recon?"

"No human witnesses saw anything and no satellite surveillance captured anything, but the investigation has just begun with local and state law enforcement assisting. Homeland is throwing every person and tek resource into this. We'll get the evidence soon."

"I don't mean to belabor the point, but it's scary, this daydreaming thing. I've never heard of it before, and I've covered the District for a while. The notion that dozens, more like thousands, of Eyes and drones in and near the vicinity wouldn't capture the exact events of this murder is mind-boggling to me."

"I hear you, but that's what happened."

"It must be terrible for his family."

"You're in your nineties and your only son dies before you. They say practically the entire Congress and even the president will be at the official funeral."

"Can you give me any leads on suspects?"

"Nothing yet, but I'm sure once they identify them, they'll send in the storm troopers hard. I don't think there will even be a trial."

Logan looks at him. "Shoot them on sight."

Steev realizes what he just said. "Please don't write that. That was me editorializing. My own feelings. Not official policy. They'll capture them."

"Dead or alive."

"Alive is the plan, but this murder is a terrorist action, which means anything can happen."

"How many of my competitors have you talked to already?"

Steev laughs. "You are all so paranoid about another beating you to a story. I haven't talked to anyone, partner, but this is what's being filtered out to the entire media. It's coming straight from the top: be transparent as glass. Obviously a lot of eyeballs in Congress and the White House are watching this one. A total media frenzy."

"In other words, all my competitors know the exact thing I learned from you now, and it's already streaming on the Net."

Steev laughs, "That would be affirmative."

So much for any edge against his competition. "Any angles you can give me? Any head-starts on leads?"

"Homeland is running this. But if I hear anything, I'll drop you a quick message."

"Good. I'll touch base with you tonight. And tomorrow morning. And tomorrow night. And every day until you give me something."

He chuckles, "Okay, Logan. I know you have to eat too, but I don't know where you expect to find your next fiery-hot lead.

There must be thousands of reporters on this one. I know you're good, but this is too high-profile for you to really beat out your competition this time."

"I always find the unique angle."

"Maybe you can brush up on your recent Jew-Christian history."

Logan looks at him. It is the first time that the two men have looked at each other for a length of time longer than five seconds without looking at their devices. Pagans even have a name for their universal, multi-tasking way of talking—tek-chatting.

"Are you giving me a tip?"

"Off." Logan turns off the record feature of his e-pad without looking. Steev leans forward and says, "Those Jew-Christians did it. That's what Homeland is going to be pushing out to the public by tomorrow. I know all you over-paid reporters are everlooking for a Watergate event, but this is all just a simple case of murder and nothing more. But there's your advance tip. Not that you'll be able to do anything with it."

"Thanks. I know you're breaking protocol for me."

He smiles. "I'll expect ten percent if it amounts to anything. I'm off for some R and R."

"More rest or more recreation?"

"I'll need to rest after all my recreating." He stands and waves to him. "Bye-ya." Logan waves back as the officer walks to the elevators to the private bedrooms.

Logan flicks on his e-pad again. The story is the number one trending item on the news stream. Not one witness—human or machine.

Jew-Christians did this? Why not some drug zombie mugger or Pagan Anarchist? Why not the CHINs, a lone Muslim, or even a political rival? It is just as he and Edison said, and the investigation has barely started: *something is not right here.*

Watergate Hotel, Washington DC (Nineteen Years Earlier)
7:05 p.m., 2 March 2070

Who lost Western Europe? The question preoccupies the

minds of the American political elite. Western Europe was the center of the international community for centuries, but it fell in mere days. The Muslims cleverly used the Old European Union and now defunct United Nations to solidify their own empire in the Supreme Islamic Caliphate and add the entire region to their territory by 2065.

America is now the only remaining empire of Western civilization. Its elite are determined not to allow the same to befall them. The American Pagan majority will preserve themselves by doing what the Western European Pagans failed to do—abolish religion, end religiosity.

Behold the Good Bible!

"We have a madman in the White House," says the elderly man with thin gray hair and piercing blue eyes.

It is one of the many private meeting rooms in the historic hotel, which has become a favorite stop for the movers-and-shakers in the District to conduct private business away from their Capitol or Pennsylvania Avenue offices, so much so that Homeland maintains a satellite office there to oversee the general security of the building.

Gathered are about a dozen well-dressed men in office-suits relaxing in single-seat lounge chairs in the room, each with a drink in one hand and a drug-cigar in the other. They are all unattractive or sinister in appearance. The one exception is a man who sits facing them all with his hands casually folded on his lap. He is above average height, with a toned, muscular build, brown hair with not a strand out of place, clean-shaven, attractive at thirty-five years old.

"You're putting me in an awkward position," he says. "The man is the president—and my boss."

"He is simply the latest temporary occupant of the office. The American people own the Oval Office and pay the bills. And for us in this room, we directly paid far more than our fair share to allow him to get there," the elderly man continues. He inhales a final draw from his drug-cigar, savors it and then exhales the green smoke. "Wilson, let's cut to it. You're the director of Homeland today, but don't be coy. We know you want the office. So instead of waiting for whatever date you have in your head, why not make the move now?"

"And we know you've been talking privately to a little devil," a man in the back says, smiling. "Lou Mestopheles—only the most powerful campaign manager in the nation."

"President Kanien will be impeached. It's a certainty," another man says; he is tall and fat.

"Nothing is a certainty in this town until it happens," Wilson says. But everyone knows he is laying the groundwork for higher elected office, even his current boss.

"The House Judiciary Committee is already coordinating action behind closed doors and those doors will be opening soon. He'll be gone," the fat man says.

"What happens when the president completes his…Three Towers? The people may fall in love with them," Wilson says.

"Who cares what the people love. We want him gone. Capitol wants him gone. New York wants him gone. He's done. We've kept the religious freaks out of the office for decades, and then one of our own turns. We will not have it," the elderly man says angrily.

"If the president is impeached, then the vice president moves into the office. Or am I missing something?" Wilson asks.

The men laugh as they look at each other and then back at Wilson.

The elderly man, smiling, says, "I don't know. Are you missing something, Mr. J. Edgar Hoover?"

Wilson can't help but laugh himself. They know too, then. The vice president is *compromised*, and if the president is impeached and he becomes the next president, it will be at the most one term.

The 20th-century head of the Federal Bureau of Investigation for thirty-seven years was J. Edgar Hoover, and if you include his directorship of the Bureau of Investigation, which was the precursor of the Old FBI, his tenure was actually an astonishing forty-eight years. It was common knowledge that he conducted extensive surveillance and kept files on not just criminals but average Americans, including Hollywood actors, congressmen, senators, political enemies, and rivals. He allowed the Mafia to form and flourish under his watch, and he did nothing about domestic terrorist groups like the Ku Klux Klan until politically he couldn't ignore them any longer. However, the secrets he knew about the political elite were breathtaking in scope, which is why everyone, including even presidents, was scared of him right up until his death in 1972.

Wilson's post as director of Homeland hasn't been all that sinister, but what he has done is vet every elected official in the District and in the nation who could even possibly get elected to federal office. Blackmail operations by the CHINs, determined to have moles within the American government, are a real and aggressive threat. Wilson is the man who knows all the secrets and the vice president has plenty of skeletons in his closet, any one of which would end his political career even in the anything-goes, all-behavior-is-relative society of today.

"I'll let you know when I'm ready," Wilson says.

"Excellent," the elderly man says. "So, why do you want to be president, Mr. Wilson?"

"Because if I'm not, this country will either be speaking Arabic or Mandarin Chinese or both in the not-too-distant future. I'm not interested in either, and neither are the American people. I personally help compile the Threat Matrix report that the president receives each and every morning with all the latest threats to the country, domestic and global. It is obvious to me, my boss's recent quasi-religious conversion aside, that this country must be *purified* of all religiosity. He doesn't understand that. Western Europe didn't act, and now they're dead. America won't make that critical mistake. Religion is simply an ideology for the weak-minded and the fanatical; we can't have either. Their crusades and inquisitions—we must have a safe and completely secular America. And, gentlemen, know this: I can tolerate anything from my friends, *except* interference in my timetable. I will not tolerate anyone interfering in my plans. Not even once. The more powerful the friend, the more powerful my retaliation will be. Nothing personal, but we all live in the deadly world of high-stakes, life-and-death, global politics. We have the Caliphate, those jackals, laughing to themselves that America is weak and decaying. We have those grinning vultures the CHINs saying the same. To protect our great nation, killing even one American that is a threat is a necessary option."

The men study him carefully. *Did he just threaten us?*

"Let's get this man into the White House," the fat man says. "That's the kind of steel-balls talk we need in the faces of the Caliphate and CHINs."

"Excellent," the elderly man says. "Tell us what to do."

Elizabeth Center, Anacostia, Southeast Washington DC
9:46 a.m., 5 April 2070

"*Jew-Christian,*" she says. Deputy Director Anita McDunn has dark eyes and short blond hair angled into her chin. She wears a black female office-suit. "That's the new term they came up with."

"I like it," Wilson says.

Elizabeth Center is the District headquarters of the Homeland Defense and Intelligence Agency. They sit in his spacious office, he behind his executive desk with her facing him.

"Our focus groups all said the same thing: '*the religious*' is too amorphous a term. To be effective, we need to target people, not ideas. Those Christians are the largest group, and then the Jews," she says. "What about Muslims?"

"We're pursuing a separate track with them," he answers.

"Understood, sir."

"There is always a segment of the population that we have to *manage* in this country. You would think that all Americans in a nation as advanced and educated as ours would have matured past these dangerous superstitions and myths. Yet we still have a segment of the population clinging to them. As someone once said: religion causes wars."

"Sir, their followers are largely uneducated and easily manipulated."

"We've now properly elevated this problem to the national

security level. How will we roll this out?"

"Communications will have a full media blast on all channels; we'll push out talking points to all Capitol offices and staffers and add the word to all Net dictionaries. We do need the president to issue a directive to cease using the words: 'religious,' 'Jew,' 'Christian,' 'Mormon,' etcetera, in favor of 'Jew-Christian.'"

"Let's not be sloppy. Add Nudist, Hindu, Sikh, Animist, Vampire, Wiccan, Warlock, Vulcan, Jedi, everything. Add agnostic too; that will force them to choose sides, and Buddhist, assuming there are any still alive."

"I think they're all dead, sir."

"Our enemies love wiping people out—Western Europe by the Muslims, New Tibet by the CHINs," Wilson says almost under his breath, then forcibly, "Everyone is either a Jew-Christian or a Muslim when it comes to religion from now on."

McDunn nods. "Yes, sir. Will the president be able to send out the directive, even with the scandal?"

"*A president* will send out the directive."

"I understand, sir."

"What did the study groups anticipate in terms of blowback?"

"Nothing we can't handle. Also, sir, I heard that you will be appointing a…Jew and Christian—I'm sorry—two Jew-Christians to be our official spokespeople?"

"Yes, they will be the public face of the initiative. In fact, all our spokespeople will be Jew-Christians. The religious will be used to end religion. A Russian leader of the past had the perfect name for them: 'useful idiots.' No need to get our hands dirty if we can find their own to do the work for us."

McDunn says, "Sir, did I ever tell you that you're a super-genius?"

"Just call me *God*."

Executive Branch Non-Public Off-Site Offices, Washington DC
10:13 a.m., 12 April 2070

"Susie B! How are you, sweet cakes?!" Bishop Joe runs down the hall and embraces Rabbi Susan.

She giggles as she's smothered in kisses. Bishop Joe is by no means a traditional clergyman. The hallway is filled with people—Capitol Hill staffers, high-level security and intelligence personnel, political contractors and lobbyists. Many watch them as they walk down the hall or wait for meetings; some stop in their tracks, aghast at the sight of Bishop Joe, wearing his black robe with his white clerical collar and large gold cross hanging from his neck, embracing Rabbi Susan, wearing a white suit and a white tie with a Star of David symbol.

A large Capitol policeman walks up to them. "Excuse me."

Bishop Joe and Rabbi Susan stop and look at him.

"Yes, Officer?" Rabbi Susan asks.

"Hello Officer," Bishop Joe says. "Are you available?" He laughs.

"This area is a no-religious zone."

"So?" Bishop Joe says.

"You can't be here," the officer says.

"And if we insist on staying what are you going to do about it?" Bishop Joe says, smiling.

"Then I'll arrest both of you."

"Good. Will you frisk me and perform a body cavity search, too?" Bishop Joe asks mockingly.

The policeman is clearly uncomfortable and doesn't quite know what to do or say.

"Let me make this simple for you," Bishop Joe says. "Call your master and tell him you're about to arrest Bishop Joseph Saint Matthews and Rabbi Susan Ben. Then have your master call the White House and tell them what you're going to do. I imagine, and this is without divine consultation, that he will tell you that Bishop Joe and Rabbi Susan are guests of the president of the United States—the new one. So honey, and I say this with the utmost religious conviction, get the hell out of our face and go fondle yourself in the unisex bathroom."

The officer glares at him, his face turning bright red.

"Bye-bye." Bishop Joe spins around to turn his back to the officer, takes Rabbi Susan by the hand, and leads her away to continue their conversation.

She bursts out laughing as the officer stands in the middle of the hallway, almost frozen in anger. The officer grabs his e-pad from his pocket and begins talking to someone.

"Joe, you are so wicked."

"I imagine he's calling his master. So Susan, we're going to be working together!" Joe hugs Susan again. "We're working for the president!" He starts to do a little dance around her. She laughs again.

Susan notices the officer putting his e-pad back in his pocket and storming off down the hallway. Guess he won't be arresting anyone.

Most major cities, and especially the District, have created "no religion zones," where no religious items, displays, or speech are allowed. However, some interpret these laws to apply to religious people themselves. The courts are inundated with lawsuits, and the rulings are a never-ending back and forth between anti-religious judges and pro-religious-rights judges.

11:01 a.m.

"Did you get his name? I'll have him reprimanded," Anita McDunn says. She touches the vid-screen on her desk: "Dial Personnel Services."

Bishop Joe and Rabbi Susan stand on the other side of her desk in the small conference room. Bishop Joe walks to her with a smile and touches her shoulder. "Not necessary. Turn the other cheek. We've let it go. You can let it go."

McDunn looks at him for a moment, then touches the vid-screen again to disconnect the line. "I can see you're going to be very good in the public relations arena."

"I'm an ordained bishop in the Episcopal Christian Church. Been preaching since I was fifteen. It's all second nature."

"Have a seat, then," McDunn says.

All three of them sit. McDunn sits in her executive chair behind the desk. Joe waits and sits after Susan does.

With a smile, Bishop Joe says, "We get to work for the president!"

McDunn smiles. "Yes, how do you feel about that?"

Rabbi Susan says, "We're deeply honored."

"Congratulations," Bishop Joe says and touches Susan's leg. "I can't call you Susie B anymore. You're Rabbi Susan now. An ordained rabbi in the Reform Rabbinical Council. Queen of the Jews!"

Rabbi Susan laughs. "I don't know about all that."

"I agree," McDunn says. "Both of you will in fact will be national leaders on this. You will work under the auspices of the office of the president, but under the direction of Homeland."

Bishop Joe is perplexed. "Religious leaders under Homeland Security?"

Rabbi Susan says, "Not the White House Office of Faith-Based Partnerships?"

This office has been kept around by presidential administrations, though in an increasingly anti-religious climate often existed on paper alone. Despite its lack of relevance, both pro-government Jew-Christians and anti-religious Pagans have pointed to its existence as proof of the harmony between religious citizens and the government.

McDunn says, "We are creating a new division, the Religious Registration Division, formally the Selective Service. With the Fall of Western Europe, the president wants to resolve this question of religiosity within the country. How do you balance the legitimate security concerns for the country in the face of religious terrorism, preserve religious freedoms, and bridge the divide between the secular and religious Americans? Quite the balancing act, but there is nothing that government can't do when it puts its mind to it."

"Religious registration?" Rabbi Susan asks.

"Yes. If we're going to do this, then we're going to need the religious community to meet us halfway. We need all Americans to support the nation's anti-discrimination and anti-hate-crime laws. Marriage freedom in all forms in all fifty-three states…"

"Amen!" Bishop Joe declares.

"What is your overall assessment of the religious community on modern social attitudes and the culture?" McDunn asks.

Rabbi Susan says, "I think the news is very positive. You

have super-orthodox or paleo-traditional churches and synagogues with individuals stuck in past, but they are the minority, and they're disappearing. We've lost a lot of people, especially the youth, who have walked away from religion because of outdated beliefs and teachings on a wide range of current issues that they're on the opposite side of. People are more tolerant, open, mobile, connected, and sophisticated. Ancient Torah or Bible principles don't work for the modern Tek World. Organized religion has been in trouble for a long time. We either adapt or die."

"Preach it, baby," Bishop Joe says, smiling.

"Are your opinions shared by most of your religious colleagues?" McDunn asks.

"I believe so," Rabbi Susan says. "They can read the writing on the walls. Religion needs to be relevant."

McDunn continues, "The reason for this new Registration Initiative is that we can no longer support self-designation of religiosity as a defense against obeying the anti-discrimination and anti-hate-speech laws of the land. The nation's third President, Thomas Jefferson, already showed us the way. He took the Bible and removed sections that he felt were inappropriate to create the Jefferson Bible. Why could we not do that with all 'holy' books? Modern people have evolved and advanced as we've gained more knowledge, gained wisdom as a result. We don't believe the world is flat anymore or that the Earth is the center of the universe. Social customs have also progressed to a more civilized, compassionate place. Rabbi Susan, we were intrigued by a research paper you did for your master's thesis at USC."

"Yes?" Rabbi Susan asks.

"Tell me about this concept of a *Good Bible*."

The Butterfly Demonicus Effect

"The fluttering of a butterfly's wing in Rio de Janeiro, amplified by atmospheric currents, could cause a tornado in Texas two weeks later." – Edward Lorenz, mathematician, meteorologist and pioneer of chaos theory, coined the term the 'Butterfly Effect'— a small change at one place in a non-linear system can result in large differences to a later state.

"Can the flapping of a butterfly cause a hurricane? Can the seizing of a book kill a nation?" – Elder Mother Esther, founding member of the Separatist Movement

Chesapeake Ranch Estates, Maryland
10:35 a.m., 2 January 2089

Calvert County is still the smallest county in Maryland. The appeal for its residents is living next to the Chesapeake Bay on the east and the Patuxent River on the west. Beautiful cliffs, scenic greenery, and a myriad of creeks make the area a virtual heaven for those who love living close to nature and those who enjoy fishing and boating.

Logan moved to the Chesapeake Ranch Estates to be in a premiere gated community that takes the security and privacy of its residents seriously, with both human and robotic guard measures; trespassers are subject to immediate arrest and significant fines. Despite the propaganda, it isn't only Jew-Christians that demand to live in their own exclusive, gated colonies.

From a mile away from the Estates, he has been under surveillance. High-class guarded communities such as his also have the further security measure of requiring auto-drive of any vehicle approaching, and only residents or authorized guests may approach.

Auto-drive takes him through the main gates, past the human-manned guard station, and a few blocks to his home on T. Clancy Street. He manually drives into his car garage, which automatically opens and closes behind him.

All homes in the Estates are the most state-of-the-art of smart-houses and run by the best A.I.; though even today, people are somewhat apprehensive about that term. They have internalized too many movies where the evil A.I. takes control of a car or home or city and kills people. But actually anything smart is controlled by artificial intelligence.

High-end smart-houses are able to generate their own limited power with solar cell capture tek, and sometimes combined with wind turbines in high wind areas or hydro turbines for homes on or near a flowing water source. But even now, at least 80 percent of a home's energy needs—as with the whole tek-city—are powered by the Grid via fusion, natural gas, or clean-coal.

"Open sesame," Logan says as he walks from the garage into the house. The door opens and closes behind him. Unlike most people, he prefers the extra security step of voice-cog (voice recognition) rather than just auto-biometric sensing. "Lights on."

The lights in the room turn on and will turn on and off as he moves through the house. The wall displays activate, showing him all the voice, vid, and text messages he's received, but it is the same display as his e-pad and his car's dashboard display—nothing that needs to be responded to at the moment.

He walks to the kitchen. "Ice blended mocha." He hears a few clicks and after a few seconds a compartment near the refrigerator opens. Down drops a cup filled with the beverage. He grabs the cup, takes a sip, and walks to his home office.

The entire house is decorated in a white-fabric-and-glass motif: all the chairs, tables, foot rests, shelves, drawers. It is a one-level, two-bedroom residence, and all his! No pets, other humans, or other robotic residents, save Mr. Café.

His home office, or as he calls it, the Command Center, isn't as impressive as Edison's, but he doesn't have to manage freelance journalists all over the world. His configuration is different but very common: Logan sits, lies back in his inclined recliner chair, and rests his arms on the padded armrests, each with one half of a keyboard under his fingers. Three vertical flat-screens automatically lower from a ceiling and stop when they are eye-level.

"Let there be light," Logan says. The computer screens flick on. The center screen is his homepage—his avatar—and he can once again see all his audio, vid, and text messages, and all the friends, colleagues, and contacts from around the world that are available to talk. The left screen displays local, national, and international newsfeeds. The right screen will be his workspace.

Who killed Lucifer Mestopheles?

He continues his Net research from this morning. There are all kinds of articles, blog entries, and journals swimming around on the Net—a typical data dump of new material. Everyone does it: governments, organizations, individuals. Dump a story on multiple Net channels to create a buzz, start a search frenzy, blunt the impact of a scandal by getting it out there first, confuse netizens by planting false stories to counteract the true stories, or vice versa. He and Edison have done this themselves so many times before.

His system is the best in quantum computers, zippy and lean software, saber-tooth encryption, mirage firewall, scatter-gun traps; impenetrable to other users, but the government could slice through it like nothing if it wanted. He links to his secure remote terminal in Australia, almost ten thousand miles away. The Australians may be paranoid about letting people into their nation, but they have no problem with people setting up remote terminals on their soil to link into Freespace—a region of the Net that is not run or sponsored by a government, where you can work free of any government monitoring or tracing. But the major downside is that Freespace is infested with cyber-pirates, who attempt to seize control of your link for their own purposes or try to follow it back to the original sender, you, where they can do such wonderful things as steal your identity or hack into your computer; dark worms, that eat any data you capture from the Net; or freddies, that corrupt any data you capture from the Net. These are just the main Net-predators; there are dozens of other types. It is very much like maneuvering through a jungle teeming with ferocious wild animals.

He does hours of queries: enemies of and threats to Lucifer Mestopheles, separate list of political competitors of; day-dreaming and AI, truth and hype; Jew-Christian enemies of Lucifer Mestopheles; list of journalists working on the investigation. The last query is not just to see all his competition on the story but to see if he has been identified yet by anyone as working on it. As his former work partner said, there weren't hundreds of reporters on it—there were thousands.

Being an investigator of any kind is tedious, lonely, and often boring work. You can spend hours, days, or weeks working on a lead and ultimately come up with nothing. Most of his competitors are excitement junkies, which is why most are so bad. Most simply follow the pack and don't have an original thought in their brains. His work is 90 percent tedious, 5 percent mildly interesting, and 5 percent amazingly fun.

The amount of data to review through the Net is beyond comprehension and requires separate passes through the different regional Nets around the world. Simple searches can be done within seconds, but the data received is the most viewed out of all the endless choices—*not* necessarily accurate, which is why queries are a must. You could do a query on the normal Net, but again it would be monitored by the government. Every real journalist avoids that like the plague when putting together an original story, especially if it's about the government. But when running a query in Freespace, you have to watch it at all times to be safe, or even better, specifically watch the code. A cyber-beast could pounce at any time, even with your firewalls.

He activates another workspace on his center screen, pushing his avatar to run in the background while he monitors the code of the search on the right screen and reads the newsfeed on the left.

He watches the code search flashing on the main screen. Logan yells out, startled—*staring at him is a large face of a man from the vid-screen.* The man studies him, then reaches to touch the screen on his side with his finger. Click.

"No!" Logan yells.

The man disappears. The code search returns to his screen.

Logan jumps out of his chair recliner to his feet. "Computer, is two-way vid activated?"

"Two-way vid is not activated," the computer voice says.

"When was two-way vid last activated?"

"Two-way vid was last activated 3.79 seconds ago."

"Who authorized that connection?"

"Right screen terminal was remote-controlled by unknown source."

"Damn!" Logan yells. "Computer, was two-way vid used to take a photo of me?"

"Two-way vid camera was activated."

"Damn!" Logan is furious. "Computer, voice recite current search on right screen terminal."

"Right screen terminal searches are complete."

Logan bends done to view the screen. The searches are done.

"Computer, download all search results."

"Download complete."

"Computer, sever all links."

"Sever complete."

"Computer, are any systems compromised?"

"Diagnosis complete. No anomalies detected."

"Computer, shut off all systems."

The three screens rise back up to disappear into the ceiling compartment. Logan is still furious. "Computer, was two-way vid on right screen recorded?!"

"Vid recording was enabled."

"Yes! Computer, send recording to e-pad."

Logan reaches into his pocket and takes out his e-pad. He touches the screen and swipes his finger back and forth. There he is! The man's image staring at him.

"You got me and I got you too, bastard!" Logan smiles. "Computer, identify sent photo."

"Person is not listed in known registry."

"Computer, access international registry."

"Searching. Person identified."

"Computer, read me the name."

"Person's name is: *You Got Me and I Got You Too, Bastard.*"

There is a knot in Logan's stomach as he looks at the ceiling and all the walls around him. He's not smiling. *His audios have also been hijacked, and they are listening to him right now.*

Washington Hilton Hotel Ballroom, Washington DC (Eighteen Years Earlier)
12:40 p.m., 2 January 2071

Smiling faces are everywhere. The crowd is howling and applauding madly. They are all as well-dressed as they are well-connected politically—the District elite class.

"Thank you, thank you." Rabbi Susan is the keynote lunch speaker. The applause is so loud that she can't even hear herself talking through the booming speakers. She feels elated and bigger than life, with a smile from ear to ear. "There are many of us, in this room even, who have a very dim view of the nation's Founding Fathers…"

The crowd erupts in boos.

"No. No. Let's not do that because one of them, our third president, Thomas Jefferson, was a prophet. He gave us his Jefferson Bible, which he forbade to be published while he was alive, for it was too far ahead of its time. You liked what I had to say about the Good Bible before?" The crowd erupts again in "yeah!" and "yes!" "Well, it is the literary descendant of his work. We reject the notion that religion has to be about intolerance and bigotry and holding onto arcane, obsolete myths of the past. Religion can be, will be, better than that! I'm Jewish. Bishop Joe is Christian. We get it. So can our religions!" The crowd erupts in applause again. "Today, the first month of the new year, 2070, we start the crusade. No religion in the public square! We shouldn't intrude on the public space anymore than the public should intrude in our places of worship! No hiding behind a holy book as an excuse for refusing to join the twenty-first century of the civilized, the modern, and the future. A future that is now! Religious, agnostic, and secular all united! The government will end intolerance, bigotry, and discrimination in all forms in this nation forever! Amend our Constitution. Amend our holy books. All Americans are equal!"

Bishop Joe jumps on the stage and runs to Rabbi Susan to embrace her. The crowd again goes mad with applause.

"And my God isn't a marriage bigot!" Bishop Joe yells with a smile. "Boys and girls: *all* marriage is traditional marriage!"

The crowd laughs and applauds.

The dynamic duo jointly wraps up the speech. Before they can even come off the stage, they are inundated by the crowd wanting to personally greet and congratulate them.

A young man pushes through the crowd to them. "Bishop Joe, Rabbi Susan. Let's do the photo shoot right here."

"Here?" Rabbi Susan asks.

"Yes, this is fantastic. We can do some shots with you and the crowd and then do a series for the cover shot."

"We're all yours," Bishop Joe says, smiling.

"Have we come up with the tagline?" Rabbi Susan asks.

"Resistance Is Futile: The New Religious Paradigm in America," the young reporter says.

Washington Hilton Hotel Ballroom
11:41 a.m., 7 April 2071

Three months later: same location, same speakers, different crowd. No one is smiling. The pastors, reverends, bishops, and rabbis sit in the large auditorium in groups of ten at round tables. Rabbi Susan and Bishop Joe stand on the stage, each at a podium. Their speech has not been well received.

"Are there any questions?" Rabbi Susan asks.

The rabbis with full beards and mustaches at the back of the auditorium, dressed in black suits, with their black head coverings called *kippot*, get up from their table and leave.

Bishop Joe, though not smiling, still has an air of good cheer. "Gentleman and ladies, we have to make this work."

Reverend Benjamin stands and says, "Thomas Jefferson was a fool. I don't care how brilliant people say he was or if he was our third President or a Founding Father or if he authored the Declaration of Independence for the United States. He was a fool, because only a fool would think he was smart enough, as a flesh-and-blood human, to perfect what is already perfect in the Word of God."

"Really, Reverend?" Bishop Joe says.

"You Pagans like making up new words," Reverend Benjamin says. "Now that I've seen this performance with my own eyes, I've come up with one for you. There's a group of Christians called the Amish who still use the term Order, not denomination or sect. I agree with them. We are an Order, and you fakers are a Disorder with demonstrated contempt for the Word of God."

Bishop Joe says, "Matthew 18:8: 'If your hand or your foot causes you to sin, cut it off and throw it away. It is better for you to enter life crippled or lame than with two hands or two feet to be thrown into the eternal fire.' 1 Timothy 2:12: 'I do not permit a woman to teach or to assume authority over a man; she must be quiet.' Leviticus 11:10: we can't eat shrimp. Do we still practice those things?"

"What exactly are you the bishop of? The circus?" Reverend Benjamin asks.

"I'm an ordained bishop in the Episcopal Christian Church. I have the full support of my church leadership, and they unanimously support this initiative."

"Episcopalians. Yes, the premiere fake Christians in the nation. Along with Lutherans and Presbyterians."

"We are all children of God, Reverend."

"So was Judas." Reverend Benjamin turns and leaves with his delegation.

Other groups in the crowd do the same. But many remain seated, and a few groups make their way to the front of the auditorium. Supportive clergy surround Bishop Joe and Rabbi Susan.

A pastor says, "Don't worry. Most will come around. At the end of the day, no one likes to be left behind."

Rabbi Susan says, "I was hoping for a better reception. We've spent almost a year talking to everyone in preparation for this meeting. I already have full support of the Reform Judaic Council, and the Conservatives have assured me that they will give us a fair hearing. Bishop Joe has secured, what, four...major Christian denominations?"

"And the entire American Catholic Council too," he says.

A female pastor says, smiling, "We're building the coalition. Soon we'll have our own United Nations of the New Age Religious."

Rabbi Susan says, "We have to work even harder, though. I want everyone aboard. The White House wants the Good Bible adopted nationally by year's end as we roll out the initiative. Everyone needs to understand that compliance will be mandatory for all religious institutions, organizations, and places of worship. No more knee-jerk resistance or sermonizing. I don't want to lose our coalition's momentum."

Bishop Joe smiles and says, "Don't worry. There is no stopping our new world order."

By late afternoon, Bishop Joe and Rabbi Susan sit with Master Pastor at one of the round tables. His delegation is only a few tables away, speaking to the bishop's and rabbi's delegations.

"Your problem is you're focused on the minutia, and politics, timetables, and deadlines. When you talk to religious folk, it has to be about the *love*. Jesus said in Matthew 5, chapters 43 and 44: 'You have heard that it was said, love your neighbor and hate your enemy. But I say to you, love your enemies, bless those who curse you, do good to those who spitefully use you and persecute you.' That is what Jesus said. You have to come at them with love to get them in the right frame of mind."

"Not scripture?" Rabbi Susan asks.

"Forget scripture. Focus on the love," Master Pastor answers. "We're talking about Christians. You get two Christians in a room reading the Bible and you get five different interpretations depending on their politics or ideology. Make it about love. Make it simple. We're talking about religious leaders too. So make it about money. The only thing short of the coming of the Messiah that will make them move is to tell them that their lack of compliance will jeopardize their tithes and offerings church money. Love of country. Love of people. Love of government. Love of harmony. Love of peace. Love of unity. Love of Jesus. Love of money. Let them pick the love they want to rally behind, but it will be love."

"Will you help us?" Bishop Joe asks.

"That's why I'm here. They don't call me *the* Master Pastor for nothing. I make things happen. Just focus on the love, and the good will follow in God's name."

Holy Cavalry Christ Church, Washington DC
7:07 p.m., 31 May 2071

It is a hastily convened meeting of a group of some fifty Christian pastors, priests, reverends, and bishops, both male and female. The man they are now looking at is Elliott Finegold, a thirty-something Jewish lawyer with short black hair, a short beard and mustache, and a two-piece black suit with a solid white shirt and black tie.

"I will save the lawyer jokes for another time. I know you are all in panic mode, but the Pagans were saying this country wasn't a Judeo-Christian nation even when America was still a Christian majority. What did you think they were going to do when we all became a numerical minority? All I can say is that Christians are definitely the dumbest people on the planet."

The Christian clergymen are not amused.

"Don't feel bad. I'm a Jew, and when everyone in the room is Jewish, I say Jews are the dumbest people on earth. My people are the original people in panic mode. We've been at it longer than anyone else, and we'll do something stupid again soon.

"The Pagans wiped out every other traditional religious-centered organization in the nation a long time ago. I'm sure most of you don't even remember the Boy Scouts or Girl Scouts, Salvation Army, Alcoholics Anonymous, none of them. First they started with the name calling: bigoted, discriminatory, hateful, dangerous. Then they kicked them out of city parks, public schools, public forums, and local meeting places of any kind. Then they passed laws to dictate and take away their freedom to pick their own board members and leaders. Then they took away their city and county funding. Why you accepted that funding to begin with is beyond me. Even we stupid Jews didn't fall for that trick. We never took government funding, ever, for our groups, we just passed the hat amongst ourselves. Then you all surrendered, just closed the doors of all your organizations operating in the public.

"It was good ol' 1954 low-life President Lyndon Baines Johnson, our thirty-sixth president, who wanted to get back at the church community that opposed him in his election, so he passed what would be called the Minister Gag Rule and overnight gave the Tax Bureau, known back then as the Internal Revenue Service, the unimaginable power to reach into every church in the nation and exert control over them. Every church had to be careful of what they said or the big, bad government would come in and yank their coveted tax-exempt status. The reality, however, ladies and gentlemen, is that in all one hundred-plus years, how many churches actually lost their tax-exempt status because of that statute? Not one. In all that time, churches all across the nation could have forcefully spoken out to their congregations on politics, education, and the culture, named names, called people out, called politicians out, rallied their congregations around real causes. Instead they did not. They avoided anything supposedly controversial.

"Now the Pagans run everything, and *now* you want to speak out. When they are now using the Tax Bureau *and* Homeland to come after Christians, Jews, anyone religious, always excluding the Muslims, of course. Now you want to fight? Ladies and gentleman, it's too late. This marathon started a century ago, and it's too late to join the race now.

"They outsmarted you a long time ago. Homosexuality to polygamy to age-of-consent abolition to the current cultural freakshow known as the pan-sexual, alt-lifestyle movement. Speak the Bible and go to jail. Speak the Torah and go to jail. The Bible is 'offensive content,' 'hateful,' 'bigoted,' 'homophobic,' 'poly-phobic,' 'pan-sexual-phobic.' Ladies and gentlemen, you were focused on who could marry whom when you should have been focused on religious freedom.

"Two items: the main one being hate-crime legislation. If they could write into law the ability to criminalize religious speech, even *with* the First Amendment, then why was it not obvious to you that they would come after the Bible too, and then its people right after that?! It was inevitable! We had the nation to our north, Canada, criminalizing the Bible as hate speech, along with all of pre-Islamic-Caliphate Western Europe. The government of the nation to our south, Mexico, tried to exterminate Christians by military force in its history. Here, they want to put in place this Religious Registration Initiative, brought to us by their fake Christian and fake Jewish puppets. Hate crime legislation was always the single most dangerous piece of law in our entire history, as the very abolishment of Christianity was the inevitable outcome, along with my Judaism and every other religion in the country. It never was about homosexuality, polygamy, or any other alt-lifestyle. It was always about creating the Thought Police and codifying into law that thought itself could be a crime. It was always about the end of religiosity in the nation! Hate crime? Even the term is Orwellian. Violent words first, then non-violent words spoken, then any word or speech interpreted as a threat, intimidation, or coercion as believed by a so-called victim. My God, 'what the victim believes'? I say 'God bless you' and they interpret it as hostile, I can be subject to fines or imprisonment or both. Soon they'll move to banning the Bible and the Torah, after this ruse of a Good Bible. They were already doing this madness in pre-Islamic Western Europe, and we all know how obsessed American Pagans are with copying their Western European Pagan siblings. They sent Bible-believing clergy there to jail, not for violence of any kind, but simply for giving sermons from the book. And their 'separation of church and state' constitutional lie, the other thing you should have been focusing on and stopping!

"Who's that Christian rabble-rouser of yours? Elder Mother Esther. She reminds me of a good Jewish mother who smacks you in the head when you need it. I like her. At least she was talking about this at the beginning of the last decade. American values and religious values used to be one and the same. Now, the inmates run the asylum. Now is the first time in the nation's history that those values have been separated violently from each other.

"Both the Establishment Clause and the Free Exercise Clause of the Constitution—Congress shall make no law respecting an establishment of religion or prohibiting the free exercise thereof—have, in essence, been nullified. The courts, a judiciary taking on powers not rightly its own, have taken sides in the culture war. And it's not ours. Every practicing religious lawyer knows that the judiciary purged all the Christians and Jews from the bench on grounds of being members of organizations that 'discriminate' or 'hold socially unacceptable and dangerous beliefs,' meaning our religions, meaning our local churches or synagogues. Ladies and gentleman, we're the 'immoral' ones for being moral. We've only barely, barely been able to legally protect ourselves using the Civil Rights Acts of 1964 and 1965. Imagine; that's how far back we have to go to find legislation in this nation to protect our rights. Mark my words, the Pagans have enough votes and enough judges in their pockets to abolish in totality the United States Constitution itself, and they're going to do it. You heard it here first. Then we'll have not a single piece of legal defense for ourselves.

"*The only option available to us is to retreat.* That's it. There's nothing to fight, because we have no weapons, no advantages, no cards to play. We just have to stand still and take the punch and hope that the punch doesn't cause so much fatal damage that at least we can survive. I really wish you all, and my useless people the Jews, had decided to fight back when it would have mattered.

"I love ancient American history myself. President John Adams, one of the good guys, said: 'Our Constitution was made only for a moral and religious people. It is wholly inadequate to the government of any other.' How prophetic he was. Morality and religion were the twin pillars of our society, and the founders of our nation knew that without either there would be no nation. Again, you heard it from my lips. The Pagans will succeed in abolishing the US Constitution. Their judiciary has always had a deep-seated contempt for the voting electorate. They've wanted to do this for a long time, and our side can't get its act together.

"You asked me here to put together a legal strategy to stop the Registration Initiative against your churches and your congregations, but again, it's too little, too late. You're over a century too late. To be somewhat biblical, forget the lawyers; that time has passed. Get the swords."

"So what are you saying?" one of the clergy asks. "You're telling us to go to war with the government. I can't believe we're even talking like this."

"No. I'm telling you the war is over and it's time to get comfortable hiding under a rock. The swords aren't for the government; they're for each other, because there are going to be a lot of people fighting to get under that rock."

California Synagogue of the Reform Judaic Council
6:47 p.m., 13 February 2074

The synagogue is being used as a meeting hall, with rabbis sitting in all the chairs facing the main stage. The chief rabbi reads from prepared remarks at the stage podium as the attendees follow along, each reading from a tablet in his or her hand.

"Rabbi Susan, our esteemed colleague, has also sent us item twenty-three," the chief rabbi says.

A commotion is heard in the back. The chief rabbi looks up; attendees turn their heads. Behind the chairs, security is trying to hold a group back. It is four members from the Orthodox Judaic Council, four men all dressed in black with black kippot and full, graying beards. The formally dressed Orthodox rabbis are in direct contrast to the Reform rabbis, who are in casual to business casual dress.

The four Orthodox push their way past the guards.

The chief rabbi quickly steps down from the stage and walks down the aisle to meet them; other rabbis stand and file out to follow him.

"This is an outrage!" the chief rabbi yells.

"We will not give you the dignity of a greeting, Chief Rabbi," the Orthodox elder says, "since your Disorder has decided to renounce its Jewish heritage and faith."

"Get out of here! This is our synagogue, and we will not allow you to interrupt our High Council meeting."

"The Orthodox will never let you whores-for-hire sell out the Jews to the Pagans," the elder yells back.

"You will not call a senior member of the Reform Judaic Council such disgusting names!" the chief rabbi yells. "The Orthodox—the Jewish madmen who live centuries in the past! Who sit in tiny rooms and read Torah all day like fanatics! The Muslims of the Jewish world."

"Chief Rabbi, at this juncture I can honestly say I have far more respect for the Muslims than I do for you. The Reform Judaic Council accepts this blasphemy called the Good Bible. The Reform Judaic Council accepts this evil called Registration. Registration? That's what the Nazis did to the Jews."

"Not the Holocaust again! All you Orthodox talk about is the Holocaust."

"Actually, we never talk about it in public, but we teach our children and remember it so it will never happen again. And here it is, happening again. If you side with the Pagans on this Registration evil, free Jewish men and women forced to register with the government, free American citizens..."

"What is the harm? Americans *already* register with the government. We've been doing so for almost two centuries! What do you think paying your taxes is? What do you think getting a national identity number and having a national identity card is? You Orthodox are consumed with conspiracies. We are all already registered! They are just streamlining the program."

"I never thought I would gaze upon a Jew so stupid as to make me want to kill him."

"Get out of our synagogue!"

"If you support this government Registration program, we will excommunicate your entire denomination."

"What does that mean? The Orthodox are Catholics now?"

"It means if you come near our enclaves, we will kill you."

The men stare at each other.

"Good," the chief rabbi says slowly.

"Consider it done. From now on, you will be Chief Rabbi *Sonderkommando* to all. Since you know nothing of Jewish history, let me remind you. They were the Jews who disposed of gas chamber victims—Jewish victims—from the concentration camps for the Nazis. Removing the clothes and valuables from their bodies. Extracting the gold from their teeth. Yes, that is you, Chief Rabbi *Sonderkommando* and your Reformers."

The chief rabbi hits the Orthodox elder in the face so hard that he breaks his hand, sending the elder staggering back to fall to the ground. The other three Orthodox attack; one knocks the chief rabbi out with a single punch, as the other two push back the advancing crowd.

Several dozen are sent to the hospital. All four Orthodox are nearly beaten to death, and the chief rabbi is dead—his neck broken from falling to the ground in the fight.

The first American Jewish Civil War has begun.

Kansas City, Kansas
4:02 p.m., 16 May 2076

The driver sits quietly in his car. As soon as the police car activated its signals, his car's auto-drive pulled over to the closest place to safely stop off the main road. The driver is a dark-tanned man with fine curly hair, dressed in a blue office-suit. The policeman, dressed in a black, short-sleeved police uniform with a black t-shirt showing, exits his police car and cautiously approaches the other vehicle; the auto-drive has also automatically lowered all the windows of the car.

"Good afternoon. Do you know why I stopped you, sir?" the policeman asks.

"No, Officer."

"It's just a courtesy stop. Your car was weaving a bit back and forth on the road, so it must be out of alignment, or the auto-drive interface may be faulty."

"Thanks, Officer. I didn't notice."

"People always think we only make stops if you do something wrong, but we make far more courtesy stops to tell people something's wrong with their vehicles. It's so easy to hop in your car and have it drive you to where you're going and not even notice these things."

"Thank you. I'm picking up my children from school. I'll take it to the repair station right away."

The policeman notices something on the passenger seat. "Excuse me, sir. What's that on your passenger seat?"

The driver looks to the book on the seat. "You mean my Bible?"

"Yes. Can I see it for a minute, sir?"

He hesitates but hands it to the officer.

The policeman opens the Bible and flips through it. "Sir, this book is illegal."

"Excuse me?"

"The Good Bible is the only authorized holy book for religious people now. This isn't one, so I'm going to have to confiscate it. Hate literature is illegal."

"What? What are talking about? You can't take my Bible. It's my personal property."

"Sir, all hate speech is federally prohibited by law. I have to confiscate it, but you can protest it in court. Otherwise, it will be destroyed."

"What? Give me back my Bible. You can't take my property."

"Sir, I will create a ticket for you and you can protest it in court."

The driver attempts to snatch it back. "Give me back my Bible!"

"Sir, do that again and I'll cite you for attempted assault on a law enforcement officer!" The man opens the door and gets out. "Get back in your car!"

The driver lunges for the Bible. The policeman attempts to hold it away from him with one hand while grabbing for his gun with the other. The man grabs the Bible now with both hands and yanks it away. The policeman draws his gun, and the man immediately drops the Bible and grabs for the gun with both hands. The two men violently struggle for the weapon. The gun goes off.

Holy Redeemer Church, Kansas City, Kansas
4:35 p.m., 16 May 2076

The driver arrives running, almost totally out of breath, clutching his Bible in both hands. He stops, sweating profusely. He gathers his strength to run across the street up the front steps of the church just as another man exits the front door.

"Pastor!" the man yells out.

"Brother Rhodes!" the assistant pastor grabs him before he falls. "My God, what happened?" The clergyman wears a sharp black office-suit with a white tie and white shoes.

"Pastor, they tried to take my Bible and then tried to kill me. I shot the one who did it."

The assistant pastor is shot in the chest and blown back into the front doors.

"No!" The driver turns to look. Four policemen are shooting at them. He ducks down and, still clutching his Bible, opens the doors. Keeping low, he drags the assistant pastor inside.

The four policemen run towards the front door with guns at the ready. One of the policemen speaks into his ear-set, "We are at the main entrance of the religious building. The suspect has entered and we're about to follow inside. E-T-A on back-up?"

One of the policemen says to another, "You shot the wrong one. I told you not to do manual targeting."

"He killed a cop! Nobody kills a cop and gets away with it."

"Backup units will be there in five minutes," the voice says through the comm.

The front doors burst open and an enraged elderly man walks out. "Which one of you killed my son?!" Senior Pastor Atticus has a dark complexion but snow-white hair, white mustache and beard. His eyes are red with fury and anguish.

"Gun!" a policeman yells.

The policemen shoot at the man. He falls back.

They hear a woman scream from across the street. "You killed the pastor!"

People pour out of their homes across the street, on either side of the church, everywhere.

East Sitting Hall, The White House, Washington DC
8:20 p.m., 16 May 2076

Bishop Joe and Rabbi Susan sit on the sofa together, watching the newsfeed live on the large vid-screens on the wall, watching a city burn—whole buildings, police cars, garbage cans, trees, anything that can. Gunfire from the ground and the air is everywhere.

"We can confirm only the same seventeen dead law enforcement personnel, with another confirmed twenty-seven injured, but the fatality and casualty count could be much higher. Civilian deaths and casualties are still unknown. The governor has declared a state of emergency, and state troops have been dispatched to the scene despite heavy civilian gunfire," the reporter's voice says.

She glances at Bishop Joe. He is quiet and sullen, watching the broadcast.

"We have Jew-Christian leaders calling for an end to the violence, but many more armed Jew-Christians are taking to the streets. We haven't confirmed yet what touched off the violence," the reporter's voice continues. "But we believe a policeman was attempting to seize illegal hate-literature from a suspected terrorist and the policeman was killed."

Rabbi Susan thinks to herself that all the work they've done over the last six years, their massive council of clergy across the country to get the Good Bible accepted by all religious communities, has been for nothing. The glory days are…over for her. When you climb up a mountain, you reach the apex, and then you have to climb—or fall—down. It's the way in politics; yesterday she was on top of the mountain, today the descent begins. They won't do it today, it may be a couple of years, maybe she'll make it past the next election, but her bosses will inevitably push her out. Bishop Joe could last longer; he's just a surrogate speaker. But she's an appointed director of a government division—a division which will be phased out as quickly as politically possible. Now is when the real politics for her begins, she thinks. She must not be the fall guy for the disaster today.

The Situation Room, The White House
11:00 p.m., 16 May 2076

Wilson may not be the president yet, but he acts like it. The president is hardly ever seen, and even the vice president acts like Wilson is the boss already. "Governor, give me the run-down," Homeland Director Wilson says.

"Sir, I have seventy-two dead and almost three hundred in or on the way to the hospital," he answers. The Governor speaks to them from the screen via vid-link connection.

"Seventy-two?!" Director Wilson says. "They said seventeen."

"We kept the real numbers from the media, but they'll find out soon enough. They always do. Director, this is a full-out ground war."

"Governor, how many civilian combatants do we have now?"

"*The entire city is at war with us.* We need military troops now! I got governors all over the damn country scared to death that the same could happen in their states. If military boots are not on the ground fast, Director, you *will* have a second American Civil War on your hands."

Wilson pauses in thought. "Governor, let me confer with my advisors. We'll call you back immediately."

"Okay, but be advised that my people are dying every second you delay."

Wilson disconnects the vid-link, and the governor's face disappears from the screen.

"How the hell did this happen?!" Wilson yells. "Over seventy law enforcement personnel dead. Over three hundred injured. A growing insurrection. What military options do we have immediately available?"

"Sir, do we really want to go down this road?" the senior advisor asks. He has a very thin frame and unremarkable features in his black office suit and balding hair, but everyone in the room looks to him. "This has the potential of becoming a real live civil war across the country. It will absolutely be so by tomorrow if the right decisions are not made in this room right now. You're running for president and your platform is the security of the nation. That platform goes out the window, if Americans are killing Americans in the streets, and so does your certainty of winning."

"The Jew-Christians have killed over seventy police officers!"

the chief law enforcement advisor yells. Even within his office-suit, his well-defined physique is apparent.

"We have to let this go," the senior advisor says. "Pull all law enforcement and troops back now. They'll stop fighting if we're not there."

The chief yells, "The police will never agree to this! What message does that send? They're criminals! They're terrorists!" He turns to Wilson. "Sir, we'll lose all of law enforcement's support and their vote."

Wilson says calmly, "I'm director of Homeland. Who else are they going to support? The vice president? I hardly think so." To the senior advisor, he says, "I can't let this go. It shows weakness, and weakness invites more aggression, not less."

The senior advisor says, "Sir, then you better be able to say, and right now, that you'll be able to put down this uprising in the next twenty-four hours. Not a week, not months—now, all of it. If it goes beyond that or if it spreads, you *will* lose the election, sir. There have been many leaders in this world in history, and not one of them could predict the end of a civil war on their own soil, not one. If you want to roll those dice, just remember the advice I gave you tonight if it explodes and engulfs any chance you have of winning the White House, or more importantly, engulfs the entire country."

The legal counsel says, "Sir, we need to focus on the other item. After all our work, we're on the threshold of getting the entire Constitution finally thrown out. No more First Amendment. No more Second or Fourth or Seventh. No more Twenty-Second. We have to get this done *before* you are elected president. I agree, let this lie for now, and when you're president, you can come back and do what you need to do then." The lawyer looks to be barely out of high school in his unkempt, tan, business casual office-suit.

The chief says, "Sir, I couldn't more strenuously disagree. This move would just encourage the Muslims. Or Anarchists. There are a lot of dangerous forces out there just watching what you do with this insurrection. What about our foreign enemies?"

Wilson stands and looks at everyone. "Pull them back."

The chief resists. "Sir, we can't."

"Pull them back, now. If it's not done within the next five minutes, tell the governor we'll send in federal troops with full tank and air gunship support and arrest *them*, not the Jew-Christians. Am I clear, everyone? Have the governor follow my orders. I know why he's doing this. He's positioning himself for a surprise challenge to me in the election. I'm going to brief the president now."

Everyone responds with yeses as Wilson walks past them. He stops at the door and says to the chief law enforcement advisor, "Tell your people, off the record, we'll be back after the election. Life is about chess. Sometimes you have to move one step back to move three steps forward the next move. We'll be back. They have my word on it."

"Yes sir. I can sell that."

Homeland Director Wilson has the president pull federal forces back from the uprising and issue a public demand for the governor to do the same. The governor ignores him and unleashes a full attack force on the Jew-Christian resistance, only to have his forces neutralized in what is classified as the Kansas Event and kept secret from both the media and the public. The governor indeed wanted to use the uprising to launch his own surprise presidential challenge to Wilson by personally leading the state government troop assault, but instead the governor is killed that day by "unusual circumstances."

Stillborn

"The bio-switch represents the greatest biological revolution in human history, rivaling the invention of the blood transfusion, the polio vaccine, and the science of human organ transplants. With this simple neo-natal procedure, through the engine of universal healthcare, we end all unwanted pregnancies and fetal terminations forever." – Dr. Albertus Good, inventor, 2061

"Be very careful what you wish for; you may get it." – The Genie

The Abortion Wars are over.
Dr. Good was an unknown veterinarian on the West Coast who, when not working at his successful animal hospital chain, spent his spare time advocating for mandatory spay-and-neutering laws in every state to end animal suffering from overpopulation. Later, he became a medical doctor, once saying in an interview, "well, people are animals too." He stated in other interviews that he did want to end all unwanted and unplanned births for *all* animals forever. In 2061, he introduced the breakthrough bio-engineering medical procedure nicknamed the "bio-switch"—officially called the "reversible reproductive biological modification of sexual organs." The half-joking "Please spray and neuter your baby today" bumper stickers were everywhere. Government would now be able to "touch" every American child—screen out disease or rare abnormalities with vaccinations or neo-natal bio-correcting. The procedure was quickly courted by government officials and offered on all national health care plans. Within a decade, 65 percent of all newborn babies in the general population were given the procedure.

Even before the introduction of the bio-switch, abortion

had already been heading to oblivion with the advances in birth control pharmaceuticals and bio-tek, changing attitudes, steady anti-abortion and anti-infanticide movements, but more significantly, the collective practice in America of simply not having any children at all.

Then came the Registry.

Federal Office Building, Washington DC
8:36 a.m., 3 January 2089

The door of the roof opens and three men in office-suits exit, each with a tablet in their hand. Suddenly from the same entrance, a young male, with yellow hair, mascara, no top, silver pants and barefoot, rushes past them. Then another and another—the flash mob of sixteen kids, male and female, in various psychedelic clothes, run past the men in office-suits.

"This is a restricted area!" the main office-man yells.

"We're going to oblivion!" the girl declares, throwing up her hands in the air.

"Yeah, it'll be superlatively fun. We're addicted to fun," a boy says.

The flash mob runs and jumps in unison off the roof of the ten-story building.

Chesapeake Ranch Estates, Maryland
1:33 p.m., 3 January 2089

Logan is still shaken by the way his Command Center was hacked so quickly and completely. Stealing a device—laptop, e-pad, tablet—is really useless nowadays, as virtually everyone keeps all files, all programs, and all data on the Net. A computer today is simply an access device for your corner of cyberspace; no data files or programs are ever directly stored on the hardware—another reason they are so thin, so light, and so inexpensive.

So the burglars moved to cyberspace, but cyber-security is so good these days. Only governments, the super-wealthy, or celebrities have to worry about the real attacks, not the average netizen. Logan is famous but not a celebrity. He's rich but not the super-wealthy. But this intruder was something altogether different: remote-accessed his vid-cam and his audios *after* he shut off his system; accessed and changed a legitimate registry file, or captured and changed the Data Stream—all in a matter of seconds.

Logan is sitting outside on the steps of his house when the mechanic arrives. The common meaning of the word has changed over the years. Someone who fixes your computer is a car-tek, a car is more of an advanced computer on wheels than anything else; someone who fixes tek hardware of any kind is called a mechanic. Logan takes him into the house and gives him a tour without uttering a word before bringing him back outside.

"I want you to replace every connection: Net and vid and audio feeds," Logan says.

"That's a lot of electronics to replace."

"This was a professional hack. They ripped through my firewalls in seconds and remote-controlled my own systems."

"Replacing all those electronics will prevent them from being able to remote in again, but if they are that good, they probably have your Net identity."

"No, I didn't use my real one, of course."

"If they followed you back to your house and remoted into those systems, you have to assume they may be aware of that too. They can set up bots to look for your presence the second it shows up on the Net."

Bots are the cyberspace equivalents of surveillance drones. They can be tasked to search for one or more ID signatures. Hacking a person's Net identity is, in common slang, "hitting the mother lode." A person's Net identity is tied to their credit cards which are tied to their national identify file—the Registry. A hacker can steal the person's money, max out their credit cards, open up new ones, and use their national identity for other illegal activities. However, if you are running around off-Grid Freespace, you're on your own; the government won't give you a new identity file, and you can't recover damages from the bank or your credit card companies. Another penalty the government uses to keep its netizens off Freespace.

"They wanted me to know they hacked me."

"Why?"

"Not important," Logan says, thinking. "How long will this take?"

"Give my team half a day. Replacing all the electronics is easy, but the testing, configuring, aligning, re-establishing all your security protocols is what takes the time. I'd also recommend adding at least one more level of firewalls."

"Do whatever you need to so they can't do it again."

"If you are really concerned, I could also wire in a kill-switch."

"What will that do?"

"Governments do it, and rich people. No matter how sophisticated the intrusion program or the hacker or cyber pirate, the Net runs on juice. No electricity, no Net. All their powers evaporate. A kill switch severs all tek connections and shuts off all direct and residual power. It's technically illegal, since the government requires you to maintain a Net connection at all times."

"Do it."

It takes only a few minutes for the taxi to arrive to take Logan to the nearby commuting hub. This time he does take the fast-track, since all his appointments will be in the District. He engages in his favorite pastime of people watching, though it's a relatively boring crop of subjects all in their office-suits with only the occasional nonconformist.

Athenus Consulting, Washington DC
6:36 p.m., 3 January 2089

"What happened?" Logan asks. "There are crowds of people on the streets, but the news says the accident happened early this morning."

Ms. Papa leads him down the hallway of her palatial offices. "Yes, it happened before eight a.m. Over a dozen of them dived right off the roof. People still want to see if they can see any blood or guts on the sidewalk, even though the sweepers scrubbed it all clean hours ago. One of the little suicidals followed his parent up to the roof. He was visiting from the Outlands and decided to text all his friends to join him for the swan-dive. The parent should be fined. That's what wireless parenting tek is for, so you can live-cam your little offspring to make sure they're not doing anything unacceptable," she says. "Those people in the outer tek-cities have no connection to productive reality."

They sit in the mid-sized office of the lobbyist firm of Athenus Consulting. Queen Papa is the founder, and after thirty-five years it is still one of the largest and most prestigious on the Hill, with a who's who client list in tek, energy, and politics. She's fifty-something with red hair, probably quite fiery in her youth, a sharp red office-suit, shiny white pearls around her neck, and black lipstick. Her accent is slight but still noticeable; another ex-pat from overseas, in her case from Old Greece. Her parents fled the country prior to the Fall of Western Europe. It seems all the Pagan Western Europeans migrated to and around the District.

"Mr. Logan, you seem to be a bit out of breath."

Logan smiles. "I had to play a bit of hide-and-seek with some competitors."

Just thirty minutes ago, Logan is running through the District streets, chased by four fellow reporters. "Logan, who are you going to see?!" he remembers them yelling. "What story are you working on?!" He manages to lose them in the crowds.

Queen laughs. "Modern journalism must be quite the adventure." She crosses her legs to get comfortable. "Before we start, Mr. Logan, I'm a bit old-fashioned. When I have meetings, I demand people look at me when they talk to me. I don't allow any incoming messages or calls from devices of any kind. Everything else will function. I can have some power coffee brought in or some drugs."

"I'll be fine without any focus stimulants," Logan says. "But how do you...?" She touches a button on her desk. He hears a tiny chirp from his device and sees a red indicator light: no Net access. "Your own universal off switch."

"So how can I help, Mr. Logan? Are you going to use my name as a source?"

"No, I'm looking for background only."

"Why me? I knew Lou, everyone in this town does, or did, but not directly. We were big fish in different oceans. He got people elected. I get the legislation shaped and passed once they are."

"Which means you know all the same people and all the gossip."

She smiles. "Well, I don't know how much of that I can tell you, on or off the record."

"Who do you think killed him?"

"I don't know. They say it was those Jew-Christians."

Logan is not surprised that she already knows, though the official announcement won't be made until tomorrow.

She smiles. "Yes, Mr. Logan, I have sources too."

"You believe it?"

"Why wouldn't I? Officials wouldn't say it if there weren't already strong evidence. I don't know much about religions, but I think his full name is some kind of evil thing to them. I stay away from religious people whenever possible. I wouldn't be surprised if it was a spontaneous act and he was just in the wrong place at the wrong time. Whoever killed him will soon wish they were never born. They'll catch them. The story seems to be done already. Just insert names of the perpetrators. Which will be any day now."

"Yes, but I always look for an original angle in a story."

"That's why you're one of the top ten net-journalists in the world." She smiles. "I have to confess, Mr. Logan. I'm a big fan myself. For years now."

"Thank you."

"I always look for your stories on the Source—everyone I know in the District does. This is quite exciting to actually be one of your contacts."

Logan, still smiling, says, "Any rumors you heard about him or his staff?"

"Mr. Logan, you're fishing. I'm not going to volunteer anything."

"Okay, your firm gets legislation shaped and passed by the elected, which means you interact with all levels in all four branches of government. As the president's national campaign manager and senior chief advisor afterwards, did Lou ever contact your firm to get some piece of legislation through?"

"Why would he do that? He was in the White House. His boss was the president."

"So what? He got the president elected, not the entire Congress and Senate, though it might seem so. Presidents need help from everywhere and anywhere to get their agendas through the Legislature."

She smiles. "You are good at this journalism thing. Okay, he did, actually. Several times."

Logan sits up straight. "Can I text record you? No voice audio, just text only."

"That's fine." She waits for him to press the appropriate button on his e-pad. It will transcribe everything said in the room. "Lou worked with the president before he was even president. Back when he was at Homeland."

"Homeland Defense and Intelligence director."

"Yes, and even before that. But when the president was Homeland director, Lou took the lead or, I should say, he took the lead from behind the scenes in expanding the scope of the Registry and all the necessary legislation that went with it."

"Your firm did the work?"

"Most of it."

"Why does that seem strange to you?"

"Why doesn't it seem strange to you?"

"He was the Homeland director, and the expansion of the Registry would be a natural extension of national security," Logan answers.

"Maybe, but I know when politicians are setting the stage for something else."

"Like what?"

"I don't know."

The Registry has existed for decades: a database of every American in the nation and tied to everything, national identification card, national tax profile, and national medical profile. Even before the Registry was made mandatory, the vast majority of Americans participated. National ID cards replaced passports and state driver's licenses, and were also used as digital cash, programmed with credit cards or direct debit from personal bank accounts, which is why they are now called digi-cards. They're also used as mobile medical records, to be accessed if a person is incapacitated, injured, or killed.

When the Registry became mandatory, it also came to be used legally to enforce anti-hate-crime statutes (designation of ethnicity, national origin, birth gender, current gender, religion if any, and sexual orientation were mandatory); medically, to ensure vaccinations were administered, but more dramatically, that the bio-switch procedure was performed on all babies born in the country; and in terms of national security, to require a DNA sample of all Americans for use in solving crime and terrorism cases. However, Jew-Christians and other off-Griders do not register (and never have), which in itself is illegal.

"Lou was a political man, but some years back, I can't remember when exactly, he suddenly became interested in science. He knew Doctor Al Good personally."

"Albertus Good, the scientist who invented the bio-switch?"

"Yes. To think that a veterinarian who spayed and neutered animals all day for a living would come up with an equivalent procedure for humans. Unwanted pregnancies and abortions completely done away with within a couple of years. He becomes a gazillionaire. Registry participation became virtually universal overnight, except for those Jew-Christians and off-Grid crazies."

"Abortions?"

"I forgot you're a young one. In the past, people terminated their babies before they were born when they didn't want them."

"That seems rather primitive. Another thing to add to my boss's Top Ten list of things we don't do anymore with the coming of the new century. So what did Lou do with Doctor Good?"

"Lou was the one that pushed the legislation through to mandate the bio-switch for all newborns in the nation through the Registry, which again to me seems out of the realm of a political strategist. It's a scientific matter. Unless there was some kind of political strategy that he knew of but no one else saw. You know, like how when abortions were made legal in the pre-modern era, they actually cut the crime rate decades in the future but no one had any idea that would be a result." She can see he doesn't understand. "If the little urchins are never born, then they can't commit crimes fifteen to twenty years later."

"I understand now. Again, very primitive."

"We can have all our shiny new gadgets and devices in Tek World, but people will always be primitive."

"That's for sure. Could it simply be that the president asked him to do it because he didn't trust anyone else? The vote consensus could have gone either way."

"True, that could have been it. The Jew-Christians at the time were so happy to see abortions not only made obsolete but rendered illegal because of the bio-switch for all newborns through universal healthcare. But then they started complaining about government-control of the reproductive determination of humankind. Can't please those people ever."

"Is there anything to it?"

"Of course not. Anyone can have their reproduction functions switched on anytime they want at any twenty-four-hour hospital or clinic anywhere. No one can ever be refused. It's the law. But in this town no one does it. Do you know the District is the host-mother capital of the nation? Everyone uses them if they want to have a kid. But it won't be long until we can reproduce non-biologically, no more child birth or surrogate birth-mothers even. I read about it. They'll be called hatcheries."

Logan smiles and says, "That's weird science fiction."

"Childbirth, eeek. What an undignified thing for a woman. That's primitive."

"Anything more to Lou and Dr. Good?"

"No, but I still think it was strange for Lou to be leading the legislation. I really think there was more to it." She smiles. "Maybe a bigger story down the road."

"If there is, I'll name you as the source in the top paragraph."

"Oh no, don't do that. Just give me a few days' head start so I can gossip to all my cocktail compatriots that I was the source. I'll be at the top of the talk for months."

"It's a deal. Were there any other notable pieces of legislation you pushed through on Lou's behalf?"

"No. All of them had to do with expanding the Registry. There were about two dozen separate pieces of legislation put together into about four different bills signed by three different presidents over the years."

"If it wasn't a spontaneous murder, besides Jew-Christians, who do you think would have killed him?"

"Mr. Logan, the simplest answer is always the answer. They say it was them, then it was them. I think the question should be why, not who."

"Then why?"

"You as a journalist always look for the angle for your stories. Lou always had an angle too. It was all about him. He never did anything unless it could directly benefit him. Getting people elected to the highest office in the land was not about politics or ideology or money with him. It was so he could call in favors for whatever he wanted in all four branches of government and he did so frequently. Working on the Registry and then the bio-switch had to have a personal benefit to him too. The rumor I heard was that Lou was having the good Dr. Good create something for him personally. Maybe the Jew-Christians found out what it was and they thought it was blasphemous to their gods or something."

Logan laughs. "You're just reciting fantasy."

Queen laughs too. "It would be a great story if it were true. Something like Lou mass-producing children directly from his own DNA. Cloning, hatcheries, the next evolution of human reproduction. Exciting, right?"

"That is just plain weird."

Queen laughs. "We live in the District. This is how it is every day. That's why people would rather commute in to work than tele-work. It's just too much fun to miss. But seriously, Lou never helped anyone unless they could do a favor for him. Who knows what Lou was up to. Probably only the president."

"I suspect I won't be able to get that interview."

Queen smiles and says, "We can both be very certain about that."

"Did Lou have enemies?"

"That would murder him? Never. This is America, not the Caliphate, the Russian Bloc, or the Spanish Americas. Beating your guy in the next election is what we do, not killing off the competition. Mr. Logan, this is all petty stuff. Your competition and the police have saturated all these leads days ago, but you know that. You have to do something radically different or your whole story will be still-born, dead on arrival. There's an archaic word for you."

"So we're right back where we started."

"Yes, we are—the Jew-Christians. Were you covering their Separatist Movement?"

"No, I started in the biz just a few years afterwards."

"You should review it, because the Registration Initiative led to that whole thing. Lou was in the center of that too. Maybe that's your 'why' for the murder. These Jew-Christians have memories."

"But that was thirteen years ago. Seems rather thin."

"Terrorism still happens today."

"But from Jew-Christians? Very, very rarely. And it always has to do with someone interfering with their communities. No, you leave them alone and they won't bother you. Muslims and Anarchists are another matter."

As Logan realized a long time ago, the strange thing is that, since the Separatist Movement, now over two decades ago, if you were to ask most Pagans if they had ever seen a Jew-Christian in their entire lives, they would say "no."

Logan adds, "But you've given me an idea."

"A new angle?" Queen's face lights up.

"Yes. I'll see where it goes."

"Good. I'm glad I could help. Everyone says it was the Jew-Christians, and I have no reason to disbelieve them. They may not be actual terrorists, but they are potential ones. 'Agitators and rioters and terrorists.' That's what the news always called them back then."

Washington DC Convention Center (Thirteen Years Earlier)

10:05 a.m., 20 April 2076

The final preparations for the photo shoot are being wrapped up. Clergy from around the country stand everywhere near the massive stage. An aide enters from the back with the White House communications director, S. Frinos.

The aide looks at the clergy and says, "Sir, they're wearing all kinds of religious symbols on their clothes and on chains around their necks. It's illegal to broadcast this publicly. Are we going to digitally erase the images and censure the words when it's time to broadcast?"

The communications director stops. "This is being done under the auspices of the White House. We can do whatever we want. The executive order was signed. Don't mention it again."

Later, he stands with Master Pastor, Bishop Joe, Rabbi Susan, and a couple of their aides.

"Thank you, Pastor, for pulling this together so fast," the communications director says.

Master Pastor says, "After the Kansas Uprising, people need to know that they don't speak for or represent the *real* religious community. The real religious community is peaceful, law-abiding, and supportive of our government."

Bishop Joe says, "Rumors are flying that government police intentionally killed two of their religious leaders."

"Let's not add fuel to the fire," the communication director says. "There are multiple investigations. All the details, good and bad, will be made public."

Master Pastor says, "What we have to get across is that we follow the law, not start insurrections. We are the new religious order in this nation and they better get aboard or find themselves permanently on the outside."

Ever since the Kansas Event, the White House has directed Rabbi Susan to take a more subdued role and to delegate more. Rabbi Susan reviews the schedule on her e-pad; her new deputy, Mr. Finkel, also a registered Jew, stands at her side.

She says, "The Registration Initiative is working. Worship centers are registering with the government and publicly agreeing to use the Good Bible for their worship services."

"It's because compliance means continued tax-exempt status for their religious institution and double tax write-offs for any donations to the religious institution by registered members," Finkel says.

"As long as it gets done, who cares why."

"Rabbi, I think we should still try to open dialog with the Orthodox," he says. "We should take full advantage of the aftermath of their religious civil war."

"The Orthodox will never sign on to the Registration Initiative. They've been the way they are for centuries—before either one of us were born. Focus on the Conservatives. They're split now, so quickly sign up as many as you can to shore up our Reform support. We need to do the same for Jews as Master Pastor has done with the Christians, lock up all the senior leadership."

"That would be easier if we didn't have certain troublemakers at every corner."

"Welcome to the world of politics." She hands the e-pad back to him. "Focus on the Conservatives."

"Do you want to accompany me?"

"No, I've been advised by the Secret Service to be more careful. Apparently, there are Jews who are calling me the new Hitler."

"That is outrageous. I'm sorry, Rabbi, did you kill six million Jews while I was out having my hour lunch? Outrageous. I bet I know who's leading the smear campaign—those fat, self-appointed defenders of all Jewish kind, the Wise Men. Troublemakers all of them."

"Focus, Finkel, focus. Forget those professional pity-peddlers and the 'everything is the Holocaust' crowd. Lock in the Conservatives."

Master Pastor appears next to them. "I couldn't help overhearing. Problems?"

Finkel nods and says, "Problems with the Jews, but nothing new. It's that Anti-Semitic League. It's like they've put a *fatwa* on the Rabbi."

Master Pastor is concerned. Though fatwa is an Islamic word for a religiously sanctioned death contract, it is often used as a kind of slang for the same in other religious circles. He asks, "Death threat?"

Rabbi Susan says, "It's not a real one. They're doing the normal scorched earth, character assassination tactic on me in the Jewish community. I'm Hitler one day, then Goebbels the next, then another Nazi killer. And 'Queen' Herod, too."

Finkel says, "Rabbi don't make light of this. They're jeopardizing your life."

Master Pastor asks, "Is this ASL group led by the Wise Men?"

Rabbi Susan says, "Yes, they've run it forever."

Master Pastor says, "I have some connections in Jewish circles. Let me take that on for you. My contacts are billionaires and billionaires know how to talk to other billionaires in terms they can understand. Where did the other half of your dynamic duo go, Rabbi?"

Rabbi Susan looks around and says, "Bishop Joe was here just a minute ago."

Master Pastor says, "Let's get this show movin' and groovin.'"

He stands in the center of the stage as the cameras engage: "We want the American people to know that we are the true face of Jew-Christians, religious people of good will. On their side are religious agitators, rioters, and domestic terrorists destroying neighborhoods and cities. They are not us. They are few and are disappearing. We, before you, do not resist the rule of law. We do not resist an end to bigotry and intolerance. We do not resist an end to violence. We are the leadership. We are the majority. Let us all stand together. Yes to Registration! No to their resistance!"

After the final vid, all the clergy pose on stage for the massive publicity shots to be blasted everywhere: Master Pastor in the center (African Methodist Episcopal Church Coalition), Bishop Joe to his left (Episcopal Church Coalition), Rabbi Susan to his right (Reform Judaic Council). All around them are the main national clergy leadership: Lutheran Churches Coalition, United Methodist Church Coalition, Unitarian Universalist Unity Churches, Presbyterian Churches of America, American Catholic Council, Baptist Church Unity, Pentecostal Church Coalition, Singing Gospel Church Coalition, New Evangelicals for Good Government, and dozens more.

I Could Kiss Arafat on the Mouth

"What a piece of work is a man! How noble in reason, how infinite in faculties! in form and moving how express and admirable! In action how like an angel! In apprehension how like a god! the beauty of the world, the paragon of animals!" – *The Tragedy of Hamlet, Prince of Denmark* by William Shakespeare, 1599-1601

"O wretched man, wretched not just because of what you are, but also because you do not know how wretched you are!" – Philippic by Cicero, orator and philosopher of ancient Rome, 43-44 BCE

(Excerpt from cover letter to Director of Homeland Defense and Intelligence Agency T. Wilson)

Dear Honorable Director Wilson,
 I thank you so much for the opportunity to present my major thesis paper from my communications program at Columbia University. My colleagues have spoken admirably of the quest of your office to find the best and brightest young minds at our nation's major colleges and universities and your concerted effort to hire from that talent pool to join the president's administration—what a deep honor! I am so impressed to see that someone at your high level within the government understands that every field and every discipline is connected when we talk about the overall national security of America—not just law enforcement, intelligence, military, tek, and politics, but entertainment, culture, and, my fields of specialty, demographical sociology and communications.
 My thesis is attached for consideration.

S. Frinos
Masters Program, Journalism, Strategic & Global Communications - Columbia University, New York

Memo to Director Wilson:

Enclosed are excerpts from the 101-page thesis of graduate student S. Frinos. We recommend him for the formal panel interviews.

From section: Introduction

{For the purposes of this analysis, the following terms will be used that are no longer part of the common language and represent concepts that may be somewhat foreign to the average person. They are: race (not as in the human race but a synonym to the word ethnicity; often used in the past, but now obsolete), White, Black, Hispanic, Latino, Native American, mixed-race, inter-racial.}

From section: The Problem

Despite the assertions, debates and lengthy writings from fellow secular thinkers, analysts, and writers, the inescapable fact is that the United States of America, no matter how large the Pagan population grows, was founded by the religious, our founding documents were founded on religious tenets, and a core center of our citizenry is religious. That admission does not deny that these people and their ideas remain a hold-over from the past, like the duckbilled platypus crawling around the plain with far quicker, smarter, more evolved, more modern fauna present. Pagans have achieved supremacy and do indeed control this country from the elite to academia to the culture. However, there is one term that all still use: Judeo-Christian. To solve a problem we must acknowledge it, not deny it. America was founded as a Judeo-Christian nation. Only by acknowledgement of that fact can we now transform the nation completely and irreversibly to what the Tek World demands it to be. Thus, our strategies for that transformation are as follows:

From section: The Objective-Subjective Construct of Race and Its Benefit to the Modern State

Almost a century ago, census demographers classified the population into thirty different categories known as *race*. Ridiculous, considering that almost a century earlier that same scientific community said there were only three races of humans.

As we know, politics played a role in this creation of race almost from the very inception of the nation. Pre-slavery America primarily used the categories *White* (light-skinned), *Negro* (dark-skinned; African), and *Indian,* or the later term used, *Native American*, (indigenous peoples of North America). Later *Oriental* was added to classify the influx of Chinese.

In early America, not all Whites were created equal, with British, German, Dutch and French occupying the top of the social ladder and Italians, Irish and Jews occupying the bottom. Once slavery became the institution of the land, Blacks on one hand were not considered people of value in terms of rights, but on the other hand were valued sometimes more than lesser Whites and other racial groups because of their capitalistic worth as slaves. Among Blacks themselves, as with other racial groups, the darker the skin, the more 'Black' one was, and the lighter the skin (read mixed-race offspring of Whites and Blacks), the less 'Black' one was. Conversely, among Whites, lighter skinned Blacks were higher in status than darker-skinned ones.

In the early 1970s, the administration of the 37th president, Richard Nixon, created a new race out of thin air: *Hispanic*, denoting origin from Spanish-speaking countries such as Puerto Rico, Mexico, or the Spanish Americas (then known as Latin America). Prior to this change, this sub-group had always been classified as White. This move was purely political, and this new classification by the government officially began in 1980. Later, *Hispanic* would be interchangeable with the newer term *Latino*.

Most of us are aware of these almost comical skin-color classifications of the past, but very few today are aware of how pervasive and powerful they were in this country and in many parts of the world, and how they even determined a person's self-identity and assigned beliefs.

The salient point is that there is no race when it comes to humans. Physical characteristics and traits that manifest over hundreds of thousands of years of evolution in different climates and environments do create distinctive traits, but not new races. What does exist is tribalism. Humans have an almost genetic need to sub-divide into separate cliques, groups or tribes.

More importantly, from the standpoint of the state, race was a useful tool to manage the population. I do apologize up front for any offense from the next example, but the Jew-Christian fable from their so-called holy book is by far the best narration of this fact that could be found: their story of Babel. All the peoples of the world unified in one language and by one purpose to build the Tower of Babel, a monolith reaching from the ground into space. What did their god do? Stop them by giving them multiple languages so they couldn't communicate with each other. The tribes of humans scattered across the world. The Tower of Babel would never be built, and its structure decayed to dust with the passage of time, no trace of it remaining.

Human unity in a state with one ruler is, for lack of a better word, dangerous. If people are unified, they can turn that unity against the state or against one or more laws or policies of the state. The loyalty of the masses in a democracy is a fickle thing. Race has played an important role in maintaining the needed disunity to ensure the masses can be properly managed by the state as desired. The obsolete term used was *ethnic politics*.

The dilemma for the modern tek-state is that 'race' is dead. The culprits are demographics, tek-culture and the Jew-Christians themselves. However, it started with the very minority group that had historically been the victim of the invented concept—Blacks.

With the election of the 16th American president, Abraham Lincoln in 1860, Blacks voted virtually unanimously for his political party, the Republican Party, which was founded explicitly in opposition to slavery and remained that way for over a century.

However, the ultimate irony is that by the late 1960s, just a century later, due primarily to the Second Civil Rights Movement and the political emergence of the new 'baby-boom' generation (Americans born between 1946 and 1964), the overwhelming majority of Black voting patterns began shifting to the historic party of slavery, racial segregation, and domestic terrorism against Blacks—and the killer of their Great Emancipator, President Lincoln.

Generational changes began again as the baby boomers began dying off, including race-centric Black civil rights leaders. The population with the deepest emotional connection to the Second Civil Rights Movement of the 1960s was no longer alive, and their descendants were either apathetic (non-voters) or independent (not favoring either party). For the first time in two hundred years, Blacks ceased to be a reliable voting bloc for either party.

Note the quotes of two of the leading, and opposing, race leaders of the middle of this century: "It is imperative that we maintain our historic Black identity and our emotional, historic, and spiritual ties to our ancestors in the First Civil Rights Movement of the 1850s and the Second Civil Rights Movement of the 1960s. We, as our great founding fathers Frederick Douglas, W.E.B. Du Bois, Booker T. Washington, James Farmer, Reverend 'Daddy' King Senior and finally Reverend Martin Luther King Jr. preached, have not made it to the 'Promised Land.'" - J. Ivory, President of the National Association for the Advancement of Colored People.

"My heart is forever saddened by the race-hustlers who refuse to die, even though we have already sealed them in the coffin and buried them in the ground. The slave runners of the Old Atlantic slave trade era, the Nazis and eugenicists of the WWII era, the Ku Klux Klan and Aryans of the pre-modern era, and now these throw-backs to the past, Ivory and the NAACP, who obviously didn't get the global memo that people stopped calling anyone or themselves 'colored people' two hundred years ago! While Ivory is in the past, the American Bi-Racial, Interracial, and Multiracial Association (ABIMRA) represents the New

America. Or more precisely, the America that always was. We denounce the NAACP, its ilk and like race organizations as we denounce the the long extinct KKK and its. Let the past remain where it belongs—dead." M. Harlim, President of ABIMRA.

The fault of Ivory, the NAACP, and similar organizations was that not only were they using identity terms and a mission that had long outlived their usefulness, but they were advocating for a group of Americans who had no connection to, allegiance with, or interest in them. The generation who cared was dead, and the generation that followed believed skin color to be as significant as having ten fingers and ten toes. Black identity as a political unifier was gone.

The problem with Harlim was the same: if people couldn't care less about being Black, or any other single race, then they would be equally disinterested in being biracial, interracial, or multiracial.

By 2050, 50 percent of Americans self-designated as two or more races. By 2060, 95 percent did. To amplify the point, respondents were self-designating as Black, White, Hispanic, Asian and American Indian, with 36 percent of them also picking "Other." In the latest census, roughly 70 percent selected two or more races, but an astonishing 45 percent wrote in human, homo sapiens, biped, mammal, humanoid, non-cybernetic biological machine, Pangean, Terran or Earther as their self-designation. Leaving aside the humor of some of the responses, it shows that a growing number view such designations as silly, meaning that at a date in the near future, most netizens will simply refuse to select anything at all. The racial designation section of the National Census is by far the least accurate section of the Registry.

There were high hopes that the created 'race' of Hispanic or Latino would replace Blacks as a reliable voting bloc, but a very interesting thing happened. Their numbers increased dramatically across the nation, but the same thing happened to this group that had happened fifty years and a hundred years prior: growing numbers self-designated as White, especially those who no longer spoke Spanish in the home.

Hispanic citizens of Mexican descent were still relatively likely to self-designate as Hispanic/Latino, but non-Mexican Hispanics/Latinos, who came to outnumber the former, were not—again rendering any collected data useless. Further to this point, there were two notable stories wherein residents of a particular city, all White, all self-designated as Black because their sister cities were in Africa; another city where all the residents were Asian self-designated as Hispanic because the city had a Spanish name.

What remains of the nearly eight-century race regime is just a handful of words. Americans have forsaken the concept and instead use the modern replacement terms to simply describe someone's physical appearance. Further, the new terrorism landscape has put the final nail in the coffin by requiring all netizens learn through primary and secondary public education how to accurately describe a person for identification purposes. White is gone; Caucasian is in. Hispanic and Latino gone. Black is gone; olive or light tan, brown or dark tan, and very dark skin or African are in. Asian remains. There is already legislation being crafted to replace the 'race/ethnicity' section of the Census with these 'national identification categories.'

What is a state to do when its people will not allow it to play ethnic politics anymore because they no longer accept the concept of race? Simple: find a new construct by which people can be divided. The state must retain its ability to pit one group against another for specific political goals and avoid at all costs the 'Babel Effect'—the unifying of the general population.

From section: The Malleability of the Masses

In behavioral science, there is a foundational fact that even first-year students are aware of: due to the innate, low intelligence of the public (an objective fact based on data) from overreliance on tek and their need to conform, it is very easy to train and condition the masses to *do anything and believe in anything*. Reconditioning is simply a matter of time and utilizing the most effective behavior modification methods over a prolonged period. Controlling the culture through the media and education through the schools gives the state the necessary abilities to mold the public to the required result and at the same time suppress independent or rebellious thought and criticism of the government.

While many of my fellow students at Columbia are fascinated admirers of uber-propagandist Joseph Goebbels of the Hitler regime of Old Germany, whose mastery of the art still stands the test of time even today, I worship Yasser Arafat, who died at the beginning of this century. Imagine that this little Muslim man got the world to hate the nation-state of Jewish Israel a mere twenty years after the Holocaust and the extermination of some six million Jews. He had the world call Israel bigoted, murderous, and even Nazi-esque. He even had Jews join in the anti-Israel campaign!

It started simply with the hijacking of language by Muslims and Arabs, taking the word Palestinian, which had always meant 'Jew' prior to the 1960s, and, presto, turning it into a word to refer to the millions of *indigenous* Arab people of Israel, except for one thing. There was no such group. Terrorism against Jews was glossed over or ignored, but slights or acts of defense against the new Palestinians were followed by knee-jerk charges of Jewish atrocities and war crimes.

As Hitler so readily learned as a young man after the Armenian Christian Genocide by the Turkish Muslim Empire starting in 1915, kill a few people and it's big news; kill millions, and it's a non-news story. You can even get the world to talk or act as if the event never occurred. In modern times, the same model was followed by the Chinese in the eradication of the Buddhists in New Tibet Province and their ability to even impose *approval* on their citizenry.

The state must be able to create these out-groups for whatever political purposes. Using proven techniques, one can easily create a new out-group or in-group. By using the culture and media in particular, the state can condition the masses to wipe away any aversion to amorality. Morality becomes a malleable construct: i.e., slavery good, slavery bad; abortion bad, abortion good, abortion bad; etc. The state becomes the final arbiter as to what is good and what is bad.

This reconditioning process of acceptance by the public is the same. The *Hat Yai* experiment conducted in Thailand showed that in a space of just ten years a population could be re-trained to go from absolute opposition to forced child prostitution, to indifference, to acceptance. Pick the new/alternative behavior or viewpoint you wish to condition the society to adopt as the norm. We shall name it X.: 1. Talk about X as often as possible and thereby make X look normal and commonplace; 2. Talk about religious institutions that support X as often as possible and thereby suggest endorsement of X by notable entities; 3. Portray religious institutions that don't support X as bigoted, hateful, backwards, and religious institutions that do support X as champions, noble, righteous; 4. Portray members or practitioners of X as victims needing government protection and support—the greater the portrayed victimhood of X the greater their moral claim on the larger society; 5. Portray individuals or groups opposed to X as aggressors needing public condemnation, and ultimately enact laws against them; 6. Make members of X always look good (use positive historic figures or celebrities if available) and hide any negative portrayals; 7. Portray individuals or groups opposed to X always as bad, crazy, bigoted, dangerous, and out of the mainstream, and hide any good portrayals; 8. To attract those undecided, show that support of X is not necessarily support of X itself but support for anti-discrimination and tolerance; 9. Make government elite reinforce the campaign to support X vocally and often; 10. Raise and use the needed money to support the campaign to make X the norm.

CASE STUDY	
Italians, Irish as unequal	Italians, Irish as equal
Jews as unequal	Jews as equal
Blacks as unequal	Blacks as equal
Women as unequal	Women as equal
Interracial as unequal (people/marriage)	Interracials as equal
Homosexuals as unequal (people/marriage)	Homosexuals as equal

Polygamists as unequal (people/marriage)	Polygamists as equal
Other marriages as unequal	Other marriages as equal
Other sub-cultures as unequal	Other sub-cultures as equal

In America, unfortunately, two significant obstacles exist—the Bible and the Constitution. For the state to have supreme control over morality and the ability to shape its people as needed, there can be no objective moral documents in existence. That is why such moral documents of any kind must be destroyed (i.e., Bible/Torah, Constitution). They draw a line in the sand that cannot be breached. The state must retain its ability to redraw those moral lines as it sees fit at any time for any reason.

In those documents are the great barriers to the abolishment of morality by the state, and by inference, the great threat to the state must then be the Jew-Christians. This population is by far the most attached to these documents and, in some sense, worships them. They would compose the majority of any resistance to nullifying these documents.

The technique of *public acceptance modification* is fool-proof. Introduce a new concept into the media/culture, then increase its exposure over time; introduce happy, friendly, and attractive spokespeople for that new concept; then reinforce it through public education and cultural indoctrination. This simple technique works every time, except on the followers of these documents—the Jew-Christians. Though their numbers are diminishing, their zealotry could ignite at anytime.

Jew-Christians are the only obstacle to this process. Previously, I spoke of how race was gone and *Black* was obsolete, but to use the term again to make the point, there is a gross over-representation of the Black among Jew-Christians. We should replicate what I call the *Arafat Process* towards these Jew-Christians, especially the Blacks and Jews, as was done to the Jewish Israelis. These Jew-Christians represent the largest bloc of voters and netizens unsupportive of the state. People are to serve the state as it's the ultimate burden of the state to ensure the existence, sustainability, growth and protection of the nation and its population.

To use a phrase coined by the American Founding Fathers, we can make a "more perfect union" by this purge of religiosity and its adherents, resulting in an ordered nation which will be a nation-state that as closely resembles 'paradise' as humanly possible.

We can be thankful that the Pagan population is a majority in America now. All public opinion analysis indicates with 99 percent certainty that such a move would be accepted, even before propaganda and public attitudinal protocols could be implemented with the necessary sociological macro-response techniques.

Memo from T. Wilson / HDIA Director, 21 August, 2075

Please notify HR that S. Frinos has been hired to serve as the new Homeland Defense and Intelligence Agency communications director, effective 1 September, 2075.

Weird People

"This is very hard for me to write. It forces me to squarely confront my past actions and to accept responsibility for the damage I have had a part in causing. I sincerely apologize for my involvement in and my founding of the AIDS activist organization ACT-UP [AIDS Coalition to Unleash Power] DC. I have helped create a truly fascist organization... The average gay man or woman could not immediately relate to our subversive tactics, drawn largely from the voluminous Mein Kampf [Hitler's autobiography], which some of us studied as a working model." – Eric Pollard, founder of ACT-UP DC, January 1992 (from The Pink Swastika)

"It seems incredible to me that Faithers were so utterly oblivious to the fact that the destruction of two-person heterosexual marriage would naturally and inevitably lead to the wholesale attempted eradication of religiosity in all its forms from society, especially Christianity. I'm not even speaking in moral or religious terms, but of particular interest, the destruction of peoples. I really can't understand it. A blind man could have seen it coming from two hundred miles away." – Mother Moses, leader in the Resistance, 2075

"For the fifth time, I don't wanna come to your cat's birthday party, freak. My dog is getting married that day." – Someecards.com

Crystal Cathedral Church, Virginia
11:02 a.m., 4 June 2076

The building, as it name hints, seems to be constructed out of pure glass. Inside, the many vaulted windows amplify the light. A few pastors talk with Bishop Joe, Rabbi Susan, and Master Pastor—now the universally recognized leaders of the national pro-Registration religious coalition.

"Have you heard of this man called Moses?" a pastor asks.

"Who is he?" Rabbi Susan asks.

"He's supposedly organizing all anti-Registration clergy, it seems nationally now," the pastor says.

"I think I heard his family members were killed in the Kansas Uprising," another pastor says.

"So they found a revolutionary for their side," Master Pastor says.

"If his family was killed, we should say something," Bishop Joe adds. "Some kind of public statement, that we grieve the loss of life and must end the violence."

"No," Rabbi Susan says. "The the whole thing is still under Homeland investigation."

"Is Moses his first name or last name?" Master Pastor asks.

"I think his last," another pastor answers.

It's not uncommon for people nowadays, religious or not, to use only one name for their primary identification, even along with a title.

"What denomination?" Master Pastor asks.

"I think he was with the Baptist church. Or African Methodist. He was a pastor with his wife before joining the Resisters," a pastor says.

It has become the established name for those Jew-Christians who fought the Registration Initiative—Resisters. The term the *Resistance* would come later.

"Rabbi, can you use your resources to find out all about him?" Master Pastor asks.

"I'll have Homeland pull his full Registry file," Rabbi Susan says.

New Atlantic City, New Jersey
4:52 p.m., 4 January 2089

Even in the shiny, pulsating land of tek-cities, there must

be space for the darker, grimier, and baser—the seedy side of town—the Outlands, the term for lesser tek-cities. If New Vegas is the model of those metropolises that transitioned smoothly to the Tek Age, then Old Atlantic City is the example of one that didn't. It is a retro-fitted tek-city, but the era when it was a major destination for travelers, especially from the East Coast, is now a century and a half past. The old traditional brick-and-mortar casinos no longer exist in America. Why would they? All gambling is on the Net now, and all cash is digital.

If Trenton, Jersey City, and Princeton, are A-plus tek-cities, then Atlantic City is a C-rated town where office-suit wearers and beautiful people are rare and the naked, metal-clothed, dark-draped, body-modified, body-pierced are the norm. Always a potentially dangerous place to go, but then that's why people came and why people lived here. If the perfect were called "beautiful people," then Goths, Vampires, Nihilists, Hedonists, Anarchists, Zombies, Nudists, Space Cadets, and Trogs are the "real people"—or the "human refuse," depending on your point of view.

Logan takes public transportation this time, taxi to bus to train to bus, even though it's by no means convenient. He'd rather not risk his personal car. He might return to find Hedonists having an orgy in it, a Nudist urinating or defecated on it, or an Anarchist ripping it apart "just because it was there."

He wears a thick black coat over his normal clothes and goggles on his eyes while he holds an air filter mask to his mouth and nose as he walks further into the city.

Every wall is a holo-wall that changes in rapid succession with various advids—all related to drugs, sex, body modifications or implants, or sports. Some are on a general ad rotation and others cater to a specific person, identifying them based on their portable devices or embedded chips to be able to sell to them. More and more people are getting chipped especially to interface with their smart-houses even when they are not carrying their e-pads or tabs, but Logan isn't into body modification or implants of any kind.

The street crowd is sparse compared to what he's used to. A

Nudist runs by completely naked except for a groin sock. A lot of people have cigarettes (simply known as cigs) in their mouths, exhaling a wide variety of colored smokes from a wide variety of recreational drugs. To think that in pre-modern America smoking actually used to be banned in most public places, and they weren't even real narcotics. Well, the anti-smoking forces were crushed like a flea when the pro-drug forces really got going—all drugs were made legal in all fifty-three states and the American territories.

For those who want to join the drug culture without their own cig, every ten feet or so are plumes, which is why Logan maintains the mask on his face and wears goggles. Plumes are about four foot high poles of various styles, weighted to the ground, that release a steady flow of psychogenic, hallucinogenic, and stimulagenic vapors for the public to sample the drugs for sale in the particular drug store or being used in the drug den, brothel, or circuit parlor they're passing. For the non-user or the uninitiated, like Logan, the vapors mess not only with the mind but with the eyes, nasal passages, throat, and even skin pores.

A bug-eyed man suddenly appears next to him. He looks grimy, with his matted hair hanging in front of his face. He only wears a loose, clear plastic vest and very tight pants.

"I'm bored," the man says, holding his crotch.

Logan says, "What do I have to do to get you away from me right now?"

"Beat me. Beat me up or let me beat you up. I just had my five-minute drugs and my groin hurts, so that's all I can do right this minute." The man starts to move closer.

In an instant, the man drops to the ground unconscious. Logan holds his stun-stick firmly.

A male and female couple dressed in black with spiky hair, tattoos, and piercings everywhere run up to him with the biggest smiles. "Stun us too," she says. Logan doesn't hesitate, and they fall to the ground.

Logan found out he had a child from a past girlfriend about seven years ago. His kid is twenty-seven. Logan was caught by total surprise and suspected the mother only contacted him when he became famous to get money, but he still felt a compulsion to be in his son's life, even if he was already an adult; she has been a useless mother raising him. The state may classify him as an adult, but his Nihilist son is anything but.

No one in Tek World gets married—people cohabitate as they please for as long or as short as they want and in some rare cases have a child or two. Marriage is such an out-dated concept, and no matter what arguments to the contrary or what the configuration, it is a religious one on top of that. The terms *husband* and *wife* were actually made illegal years ago, so the proper term is *partner*. Such irony. The Marriage Wars went on for over fifty years and by the end *all* marriage was made legal, but the side that won discarded the practice altogether. But not the Jew-Christians, they're the only ones in society who still get married—always two-person, male-female, over the age of eighteen, couples exclusively.

Sprocket stands at the corner waiting for him, dressed in black skin-jeans and a ripped up t-shirt covered by a thin, plastic leather jacket with a flimsy hood attached. His long dark brown hair is disheveled except for a casual part to keep it out of his dark brown eyes, barely.

Logan reaches him and looks at the buildings around them: a v.r. game parlor where the hardcore gamers come to play the latest games in large rooms with full computer-generated virtual reality interfaces; next door, a male, female, she-male, male-she and dual-gender hermaphrodite workers hover around the doors of a brothel and a drug den.

"Hey boys, me love you long time," one of them says.

Logan isn't amused and looks at his son. "So which one were you in?" he asks.

"Daddio, you might as well be a JC with your judgmentality."

"What's a JC?" Logan knows, but he asks anyway.

"Are you kidding? Jew-Christian, of course."

"I have to be sure, with all the acronyms youth use today. And there's no such word as judgmentality. But to move the conversation along, I'm just asking a question."

"I was in all three."

Logan pretends not to be annoyed. "When are you completing

your Registry file? You need to pick your sexual orientation." Legally, people are required to self-identify their gender and sexual orientation for census reasons.

"Daddio, you need to red light the verification thing."

"You can't remain in unverified status forever. They'll start fining you."

"Let them. I don't have any bank accounts with money."

"What happened to the one I opened for you?"

"Daddio, you really are mad. I was in the v.r. game-room, not the drug den or the brothel. But I pass by the plumes every chance I get to suck the fumes. Deliciously good inhale. And I am going to a circuit parlor later tonight."

Drug dens, where addicts congregate to indulge their habits, are very popular. Prostitution has also been legal for decades, but often the brothels are zoned to be on the outskirts of the tek-cities. Circuit parlors are basically group hotels where people on the circuit can meet for their liaisons.

"You closed the bank account I opened for you again? Why do I bother? And I'm not mad. I can't tell you what to do. You're an adult."

"And you're only thirteen years older than me, so you definitely don't have more wisdom than me."

"Thanks for spitting in my face again. If I had known you existed at birth, I would have been around, and you would know I had more wisdom in my little body at thirteen than you do now, almost-thirty offspring."

"Doubt that. Maybe you should have made better choices with those you inseminated."

"Okay, I'm leaving. You're in one of your moods."

"Okay, okay, Daddio. You're so sensitive today. What did you want to talk to me about?"

Logan pauses to calm himself down. How do offspring always know the buttons to push to anger you so easily?

"My sources say the best off-Grid tek-heads are Jew-Christians. Is that true?"

His son grins at him without saying a word.

"Is it supposed to be a secret? Who would be the best group

to approach to find a real tek-head in the Jew-Christian world? I need the best off-Grid one out there," Logan says.

This is Logan's ace-in-the-hole. None of his competitors would think to go to the very people said to be complicit in the Lucifer Mestopheles murder.

"Hacker, tek-head, or tek-lord?"

"What's the difference really?"

"Hackers or tek-heads are for the simple things. Tek-lords—they can do freaky tek-whispering. Real tek-magic skills. Tek does what they command. The rumor is that some tek-lords can even hack into the Grid and the Registry. But all rumors."

"Tek-lord then. Who to approach?" Logan asks. "Nihilists, Hedonists...?"

Sprocket puts up his hand. "Daddio, I hear you. I'll do the run-down. Nihilists believe in nothing and spend most of their time doing drugs. A Nihilist is an ex-Hedonist bored of sex or a Zombie-to-be, that's unless they euthanize themselves beforehand."

Logan removes his mask from his face. "Don't you consider yourself a Nihilist?"

Euthanasia is also nationally legal and, though not widely reported in the media, suicide by drugs is quite common. Logan hates the word—a euphemism that hides a terrible act, in his mind.

Sprocket looks at him. "Daddio, red light those emotions. I'm a quasi-Nihilist. And I'm not planning to commit suicide. At least not today." He smiles.

Logan is not amused.

"You're mad again," Sprocket says.

"No, I'm not."

"You didn't know I existed for twenty of my twenty-seven years on this blue marble Earth. If I exited to oblivion, why would you care?"

"I guess as a Nihilist, you wouldn't understand. Give me the rest of the run-down."

"Well, Hedonists are just into sex. Zombies are slaves to the drugs. Space cadets are not mentally connected at all; they believe they were abducted by aliens and were experimented on. All they do is wander around, talking to themselves, and doing nothing."

"Like Nihilists."

"We don't talk to ourselves. That would be doing something."

"Not looking promising."

"Daddio, I'm not finished. Goths wear their black clothes, black tattoos, black piercings, but not all of them are Nihilists, Hedonists, or Zombies. Did you know some of them are JCs?"

Logan is surprised. "Really?" If a Jew-Christian wanted to hide in the general population that would be a good way to do it. "Hiding in plain sight."

"And Trogs."

Trog is the common slang for those who hate tek—they avoid not only using it but even being near it. For the average tek-dweller, it's a state of being so alien, so deranged, so inhuman. People cannot live without the mechanization of the Tek World.

"But Trogs hate tek. That's why they're called Trogs."

"Daddio, two kinds of Trogs—those who hate tek and those who hate tek controlled by the government but are very much tek-heads. If you don't have any contacts, find a JC Goth to get you to a JC tek-head Trog, and they'll get you a JC tek-lord."

"I learned something today."

"What?"

"My offspring actually knows something I don't."

Sprocket smiles. "Okay, I'm sorry I was in a mood with you before."

"It's okay. How do I find someone from one of these two groups? And how do I get them to talk with me? To the JC, I'm a Pagan. To the tek-head Trog, I'm part of the Grid. Why would they trust me?"

"You need a go-between. Someone who knows you and knows them. Otherwise it will be a big red light all around."

"Then who do I need to talk to so that it is a big green light all around?"

"Daddio, think fast! You're losing the window of opportunity!"

"How much?!"

Sprocket smiles. "I was thinking you were starting to get senile already."

"If I am, then you're right behind me. But you don't believe in money."

"I don't believe in bank accounts. I got tons of money. Off-Grid, Daddio, off-Grid."

Evangelical Lutheran Church for the Master, Virginia
11 a.m., 28 June 2076

Bishop Dyna takes center stage to overlook the Sunday worship service. Her co-clergy are Bishop Edna—also her wife, visiting from another church—on her left and Reverend Eunice on her right; they stand back a bit with arms and hands outstretched. Bishop Dyna looks down at her feet and suddenly notices water rising above them. She bends down and takes off her shoes, then rises to watch the waters again. No one else sees what she is seeing. *Am I hallucinating?*

Bishop Edna and Reverend Eunice look at each other, concerned.

Bishop Dyna looks up. A congregation of about twenty-five people sits in the pews, all spread out in the modern church that could seat five hundred. She jumps down from the stage and runs down the aisle and out of the building. Everyone else looks around in bewilderment.

Bishop Edna and Reverend Eunice look at each other again from the stage, not knowing what to do or what has just happened.

Washington DC Convention Center
11:02 a.m., 4 July 2076

The Marriage Wars are over.

The gathering: a man with his seven wives, a woman with her three husbands, a woman with her pet, an elderly man with a little girl, a bearded woman with a man wearing a dress, among many other civilians mixed in with the clergy of the National Religious Registration Alliance.

A few pastors are visibly nervous about the gathering.

"What is this? I thought we were promoting the Registration movement among religious Americans—leaders and laypeople," a reverend says.

Bishop Joe says, "It's all connected, Reverend. We're breaking down all the walls at one time. We're showing the world that the new religious in America have left all the bigotry and intolerance behind. That's why we embrace Registration. That's why we embrace the Good Bible."

"Is that a man or a woman?" another clergyman says, looking at the group. "And that woman has a dog? What's that supposed to be? The dog is her husband?"

Rabbi Susan tries to change the subject. "The fastest-growing religious group in America has been those with no religious affiliation at all. And that's because our religious institutions have not been attractive to the masses in modern tek-society, especially young people. Organized religion has been declining for a long time, and we better change or we'll go the way of the dinosaurs."

"And this is the solution?" the reverend asks. "A man with twenty wives? An old man with a toddler as a wife? A woman marrying a pet? What kind of madness have you brought us into here?"

Bishop Joe says, "Reverend, one of the wisest men in the Bible, King Solomon, had a thousand wives."

The reverend looks at him. "That's not even remotely funny, Bishop. Who was the wise man in the Bible who had a pet for a spouse?"

"Everything should be legal when it comes to consenting adults," Bishop Joe says.

"A child is not an adult," one of them says.

Bishop Joe ignores the comment. "People should be able to marry whomever they love. Why are we still trying to tell God's children that they can't marry who they love? We live in the modern Tek World. In the end, who are we to judge? Only God can judge."

"That's not Biblical doctrine or teaching, Bishop. None of that is."

"Gentleman, I'm proud to be a Christian and a member of one of the leading mainstream Protestant movements that has led the way on tolerance and marriage equalization and modernization. We have led the way in recognizing non-hetero unions for decades. So this isn't new. We're just expanding the tent for everyone."

Rabbi Susan says, "Reverend, you may feel some in the coalition may be out there on the fringes, but let's not be distracted from our purpose here. This is a march for freedom and tolerance and dignity and the future. That's a message we can all rally around. That's why we're here for the march. Do you know what these images will do when they go viral? The power of these images. This is what the people will point to and talk about. The New Religious Paradigm in America. Religion that tolerates all! That's power."

Bishop Joe smiles and says, "That's God-power!" He grabs the reverend by the shoulder. "And it's the Jesus thing to do, Reverend! Can I get an amen?!"

The reverend and the other clergymen pause for a moment. The reverend says softly, "Amen."

At the other end of the gathering a few of the pan-sexual members walk up to Master Pastor.

"Can we talk to you privately?" asks the he-she.

"Of course, what do you need?" Master Pastor asks.

"Well," the she-he says. "We want to be on record that we don't want the homos to be in the center. They are so bossy and think they are so superior. They always try to crowd us out. Put them on the outside or in the back. That's what they always do to us. There are six genders, after all, but they'd have you think there are only four."

Master Pastor smiles. "We'll make everyone happy."

With cameras and reporters swarming around them, the rally makes its way down the street, cordoned off by police. The clergy walk with arms linked in rows of seven people each. Bishop Joe and Rabbi Susan, Master Pastor, and notable elected officials lead the march. Thousands of fellow clergy and citizens representing all marriages and alt-life styles follow.

God's Little Church, Maryland
1:06 p.m., 9 July 2076

The pastors sit across from Bishop Joe and Rabbi Susan. Their faces are sullen.

"Pastor, you need to understand that this is going to happen. The pro-Registration religious movement is growing across the country," Rabbi Susan says. "You represent a key coalition of churches who haven't joined either side. We want you on our side."

"And like it or not, this is national now. It's going to happen. The votes in Congress are there. No religious speech against any lifestyle will be sanctioned. It's done," Bishop Joe says.

The pastor looks up in the air and says, "What was that saying from my late father? 'Everything can be marriage. And when everything is marriage, nothing will be.'" He looks back at them. "You mean marriage as defined as a union between two or more biological things, you're ignoring your Sid and Nancy people, you already have the Woody A. Clubbers, and you'll need to change it again so someone can marry a robot. I'm surprised you haven't thought of it already."

Sid and Nancy was the woman—Nancy—who was leading the charge for people to be allowed to marry their pets, in her case, her dog Sid. The Woody Allen Club was an organization that grew out of the movement to eliminate all age-of-consent laws in all fifty-three states and thereby eliminate any existing pedophilia laws. WAC also advocated the end to all anti-incest laws.

Rabbi Susan says, "Use of the Good Bible in your church will soon not be voluntary, Pastor. It will be law. Hate-speech will not be tolerated in any church or synagogue. We didn't allow supporters of slavery to prevail or supporters of skin-color segregation to prevail."

"Are those the talking points you're using with the public?

We're synonymous with the Klansmen and Nazis of the past? There's only one problem with your propaganda, Miss Susan and Miss Joe. We never lynched anyone, hanged anyone from a tree, set anyone on fire, hurt anyone, killed anyone. The only thing we've done is pray and worship God, give to charity, help the poor, provide for and raise our families. Asking for nothing, but to be left alone." He stares coldly at them. "Your little sidekick is just a traveling circus show of sin wrapped up in a false cloak of religion. You on the other hand seem to enjoy the destruction you're unleashing among your people, my people, all to be the center of attention, to be able to tell your Pagan cocktail-set buddies in the District that 'I get to speak to the White House every day.'" He points his finger. "You both are going to get what you deserve one day. Your Pagan masters will eject you from the property to be picked up with the trash one day. Mission accomplished, they will say to you. Go join your own kind. But we won't take you back either."

"Please don't feel this is some anti-religious, anti-Christian crusade and that you're all being singled out. These laws apply to everyone," Rabbi Susan says.

"You're joking, of course," the pastor says. "This is a crusade against *us*."

"The only way you will get my Bible is from my dead, cold hands," the other pastor says.

"I'm sorry you feel that way. As the director of religious affairs, I'm simply upholding the laws of the land. No hate-speech in written, verbal, or digital forms will be allowed anymore. All Americans must register with the government, no exceptions. All religious institutions must register, as a condition of their tax-exempt status, and use of the Good Bible is a further condition. Pastor, we're trying to do the same thing you are: make a better world for everyone in this country. This is not a grand conspiracy to get Jews or get Christians or get Mormons or any other religion. We are simply upholding the laws of the land. Equal rights and tolerance for everyone."

"Your shiny tek-cities, flashing signs and computer-controlled machines. This is what you have labored to create—Neo-

Sodom and Gomorrah. We want no part of your Tek World."

The pastor says, "Intolerance of some things is a virtue. You use the word intolerance as a trick to confuse people into believing that opposition to something that is wrong or immoral or not in keeping with the Bible is bad. You may be able to fool most of the people most of the time, but we are not those people."

"Tell me what the hostility is all about," Rabbi Susan asks. "We can figure this out. Our coalition is big enough for everyone. Why are you afraid of unity?"

The pastor shakes his head. "You truly don't know, do you? We're not afraid or against unity. We're against *your* unity. How can you call yourself a religious leader? If you reject everything that the Bible declares, then what the hell makes you different from the Pagans? Rabbi Susan, do you believe in God?"

Rabbi Susan at first starts to answer emphatically but stops for a second, then, aware of her own hesitation, answers, "I've never been asked that before. It's silly. I'm an ordained rabbi of the Reform Judaic Council."

"You didn't answer my question."

Rabbi Susan says directly, "Of course. Yes."

The pastor and the other clergy stare at them. He says, "Have a good day."

Not even a closing "God bless you." The pastor leans back and folds his arms. He will not be shaking their hands or ending the meeting with the customary prayer. Rabbi Susan and Bishop Joe slowly leave the room.

Another pastor says, "Another excuse for the government to create their damn database of Americans. Four hundred years it categorized people based on skin color so it could give light-skinned people goodies and beat up the dark-skinned ones. Then for some fifty years it gave its goodies to dark-skinned people and beat up the light-skinned people. They only stopped because they couldn't do the skin-color game anymore. Then they moved to categorizing over who or what or how many a person sleeps with. Now they're obsessed with knowing who your God is. Do religious folk honestly think all this gathering of information is so they can send each of us a box of chocolates?"

The main pastor looks at his aide. "It's real now. We are officially in a state of war."

The aide says, "The Jews are collapsing from their own intra-religious war."

"Who's winning?"

"The Orthodox are intact. But the Reformers and Conservatives—when their war is over, there may not be a Reform or Conservative Jewish movement left."

The pastor sighs. "What about us? Who's intact our side?"

"We're worse off than the Jews. We're just not fighting in the streets against ourselves yet. The government has the Episcopalians, Methodists, Lutherans, Unitarians, Catholics in their pocket. Master Pastor has almost everyone, the entire Christian leadership across all denominations. Baptists, Presbyterians. He claims he even has the Evangelicals and Pentecostals."

"It's a game with him. He's signing up the leaders but not the people."

"What can we do? Non-denominational, un-affiliateds like us don't have any power. It seems like it's over," the aide says.

"We are the righteous on this one. And by God, when one puts righteousness and goodness in a box with corruption and evil, only goodness will triumph after the messy process."

The aide says, "Pastor, I was raised on a farm. If you take the greatest wine in the world, aromatic and bold, crisp and refreshing, and mix it with feces, in the end all that remains is crap."

Temple Israel, Miami, Florida
5:34 p.m., 20 July 2076

The synagogue is in chaos, with lots of yelling from the hundreds of attendees in the seats facing the stage where the seven-member Conservative High Council sits. The head rabbi stands in the center and holds up his hands to try to calm the crowd.

A man carrying a metal baseball bat gets up from his seat and walks onto the stage. The head rabbi watches him, as does the High Council, with confusion at first, and then with fear.

"Head Rabbi, if you don't immediately sit down and shut up,

I will take this metal bat and beat you to death right now, here and now!" the man yells. He raises the bat, holding the handle with two hands as if readying to swing. The Council remains frozen seated in their chairs; the head rabbi runs to his chair and sits down. People in the crowd watch in astonishment, some seated, some standing. The commotion lowers to whispers.

A woman walks up to the microphoned podium on the stage. The man stands behind her, holding his metal bat in his right hand, its end touching the ground.

"*Boker tov*. My name is Tova. And this is my husband, Mr. Tova," she says. "Excuse our blunt nature, but we've just returned from living in Israel for about ten years carrying guns and machine guns and knives wherever we went since the Muslims there are waiting every second to wipe Jews off the face of the planet. So my husband and I said, let's move back to America, bring the kids, and move to where Jews are safe, where Jews are strong, where Jews know how to stand up to persecution. And what do we find? Not Muslims destroying Jews or Pagans destroying Jews. Jews destroying Jews! It's like nothing changes in our history.

"We have a choice right now, right here. We will not allow Conservative Judaism to collapse. These men sitting behind us have the audacity to call themselves our High Council and fiddle around with triviality while New Jerusalem—America—burns. You have a choice! Either stay in this building, which has ceased to be a synagogue, a place of honor and worship, since our esteemed High Council has used it as a place to collaborate with our enemies. Or you can leave with us now to re-start the real Conservative Jewish Order by voting for a new High Council. One that doesn't collaborate. One that looks out for its people, its families, and its communities. One that honors God and our holy Jewish texts. So let them remain here to confer with their Pagan masters in the Capitol—we will not be here. And if it's only myself, my husband, and our children, then so be it. We will be the New Conservative Jewish Order. This will then be the home of the New Reformer Disorder."

Tova steps down from the stage with her husband. Up the aisle they walk, and each row empties with people following. In moments, the synagogue is empty—except for the seven-member High Council.

Location Unknown
11:58 p.m., 5 January 2089

Logan stands at the corner, waiting. Still in his thick black coat, his air-mask now firmly fastened over his nose and mouth by a plastic strap. He has met many an informant in a secluded place for a story, but this area is way out of the way. There is no one around, no drone fly-overs, no visible Eyes at all. He doesn't like it.

A group of four people appears from around the corner and walk towards him from twenty yards away. They are dressed in black and their faces are obscured by black hoods, *but they all have glowing yellow eyes.*

This is not good. They could be the people he's supposed to meet or they could be a group of Nihilists or Anarchists looking for a lone victim to assault, or worse. He thinks to himself that he could be brave and wait it out. However, he isn't brave and he isn't a fighter. Contrary to the movies, when one guy takes on four guys, the one guy loses every time.

Logan runs. He hears the four men laughing hysterically behind him. *Suddenly his back is hit hard by an object.* As he's running, he turns his head back to look down at the ground. It's not a rock or bottle, but a strange black ball of some kind with a steady red light.

The four men are gone, so he stops running and slowly walks back to the object. It could be dangerous, but he stares at it.

"What do you want?" the object says in a deep-bass mechanical voice, startling Logan.

Logan steps closer. "Who are you?"

"I don't have time to waste, Mr. Logan. This is Goli, the tek-lord."

The Math That Lost America

"Pay no attention to that man behind the curtain." – The Wizard of Oz

Threat Matrix Memo to President (Classified "For Your Eyes Only")

Mr. President, I bring an urgent matter to your attention—doubly so, now that we have witnessed the real-time Fall of Western Europe. The inescapable fact, Mr. President, is that the United States is dying! I realize that you will on first reflection want to dismiss my declaration, feeling I'm engaging in tiresome hyperbole. However, we will inevitably cease as a world superpower, as predictably as Western Europe ceased to exist—their fall predicted many decades ago—unless you act.

America has several critical vulnerabilities:

The National Debt – Our third president, Thomas Jefferson, said it best: "It is incumbent on every generation to pay its own debts as it goes. A principle which if acted upon would save one-half the wars of the world." Our nation has not only been spending its children's money for decades but its grandchildren's and great-grandchildren's. The nation has been spending more money than it takes in for over a century, but this practice will reach its end and has already affected our strategic and tactical planning and decisions domestically and abroad. The interest on that debt has again become our single largest item of the budget. Having come from the budget and finance side of the government sector as director of the Office of Budget and Finance (the merging of the Old Office of Financial Research and Congressional Budget

Office) before moving into my current position, there is no better example than the creation of our super agency, the Homeland Defense and Intelligence Agency, which was a merging of the Old Department of Homeland Security, Federal Bureau of Investigation, Central Intelligence Agency, Defense Intelligence Agency, and National Security Agency. This, as with all our initiatives for government efficiency, was not driven by the desire for government efficiency, despite media hype to the contrary, but by the realization of a certain date when we would no longer have the money to run all of these agencies simultaneously. The founders of the nation should have included among the Articles of the Constitution one wherein government expenditures could not exceed a certain percentage of GDP during peacetime and a higher level during wartime. But these eighteenth-century men could not have foreseen everything. The enormity of the money we owe to various nations, especially the CHINs, and to a lesser degree the Russian Bloc and Australia, has left us with the inability to fully keep pace with our domestic obligations—military, education, and entitlement spending. All manner of financial strategies (and gimmicks) have been exhausted, such as closing all overseas bases and returning all troops to the homeland, implementing proportional rather than majority funding for the United Nations and NATO (this should cease altogether now that the Caliphate has taken control of Western Europe), imposing a national sales tax on all physical and Net purchases, additional vice tax on all prostitution, recreational drug, and sporting activities, automatic assessments on all bank transactions by individuals and corporations, elimination of all Congressional earmarks, increased energy sales to the Spanish Americas and the Asian Consortium, and further nationalization of industries within a capitalistic framework. Our dire situation is further exacerbated by a shrinking domestic tax base due to declining birth-rates, rising suicide rates and increasing off-Grid populations. There are now plans through executive order to eliminate all bonuses and cost-of-living increases for national government workers, impose salary caps, and mandate bi-weekly (to start) furlough days for workers not under the Homeland Defense and Intelligence

Agency or otherwise directly related to the government security and intelligence communities.

Economic Terrorism – With our current national debt status, it would follow that others would try to hasten our financial implosion. We currently borrow nearly fifty-five percent of every dollar we spend. Both the CHINs and the Islamic Caliphate are aware of our precarious financial situation, as are lesser global powers, but only the former two have the means to capitalize on the knowledge. They can, through cyber-war or even traditional financial means, cripple America's economy by calling in our debts, forcing a renegotiation of our debt at higher and higher rates, closing key economic markets to our physical goods and services, or shutting off, or disrupting, the Net-bridges to their territories to block Net-commerce.

Cultural Degradation – The rise of Nihilist, Hedonist and Anarchist cultures will eventually threaten normal secular society by their anti-work mindsets and physically destructive behaviors. Physical government force may be required soon, with the strong possibility of riots, insurrection, and domestic terrorism resulting.

Welfare State Time-Bomb – The rolls of those Americans receiving government assistance transfer payments have increased to 85 percent of our population. The rolls are expected to further increase with the coming mass immigration of secular populations from Old Europe as a result of the Fall of Western Europe. None of this is remotely sustainable for even the short term. Also, continued welfare fraud from criminal cartels primarily in the Spanish Americas and the Russian Bloc, though at the margins, still represents an ongoing threat to the solvency of the funds.

Civic Center Degradation – The implementation of tek-interfaced voting systems on local, state, and national levels did result in an increase of voter participation in the electoral process decades ago. However, voter apathy has returned us to the days of single-digit voter turnout in local and state elections. National elections, despite voter tek advancements, still hover below 50 percent and have even dipped to as low as 25 percent in recent years. This apathy has a direct correlation with national legalization of recreational drugs and prostitution, the steady consumption of entertainment and vid-games, the rise of negative cultures (as noted in the preceding paragraph), and even the use of tek itself. We no longer possess a reliable civic center or foundation of core netizen voters to help guide the country in solving its problems, and as a result, the federal government must take over more local and state control and view its function as a stern caretaker of the American people rather than as a public servant. The federal government has already taken over the local policing of most tek-cities in the nation, because most states so mismanaged their funds that they could no longer afford their own state police. Our current form of democracy, more precisely a representative republic, that was put in place 289 years ago has run its course and no longer has the political cohesion necessary to run our nation-empire. The dictatorial model of our global enemies affords them the political agility needed to effectively advance their empires, and we must adapt accordingly or follow the fate of the former Western Europe.

At the writing of this report, America remains the last remaining empire of Western civilization. Mathematical projections calculate the nation has only a decade and a half of sustainability left at the most, barring any catastrophic crises, after which time the country will neither be able to economically sustain nor to militarily protect itself adequately, as we will run out of all financial resources and debt-borrow options will no longer be available to us. Unfortunately, we have reached the threshold of individual and business taxation for Americans; unlike citizens of other countries, they will not tolerate more, and to impose it would invite a national crisis which, as mentioned before, we cannot risk.

We are at a grave national security crossroads and executive action must be implemented without consultation or approval from the legislative or judicial branches, or the public. Our prestige, our superpower status, and our very nation are at stake.

Let us not forget that the top global economists agree that it was the financial crisis in Western Europe at the beginning of this century which marked their final decline; their weakened state allowed them to be conquered from within by their Muslim masses.

Recommendation: The nation must create a 'supremacy of fear' framework through our security and intelligence communities by identifying enemies, real or imagined, domestically and abroad. America needs a new domestic enemy to rally against. This is the only feasible way to reverse our current decline and ensure the elevation of the United States to the status of sole superpower of the planet with certainty well into the twenty-third century. We must give Americans a reason to hand over most of their discretional income to the government.

Our decided course of action must be aggressively implemented, and any domestic or global threats to these plans must be eliminated to ensure their full, and clandestine, completion. The Anti- and Counter-Terrorism Industrial Complex must be defended to the very last American, because without it there will be no America. My assessment is also shared by the Terrorism Threat Work Group.

Action must be forced now as we cannot digitize enough money, or we will irreparably devalue the American dollar and trigger an immediate collapse of our currency and the nation. In short, the math is not on our side.

Torrey E.C. Wilson, Director of Homeland Defense & Intelligence Agency, United States of America, 21 August, 2065

Scare(y) Decisis

"US Constitution is unconstitutional." – Circuit Judges Alfred T. Goodwin and Stephen Reinhardt, Federal Appeals Court, San Francisco, 2002 (overturned)

"US Constitution is unconstitutional." – The United States Supreme Court, 2079

The death of the Constitution.

The first session of the US Supreme Court on 24 September, 1789 began with a four-hour Communion service.

Hey, ho! The witch is dead, the witch is dead, the Catholic witch is dead! Hey, ho, the Catholic witch is dead!

The song was popular in many atheist circles. In Western Europe, the 2030s marked the rise of the Muslim majority, but in America it was the rise of the anti-religious atheists. However, the US Supreme Court remained the last bastion where the religious had a foothold, but with the retirements and later passings of John Roberts, Antonin Scalia, Clarence Thomas, Anthony Kennedy, Samuel Alito, and Sonia Sotomayor, not only was the Court absent a Catholic majority but a religious majority. The song of Sotomayor's passing was seen as over the top by even the secular public. The old terms *liberal* and *conservative* were also made obsolete by an ever-growing libertine citizenry, eroding cultural norms, vanishing traditional morals and the fact that debates over the size of government had ended—government controlled everything, and Americans were fine with that. The venom had solely to do with anti-religious bigotry.

The reconfiguring of the US Supreme Court from a religious

to a secular majority would set the stage for the most dramatic change to America since the very founding of the nation.

Stare Decisis—definition: Black's Law Dictionary—was the legal principle by which judges were obligated to stand by decided cases; to uphold precedents; and to maintain former adjudications. However, the highest court, the US Supreme Court, had always retained the power to implement or reverse any law that it wanted.

The fact that many presidents saw the Constitution, with its articles and amendments, as an inconvenience to their political goals was by no means a new thing. However, no other American president in history had ever before breached this judicial firewall so completely as Homeland Director and presidential candidate T. Wilson.

Outskirts of Tek-City, Virginia
3:35p.m., 29 June 2076

Bishop Dyna runs through the streets barefoot, as if possessed. She has been running for hours, ignoring the traffic, flying drones overhead, people, everything. Sometimes it's funny how seemingly insignificant things you do in the past can have such profound implications in the future. How running three marathons a year for fifteen years has led her to this moment: *there is a good chance that she will be dead by week's end.*

It is dusk when she reaches her destination—the Jew-Christian walled city enclave of Restoration. The Pagans and pro-Registration Jew-Christians call them ghettoes, but now that she looks at the city, she is offended by the word, and more so that she has used it herself.

Ghettoes historically were a section of the city where groups lived, voluntarily or involuntarily, due to legal, social, or religious pressure. Later it was the term for overcrowded urban centers, back in the time of skin-color segregation and the decades afterwards.

This is what it has come to—Jew-Christians across the nation creating self-segregated communities known as *enclaves*, with high walls, sophisticated security, armed gunmen, and sometimes attack dogs. The propaganda says that the fledgling Resistance is losing and their numbers are declining, but is that really true? The Jews seem on the verge of collapse, but the Christians seem to actually be standing their ground. Christianity is now permanently divided into pro-Registration and anti-Registration camps. Her pro-Registration alliance is about to win the war, everyone says so. So why does she want to change sides?

Bishop Dyna reaches the wall and stops; it is gray, stone-bricked, and impassable with no windows or entrances visible. She cannot see anyone but knows she's being watched by vidcams, probably from when she was a mile away or more. She could call out to them but they will not listen or respond; she's been excommunicated. The fact that they all call themselves Christian is irrelevant. They are separate peoples now.

She is about to touch the wall with her outstretched arm but decides not to. She cannot provoke them in any way. She sits down on the ground and wraps her arms around her legs as she rests her head on her knees.

"I have to do something bold. I know. *I will just sit here and die,*" she whispers to herself.

The Greatest Church of the World, Maryland
10:13 a.m., 4 August 2076

Everyone is preparing for the rally. It will be another major National Religious Registration Alliance event. Master Pastor stands in front of a crowd of clergy, aides, and volunteers. He motions to Bishop Joe and Rabbi Susan but they signal him that they will join him shortly.

Bishop Joe says, "What's wrong?"

Bishop Edna stands with them almost on the verge of tears. Reverend Eunice stands with her putting an arm around her shoulder.

"She's gone. Dyna is gone," she says. "Someone said they saw her running in the streets."

"Where?" Rabbi Susan asks.

"To one of those Resister communes!"

"Why would she go there?" Rabbi Susan asks.

"I don't know. She just ran out of our church service. You have to help us. They could kill her or torture her or worse!" Bishop Edna yells, eyes tearing up.

"It will be all right, Bishop," Reverend Eunice says, hugging her.

"We'll find your wife," Bishop Joe says.

"If I have to get Homeland involved, I will. We'll find her," Rabbi Susan says.

"There is a rumor that people are disappearing," Bishop Edna says.

"That's not true," Rabbi Susan says. "It's Resister propaganda. That's all they have left."

"Let's get this event done," Bishop Joe says.

Maryland Streets
11:43 a.m., 4 August 2076

The rally marches down the streets, flanked by motor-bike police—Master Pastor, with Bishop Joe and Rabbi Susan on either side and hundreds of other clergy, volunteers, aides, and citizen protestors all around them following.

They near the Resister enclave, the closest walled community of anti-Registration Jew-Christians. The imposing wall is at least ten feet high; the top lined with razor-wire and surveillance vidcams spaced every few feet.

The media is already set up at the wall as the marchers approach en mass. Everyone takes their choreographed positions: Bishop Joe moves to the center, with everyone flanking him and the media filming.

"Good day, people of America. We are gathered here today, our esteemed National Religious Registration Alliance, to support our government, its policies, and its Registration Initiative. We have a message for the shrinking numbers of anti-government religious hiding inside behind us: Tear down these walls!"

The crowd erupts in applause.

Evangelical Lutheran Church for the Master, Virginia
6:11 p.m., 4 August 2076

They are gathered in the church's main meeting room upstairs. Bishop Edna sits at a table with Reverend Eunice, and standing around them are other clergy members. They are planning the events for the next week, but the mood is somber.

At 6:12 p.m., Bishop Dyna appears and walks into the room. All talking ceases and all eyes turn to her; the silence is deafening.

Dyna approaches the table and stops. She seems different somehow to everyone. Dyna reaches into her inside vestment pocket and places a folded piece of paper on the table. In a world of e-pads, tablets, and digi-paper, only the religious still use pens and physical sheets of paper. She reaches into her pocket and places a sealed envelope on the table next. Dyna makes no eye contact with her wife or anyone else until she reaches to remove the clerical collar from her neck and tosses it onto the table as well. Bishop Edna stares at her with eyes tearing up. Dyna says nothing, turns and leaves.

Everyone looks at each other in total confusion. Bishop Edna stands and, with tears streaming down her face, moves to go into another room at the back.

"Bishop, what is happening? Where is Bishop Dyna going?" Reverend Eunice asks.

"Bishop, what did she leave in the letter and the envelope? Aren't you going to read them?" another pastor says.

Bishop Edna turns to them and says, "You have my permission to read them. I know what they say already."

Reverend Eunice stands. "What do they say?"

"The letter says she's resigned from the church, our church. The envelope contains a letter saying she's officially divorcing me and her wedding ring. Tell everyone that Dyna has joined the Resisters and is not to be allowed entrance into the facility, and the authorities are to be notified and called in if she is ever seen again. She must be considered a domestic terrorist from this day forward."

There are gasps, and everyone looks at each other. Reverend Eunice grabs the letter and opens it. The other pastor opens the envelope and a gold ring falls out.

The Greatest Church of the World, Maryland
2:02 p.m., 9 August 2076

His glass-paned mega-church is massive, with twelve-foot vid-screens on the high, vaulted walls, flashing lights, a hundred-person chorus with a twenty-four piece band. The congregation of the church is often ten thousand strong for each of its three Sunday services, two Saturday services and single Wednesday service. Master Pastor conducts services in his purple robe over one of his expensive office-suits.

"Let's get the show movin' and groovin'!" Master Pastor yells.

The huge congregation responds with yeses, amens, "yes Master Pastor," and thunderous applause. Every Sunday, Saturday, and Wednesday, he hosts a worship service called the Big Show for thousands of church attendees and millions more via broadcast. He stands as one of the biggest religious icons in the nation and is on a first name basis with elite leaders from around the world.

Members of the National Religious Registration Alliance wait in the back of the church to watch the Big Show—Master Pastor giving a fiery sermon with passionate and loud participation from the congregants in the form of shout-outs of "amen" and applause; the gospel chorus, each member clothed in flowing purple robes, with the Master dancing on the stage; church go-ers giving their tithes and offerings by swiping their digi-cards over a machine that looks like a small twine-woven basket passed from person to person, row to row; church announcements and recognitions; and finally a dismissal of the congregation. The Show is electric, lasting two hours, but the final service of the day can last over three.

"Congratulations!" Rabbi Susan says.

Rabbi Susan grabbed Communications Director Frinos as soon as he entered the church at the back of the main congregation hall while people exited. She pulls him over to a side corner.

"Thank you, Rabbi Susan," he says.

"Is your move from Homeland communications director to White House communications director a not-so-subtle indication that Director Wilson will be our next president?"

Frinos smiles and says, "I can neither confirm nor deny such rumors."

Rabbi Susan smiles too. "Just remember I already voted for him."

Frinos says, "So did I—multiple times."

They laugh.

"I do have a question for you," he says. "How good are the others in the coalition at keeping discrete matters to themselves? Keeping things secret?"

"Depends on the information," she says.

"I'll just tell you for now. We seem to have a number of pro-Registration clergy who may have gone over to the Resisters—some openly, some have simply disappeared."

"I don't think we should worry if a few people get cold feet and run over to them. They'll all be back. No one likes to be on the losing side."

Frinos holds his e-pad to her face. "I have a list of over two dozen."

Rabbi Susan is shocked as she reads. "Those are members of our Alliance leadership itself."

"Exactly. Should we tell the others?" Frinos asks.

Rabbi Susan thinks for a moment. "No. It will just distract them. Our side is growing, so it doesn't matter."

"Aren't these major defections?"

"They'll be back."

"Rabbi Susan, I'm sharing this with you in confidence because you and I are actual paid staffers on the administration. Everyone else is a volunteer. What are these walled communities called again?"

"Enclaves."

"These enclaves are popping up all over the country. I'm not a genius, but if our alliance of religious is growing, then why are we seeing more of these Resister enclaves popping up all over the place?"

"It could be just a matter of people moving out of the city."

"Rabbi Susan, please don't shovel propaganda at me. That's what I do for a living. When I say that the Resisters are collapsing and joining the Registrant side, I want there to be truth to it. So does our next president. We need to put a stop to the growth of these enclaves."

"I'll talk to my chief deputy. We'll take care of the Jews."

"Good. Master Pastor will take care of the Christians."

4:52 p.m.

At the front of the church near the main stage, they are holding a major meeting. It has become common for the pro-Registration clergy leadership to meet here, and Master Pastor is always eager to host the gatherings.

"We will tie it to our new 'Tear Down These Walls' campaign," Frinos says to Bishop Joe.

Bishop Joe smiles. "God always said I'd be a superstar." He looks up towards the ceiling and says, "My close-up, God, I'm ready and even have my make-up on."

Everyone smiles or laughs. Bishop Joe is such a character.

At 5:12 p.m., a man enters the church congregation hall, well dressed in a black office-suit with a white shirt and tie. Master Pastor and a few others notice him the moment he passed through the main doors. He walks up to them carrying a stack of folded pieces of paper.

Everyone now notices him and stops talking.

"Can we help you, sir?" one of the pastors asks. "Are you here to join the National Religious Registration Alliance?"

"Thank you, Pastor, but no." The man smiles and looks at Master Pastor. "I hear you've been inquiring about me, sir."

He hands Master Pastor a sealed black envelope from the top of the stack of papers and hands out the rest to the others. He skips Frinos, Rabbi Susan, and Finkel.

"You call us Resisters, but we actually prefer *the Resistance*. I used to hold various odd jobs around the world helping Christians and other people of good will; now I'm a general in this little war between us. You and your Pagan masters love to refer to us as domestic terrorists, even though we have never committed or attempted to commit such an act, ever. Except if you consider protecting ourselves, our families, and our communities from your storm troopers, who like to shoot religious people dead for carrying the Holy Bible. My name is Moses. General Moses."

Everyone freezes. *The leader of the Resistance is standing right in front of them, all alone.*

"The letter you now have in your possession is a formal pronouncement of excommunication. As of today, because of your collaboration with the Pagans in the destruction of your own people, you are no longer recognized as Christians. No one will acknowledge your existence or speak your names. If you come to any of our enclaves, you will be refused entry. If you try to force your way into any of our enclaves"—he pauses as he looks at all of them—"*you will be killed.*"

Everyone stares at him.

Moses turns to Rabbi Susan. "Your people will be delivering a similar letter to you directly. We have also signed an accord with all anti-Registration Jews and Mormons, and they will recognize your excommunication, and we will recognize theirs."

Excommunication had meant many things in the two-thousand year history of Christianity: depriving a person of church membership, cutting them off from all fellowship with members of the church, depriving them of the privileges of church membership, or cutting them off from Communion. In the early church, excommunication might as well have been death, as the church was the center of all life. But in pre-modern times, it was so rare as to be obsolete. Now, the severity and the commonness of this practice have returned.

Rabbi Susan says, "Excommunication is an obsolete *Christian* practice."

Moses says, "Actually, we Christians got it from Jews. The word was *herem*. You should know more history…rabbi."

"So you are the man named Moses," Master Pastor says. "We

don't recognize your excommunication, because you have no authority over my church, or any others."

Moses steps closer to Master Pastor. "I'm sorry, sir. I don't think you understand what has just transpired here. This isn't mere excommunication. This is the permanent separation of our people. This is our people entering the Ark of Noah and shutting the doors closed forever with your people, the so-called Christians who think and act the same as nonbelievers, collaborators, fakers—plastic Christians—on the outside as the flood of despair and destruction rises to engulf you all. This is a divorce, and we have sole custody of the Word of God and the faith. If you don't recognize the gravity of the situation now, sir, give it time. You will."

The men stare at each other. Master Pastor glares at him with contempt. Moses smiles and glances at Bishop Joe. "Bishop Joe?"

"Yes?"

"Don't come near our enclaves ever again, sir. We don't stand in front of your house with your family. Why do so with us? If you visit any of our enclaves again, we will visit you. Am I communicating to you in a way you can understand, or do we need to have a separate talk with one or both of your husbands…or one of those boyfriends of yours?"

Bishop Joe answers, "No, my ears are very attuned to threat talk."

"It's nothing personal. It goes for all excommunicated collaborators."

"I don't take it personally," Bishop Joe says.

Master Pastor rips up his letter slowly and defiantly and says, "Jesus told us in Mark 12:17 to 'Give to Caesar what is Caesar's and to God what is God's.'"

Moses smiles and says, "So many profess they believe in and devote themselves to God but in reality act as if He doesn't exist. I was told that you have the power to cite scripture in all the wrong places—as does the devil. There were 'Christians' like you during American slavery and skin-color segregation times. I'm sure real Christians of the time were as unimpressed by their citing verse to support serious sin and intrinsic evil as I am by you now, when Caesar is once again attempting to destroy God's chosen people. But the Lord Jesus Christ did say in Matthew 21:10-11, 'At that time many will turn away from the faith and will betray and hate each other, and many false prophets will appear and deceive many people.'"

Master Pastor says, "Proverbs 12:15 says: 'Stupid people always think they are right.' Mr. Moses, our side grows, and we do not acknowledge you, your Resisters, or your meaningless, illegitimate excommunications."

Moses says, "Proverbs 12:20-21 says: 'Those who plan evil are in for a rude surprise, but those who work for good will find happiness.'" To everyone, "I've delivered what I came to deliver in word and in action. I'll be taking my leave of you."

Master Pastor says, "I'll be sure to visit you in prison, as it will be your inevitable destination and…"

Moses interjects, "I hear your government masters have become quite adept at putting Jews in prison. We Christians, however, won't be joining them—ever."

Master Pastor continues, "Then I'll be sure to visit you at the morgue. I did want to continue our battle of the verses."

Moses says with contempt, "The Bible is not a game, sir. Verses, God's words, are not linguistic toys. Proverbs 26:11: 'As a dog returns to its vomit, so a fool repeats his folly.' Good-bye, honorable prophets. The separation is complete and everyone is now on their chosen side—forever."

Rabbi Susan says, "Why are you fighting us and walling yourselves up in those gated communities? Most Christians will never go back to this new segregation, living in ghettoes, even if it is self-imposed. All Jews universally condemn and oppose this religious-based self-segregation. Even organizations like the Anti-Semitism League, run by the Wise Men, who are by no means supportive of Registration, condemn it."

"I'm sorry, Rabbi Susan," Moses says. "Didn't you hear?"

"Hear what?"

"The Conservative Jews threw out the old High Council and voted in a new one. The Conservatives have joined the Orthodox Jews in formal opposition to all government registration initiatives. All smaller Jewish Orders are already aligning with both, and joining the Resistance as a whole. You will be seeing many more excommunications." He smiles. "Enjoy your life outside the Ark." He raises his hands and yells, "Then Elisha prayed, 'O Lord, open their eyes and let them see!'" He turns and walks out of the church auditorium.

Master Pastor is already on his e-pad: "There's a man walking out of the church now. Arrest him. He's one of the terrorists."

Rabbi Susan looks at Finkel and says, "Get on the line and call around to find out what he's talking about."

Finkel takes his e-pad from his pocket and begins to dial.

Everyone is somewhat frantic: reading the excommunication papers Moses gave them, talking on their e-pads, talking amongst themselves. A few policemen run into the church.

"Where is he?" one of the policemen asks.

"What do you mean? He walked right out the front door," Master Pastor says.

"No one came out. We were standing right there," the other policeman says.

Master Pastor yells, "He must still be in the building!"

"We'll lock it down," the policeman says. "We already have a manned perimeter around the church."

"How many drones do we have?" one policeman asks another.

"We already have one in the air." The policeman says.

Master Pastor looks to the other clergy. "Find him!"

More drones fly to the church and hover above. More police cars arrive. Policemen enter the church in force, while others shore up the outside perimeter. The police and clergy search the building room by room. All vid surveillance from the Eyes is reviewed; the man Moses entered but never came out. But after a thorough visual search, aided by full scanners, they find nothing. General Moses has vanished.

Location Unknown
12:07 a.m., 5 January 2089

Logan stares at the strange black ball with the steady red light.

"How do I know it's really you?" Logan asks. "You say you're Goli the tek-lord, but I can't see you, I can't verify it. You could be some five-year-old sitting in his diapers at his e-pad with a voice changer."

"Mr. Logan, your go-between contacted me, not the other way around. And as a side-note, five-year-olds don't wear diapers. Don't you Pagans know anything about children aside from the reproductive act itself? You're wasting my time, so tell your go-between, your bio-son—I believe that's the term you Pagans use—not to contact me through intermediaries again."

"Wait a second. Is there a way we can start this first contact over again? It seems that we've both managed to annoy each other," Logan says. "I just wanted to verify it was you. I expected that our first contact would be over the e-pad and not through some talking black orb."

"Communication via a consumer e-pad is not secure, and neither is any other device you use. Mr. Logan, you have five minutes. I'm starting the countdown now."

"Until what?"

"Until I disappear and the black orb blows up in your face."

"I'll assume you're joking on the last part. I need two things: a Jew-Christian and a tek-lord. I know you're the second, though I don't know how good, but I need to confirm the first."

"Jew-Christian? What's that?"

Logan looks at the black object for a moment. Surely he knows the term.

"I don't understand," Logan says.

"Let me give you another piece of advice, Mr. Logan. That is an extremely offensive term invented by the White House to create a sub-class of Americans out of thin air, specifically to persecute and direct hatred and violence against them. You Pagans claim to be so evolved and tout your tolerance as your great Tek World virtue, but the truth is you blindly hate the religious."

"You called me a Pagan."

"Isn't that the term that you gave yourselves?"

"Well, I guess it is."

"Are you offended by the term *Pagan*?"

"No," Logan says. "Okay, so what term should I use?"

"Faither. Non-Muslim religious people are called Faithers."

"Okay, I won't make the mistake again."

"You Pagans have no respect for religious people."

"I'm sorry. Religious people should be respected."

"Especially when your own atheism is a religion too."

"I've never heard that before."

"Your own courts ruled as such."

"That must have been a long time ago."

"Actually, only your own Nihilists and Hedonists are without religion. You Pagans certainly are religious."

"How are we a religion?"

"The certainty that there isn't a God is as much an act of faith as the certainty that there is."

Logan pauses for a moment. "Okay, you're right. I'm sorry for offending you. So are you a Faither tek-lord, then?"

"Yes."

"How good are you?"

"Why?"

"Faithers are off-Grid, and I need a Faither tek-lord who can do a hack for me from off-Grid into the Grid."

"Hack into what specifically in the Grid?"

"Washington DC Metro Park's fixed and drone surveillance."

"Such a hack is a felony, Mr. Logan."

"That's why I can't use my normal sources. None of them are truly off-Grid."

"If I did such a hack, they would never find me, but with such data they could immediately designate you as a terrorist. The Grid could strip your story and even your existence from the Data Stream."

The Data Stream is the sum total of all the data flowing back and forth through the Net—text, vids, audio, code.

"Not if I get my story out on the Net first."

"They've done it before, why wouldn't they do it again with you?"

"The story itself will protect me."

"You Pagans in Tek World have strange notions on what does and doesn't protect you."

"What do Faithers call the world they live in?"

"Faith World."

"So can you do the hack or find me one of your colleagues who can?"

"You seem certain that it can be done."

"My bio-son said you tek-lords can do the impossible. So I'm accepting his faith in you."

"Faith. Interesting for a Pagan to use that word."

Logan smiles. "How much time do I have?"

"Five minutes are up. But I uploaded a number to your e-pad."

"You linked into my e-pad? What number? Your phone number?"

"No, Mr. Logan. My payment. And tek-lords don't accept digital currency."

"What other type of currency is there?"

"Physical cash."

"Physical cash disappeared from the world decades ago. You know that."

"I'm fully aware that the planet is cashless, except for those of us who do not wish to be assimilated into that system. The instructions have also been downloaded for you."

Logan now looks at his e-pad, and he is stunned. "This is a lot of money, digital or otherwise. I can't pay you this amount."

"Then you can find someone else to get you the classified Homeland surveillance vid on the murder of Lucifer Mestopheles."

Logan pauses and stares at the black orb's red light. So Goli, the tek-lord, knows what he's investigating. If he plays games, this tek-lord could vanish. None that he knows are this good. Besides, he is already impressed with this Faither tek-lord.

"Okay, I'll pay you the money. But how long will it take for you to get the information?"

"Mr. Logan, I already have the information. I hacked and downloaded the vids while we were talking."

"That's impossible. No tek-lord is that good. Impossible."

"You Pagans live in a tek world of data streams, binary code, AI algorithms, mobile computer interface devices. You have so convinced yourselves of its reality, when the simple truth is that Tek World is and will always be an illusion—imaginary creations of electricity. I found the vids you're going to pay me for as easily as you just scratched your nose."

Logan has just scratched his nose. So the tek-lord is watching him real-time too, probably through the government's own Eyes.

"The government has tek-lords too. No way you're so good and they're so bad. No way you can break into their system with such ease. I may not be a tek-head, but I'm not stupid. Convince me or I walk away. I'm not gullible and you're not going to play my need to get this info against my own common sense."

"I'm already inside the Grid. *A ghost in the machine.* Bye, Mr. Logan."

The red light of the black ball switches off, and then red sparks fly out. Logan jumps back, fearing it will in fact explode, but instead the orb dissolves into black dust. Logan walks back to the spot, but the wind blows the dust away to nothingness. This tek-lord is good.

Ghosts in the machine is a theory never proven but written about from time to time, about a group of tek-lords who live—able to access and go as they like—undetected in the Grid mainframe itself. The overwhelming consensus is that it is all an urban myth, virally spread through the Net by infantile Anarchist hackers to worry governments.

But maybe not. Logan thinks to himself, *Let me get this tek-lord his money.*

USA, 14 June 2080

The news has broken everywhere, all over the world. Just four months ahead of the next presidential election, the United States Constitution has been abolished. Chief Justice Jett, writing for the majority opinion, stated: "Despite claims to the contrary, the United States Constitution has always been a religious document and as such is incompatible with the pluralistic society of modern times. A new, secular document must be fashioned, devoid of all religious utterances or concepts. The spirit of the nation's highest law of the land can certainly be maintained without spirituality or any other superstitions."

Justice Atom wrote in a supporting opinion: "The United States Constitution is a guide and has never been a straitjacket for the highest court. Justices throughout the history of the nation have not only come to rulings completely opposing the very words of the Constitution, but have even fashioned whole new laws and legal concepts out of thin air, like the proverbial magician pulls the proverbial rabbit from a hat. Justices have always rendered their opinions first and then engaged in legalistic gymnastics to fashion an opinion supposedly based on the Constitution and the intent of its founders. The Constitution is illegal in our modern times, being based on religiosity, and a new one should precisely, without interpretation or ambiguity, lay out to the letter the powers and capabilities of all branches of government, including the Supreme Court. This clarity will return the court to its sole role in reconciling conflicting laws and policies from the other two branches of government, rather than its current construct, wherein it has become a second, but unchecked, legislative body unto itself."

Justice Stein, writing the sole dissent, said: "This ruling should not come as any surprise to those who have watched this branch of government over the decades. Though I will undoubtedly be accused of being a closet religious devotee, despite a lifetime of staunch atheism and a record of staunch opposition to religiosity of any kind in the public square throughout my career, the Constitution is a secular document; the mere fact that its original authors were religious is irrelevant. This document has been the greatest bulwark against the tyrannical tendencies of government and the greatest platform for individual freedom in the entire history of the world, despite a steady erosion of those legal underpinnings over the years. The brilliance of this document is that it said that our unalienable rights came from some invisible supreme being. I say, as a jaded atheist, what a stroke of genius. Americans could be reassured to know that this entity could not be bribed, intimidated, threatened, or tricked to give away our freedoms. Can anyone honestly say the same of our current government leaders? We probably lost our freedoms a long time ago, but we at least had some left. With the abolition of the Constitution, we'll have none."

The newsfeed has been consumed by the announcement and analysis of the legal bombshell. "The story of the century!" The new Rule of Law has been officially enacted to replace the Constitution. Millions pour over the Net-document, every paragraph, every sentence, every word.

Key provisions: The Marriage Modernization Act legalizes marriage between two or more entities in all fifty-three states, regardless of gender or sexual orientation, with states able to set restrictions on age of consent, whether partners can be related or not, and whether an entity must be a human or not; anti-hate-crime laws are expanded to all fifty-three states, superseding all state or local free-speech laws, and other than the Good Bible and the Koran, all holy books must be approved by the government; private gun ownership, including the right to carry concealed weapons permits is outlawed for everyone except government law enforcement and military; the Registry is now mandatory for all Americans, as are the bio-switch procedure on all newborns beginning 1 January, 2081, with DNA sampling, and Census participation, which mandates self-designation of gender and sexual orientation; homeschooling of any kind, parochial schools (Islam exempt), and even private secular schools are outlawed.

Besides the massive expansion of government powers to monitor, watch, trace, track, investigate, question, and, if need be, detain Americans in the name of national security, is the change that everyone expected—the Rule of Law rescinds presidential term limits.

Torrey E.C. Wilson is elected to the office of president of the United States in November 2080. Full ratification of the new Rule of Law by all the states is expected.

Trog-Land

"Don't go near that elevator—that's just what they want us to do...trap us in a steel box and take us down to the basement!" – Raoul Duke, *Fear & Loathing in Las Vegas*

"Please, please I don't want my soul tethered to the Net, my mind impregnated by the Data Stream, or my body enslaved by the Grid. I am a Homo Sapiens, dammit, and I can be a Trog and live in the soup if I want to!" – Pagan Paul

Nine years ago, the National Religious Registration Alliance launched their media blitz in the Rose Garden of the White House with the then president and several political dignitaries. Pastor Joshua and Assistant Pastors Charity, Seth, and Luke were all there—supporters representing their church leadership.

Pastor Joshua has a medium complexion and very short, thin, wavy black hair. He is led to the photo booth, where digital photos are taken of every angle of his face and upper torso and a holographic image is rendered of his entire body. His fellow thirty-something Jew-Christian "terrorists" are run through the same police routine. Charity has fair skin and dark blond hair with large curls; Seth is bald with a well-groomed mustache and goatee; and Luke has long brown hair with green eyes.

US Federal Courthouse, Richmond, Virginia
1:55 p.m., 11 November 2080

The four detainees are led by two court policemen into the courtroom single-file, dressed in orange jumpsuits and full wrist, arm, ankle, and leg shackles. The policemen bring them to the arraignment table in the center of the room.

The judge, in a shiny black robe, is already seated on the bench, a very imposing black marble structure overlooking the courtroom. The room is practically empty—by design—except for the defendants, two court policemen, a defense attorney, and the main bailiff standing to the side of the bench.

The defense lawyer stands from his front row pew seat and walks to the defense counsel table. "Elliott Finegold for the defense, Your Honor," he says. "I am representing all four defendants." He is dressed in a two-piece black suit with a solid white shirt and black tie.

"Have you submitted all the necessary identification files with Central?" the judge asks.

"Yes I have, Your Honor," Elliott says.

The judge touches the screen of his in-table tablet to pull up the case. He reviews it. "Mr. Elliott Finegold, your identification has been recognized and approved. I'm sure I don't have to state that any religious utterances of any kind are forbidden in my courtroom."

Elliott says with annoyance, "No, Your Honor, you don't have to state such."

The judge looks at him for a moment. "Are your clients ready to enter a plea?"

"Yes they are, Your Honor," Elliott says as he motions for all of them to stand.

"Enter your pleas," the judge says. "Three counts, all related to domestic terrorism and conspiracy charges."

Elliott looks at them and says quietly, "One at a time, left to right. Do not say anything but your plea."

Pastor Joshua smiles and yells, "Not guilty!"

Charity says, "Not guilty."

Seth says, "Not guilty."

Luke says, "Not guilty."

Elliott addresses the judge. "Your Honor, I move to have this case dismissed on all charges."

"On what grounds?" the judge asks with amusement.

"On the grounds that no evidence has been presented, nor

is there even a representative from the prosecution present. Is the prosecution not even required to attend and try their case in person in your courtroom, Your Honor?"

The judge smirks, "Naturally your clients are innocent. A Jew-Christian lawyer defending Jew-Christian criminals."

Elliott stares at him in disbelief. "Your Honor, I demand to have you removed as presiding judge of this case!"

"Motion to dismiss denied. Motion for change of venue denied."

Elliott is angry. "Firstly, I'm a Jew and not a Jew-Christian. Secondly, my clients are Christians, not Jew-Christians. Thirdly, if you think I'm going to tolerate you bigoted Pagan fascist pig, you have another thing coming. Fourthly, if you think I'm going to tolerate you convicting my clients without any evidence presented or even a trial, you have another thing coming. I never imagined that I would live to see the day when Islamic Caliphate and CHIN territory were freer than America."

"Shut up, you!" the judge yells. "Open your mouth again and I will hold you in contempt of court and have you put in jail. Do I make myself clear?"

Elliott glares at him, but says nothing.

Pastor Joshua yells, "Your Honor, he won't say it, but I will. He has utter contempt for you, as do we. Can I get an Amen?"

The other three defendants smile and yell "Amen!" All four of them start to talk amongst themselves.

The judge activates the courtroom silencer. The device, which looks like a series of connected black boxes, emerges from the top of the wall above the judge, aimed at them. All of them stop talking as soon as they see it emerge from the walls. They stare at the judge.

"So, Jew-Christians know about the silencer," the judge says. "Mr. Elliott Finegold, you are held in contempt of this court for failing to control your clients, breach of this court's speech codes which prohibit religious utterances of any kind, and, though I love pigs personally, for referring to this esteemed court as anything but 'Your Honor,' 'my master,' or a like phrase. That's three violations of my court. That is a thirty-day sentence for each and a ten-thousand credit fine for each. You will be remanded to the Massachusetts Correctional Institution, Cedar Junction for ninety days, and your bank accounts will be debited immediately for the thirty thousand credits. I know you can afford it. Any other questions, Mr. Finegold?"

Elliott remains quiet.

"I didn't think so," the judge says, smirking. He pushes a button on his desk to turn off the silencer. He glances at the bailiff and nods.

The doors open, and two policemen enter with three men in office-suits.

"Good morning, Your Honor," one says. "I'm the lead agent with the Homeland Defense and Intelligence Agency on the case. We'll take custody of the four defendants from the State. We have transmitted the federal transfer authorization and, with your permission, will take them into custody for immediate transfer to Super-Max Wallens Ridge State Prison until commencement of the trial."

"You will not take my clients anywhere!" Elliott yells at them. "There hasn't even been a preliminary hearing. No evidence has been presented. My clients have rights!"

The lead agent says, "That evidence is classified, Your Honor. Mr. Finegold well knows he doesn't possess the necessary clearance to view it."

Elliott yells, "Your Honor, my clients get to choose their defense counsel, not the government!"

The judge says, "Your clients have been designated terrorists by..."

"Based on what?" Elliott yells. "Because the government says so? Were American rights abolished while I was sitting in the park having my lunch? The government can't just declare someone a terrorist on a whim."

The judge leans forward. "Yes, Mr. Elliott Finegold, they can." He scrolls through files on his in-table tablet. "You don't like the rules of this country, Mr. Elliott Finegold? Then you can go live in Caliphate or CHIN territory *after* you serve your time in jail. Bailiff!" To the lead agent, he adds, "Your transfer order is approved."

The lead agent says, "Thank you, Your Honor."

Elliott is boiling mad. Pastor Joshua turns to him and says, "We'll be okay."

Elliott says, "I'm a Jew, so there's no 'turn the other cheek' in my theology. I'm not going to let them get away with this. Legally, I'm *very* dangerous."

Pastor Joshua smiles and says, "Then we'll meet again soon."

The federal policemen lead the four defendants out of the courtroom. The bailiff walks to Elliott and handcuffs his hands in front of his body. Elliott stops to glance back at the judge. The two men stare at each other for moment.

Elliott says, "And the Pagan said: free speech for me, but not for thee."

The judge smirks. The bailiff pushes Elliott out of the courtroom.

His clients and the government agents disappear into an elevator. As Elliott is led by the bailiff down the hall, his eyes start tearing up. The bailiff almost starts to laugh; the Jew-Christian is crying. Suddenly Elliott stops in place, his eyes red and the tears now streaming down his face.

"*Terrorist!*" Elliott yells at the top of his lungs.

All courthouses and government buildings are smart-buildings: every person that enters is identified through a direct link to the Registry, scanned by "see-thru" tek and monitored by hidden Eyes throughout the walls and ceilings. Listening devices are also embedded in the walls, and certain words can trigger certain automatic protocols. "Fire!" auto-starts sprinklers and whitewater cannons to terminate any possible fire and exit doors flash bright colors for people to escape through until fire suppression personnel arrive.

But the most feared command is "*terrorist,*" or any similar phrase. By law, people are required to report any possible terrorist activity. As a citizen, if you do not report such activity and an attack occurs, you could be liable for criminal penalties and open to civil lawsuits by any victim of the attack or their families. Government smart-buildings go live with a variety of weapon systems to stun or shoot a suspect or suspects.

The building identifies who has yelled the command, and a dozen armed courthouse police run to Elliott. The bailiff is dazed as Elliott waves down the policemen.

"I heard him, sir. It's the judge. Judge Heronimus Porter. He said his mother was a Jew-Christian and Pagans killed her and that he's going to blow up everyone and then go kill the president. I think he has bombs under his robes. You have to stop him! He could kill us all!"

The policemen bolt away into the courtroom. Elliott's demeanor changes and the tears are gone. The bailiff gives him a bewildered look which quickly turns to rage, and he begins to punch Elliott viciously. Elliott falls down, and the bailiff begins stomping on him.

In an instant, the bailiff is shot by stun guns—standard procedure after a terrorist alarm, subdue anyone running, fighting, or possessing a weapon. A couple of police appear and pull the now-unconscious bailiff up and handcuff him. They leave Elliott on the ground.

The judge is dragged out of the courtroom by several police. He has been stripped completely naked. His arms and legs are shackled. His mouth is gagged by a device resembling the bottom portion of a mask. His face is bright red, and he struggles helplessly to speak. He is so enraged that his body trembles.

The two men stare at each other. Elliott will be taken to jail for his ninety day sentence. He will petition to have the sentence set aside, and his petition will be granted; after all, the presiding judge has been arrested on suspicion of terrorism. Elliott will sue the government for assault by one of its agents, and his suit will be granted; after all, this bailiff was in the employ of a presiding judge arrested on suspicion of terrorism. He will serve maybe two days in jail, get his money back, and receive a monetary settlement from the government in a few months.

The judge will be held and interrogated for at least ninety days. If the government doesn't believe in his innocence, he could be in custody for six months to a year under indefinite detention protocols. If he's released, he will file a counter-suit for defamation under color of national security—in layman's terms, falsely and knowingly accusing someone of terrorism. A very serious charge, with a mandatory minimum five-year prison sentence for those convicted and, since this is against a federal employee, an additional ten years in Elliott's case. But Elliott is not concerned. He's not only legally gifted but politically savvy. It's already in the air: President Wilson is creating an entirely new judiciary across the nation. Judge Porter will be in Homeland custody while he should be brown-nosing the new regime. By the time he is released his federal judgeship will be gone, given away to others. Elliott has many lawsuits pending against the government, and they will want to settle all of them to close the books on all cases of the Old US Constitutional era. Elliott will offer a deal to settle the lot, for a lot of money for his clients and himself and open immunity from any possible charges or lawsuits from anyone (namely Judge Heronimus Porter), and it will be granted.

The judge is boiling with rage. He knows all this, but he is unable to say even one word. The police lift him up and carry him away for transport to Homeland. The unconscious Bailiff is carried away for transport to federal prison. Elliott is made to stand and led down the hall by a new bailiff for transport to a state prison.

Elliott smiles. When he gets out, he'll be able to carve out a very nice living protecting people from being falsely accused of terrorism in this new, post-US-Constitutional America. Maybe Judge Porter will be a client. No, let the Pagans get their own Pagan lawyers. He will defend only Faithers.

Outside, his four clients are already seated in a federal prison transport van and shackled to the seats of the back compartment by federal police. Two agents sit in the front cab.

Virginia Freeway West 64
2:55 p.m., 11 November 2080

The federal transport van speeds along. Following twenty yards behind the van is another car, with two more agents in the front and the lead agent in the back seat.

"Sir, the courthouse we just left had an incident report of a terrorist suspect," the agent in the passenger side says.

"Anyone apprehended?" the lead agent asks.

"Yes, one person, apparently a courthouse employee. No other details."

"Why weren't we notified to provide backup?"

"Courthouse authorities said they didn't need any. Suspect was detained and transported to Homeland."

Bam! The three men watch as the federal prisoner transport van ahead of them is hit by some kind of projectile. The front cab of the federal transport van rips away from the other half of the vehicle. The back half of the van swerves left and right, sparks flying, until it stops completely.

Fifty yards ahead of both vehicles on the road, an SUV speeds to them. It reaches the damaged transport van and dead-stops ten yards away. Its windows lower and bullets fire at them.

Their car stops too. Bullets hit the bullet-proof glass. The lead agent yells, "Call for backup! Federal prisoner escape in progress!" He and the other agents exit the vehicle and return fire at the approaching SUV.

"Take out that vehicle!" the lead agent yells. One of his agents shoots his tek-machine gun—the SUV explodes.

"Sir, drones en route," the other agent says.

The three agents run to the damaged transport vehicle with guns and rifle at the ready. They reach it and are shocked. In the driver's seat is a humanoid robot—the blast has destroyed most of its head and torso. The human drivers are gone. The back of the van is empty—the prisoners are gone!

Location Unknown
2:55 p.m., 11 November 2080

General Moses hugs each of them: Pastor Joshua and Assistant Pastors Charity, Seth, and Luke, as they exit the replica federal transport van. Surrounding them in a circle are his civilian security, men and women, watching every building around them and the sky, their hands in their jackets holding weapons not externally visible. One of them is Dyna, dressed in black. She has a tattooed black tear just under her right eye.

Oval Office, Washington DC
8:05 a.m., 5 November 2088

The newly elected President Wilson sits at his Resolute desk in the Oval Office. A smiling Lucifer Mestopheles, dressed in a red-brown leather office-suit and his trademark silver-pointed, yellow-brown snakeskin shoes, sits in the chair across from the desk. His newly appointed Homeland Defense and Intelligence Agency director, Anita McDunn, has finished her briefing.

"Thank you, Anita," Wilson says. "That'll be all."

"Yes, sir," she says. "And thank you again, sir, for the promotion. I'll do my best to follow the high standard you've set for all of us."

"You'll do fine. Just remember two things: you aren't the new Homeland director. You are and have always been the Homeland director. It's just that now people have to address you as such. Make people either fear you or respect you. Nothing else," President Wilson says. "Secondly, my directive to you: there are always people plotting against this country. There is never a time when people are not plotting against this country. If there is ever a time you are not uncovering plots against this country, then you're not doing your job."

"Yes, sir. Thank you, Mr. President."

She grabs her folio case from the chair and leaves the office.

"Good choice to succeed you," Lou says. "What's on the agenda?"

"Implementing the new Constitution must take precedence. I need to make sure we get full acceptance, ratification, and implementation in all fifty-three states as quickly as possible—within in my first hundred days."

"Soon we'll be able to implement the Project."

Wilson looks at him. "I'm president now, so time is on our side."

"Don't get too cocky. The talking monkeys have a habit of

surviving. We are so close. Everything we've fought for, for so long, is within sight, within grasp. A new tek-paradise. First America, then beyond. Nothing will be impossible."

"Yes, we are close now."

"What's troubling you, then?"

Wilson says, "We need to find new 'useful idiots'. The Jew-Christians we put in charge of expanding the Religious Registration Initiative are falling apart. More of them are disappearing or joining outright their so-called Resistance Movement. It's becoming a new problem unto itself."

"I don't understand any of this," Lou says. "It's as if something stirred them up. But it will make it all the easier to implement the Project later."

"Yes."

"If you need new useful idiots, then find different talking monkeys. How about the Vampires? I think that would be quite *interesting*." Lou cackles.

"They'll do," Wilson says. "They're all the same to me."

Trog-Land
2:12 a.m., 6 January 2089

Logan had to take three taxis to get so far away from the main tek-city. The taxi driver is a rugged guy, but even he is nervous about being here, and he refuses to wait. Even before the cab stopped they could hear the screaming, yelling, and who-knew-what other sounds of the urban chaos and anarchy of Trog-land. Even the Outlands are safer than this.

"You sure you want to do this?" the taxi driver asks. "I can tell you're not a Trog or any other life-form that would be here."

"Yes," Logan says. "I'll be okay. Just show up at the location I gave you in exactly thirty minutes."

"I'll be there, but I won't wait. And sir, if you get in trouble, no policeman will set foot here at night. They won't even send in drones. It would be hours before they find your body."

"The Jew-Christians live here?"

The taxi driver laughs. "You listen to too much propaganda.

The Jew-Christians live beyond Trog-land."

Logan has to step around Statues, drug zombies that freeze in place for seconds, minutes, or even hours at a time, whether standing or sitting or doing whatever else they were doing when their narcoleptic attack happened, a side-effect of the combination of drugs they use. There are normal drug zombies running around who look like living skeletons, with half-closed eyes or bug eyes. He passes Space Cadets, mentally unbalanced people wearing some kind of space helmet on their head, and sometimes nothing else, convinced they were abducted by aliens. People are lying everywhere on the ground, sleeping, talking to others or themselves, having sex or doing drugs. Most of them are "pleasure all the time" Hedonists, others are just unconscious, others are dead.

"Why don't you just sit with us, sir?"

Logan is startled at hearing the word "sir" in this place. The girl looks like an angel, even with her somewhat dirty face and wrinkled, scarce clothes. She must be in her twenties, maybe older; he's never been good at female ages. All around him he can hear the violence of various Nihilists, Hedonists, and Anarchists beating each other up.

"You should sit with us, sir," she says as she takes his hand.

"I do have a purpose or I would."

She smiles. "That's very good, sir. You should hold on to that as tight as you can."

He hesitates before walking away. He looks at the little open shack where she wanted to take him and sees people just sitting together talking, laughing, playing cards or retro board games. It is a place to congregate for simple platonic human contact, without any tek or drugs.

King Street Metro Station
10:37 a.m., 6 January 2089

Logan has had no sleep. He still remembers the girl, that moment. His e-pad beeps—a message, probably from Edison. The moment is gone.

This is a first for him. He has never touched physical cash before. It isn't just the Faithers who don't accept digital currency—another quirk of anti-government paranoia. So what is one to do in a cashless society to pay one of these off-Griders who loathe any connection with the government or the Grid? Logan hadn't even known there was such a thing as physical currency anymore, but there is—one can buy anonymous cash chips from off-Grid places like drug shops. The one he went to had a line out the door. The only down side is that whoever buys them is instantly flagged on the Grid, like a loud announcement to the government that one is about to do something illegal. However, Logan has no choice.

Logan thought the tek-lord would demand he go to another secluded place, but he instead insisted that Logan take the most public of transportation and travel to a very busy part of the tek-city for their rendezvous.

Logan wears a backpack filled with the cash chips as he walks down the street. He suddenly stops and looks back. People are everywhere, hustling to and from their destinations. He stares awhile and studies as many of the people as he can, giving each a nickname based on some outstanding feature. He does this for about five minutes before turning around and continuing to the train station to catch the next fast-track into the District.

For their meeting, the tek-lord has chosen, of all places, the Garden, the very place Lou was murdered. There will probably still be a ton of police there, but he will probably know many of the officers. Hopefully, none of his competition will be there and notice him. That reminds him: he takes a baseball cap out of his jacket and puts it on his head, then puts on his dark glasses. Not a great disguise, but it will have to do.

The fast-track into the District departs every ten minutes. He finally enters the bustling station. Large digital wall displays and arrows lead him to his train. Walking briskly, he swipes his digi-card to automatically pay for the ticket as he passes through his departure gate. He hears his e-pad beep: payment accepted; e-ticket received.

"Fast-track to the Capitol departing in five minutes," an automated male voice sounds off on the overhead speakers.

Logan reaches the platform with the waiting train. From the lights just above the doors, he can tell which cars have empty seats and which don't—green for available seats, red for filled to capacity. He enters the car in the middle of the five-car train. Early morning and late morning fast-tracks have as many as ten cars, and if there is a special event, twenty cars are common.

As he sits down in an empty seat, he looks around at the people. Some alone, some with pets, couples, families; some dressed up, some practically naked; some seem to be locals, others look like tourists. People are still getting on the train.

Logan's eyes focus on a man: Button Nose, one of the faces he had memorized on the street. A tiny nose, lean face, tan office-suit, and dark hair. The man may be following him, but it could also be a coincidence.

Big Curls enters the train next, then Red Sunglasses, then Scary Woman With the Long Black Hair and Big Chin and Stupid Hat, then Trench Coat. He can believe a few people he noticed would be getting on the same train as him, but not *all* of them.

Logan stands and yells, "Why are you all following me?!"

Everyone in the compartment stops what they are doing and looks at him.

Logan takes out his e-pad and touches the screen to prime the camera feature. He walks to Button Nose and snaps his picture. "One!" The man glares at him with menace. "Two!" he snaps Scary Woman. "Three!" he snaps Trench Coat. "Four!" He snaps Red Sunglasses. He walks through the car, snapping all of their photos. Some of them ignore him; others stare at him with annoyance or contempt.

He looks around again. Everyone continues to watch him carefully.

"I got your pictures and...there, I've emailed them to my friends. In ten seconds, we're going to have all of you identified, and then I'm going to post all your photos on the Net," Logan says. "You can all go home now. I know who you are, and I've memorized your faces, so you won't be too effective following me anymore."

"Fast-track to the Capitol departing in one minute," the automated voice sounds.

Logan sits back down but continues to look at them. Button Nose exits the train first, then Trench Coat, Scary Woman, and all the rest follow. They stand on the platform watching him.

"Doors closing in thirty seconds," the automated voice says.

Trench Coat walks up to the car and yells to Logan, "Are you sure you got all of us?"

Logan says, "No, but I did get you. Go back to Surveillance 101 school. And lose the trench coat, moron."

People laugh as the doors close with Trench Coat watching him. The other "followers" also continue to stare at him from outside the train. He can see all their mouths moving, obviously talking on their ear-sets to someone.

Logan sits back as the fast-track speeds out of the station. Through his dark glasses, he scans the other people in front of him in the car. Most are back to doing whatever they were doing before, but some are still looking at him. Are there any others following him? Who sent them?

The Garden, Washington DC
12:02 p.m., 6 January 2089

Logan has tried everything he can to see if he is being followed again, doubling back, stopping suddenly, walking around a block two or more times, but he hasn't seen anyone. However, he knows full well that if the government really wants to follow him without him knowing, they can do so easily. With Eyes everywhere, all they have to do is guide their agents by talking to them via ear-set.

Logan tries another method and sprints to the center of the Park, then turns—no one following. "Okay, enough of this," he says to himself.

He walks around the Garden and studies all the people he sees. There are probably hundreds in the park. He doesn't see any police, though, which is strange. Where is Goli?

A strange-looking man enters the park and walks directly

towards him. Logan immediately stops and stares at the figure approaching him—he has a very thin frame, dressed all in black clothes, but his head—his head is a perfect globe, no eyes, ears, mouth, nothing. The figure stops right in front of Logan and just stands there.

Logan looks at him, not knowing what to do. "Who are you?"

"How are you, Mr. Logan." The man's voice is not sounding from his invisible mouth but directly in Logan's left ear-set. "It's Goli, of course."

"How are you doing that?" Logan asks.

"My robot will visually monitor the area on a three-sixty degree axis, jam any incoming surveillance signals, and prevent any signals from remoting into any of your devices. Take the face mask from the robot and place it on your mouth to prevent any vids from reading your lips."

The robot man hands him the mask, and Logan covers the lower half of his face.

Logan says, "Is this good?"

"Yes," the voice says in his ear-set.

"Your voice is different, Goli the tek-lord."

"You Pagans change your genders all the time. Tek-lords change their voices and identities."

"I guess this means we'll never meet," Logan says.

"We are meeting, Mr. Logan," the voice says. "Do you have my payment?"

"Yes," Logan says.

"Give it to the robot," the voice says.

Logan takes off his backpack. The robot takes it and holds the bag with both hands.

"Is it going to count it?" Logan asks.

"It already has," Goli answers.

"For a Trog, you do have the best tek."

"Mr. Logan, *most* Trogs have the best tek. That's how we're able to stay off-Grid."

"Makes sense. Can your robot tell if I'm under surveillance now?"

"You've been under surveillance since last week when that

man's face appeared on your home screen and took your photo."

"How did you know that? You couldn't possibly know that."

"And today, you embarrassed a bunch of their agents and got them to get off your train."

"How do you know that? Who's tracking me? You or the government?"

"The government is tracking you. And I'm tracking them. All I did was hack and copy their surveillance files on you."

"How? Are you that good, that you can hack into government files so easily?"

"Where do you want the vid and audio files downloaded?"

Logan pauses, and his mind races in a million directions. "I—I don't know where they should be downloaded. I don't know what device I have that is safe."

"None of them are."

"Tell me what to do then," Logan says.

"Mr. Logan, shake hands with my robot."

"What?"

The robot takes Logan's hand and shakes it vigorously.

"Biometric data received," the voice says.

The robot takes Logan's right arm and lifts up the sleeve. It then pulls a silver band from its robot arm and wraps the device around Logan's wrist. It locks.

"The files are downloaded onto this wrist device. Only you can access them."

"Just so I'm clear, what vid and audio files are downloaded?"

"The vid and audio files from the day of the murder. What you asked for."

"Why are you doing this for me? You're a Faither. And I'm a Pagan."

"Yes, this evil man is dead, but your interests and ours align—this time."

"I must be the luckiest man in the world to meet a tek-lord who can hack and maneuver the Grid and the Net so easily, with its collection of millions and millions of different computers, systems, and networks."

"Quadrillions, Mr. Logan, not billions or trillions, quadrillions. And then there's the Net software, protocols, bridges, and the code itself. And that's just America. Also, the Grid doesn't *daydream*. Your Tek World is so much more vast and dangerous than you're prepared to handle. The Grid monitors your Net traffic transactions, your texts, your emails, your vid traffic, your audio traffic, your personal files. Everything is stored—forever."

"I know it's a strange concept for you, but I know that already. So does the public, but we really don't care."

"You don't care if you don't have any privacy from the government at all."

"No, we don't care. It's the price of living in a free, safe tek-society."

"You don't care the Grid can tap your audio or vids, spy on you without a warrant anytime, all the time."

"No, we don't care. Do you know how incredibly boring the average person is?"

"Yes, Faithers and Pagans are different species of the human race now. One day, we will have to live on different planets, as the gulf between us will be too great."

"I hope not. Personally, I'm still holding out hope for us all to be one big happy human family again."

The voice laughs. "You're a decent man, Mr. Logan. Explains you becoming what we Faithers call more *traditional* in your older years. But do you care if this Grid kills people?"

"If it's terrorists, no."

"What's a terrorist? Not your definition, the government's definition."

"I know the definition. I've done numerous stories on the subject," Logan says.

"You just think you do. This evil man whose murder you're investigating became a threat. Your law enforcement buddies lied to you. The reason the vid of the murder is unavailable to law enforcement is because Lucifer Mestopheles, the President's own chief aide, has been classified as a terrorist, and all related vid, audio, and data files were classified far above the security clearance of your law enforcement buddies."

"So Faithers didn't kill him," Logan says.

"Mr. Logan, you've known that from the very beginning."

"Why?" the male asks.

"Because everyone must know that no matter how high you rise, I can still utterly destroy them,"Lou says.

"He thought so," the female says.

"What was that?" Logan asks, but he already recognizes the voice of the late Lou Mestopheles.

"A segment of the audio from that day."

"You did get the files. What is he talking about?"

"When I read your story on the Source, I'll know. And Mr. Logan?"

"Yes?" Logan says.

"*You are currently classified as a terrorist.*"

"What are you talking about?"

Suddenly Goli's robot starts to run away.

"Mr. Goli, how do I contact you again?!"

"There's a remote number included, but you can only use it once," the voice says and disconnects.

The robot runs slowly at first but then increases to a breakneck speed. A police car stops along the side of the road, and policemen exit with guns already aimed at it. A couple of globe-drones whiz through the air towards the robot.

Logan doesn't wait; he runs in the opposite direction. It dawns on him: non-government robots are illegal anywhere in District—so how did Goli's robot just walk into a national park without immediate interception by law enforcement? This guy is better than good.

He hears an explosion and turns back for a second. Did the robot self-detonate, or did the policemen or drones blow it up? He will never know; he continues to run away.

The Man Made Out of String

"It was the best of times, it was the worst of times, it was the age of wisdom, it was the age of foolishness, it was the epoch of belief, it was the epoch of incredulity, it was the season of Light, it was the season of Darkness, it was the spring of hope, it was the winter of despair, we had everything before us, we had nothing before us; we were all going directly to Heaven, we were all going direct the other way..." – Charles Dickens, *A Tale of Two Cities*,1859

"It was the worst of times, the best were no more; it was the age of insanity, wisdom was no more; it was the time of nihilism, faith was no more; it was the endless winter of despair, the spring of hope was no more; we had nothing before us; everything we had was no more; we were all going directly to Hell, only the last of the Chosen were going the other way. No amount of Tek could ever be a substitute for a Soul. This whole sorry mess could have all been avoided." – Dee Tocqueville, *Do I Need to Wear a Towel on My Head to Be Somebody in This World and Other Inappropriate Rantings from an Old Exile from Old France Living in America*, 2101

West Wing Offices
7:05 p.m., 24 December 2088

Lou looks up from reading the tablet on his red desk. He angrily looks at the aide, a young man dressed in a black office-suit.

"When did this happen?" Lou asks. He is dressed in a red leather office-suit, a red leather fedora on his bald head and his trademark silver-pointed, yellow-brown snakeskin shoes.

"Sir, I—Shouldn't you consult with the president?" the aide asks.

"I am asking you a direct question, pigeon vomit! When did this all happen?!" Lou yells, the pockmarks covering his leathery face seem to darken and deepen.

"When the president was first elected. Eight years ago. I assumed..."

Lou commands, "You are to have all material on the project on my console—now!"

Executive Area Outside Oval Office
9:06 a.m., 25 December 2088

The celebratory streamers and signs are still hanging throughout the White House; President Wilson wins his third election!

White House staff notice Lou passing the Secret Service guards to approach the Oval Office. He is not smiling, and says nothing to the executive administrative aides sitting outside the office. They are taken aback as he marches past, opens the Oval Office door, and enters without even being announced.

President Wilson sits at his desk reading the presidential daily briefing on his tablet. He is but a silhouette in the dim interior against the natural light coming in through the large Oval Office windows behind him.

"You stupid, stupid man," Lou snarls at the president.

"Good morning, Lou," President Wilson says.

"Did you think I wouldn't find out? Did you think I would not react when I did? We agreed on the proper course. We spent years carefully moving. We were so close to a garden void of all religiosity. All this time I wondered why it went wrong, what caused our setbacks, and to find out *you* were the one. Why would you implement it back then? You couldn't wait patiently. Now you plan to re-activate it. You will terminate the execution of Project Purify."

President Wilson glares at him coldly. "I will not."

"Darwin was wrong about most things, but he was right about the effect of external force on humans. You have caused the Jew-Christians to *evolve*. I can't allow that."

"Then I accept your resignation."

"In the real world, Mr. President, the devil is more powerful than any god."

"I just got elected to a third term. What are you president of?"

Lou smiles and says, "This is so beyond your petty lust for power."

"Your services will no longer be required. I can get elected by myself now." Wilson stares at him. "Do you remember the way out, or do you need a Secret Service escort?"

"Yes, God." Lou smiles. "You managed to hide this from me for eight years. Jeopardizing all the projects we've been working on. Knowledge of one could lead to knowledge of all. Our plan was to keep everything in the dark." Lou's smiles slightly as he coldly stares at Wilson. "So you want it all to come out into the light?" Lou turns and leaves the Office.

Wilson says, "Goodbye, Lou."

Oval Office (Eight Years Earlier)
8:35 a.m., 5 November 2080

It's the day after the election, and though it may not be until January 20th that he's officially sworn in, President-Elect Wilson already has an office in the White House.

The celebratory streamers and signs are still hanging throughout the White House; President Wilson wins the election! The room is jammed with the victory election team: campaign leaders, aides, volunteers, and donors. People are dressed in colored office-suits of reds, blues, yellows, and silvers.

"What are these names they call me?" Wilson asks as he reads from his tablet.

"Mr. President, you can put down the device for a minute. Celebrate, drink, relax," another aide says with a drink in his hand.

"The Jew-Christians already have different nicknames for you. President Galerius or President Haman or President Boggs. None of the references are complimentary," the first aide answers.

"What do they mean?"

"Not important, Mr. President. All just silly nonsense."

"Surprised they haven't called me Hitler yet. You're not officially a president of the United States unless a segment of the population hates you and wishes you dead." He smiles as he hands his tablet to an aide. "Time to celebrate."

"Where's Lou? How can your national campaign manager not be here at the party?"

Wilson smiles and says, "He never attends the election parties of any of his clients. It's just his way. But do send him a text: Rest up for the remaining week, because Sunday he officially starts as my chief strategic aide. We have a new world to re-create."

Location Unknown
6:40 p.m., 20 November 2080

"Let's be very direct here. What do you want? What do you need?" the voice says.

Deputy Finkel sits facing him, not answering yet.

The other man continues, "I have taken the proactive step of compiling a list of possible items of compensation."

Finkel picks up the tablet from the coffee table between them.

"What about the Christians?" Finkel asks. "I'm not even going to consider this unless they've already signed on."

"Your Christian counterpart already signed—yesterday." The president's advisor sits further back in his chair.

"You do realize that if the contents of this ever came to the attention of the Resisters, the reaction might be one of extreme violence."

"Amateurs we are not. The contents of the tablet are biometrically coded to you alone. Understandably, secrecy prior to implementation is of prime importance. This matter now falls under national security. What do you want?"

"I'm going to rebuild our Temple."

"Temple?"

"The one the Romans destroyed. I'll be revered. It's a Jewish thing. Not important to you. I want to have a large statue of myself nearby, just like we do for our American presidents. Maybe at the entrance, or maybe duplicate ones on either side, like I was twins. I had a twin brother. He died when I was born. King Herod built the Second Holy Temple. I'll build the third."

"This Herod must have been a great man for Jews, then."

"No, his many architectural wonders aside, he was a paranoid mass murderer."

Oval Office
11:39 p.m., 22 November 2080

Except for the Secret Service detail outside the offices, President-Elect Wilson and three members of the presidential staff are the only ones in the West Wing.

"I don't want the vice president to know," President Wilson says. "The idiot couldn't keep a secret to save his life."

"Do you want any of your senior staff involved aside from the Homeland director and attorney general?" an aide asks.

"No."

"Not the interior secretary?"

"This will be a classified security matter, not a land issue."

"What about Lou?"

Wilson pauses, thinking. "No. I will inform him at a later date."

"With your signature here, we will formally begin Project Purity, Mr. President. No one outside this room will know of the Project until it is fully implemented."

District Clothiers, Washington DC
11:05 a.m., 25 December, 2080

Finkel smiles as he looks in the mirror. He admires the new office-suit and especially the new classic white loafers that feel as if they were made for his feet alone.

"You look very distinguished, sir. New promotion, new division, new staff, new suit," the tailor says.

"I'll take it," he says. The watching salesman smiles at him.

Finkel struts down the busy street in his new purple suit as he makes one vid-call after another to brag and gossip. He is so wrapped up in the moment that he doesn't notice a tall, thin man walking up fast behind him. Finkel is about to turn the corner when the man behind him pulls a pen-like device from his pocket.

Finkel awakens tied to a chair in a darkened room. His eyes dart around wildly as he tries to remember what happened. He was walking, then he felt a pinch on his neck and blacked out. He was falling, too. He looks around again.

The room is empty, or so it seems. A light directly above his head on the ceiling is the only illumination. The man appears from the darkness with a chair and stands in front of Finkel.

"I've never met a high-ranking government official before. Should I bow or kiss your feet?" The tall, thin man sits in the chair.

Finkel's eyes are now starting to adjust, and he can make out three men standing against the walls in the darkness, watching him.

"You must have me mistaken for someone else," Finkel says.

"No, Deputy Director of Religious Registration Finkel, we don't. How's your boss, fake Rabbi Susan?"

"Is that what this is about? You're trying to hurt Rabbi Susan? The entire power of the American government is going to come crashing down on you all," Finkel snarls.

The man leans in. Finkel leans back, scared now.

"Tell me about Project Purify."

Finkel at first can't believe his ears. "How can you…? Who are you?" Finkel realizes he has just confirmed the Project's existence.

"I'm a Christian, Mr. Finkel. Though your comrades call us terrorists."

"We will not be intimidated by you."

"All Jewish Orders have unanimously decreed that Rabbi Susan is not to be harmed in any way as part of her excommunication. She will die alone and broken in old age. You, Mr. Finkel, are another matter."

Finkel stares at him. The man then places Finkel's e-pad on the floor right in front of them. The screen of the e-pad changes from one rainbow color to another. On the side of the device are flashing red, blue, and green lights. Finkel can barely take his eyes off of it; he glances up at the man. They stare at each other for what seems an eternity. As the moment goes on, restlessness and nervousness make Finkel start to tremble until he can't stay silent any longer.

"What do you want?!"

"I told you already: tell me about Project Purify."

"I don't know what you're talking about."

"Mr. Finkel, do we have to hurt you? I suspect you have a very low threshold for pain."

"Do whatever you like. I can't tell you what I don't know."

The man leans back. "That is unfortunate, that you will not cooperate. You leave us no choice." He stands.

"You can't touch me!"

"Why is that?"

"I'm a Jew, you're Christian. You can't touch me! Or are you Christians returning to your history of killing Jews again?"

The man gives him a smirk and moves to behind the chair Finkel is tied to. Finkel cowers, expecting the worst, but instead feels his restraints loosened. The man stands in front of him again.

"The dark Christians, Mr. Finkel, the ones who did kill Jews, haven't walked this earth for centuries, and their lands of Western Europe have been cursed ever since. The New World Christians who founded America are not them and have never been them. Are these the lies you spread when you talk to your Pagan masters?"

Finkel stays quiet.

The man continues, "You're free to go, Mr. Finkel, since you won't cooperate. Go."

The lights in the room turn on, and he can see that there are actually five other men standing in the room. One of them opens the door.

"Go," the man repeats.

Finkel's looks at the open door then back to the man.

The man says, "Did you honestly think any of us would stand by and let you round up Faithers and imprison us in your great grand ghetto? So easy for your Pagan masters to buy you off to betray your own people. We're truly back to ancient Roman times. Finkel, the new Herod. Master Pastor, the new Judas. Project Purify will never be allowed to go forward."

"If you already know about the Project, why do you have me here? Why ask me if you already know? And that's not what the Project is!"

"You hate your people that much? What did they promise you to betray your people?"

"You don't know anything! I don't hate my people. I'll be a savior for my people. The Pagans are too strong. Western Europe is gone. There's the Muslims and the CHINs. We must be about survival and not confrontation. I'll be the ultimate overseer of all Jews in the world. What's wrong with that? I will make sure my people are safe, after we get rid of all the troublemakers. The Pagan majority may rule this country, but my people can still prosper and survive even as a minority. We've done it before, we've always done it. You crusaders can fight them on your own."

"The Holocaust got rid of a lot of troublemakers, too."

Finkel says, "Stop with the Holocaust and Hitler. The damn Nazis have been dead for over a century. I want to protect my people, not get them destroyed like you Resisters."

"The Nazis are gone, but not their final solution policies it seems. We know about the Project, Mr. Finkel. We've seen the lists. You have a lot to explain to your people."

Finkel says, "What do you mean?"

"This room is bugged. This was not for us. Everything we've said, you've said, is being listened to by your people. That's why we brought you here. They needed immediate confirmation of the Project, which you have so graciously provided."

"I don't believe you!"

"Faithers being rounded up by Pagans into a great grand ghetto under the name of Project Purify. Now what Jew wouldn't want to be a part of that?"

Finkel stares down the hall, then looks back at the five men and finally their leader.

"What are you going to do to me?"

"Nothing," he smiles. "You said so yourself, you're a Jew and we're Christians. We can't harm a Jew. Only Jews can harm another Jew. So go."

"What's waiting for me outside?"

The man smiles. "*Other Jews*, Mr. Finkel."

Finkel bolts out of the room down the hall. He's heard enough.

He expects to exit into some ultra-secluded part of town, but he is actually in the heart of the tek-city, though he has no idea where. People are everywhere, and at first he feels a sense of relief—no one could possibly hurt him in public—but that quickly becomes fear. His attackers could be anyone.

Finkel grabs the e-pad of the first person who walks past him. The man is furious.

"*Allahu Akbar!*" Finkel yells and then starts talking gibberish, waving his hands around wildly and rolling his eyes.

The man runs away as fast as he can. Nearby people also move away. "*Allahu Akbar,*" the cry of a Muslim bomber, can always thin a crowd or empty a room.

Finkel dials quickly. "Susan, it's me! Help me! I was kidnapped! They released me but I'm still in trouble. GPS me and help me now! Get everyone here. Everyone! Yes, that's the street I'm on now. How far away are you? Okay, I'll get there. I'll leave the line open."

He looks all around nervously and puts his stolen e-pad into his pocket. Rather than stand directly in the middle of the street, he moves to the side. *Then he notices her.* She is above average in height, wearing a medium-length red dress, and her face is covered by a bright red, hooded cape. Though still a good distance away, he immediately notices the Star of David necklace around her neck and the hooded cloak itself. She stands motionless, and though he can't see her face, it is clear she is staring directly at him.

What heightens his fear is that she isn't alone. He sees one and then two more and realizes there are about a dozen of them around her. The men wear black pants and combat boots, skin-tight, skin-colored tops on their chests. On their heads are life-like wolf head masks with silver eyes. In the center of their chests are Star of David symbols. He has heard rumors of these new Jewish agitators: the Wolf Pack.

Finkel runs. He turns the corner and runs smack into a group of Vampires. They are all dressed in black, tank tops, tight leather pants or skirts, platform shoes or heels. Some have jet-black hair, some have purple or orange hair, some are blond. Most of them have piercings: nose, multiple ear lobes, eyebrows, and all are liberally tattooed. But the two things that stand out: their eyes (red, orange or yellow) and their teeth (fangs).

"Jesus Christ hell!" yells one of them. "What is your mental derangement walking, bag of blood?!"

Finkel realizes his good fortune. Vampirism was designated as a religion many years ago, and their membership has risen and decreased seemingly based on the latest vampire-themed movie or series. Technically, they're classified as Jew-Christians too, but no one in the public has ever called them that or considers them Jew-Christians. They are Nihilists or Hedonists with fang dental implants and different-colored cornea transplants. A religion born from a fiction book written 183 years ago.

"They're coming for me! You have to help! Name your price and I'll pay it."

The Vampires start laughing hysterically.

"Who cares about money, bag of blood?" one of them says.

Finkel looks nervously back around the corner and sees them: the red-cloaked woman and her wolf-head companions. They are walking so casually, it seems as if they feel, or know, he cannot escape them.

Finkel turns back to the Vampires. "Look!"

The Vampires join him and look around the corner. They immediately stop laughing.

"Is it the ones with Red Riding Hood?" one of the female Vampires asks.

"Yes," Finkel answers. "If you…"

The lead Vampire pushes him back. "Red Riding Hood is yours. The werewolves are ours. Vampires hate werewolves."

The Vampires walk around the corner and assemble shoulder to shoulder. They bar their fangs in unison and scream, flexing their hands as if they were claws.

Finkel watches his new recruits with satisfaction. The Vampires rush the Wolf Pack and the groups collide. The Vampires have fake elongated nails, but the Wolf Pack seems to have real claws, and they rip at the Vampires' flesh. The Wolf Pack attacks in an intense melee of punches and kicks. The Vampire victims are pummeled far past consciousness. Blood is everywhere.

The red-cloaked woman walks right through the violence towards Finkel. He runs.

A hotel doorman is almost knocked down as Finkel races past him. He runs to the elevators as a door opens and people get out slowly. They suddenly duck and move away from something behind him.

"Owww!" Finkel yells. Something has hit and embedded itself in his shoulder blade. He dives through the elevator door just as it closes.

"Penthouse!" he yells to the computer.

"Penthouse floor," the computer voice confirms.

Finkel is now practically crying from the pain but cannot reach the projectile in his shoulder blade, no matter how he contorts his body and arms. The doors open, and he gets to his feet and stumbles out. The hallway is empty and he stops to reach into his pocket for the-pad.

He hears a beep and another elevator is opening. He can already see the red cape. Finkel runs down the hall; she bolts out of the elevator after him.

The hallway dead-ends at a large vaulted window with a view of the tek-city for miles around. He stops and turns as he watches the red-cloaked woman run towards him.

"Stop! You don't need to do anything to me! Just stop! Stop!"

She reveals a gun.

"Don't shoot me!" he yells.

"I'm not going to shoot you, Herr Herod," she says with a thick German accent. She shoots out the glass behind him. Finkel is stunned and tries to cover himself as pieces fly everywhere.

She jumps and, with both feet, kicks him out the window. His scream fills the air—until it suddenly stops.

Rabbi Susan drives up in her car and stops.

"This is where the signal is. At this building. I had it clear and then it just stopped. What are you showing?" Rabbi Susan speaks to the dashboard.

"Director, the signal stopped for us, too," says a male voice on the other end.

Rabbi Susan notices some kind of commotion on the adjacent side of the hotel building. Something is happening. She is about to exit her car when she sees the woman with the concealed face, dressed in a red, hooded cape which flaps as she moves. The red-cloaked woman stops and is staring at her. Susan watches her with a look of fear.

Red Riding Hood walks slowly to the car. She raises her right hand, and in the center of her palm, a Star of David is etched in bright yellow. Rabbi Susan pulls back from the car window, and the woman hits the glass with her palm so forcefully that Susan turns her face away and dives to the driver's seat, closing her eyes and covering her head.

Moments pass, and Susan opens her eyes and then slowly looks up. The woman is gone, but all around the area are police sirens, crowds, and globe drones hovering in the air.

Office of Religious Registration Annex Building
3:00 p.m., 25 December 2080

When she first arrived, in a panic, the agent-in-charge informed her that she shouldn't go anywhere without an armed detail and driver. Members of the Registrants are in hiding, including Master Pastor, fearing Finkel's murder might be part of a wider conspiracy.

Rabbi Susan sits on the couch, her eyes red from crying. One of her aides enters the room.

"Rabbi, I was able to reach his family. I told them you offered to handle all the funeral arrangements, but they insisted they would do everything."

"Whom did you speak to?" Rabbi asks.

"It was a relative. His mother had to be sedated."

Rabbi Susan looks away from her for a moment. "I wish I could be sedated."

There is a knock on the door and it opens. Two women and a man are allowed in by a Secret Service agent. Rabbi Susan stands and extends her hand in greeting, but they don't shake it.

"What's wrong? You heard, right?" Susan asks.

One of the women, a Reform Judaic Council leader, says, "Yes, we heard about Finkel."

"What's wrong?"

"Didn't you hear about the others?"

"What? What happened?"

"They killed others, too."

"My God! No! Who?" Rabbi Susan sits back down on the couch.

The aide looks at her. "Sorry Rabbi. I didn't get to tell you yet. That's why we have heightened security."

"What is Project Purify?" the other Reform leader asks.

Rabbi Susan looks up at her. "What?" she asks.

"Don't pretend you don't know. What is Project Purify? That's why Finkel was killed."

"I have no idea what you're talking about," Rabbi Susan says. "And Finkel wasn't killed. He was murdered! What's wrong with you?"

"So your deputy director knew, but not his boss—you? We don't believe you, Susan."

Rabbi Susan jumps up. "Our friends were killed today. Someone may have tried to kill me too. And you're accusing me of things!"

"If they wanted you dead, Susan, you would be."

They look at the aide. "What is Project Purify?" one asks.

The aide is quiet but obviously knows something. Rabbi Susan grabs her by the shoulders.

"Answer her!" she yells.

The aide says, "I can't. It's classified and they haven't been read into the program."

"Then tell me," Rabbi Susan commands.

"You haven't been read into the program either."

"You run some kind of office, Susan," one of the women says. "Your employees know but you remain in the dark. Or so you want us to believe."

"We're here to formally let you know that the Reform Judaic Council has revoked your rabbinical standing," the other woman says.

"What?" Rabbi Susan says. "I am an elected member of the Council, and you can't just revoke my rabbinic authority without cause. There is a process, and that process hasn't been followed."

They laugh. "It doesn't matter anyway," one of them says.

"Why not?"

"The Reform Judaic Council was disbanded an hour ago."

Rabbi Susan shakes her head. "What are you talking about?"

"You weren't notified because of your complicity with this Project Purify."

"What are you talking about?! What is this Project Purify?! I don't know anything about this!"

"We are going to plead our case to the Conservatives or the Orthodox. Whichever will listen and revoke our excommunications, whichever grants us a reversal, will be the one we join."

"Why would you do such a thing?"

"Because, my dear Susan, you will soon be the last remaining member of the Reform Jewish movement. Not only was the Council disbanded an hour ago, but the entire denomination disbanded. Everyone is going into hiding or running to the closest Jewish enclave for asylum."

Rabbi Susan stands there, frozen.

"Did you honestly think you would be able to get away with this? Herding all Jews and other religious orders into some great internment camp in the center of the country. The Nazis did the same thing to us. And the Communists after them. And the ancient Egyptians, the ancient Romans, and Muslims in the past. Relocating us to one place or another for our own good. Just before they start killing us. You did it Susan, you did it. Not the Resisters, you killed Reform Judaism. And whatever we can do to stand with the Resistance, we're going to do, to stop this conspiracy against us. Whatever we need to do to stop you, the Pagans, the president, we'll do."

"I'm sorry, but any threat made against the president of the United States in any form must be reported to the proper authorities," Rabbi Susan says in an almost robotic, pre-programmed way.

They look at her with contempt.

"You do that, Susan. The rabbi of no one. The Jew who belongs to a movement of just herself. Have a nice life."

They walk to the door and one turns: "And one more thing, Susan. If I ever see you again, the decree by all Jews not to touch you in any way aside, I'll kill you."

"I know you don't care what I have to say but I swear I don't know anything about any of this," Rabbi Susan says.

They watch her with disgust and leave the room. The aide looks at her.

"Should I call Homeland before they get out of the building? They threatened to kill you. They threatened the president."

Rabbi Susan says, "You don't need to do that. You have other concerns."

"What other concerns, Director?"

"You're fired. Leave the building immediately."

The aide says nothing and slowly leaves the room.

Rabbi Susan sits back down on the couch.

She looks at the publicity photo of their first National Religious Registration Alliance gathering hanging on the wall, with all of them smiling—Master Pastor in the center, Bishop Joe on the left, herself on the right, and dozens more clergy flanking them.

Earlier

Lutheran leaders Edna and Eunice address the clergy gathering at their church.

"What do we do?" one of the other leaders asks. "People are dead. They say Master Pastor has fled the country."

"The government may come after all of us now, even Registrants," another one says.

Bishop Edna says, "Honestly, I don't care what you all do. All this has made us rethink all our assumptions. We no longer believe it's possible to be part of the pan-sexual movement—which I'm proud of—and a Christian. Christianity is a heterosexual only, the Bible-is-the-only-truth with a capitol 'T', boys club and I'm finished with it. Who are we deceiving? The majority of the population will always be hereto anyway, no matter how much we gain. If I have to choose between my identity and God, I choose my identity. I renounce Christianity. I renounce religion."

The group is astonished as Edna and Eunice leave.

Earlier

The crowds are kept behind police barricades, but people take pictures with their e-pads. The police are laughing at the dead Finkel, his remains covered.

"So that's what a Jew-Christian looks like when he falls thirty stories and splats. Aren't they supposed to be able to rise from the dead?" The policemen break into more laughter. They suddenly notice him.

Bishop Joe stands there, glaring at them. The police stare back, now quiet. They didn't even see him before. Bishop Joe is boiling with hate; he turns and disappears into the crowds.

Office of Religious Registration Annex Building
11:58 p.m., 25 December 2080

Rabbi Susan sits alone, thinking—so my bosses have been keeping secrets from me, probably right from the start. The first chance I get to return the favor, I will take it. Where's Bishop Joe? Where's my own family? Will my mother take my calls?

She won't learn until much later, but in the space of a week, aside from Reform Judaism, the Christian denominations of the African Methodist Episcopal Church Coalition and Episcopal Church Coalition have collapsed. The Lutheran Church Coalition, United Methodist Church Coalition, Unitarian Universalist Unity Church, Presbyterian Church Coalition, American Catholic Council, Baptist Church Unity, Pentecostal Church Coalition, Singing Gospel Church Coalition, New Evangelicals for Government are gone—members joining the Resisters or going underground, some walking away from Christianity altogether, some leaving the country. Though it will not be publicly acknowledged for years, the National Religious Registrant movement is over.

The West Sitting Hall, The White House
9:08 a.m., 27 December 2080

The original White House building, though imposing, is surprisingly small, especially when compared to the presidential palaces of the leaders of the other superpowers. It was created to intimidate foreign heads of state, and for the most part continues to do so in its own small, but majestic and non-tek way—though it is far, far from non-tek.

The Secret Service has very strict room capacity rules, which it enforces without hesitation, but today is not an ordinary day. Seven governors, their aides, the president, and his aides crowd into the Oval Office, along with four Secret Service agents—one at each exit and another two behind the president at the wall.

"When were you planning to tell us, Mr. President?" Governor Chauncey yells.

President Wilson says angrily, "That is a top secret project, and the very mentioning of it is a breach of national security."

"Then maybe, Mr. President, you should do a better job of disciplining *your* staff," Governor Chauncey scoffs. "The question on the table is when were you planning on telling us? You're talking about the federal government unilaterally seizing state land without the consultation or approval of the governors or legislatures of those states."

"Governors, this is not the ominous thing whoever leaked it has led you to believe."

"Rounding up Americans to be imprisoned on land in the center of the country," says Governor Stillman. "Sounds ominous to me."

President Wilson laughs. "Is that what the allegation is? Project Purify is a relocation program to move Jew-Christians to a federally created and protected city-size reservation. It will be their own homeland and should end the hostilities and the violence. We even designated administrators, their own, to be their representatives and liaison with the government. They will run their own internal affairs. This is not a new concept, and other presidential administrations have done it in the past, decades and decades before any of us were born. A lot of time and resources were put into devising and implementing this program."

"What happened to Governor Turgood in Kansas?" Governor Sabe asks.

President Wilson hesitates. His look tells them all that they shouldn't know about this *incident* either.

"He was killed in an accident," President Wilson says.

"How?" Governor Sabe continues.

"It's still under investigation."

Governor Melnor turns to Governor Sabe and says, "He was in his state office and several drones crashed through the windows, snatched him up, flew him thousands of feet in the air, and dropped him to his death. His body exploded when it hit the ground. They had to scrape his DNA off the police officers who were at the scene of the impact."

"I thought drones could only monitor," Governor Sabe says.

"Obviously not. Looks like they can grab Americans too, and drop them to their deaths," Governor Melnor says.

President Wilson yells, "That is not true! Domestic drones are not designed to do anything but surveillance. We don't know how Governor Turgood was killed exactly. It's under investigation."

"After all these years? We know drones are not the flying vidcams you want the public to believe, but flying robots. And that there are many types. Do you have any kill drones on American soil?" Governor Stillman asks.

"You know the answer to that. Kill drones are only used if we have full authorization from the state, the governor."

"At all times, or can a president bypass that order for any reason? You know, such as seizing state land without our authorization," Governor Sabe asks.

"If we are tracking terrorists in real time and Homeland deems it necessary, then yes."

"So kill drones can come into my state or another without our knowledge. Surveillance drones, kill drones, and whatever others you've created?" Governor Stillman asks.

"That's classified, Governor."

"Ones that can snatch Americans up in the air and drop them to their deaths," Governor Melnor repeats.

"That's not true, Governor!"

"Mr. President, with all due respect, you've hidden a major federal initiative to *relocate*—to use your word—Jew-Christians into some kind of concentration camp in the middle of the country," Governor Chauncey says.

"I object to that term!"

"Choose whatever words you like. Internment camp, then," Governor Chauncey says.

"I object to that term too."

"Reservation," Governor Stillman says.

"Federally designated homeland in America," President Wilson says. "The Jew-Christians have a homeland in Jewish Israel. They'll have one here too. That's all."

During World War II, the United States government under the Department of Justice relocated over 110,000 Japanese-Americans and some Japanese nationals living on the Pacific Coast to twenty-six permanent or temporary detention camps. The War Relocation Camps or "exclusion zones" were enacted by President Franklin Delano Roosevelt's Executive Order 9066 some two months after the Pearl Harbor attack. The constitutionality of the order was further upheld by the US Supreme Court. Other presidential proclamations designated not just Japanese nationals as enemy aliens, but also Germans and Italians, though on a far smaller scale.

"And if they don't want to go?" Governor Sabe asks.

"It will be a mandatory order, Governor."

"Tell me, Mr. President, is it something in the paint?" Governor Chauncey asks.

"Excuse me?"

"Your predecessor was some kind of necrophiliac in his spare time, the president before that heard voices and went Jew-Christian crazy and seized control of New York City to create the Three Towers, and now you plan to round up the Jew-Christians and force them onto some kind of reservation. Are you trying to start another civil war, Mr. President? Did you not learn your lesson after the Kansas Event?" Governor Chauncey asks. "So again, is there some kind of psychedelic drug in the paint in the walls that makes occupants of this office go crazy?"

"I did learn my lesson. That's why we're doing this. To ensure peace, stability, and order in the nation. They refuse to comply with the law, then this is what we'll do. Non-compliance will not be tolerated by anyone."

"If you pass a law and ninety percent disobey, do you think that maybe the problem is you, Mr. President?" Governor Sabe asks.

"No, I don't, Governor. It tells me that ninety percent of the people need to be in jail."

Everyone looks at him, astonished at his answer.

"Do all of you think this is a game? What do you think the Caliphate or the CHINs will do if they perceive us as weak? My job as Homeland director was the safety of America. As its president, that duty increases ten-fold."

"This reservation sits in four states. Did you ever plan to get approval from their governors or state legislatures?" Governor Stillman asks.

"I don't need to. This is an eminent domain action under national security."

"Are you making this up as you go? Eminent domain is to take land for the public good. Not to seize whole sections of a sovereign state," Governor Melnor says.

"Kelo expanded those powers. It doesn't have to be for public good. It can be for private use, so why not national security?" President Wilson says.

"Mr. President, there is no Constitution. So there is no Kelo,"

Governor Stillman says.

Kelo versus City of New London was a case decided by the US Supreme Court back in 2005 which involved the government using eminent domain to transfer land from one private owner to another for the purposes of economic development. The court held in a 5–4 decision that the general benefits a community enjoyed from economic growth qualified such redevelopment plans as a permissible "public use" under the takings clause of the Fifth Amendment. Many cited this case as opening the flood gates for government, especially municipalities and states, to seize private land to re-create cities into modern tek-cities.

"That's what we're here for," President Wilson says. "To finalize the country's new constitution."

"Yes, Mr. President, that's why we're here. And why I'm here. To tell you that my state will not be ratifying this new Rule of Law," Governor Chauncey says.

President Wilson looks at him angrily. He can see from the faces of the other governors that they are of the same disposition.

"None of us will, Mr. President. This Project Purify. Kill drones killing governors. What other secrets are you hiding? We thought you wanted to get rid of the Constitution so you could get rid of presidential term limits, and we were okay with that as long as it stripped all religiosity from our supreme law and other annoyances. But you seem to have other things on your agenda. We're not ratifying this new constitution of yours," Governor Sabe says.

"We've been working on this document for two damn years!" President Wilson says.

"Let us work on it some more. I'm sure if we spend another few months on it, we'll get it to where it needs to be," Governor Stillman says.

"No," Wilson says. "That is unacceptable. It must be done now. When you leave the White House today, we need to be able to walk in front of the cameras in the Rose Garden and announce to the world that America has a new constitution, our new Rule of Law."

"I said we're walking out of here now and we'll get back to

you," Governor Chauncey says.

"I'll hold all of you here for as long as it takes."

Governor Chauncey laughs. "You don't scare me, Mr. President. You want a war with the Jew-Christians *and* all fifty-three states, then be my guest, but I'm walking out of here now."

Wilson walks to his executive desk and grabs the tablet resting on it. He goes over to Chauncey and hands it to him.

"Do you want the same thing to happen to us that happened to Western Europe? Religious fanatics rising up and seizing our country? Our religious must be contained and managed. That is all Project Purify is. That's it. People still ask 'Who lost Western Europe?' Do you want the same to be said of us in the future— 'Who lost America?' Governors, tell me what you want. I don't care what it is. We'll amend the Rule of Law right here, right now. It's more important to me that it gets done. My only must-haves are the repeal of the presidential term limit, which you already know, and a permanent exception to any free speech claim when national security is at stake. We Pagans can lionize the late, great Justice Hugo Black for laying the legal groundwork for us to be able to remove all religiosity from the public square, but the man was a fool when it came to national security—allowing the media to publish classified material. Old President Nixon versus the old *New York Times*, I choose Nixon. Or two decades later the courts allowing the media to publicly reveal how we used banking transactions to track and monitor terrorists, or that we did warrantless eavesdropping on possible terrorists. These media all got journalist awards when they should have been convicted of treason and executed. Presidents must be able to keep data out of the public arena at their discretion to protect this country and its people. Those two are my only must-haves."

"Everything else is on the table?" Governor Melnor asks.

"Yes. We must finalize this now."

"Before we start, we want it in writing that, one, Project Purify is terminated right now," Governor Sabe says.

"Done."

"Two, all of us will be read into the program so we can see for ourselves what the initiative is—was," Governor Melnor says.

Wilson nods his head. "Done. And you will see it is nothing ominous."

"Three, you are to leave those Jew-Christians alone. Let them stay in their ghettoes. They are staying away from us, then stay away from them," Governor Chauncey says.

"Done." Wilson says. "And four, no one will mention the Project to anyone outside this room. Not to your staff, your partners or bed-buddies, anyone."

"Mr. President, your ban on exclusive gated communities is out. That is to become an American right. That's fine for the masses, but the elite? No damn way. The police protect the public. The elite must be able to protect themselves," Governor Melnor says.

"Forget about the Jew-Christians. Their ghettoes are far removed from our tek-cities, but the stupid law you've proposed would prohibit our own gated communities. Unacceptable," Governor Stillman says.

"And making private schooling and home instruction of any kind illegal? That's out. Are Jew-Christian schools and home-schooling such a threat to you? Your fixation with them has to stop," Governor Sabe says. "Do you want a war with the rich? My offspring will go to whatever damn school I want. I want them in an exclusive school and I'm paying for it."

"Anything you want," President Wilson says.

"Then we need to add a fourth branch of government—a Supreme Senate, made up of all the governors, to approve all police actions that supersede a governor's authority. You'll need a majority of us to move against any state," Governor Chauncey says.

"That is unacceptable. The Oval Office must have the full authority to protect America."

"Yes, because governors of states have no interest in protecting the people of their own states," Governor Stillman says sarcastically. "Are you planning on abolishing the fifty-three states, Mr. President? Is that your ultimate goal?"

"That is ridiculous."

"Because that's what it sounds like to me, if you can take our land whenever you want, send in federal troops without our permission, send in kill drones without our permission. It seems you will have all the power, and the governors, Senate, Congress will have none," Governor Stillman continues.

"Governor, we worked two years on this document. Wasn't that you in the room with us, or was a clone?" President Wilson says. "I will not let you risk a constitutional crisis. The US Constitution has been abolished. We must replace it now, in an orderly and public fashion, with the new supreme governing document for the nation."

"We need to establish quite clearly which jurisdiction has sovereignty over what. You seem to be of the opinion that, when in doubt, the sovereignty is yours. That is not what we agreed to. Otherwise, not only is having states meaningless, but so is having separate branches of government. My idea is to have a Supreme Senate," Governor Chauncey says.

"I will not let you paralyze the entire government by refusing to act. Paralysis would lead to collapse," President Wilson says.

"Or civil war," Governor Stillman says. "The governorship and the legislature run my state and not you!"

"Do you honestly think I want or care to run a rabble of fifty-three states?"

"Then put the damn words in writing! What are we arguing about then? Put it in writing and we'll ratify it. Otherwise, none of us will rubber-stamp you becoming the emperor of America. We got one damn emperor on the planet in the Muslim Caliphate. We don't need another here," Governor Chauncey says.

"We need to set clear, unambiguous standards. We'll be setting precedent for the next two hundred years or more if we do it right," Governor Melnor says.

"Mr. President, I don't think you fully appreciate the fact that we're having serious misgivings about this new constitution. I cannot fully say that I trust you. Say what you want about the Founding Fathers. Just because most were Jew-Christians doesn't mean they were incorrect in their fear of government tyranny," Governor Xavender says.

"I agree completely. We need to tone down the language. The public mustn't think it's some kind of document for a new quasi-dictatorship or oligarchy," Governor Zeta says.

"Yes, and does it have to be so long? What is with attorneys? The Old Constitution was three pages. The Rule of Law is hundreds of pages," Governor Melnor says.

"We should write it. The governors," Governor Chauncey says. All the governors nod in agreement.

The door opens, and another Secret Service agent enters and walks to the president.

"Mr. President." He motions Wilson away from the crowd. "There's been an incident, sir."

"What is it?"

"Should we vacate the Oval Office, sir?" the agent asks.

President Wilson takes him to the corner of the office. The agent whispers to him. The President walks back to the crowd of governors. He touches a spot on the wall. A large vid-screen lowers from the ceiling. "Link vid to screen," he says to the agent.

The agent talks into his wrist. After a few seconds, the picture becomes visible to everyone. A massive mural painting, twenty feet by twenty feet, sits in a field. In the center is a demonic-looking President Wilson with a gold crown on his head. On one side of him is Deputy Director Finkel with a Star of David on his chest and a white paper crown; on the other side is Master Pastor with a cross on his chest and a matching white paper crown. On the outsides of them, are a smaller Rabbi Susan, on one side, with a floppy three-pointed jester's cap introducing Finkel with both hands; and on the other side is Bishop Joe with his own jester's cap introducing Master Pastor with both hands. On either side of them are the governors—in fact, the very contingent of governor's in the Oval Office with the president right now, and each with the lower half of the face contorted in skull-like smiles, each wearing a gold crown. They each have a unique pose or gesture: Governor Chauncey raising his right arm with a short riding crop, as if about strike, using it as a weapon; Governor Melnor with tiny arms and feet in her mouth; Governor Stillman with his head tilted forward as if to use his forked ponytail as a weapon; Governor Bear holding a pitchfork; Governor Sabe with flying insects around his head and on his shoulders; Governor

Zeta with a disembodied head gnawing on her ear; Governor Xavender holding a pile of reddish goo in his hand. Disturbing doesn't even begin to describe the picture.

"Tell them where it is now," President Wilson says.

"Outside Camp David, sir," the agent says.

"How long has this thing been there?" Governor Sabe asks.

"It appeared yesterday," the agent says. "We waited on notification because of your election events. But when we saw the same governors here now, we had to say something."

"But…they're wearing the exact clothes that we're wearing now," Governor Melnor says.

Everyone now notices the fact, looking at their own clothes and each other in astonishment.

Governor Chauncey looks at Wilson. "Leave those Jew-Christians alone! This is that voodoo paranormal witch-stuff you read about where they make people swallow their own tongues or make you see dead people."

Governor Stillman asks, "Do we still have the article universally banning private gun ownership and concealed weapons?"

"You know we do," President Wilson answers.

"I change my mind. I agree with the Southern governors now," Governor Stillman says. "Let's take that one out. Leave it to the discretion of the states. Who knows what may happen in the future."

Governor Melnor says, "I am incredibly disturbed right now. I hate to use Jew-Christian moralistic terms, but that mural is downright *evil*."

President Wilson looks at the agent. "I want it destroyed now."

"Yes, sir," the agent says. Wilson notices that he wants to tell him something but the agent exits the room.

President Wilson announces, "I need all of you to focus and forget their stupid mural. We must do what we came here for: modification, ratification, and implementation of the nation's new constitution. It must be done and finalized before the inauguration. Remember our mandate when we started this two years ago: to begin the second great age of America."

New Atlantic City, New Jersey
7:53 p.m., 6 January 2089

"I know who killed Lou," Logan says. "Our instincts were right."

He is back in the seedy part of the outer tek-city where he met his son before. It is virtually impossible to buy an anonymous e-pad anymore because of national security, but for the right price, you can buy a stolen one.

"Please tell me you're on a secure line," Edison's voice says.

"Even better. An off-line one."

"Even worse then," Edison says. "Come in now."

"I need to go home first."

There is a pause on the line, a long one. "Why do you need to do that?"

"I have to. I have to kill the systems I don't need and remote link the ones I want. I had a mechanic do some work on the house so I can't remote in anymore. I have to do it manually."

"Listen to me carefully. Do not go home. Come straight here. At hyper light speed, now."

"You've been to my home. The security is nothing to scoff at."

"You've been to my home, and I scoff at your security. Please let's not joke about this. Come here now."

"Afraid you may lose the story of the decade?"

"Actually, I'm afraid of something else. Let's not joke about this. Get over here now. I can feel myself starting to age at an accelerated rate."

"It's done."

"What?"

"The story. I wrote it before I called you."

"My ageing has stopped. What else?"

"You know how to get it."

"I do?" Edison's voice pauses. "I do."

"And I don't know if you remember them, but I also contacted a Bishop Joe and Rabbi Susan—they were the highest-ranking Jew-Christians in the Wilson administration when he was first elected. I wanted to get them on the record too, for background."

"I wish you hadn't done that."

"I had to. We need to get everything we can. The story will be a bombshell."

"What did they say?"

"Bishop Joe was hard to find. He's some crazy recluse now, cursed at me and then gave the line to his robot, who also cursed at me before disconnecting. Susan started crying and disconnected."

"Bloody hell. This could be an atomic bomb story."

"Exactly. This one will make you rich all over again."

"Forget that, get over here."

"I'll be there as soon as I get home and do what I need to do."

"Can you just do this one thing for me? Just come here first and we'll all go."

"Edison, I'll be fine."

"I wish at this moment you were a Jew-Christian, because I wouldn't have to beg you to listen to those innate animal instincts I know are yelling in your brain, telling you not to do what you're going to do. Watergate Syndrome isn't worth a toe-tag, Yank."

Journalists so obsessed with getting *the story* to topple a government, the story to be talked about for decades, the story to make the journalist immortal, had a name for the mindset: Watergate Syndrome.

"You have the story and all the files, so start your editing magic. I'll be there before you're done."

"No! Please don't run around in the dark. Wait until the sun comes up."

"Thanks Edison, I'm sincerely touched. I'll see you tomorrow by 10 a.m.," Logan says confidently. "And without a toe-tag."

Logan disconnects the line. He walks to a group of Goths standing around a metal rectangular garbage can containing a roaring fire. They are dressed in black and wearing black make-up. Logan tosses the e-pad into the flames as the Goths throw bottles of liquid inside. The flames rise higher and get hotter. There will be nothing left.

The West Sitting Hall, The White House

5:08 p.m., 27 December 2080

It has been an extremely hectic day. The president-elect, the governors select—the appointed executive board of the nation's governors—and an army of aides have finalized the nation's new constitution. The governors are gone and the agent is now free to talk to the president in the Oval Office.

"Sir, there was something else left at Camp David aside from that mural that is more disturbing."

President Wilson stares at him concerned. "*More* disturbing? What is it? Am I supposed to guess?"

"Sir, do you have any siblings?"

"Of course not. You know that. What is it?"

"We'll show you, sir."

The agent leads the president down the hallway, three Secret Service agents following. It takes them a few minutes to get to the presidential garage, where even more Secret Service wait, some around a white van. As they approach, another agent opens the back door, and a man who appears to be some type of doctor dressed in white scrubs jumps out.

The agent gestures for the president to look inside.

Wilson is more than disturbed at the thing lying on the silver gurney inside the van: it looks like a shrunken and dead version of himself, naked from the waist up; from the waist down, it has the sickly body of a thin snake tail. The entire figure is covered in putrid sores.

President Wilson asks, "Is it real?"

"Actually sir, it's fake. Some kind of advanced plastic-polymer. Any kid in school could make it."

"So why am I here?"

"The entire thing is…covered in your DNA, Mr. President."

"Meaning what? Hair?"

"The forensics team says that it's covered with enough saliva to fill a five-gallon drum. It's your saliva, sir. Fresh saliva."

President Wilson steps back from the van and gives him an incredulous look. "How would they get that?"

"Sir, forensics said it was as if they came into your room night after night and extracted your saliva from your mouth over the course of months or…longer."

"Enough!" President Wilson says and walks away from the van, furious.

"Sorry sir. It's the most bizarre thing we've ever come across, and you know that Secret Service sees strange things every day when it comes to protecting you."

President Wilson looks around, seething with anger.

Logan's Home, Chesapeake Ranch Estates, Maryland
8:00 a.m., 7 January 2089

There is no place like home as the saying goes, even if there is an element of danger. He left New Jersey as soon as he knew it would be light again when he arrived. Logan had called ahead to the main security station and asked them to send two guards into his house to make sure that it wasn't broken into. They did so—including doing full scans for any humans or foreign tek (spying devices, mini-robots, etc.) planted in the house. They reported that the house was completely empty.

The auto-drive takes his car down one street, to the next, to his house, into the garage, which opens and closes.

As he enters the living room, Logan says, "Open sesame. Lights on. Displays on." He is glad he had the mechanic add all the security enhancements to his systems. He won't be staying long at all. Kill or remote his systems and get back on the road. The story will be a bombshell even to a public that is not easily shocked.

He walks to his Command Center: the long inclined recliner and the three vertical vid-screens automatically lower from their ceiling compartment and stop at eye-level. "Let there be light," he says, and the computer screens flick on, and padded armrest keyboards rise from the bottom of the recliner. The center screen shows all his audio, vid and text messages—he has thousands of them—and all the friends, colleagues, and contacts from around the world available to talk—he hides his availability.

Logan jumps into the recliner and lies back to read the left screen displaying local, national, and international newsfeeds. "Work, then warp drive out of here."

Logan's mouth has not even closed before a five-foot bundle shoots down his throat from behind the center computer screen. *The Man Made Out of String's tiny eyes observe as it pulls the rest of its thin body into Logan's throat.*

Logan jumps up from the recliner and desperately tries to pull the creature from his mouth, but it has already extended into his esophagus and stomach. His eyes tear up and he gasps for breath as he frantically runs around the room. He grabs for the e-pad from his pocket to text for help. Logan collapses to the floor.

Edison's Place, Arlington, Virginia
4:50 p.m., 8 January 2089

Edison sits in his office, without his clear glasses, looking first at the vid-screens, then his tablet, then his e-pad. He is so restless he can barely sit in his own skin. Logan never did show up at 10 a.m., and no one can reach him.

BB Bunny slowly walks into the room, her dark mascara running down her cheeks mixed with tears. Edison looks up and he immediately knows it's bad.

"He's dead," she says.

Edison just stares at her. He cannot speak.

"Logan's dead. Did you hear what I said?"

Edison rises from his chair, feeling light-headed. He holds onto the chair to keep his balance.

"Logan is dead!"

"Shut up!" Edison yells. "I heard you. Saying it over and over again doesn't change the fact."

BB Bunny starts to sob again.

"Stop crying! That doesn't help either," Edison yells.

The words just make her cry harder, and she sits on the floor yoga-style, her head lowered.

He walks over to her and kneels down. His voice is softer and hushed. "Listen to me." He puts his hand on her shoulder.

She looks up at him. "You knew this was going to happen,

didn't you?"

"Listen to me. I'm leaving the country now. I can run my business from anywhere on the planet. I can get an entrance visa for you too."

"I'm not leaving my country."

"Sometimes you don't have a choice."

"I'm not leaving."

"We have to disappear now. Whom can you stay with?"

"I'll find someone. That's easy."

"What about that military guy you mentioned? He seems stable."

"No, he's too stable, and he's supposed to be moving to New York. I hate New York."

"Good. Off to New York you go. Men like that kind of thing, a woman just showing up to be with them. I'll leave the country and run operations from overseas."

"But the house? My place?"

"Is it worth dying over?" He stares at her.

She thinks for a moment. "No."

"Our lawyers with their slime can handle the sales and the moving. We go straight to the airport now."

"He didn't listen to you, did he? I heard you talking to him. You told him to come here and he didn't listen. Now he's dead."

"Go straight to the airport now. In fact, I'll drive you."

"What about Logan? Are we not going to do anything for him?"

"There's nothing we can do but make sure we don't join him any time soon."

He lifts her up from the ground and grabs a few things before leaving the building. They get into his SUV, and Edison gives a final look at his mansion as they drive off. He knows he will probably never see the place again.

White House Offices
8:28 a.m., 7 January 2089

The Homeland Security director walks into the West Wing

conference room. The man sitting patiently on one of the plush chairs in the corner sees her and stands. He's dressed in a one-piece black office-suit, with a red shirt underneath and a silver tie. His red eyes shimmer in the light—the man is a Vampire.

McDunn says, "We're glad to have you, sir. How should I address you?"

"Thank you. It's all my pleasure to work for the president of the United States. Just call me Bloodgood. Your Vampire slave." He gives her a big smile; his fangs almost seem too big for his mouth.

Philadelphia International Airport, Pennsylvania
Morning, 9 January 2089

He didn't feel comfortable staying in the District, even to just fly out of Ronald Reagan New International Airport. Edison boards the hyper-sonic luxury jet bound for Melbourne, Australia. He sits in his large, plush recliner seat, staring out the window. He holds back tears at the loss of another good friend and possibly of another nation he has called home. He is not looking forward to seeing the French again, so many of whom migrated to Australia after the Fall of Western Europe.

He now thinks about the man who most likely killed Logan; the same who killed Lucifer. I will avenge my friend, Edison thinks to himself. I'll dump the entire story on the Net for all to see and know.

"I blow you a kiss, Emperor Wilson, straight from my black heart," he whispers as the hyper-sonic jet starts its taxi down the runway for departure.

Department of Homeland Defense and Intelligence Agency Security Dispatch / 10 January 2089

Notify HOMELAND that illegal download of classified data to Net was successfully intercepted. Specific Data Stream block was quarantined, shredded, and force-deleted. No unauthorized subjects have become privy to data. Source of potential classified leak: Edison Blair, ex-citizen of Old England, emigrated to United States in 2065, now in Australia. Covert rendition team in Australia activated to intercept.

THE PROTESTANT ORDER

(The Rise of the Resistance)

America

It's Always Sunny in Hell

"Hell isn't merely paved with good intentions; it's walled and roofed with them. Yes, and furnished too." – Aldous Huxley, English writer, intellectual (died Nov. 22, 1963)

"The safest road to hell is the gradual one – the gentle slope, soft underfoot, without sudden turnings, without milestones, without signposts." – C. S. Lewis, English writer, intellectual (died Nov. 22, 1963)

Nearly four centuries after Christ, Christianity was still a small religion on the planet. For Christianity's first thousand years there was nothing else besides the "holy, catholic church" (catholic simply means "universal"). Not until several centuries after Christ did the church begin to develop into the *modern* Roman Catholic Church.

But early Christianity may not have survived in the face of intense persecution from ancient Rome, and the church was focused primarily on its survival. Then came the conversion of Roman Emperor Constantine in 318 AD. Some would say the church was assimilated by the empire, adopting its governmental structure with geographical provinces ruled by bishops. Later bishops emerged as the preeminent rulers of major cities such as Alexandria, Jerusalem, Constantinople, and the capital of the empire, Rome—ironically the very place the Apostles Peter and Paul were believed to have been killed by the Romans centuries before.

Historically, Roman Bishop Leo I (440-461) is considered the first official pope, and he was the first to claim ultimate authority over all of Christendom. Asserting papal authority, he wrote that Christ had designated Peter and his successors the "rock" on which the Church would be built. During the Middle Ages, from 500 BC to the 1500s, any Christianity other than the Catholic Church was a heresy—punishable by death.

Then Catholicism splintered. In 1054 was the political split of the Eastern Orthodox. However, more significant was the bloody Protestant Reformation from 1517 to 1648 led by Martin Luther. Protestantism too would also splinter into many, many different denominations with time.

Of all of them, the pacifistic Anabaptists are actually descendants of the most radical wing of the Protestant Reformation. The most traditional of them are the Old Order Amish.

Amish Quarter, Pennsylvania
8:35 a.m., 14 September 2088

Amish Quarter is one of the largest remaining East Coast communities of the Christian Order known as the Amish. To visit is like stepping through a doorway back in time: it is a large, rural community of about eight hundred residents with a way of life that has remained virtually the same for over two hundred years. All around them is quite another matter. The Quarter sits in the southeastern tip of the state, with Philadelphia the closest modern tek-city to them—only one hour away by freeway.

The Amish are not blind; they can see the ever-advancing Tek World around them. While the Quarter has plush fields with quaint family homes and simple general-use buildings, the outside world is made of towering structures of glass and steel, high into the sky. By day this world can be easily ignored, but at night even though many miles away, the pulsating neon lights and digital signs and loud audio invade their peaceful sanctuary.

Amish Quarter and Pennsylvania have had a pact of sorts for many decades, despite the Pagan majority: stay away from the Quarter; the Amish are of no concern. Previous Pennsylvanian governors even went so far as to declare Amish land a state recognized reservation approved for use by these specific Jew-Christians. But the average Pennsylvania tek-dweller views them as throw-back oddities from the stone ages to be internally mocked and externally avoided: robots farm, not people, and who drives horse-drawn buggies anymore? To the Pennsylvania government, the Amish are a state historical treasure, like the pink mountain laurel and the ruffed grouse, their state flower and bird respectively—and similarly on the verge of extinction.

Amish Quarter was founded only some thirty years ago, breaking away from other Lancaster Amish communities due to their own population growth and need for land.

For the Amish, anyone non-Amish, religious or secular, is called 'English.' Given all the ex-patriot British who fled the Fall of Western Europe to America, most people mistakenly think they are referring to these New Americans. The Amish are not aware of such terms as *Tek World*. To them, the outside world is called the "English world," "Devil's Playground," or simply the "Playground."

Homes in the Quarter all look the same: simple two-story white-brick houses, well-kept, plush green lawns, and accompanying crop fields, gardens, or both of varying sizes. The fields grow an extremely wide variety of crops, from asparagus to zucchini, and they have many types of fruit trees. The homes with barns and grazing land keep any variety of animals: cows, goats, pigs, chickens, horses. Probably the most technologically advanced thing on the Quarter is its rich imported soil.

Decades of foot traffic from people and animals have created a network of roads connecting every building in the Quarter. Kristiana walks casually back to her home where she can already see her father working in the vineyard. Parts of their vast fields grow different varieties of grapes, but for the past ten years her father has also been making wine to sell on the market. They have the only vineyard in the district and windmills dot their property providing power to the fields—a sanctioned exception to Old Order Amish rejection of modern tek.

She looks up: another flying Dutchman, as the Amish youth call the massive jumbo jet sky-ships of the English flying out of their main airport to destinations unknown. There was a time when sightings of planes were rare but now they are quite frequent and very close to the Quarter. They used to fly so high as to be dots in the sky. Now they fly low enough so that Amish children on the ground can almost see the faces of the passengers through the plane's windows. The children may be captivated, but Amish adults are quite suspicious of the growing proximity of the planes above their homes.

Kristiana has a slim build, very fair skin, light brown hair worn in a bun, and green eyes. In standard female Amish dress, she is wearing a white bonnet, long-sleeved calf-length blue dress, black shoes, and stockings. Her father stops working for a moment when she reaches him; he too has green eyes. He wears dark denim pants, a light blue shirt with the sleeves rolled up, and suspenders. A wide-brim straw hat sits on his head—something Amish men have worn for almost 160 years—and a full brown beard that is starting to whiten. Like all Amish, the men don't shave their beards after they marry.

"A flying Dutchman, Father," she says.

He looks at her and can't help but smile. "Good afternoon, Kristiana."

"Oh, sorry, Father," she says, almost blushing. "Good afternoon." She smiles again.

"You are easily distracted by the English," he says.

"Oh no, Father, not at all."

"Where did you get the phrase 'Flying Dutchman'? Have you been watching movies again with Pagan Paul?"

She looks away sheepishly. "I must have heard it from someone, Father."

How the name of a ghost ship doomed to sail the seas for all eternity became the name of the English passenger planes in Amish slang no one could say.

"Kristiana, you often forget I used to be your age."

"Really, Father? Did the English invent planes yet?" She smiles. His daughter is one of those people who have an infectious smile and an even more infectious laugh.

"Are you sassing me again, Kristiana?"

"Of course not, Father."

"You do know God made me on the eighth day, so I was

made long before the English machines."

Kristiana bursts out laughing. "You were here before the dinosaurs, Father!"

Her father starts to laugh too. She can always distract him from his field work. "Kristiana, go do your chores. You can do your comedy at the dinner table tonight."

She smiles and says, "Yes, Father." She starts towards the house, then stops. "Oh Father, when can we talk privately? I don't want to talk with Mother and everyone else around."

His disposition changes immediately. He knows what it's about. "What is there to talk about?"

"I'll be eighteen, Father."

"Yes."

"I did promise to stay a full year."

"Yes, you did."

Kristiana looks at him, perplexed. "You're not going to try to talk me out of it again?"

"No, not this time."

"Is this a parental trick? Because I'm not changing my mind this time, Father."

"I know. No trick."

"Is Mother going to try to stop me?"

"Not her either."

"I don't understand, Father."

"Did you already tell Pagan Paul that you are really going on *rumspringa* this time?"

"Not yet, I wanted to tell you and Mother first."

"Good. Go tell him now, and I'll go tell your mother so she isn't surprised at dinner tonight."

"Right now? Don't you want me to start chores?"

"No, tell him first and do your chores afterwards."

Kristiana is still suspicious. "Okay, Father."

She turns around to walk out of the Quarter. He watches her sadly. She is the middle child of his five, but in most ways she is the smartest and most mature—except in one area, her insatiable curiosity for life. Here in the Quarter such a trait is welcome, but in the Playground it could have deadly consequences. But there's no stopping her, no dissuading her; she's wanted to leave her Amish enclave since she was a child to "see the world." It is customary for Amish children to do so between the ages of sixteen and twenty-one for the rite of passage called *rumspringa*, which literally means "running around." Some are encouraged to leave their communities, and others, like Kristiana, are eager to do so. They have the opportunity to experience the pleasures and conveniences of life in the outside English-world, all forbidden under the Amish way of life. For the Amish, this temporary exemption from the rules of the church is a precursor to the most important decision in their lives: deciding whether to stay in the English-world or return to permanently join the Amish church and be baptized, get married, raise a family, and live out their lives in the Amish way. His own father had told him as a young man, "You have to face the temptations before you can reject them."

Few children actually decide to venture out into the English-world, but Kristiana was born an adventurer. For those that do go to "be wild," virtually all return to join the Amish church. But it has changed so much. When he went through his rumspringa as a young man just past the age of seventeen some thirty-two years ago, it was still relatively safe, and he stayed in the Playground for almost four years. However, it was clear even back then that there was a growing hostility towards anyone religious. Now his precious daughter wants to visit the place. He and his wife successfully persuaded her to forego her trip for a year, but it only postponed the inevitable.

It takes Kristiana only a few minutes to walk to Pagan Paul's home. His shack is a mile away, just outside the Amish Quarter. It stands all by itself on a small hill—one story, logs and mud-brick construction, oval windows, surrounded by a chain fence. She sees smoke rising from the chimney, the sign that he's in.

Everyone calls him Pagan Paul. No one knows his full name, even after all this time. Kristiana, like all the children and adolescents in the Quarter, has known him all her life. He was instantly popular with them when he arrived some fifteen years ago with his endless stories of the English-world, the music and movies he shares with them from time to time (both forbidden by Amish church law), and most of all, his quirky personality. He is the self-appointed protector of the Quarter.

The bishop, preachers, and elders, including her father, didn't accept him as a permanent fixture of the land until about seven years ago. He is a taste of the English-world living among them. The adults knew of his corrupting influence on the children with his music and movies, both G- and PG-rated, terms which to this day she still doesn't really understand. Her father confronted Pagan Paul about five years back, and after their meeting he walked out of the shack and never said a negative word about the man again. Aside from Pagan Paul's full name, that is the other mystery: how did he win her father over? Or at least get her father to simply accept his presence? What did he say? What did he do? Whatever it was, he won over her father and all district elders.

Kristiana knocks on the door.

"Yes, yes. Come in!" a voice yells from inside.

She opens the door and enters. As is customary she leaves the door open. She can smell the nice aroma of something cooking in his tiny kitchen. She has always suspected that it was his culinary skills that won over the elders.

"I should blow up my entire house with dynamite!" Pagan Paul now appears, rising from the floor with a large, circular disk flashlight strapped to his forehead. He looks at her, and the beam shines right into her eyes.

"No! Why do you want to blow up your house?" Kristiana shouts with a smile. Encounters with Pagan Paul never disappoint. "Why do you have the head lamp on again? It's too early to search for wires."

"Do you know that roaches can survive a direct nuclear blast? You can cut off its head, put it in a sealed gas jar, and it will live for two years and still be able to give birth to hundreds more."

Kristiana bursts out laughing. "That's not true. No insect can do that."

"I would blow up the entire house with dynamite. I can't even tolerate one of them. They pay me no rent and pay me no money for groceries." He suddenly sniffs the air and runs to the kitchen stove. He lifts the lid off one of the pots and then stirs it with a large wooden spoon. "But then I'd have no house, and they would stand there on the ground, smiling their small, sick smiles and waving around their small sick legs of six. 'We can survive an electromagnetic pulse blast or a nuke strike, but not you, human.'"

"What are you going on about now, Pagan Paul? Now you're looking for insects and not wires anymore."

"Roaches are not insects, they're alien invaders." This time he smiles. He's joking now. "I look for the wires daily, that's how I found the little invaders. I wonder if I can make some miniaturized dynamite and blow them up that way."

She is trying not to laugh again, but can't help herself.

Suddenly he asks, "Kristiana, what are you plotting today?"

"I'm not plotting anything," she says, smiling.

Pagan Paul is of average height and weight, has brown eyes, always looks like he needs a shave and he now has a very nice crew cut, unlike the scraggly mop top that used to be his hair years ago.

"Tell me a new story," Kristiana says.

"I know you didn't come here for that. I tell a new story every time you see me. So what are you plotting then?"

"You always ask me that, but it so happens that I am this time. I'm going to visit English-world for my rumspringa. I just need to decide when I'm leaving."

"That's why you came?"

"Yes, Father told me to come here and tell you."

The happy expression on his face is gone. "Why would you go there?"

"I've always wanted to go. You know that. I've been talking about it for years. And you know I was going to go a year ago."

Pagan Paul turns off the stove and removes his apron. "Sit down for a moment."

Kristiana walks to his tiny dining room table—basically the kitchen, dining room and living room are all one big room. She sits down, and Pagan Paul joins her at the table, sitting across from her. He removes the flashlight strapped to his head, turns off its light, and puts it on the table.

"Do you know why I'm here?"

"What do you mean? Here at Amish Quarter?"

"Yes."

"You told us many times before. You wanted to live in a nice, quiet place, so you picked here."

"No. That was my cover story, but the truth is different. I'm crazy."

"Crazy? No, you're not. You're just a bit eccentric."

"Crazy I am. I ran away from the outside world—Tek World. What you Amish call English-world."

"You told me once before. I thought you were joking. You said invisible rays were melting your brains."

Pagan Paul laughs. "So I did tell you. I'm forgetting things."

"Yes, you did."

"Well, I wasn't joking. I am a member of the Brotherhood of the Tinfoil Hat Society."

Kristiana laughs. "What is that?"

"The outside Tek World is saturated with these invisible rays that come from all their machines. Electro-magnetic waves that go right through your body. They made my head hurt. The rays were killing me, so I had to get away to places where the rays couldn't get me. No electro-emission towers anywhere nearby. Far away, so I came here. Now I can live. The headaches, migraines, progressive memory loss, tumors are all gone, ever since I came to live in the Quarter."

"Invisible rays do that?"

"To people like me, yes. It's how they control you. These invisible rays. And the updates. It used to be just portable devices, but now everything is computers—the car, everything in the home, even the house itself." Pagan Paul seems to drift off as he talks. "Their machines won't work without the latest update. Lies! It's so they can control you by controlling your machines. Tie you to the Net. Enslave you to the Grid."

"I have no idea what you're talking about."

"It's the English box I showed you that day when those tourists visited the Town."

"Oh yes, their technology folding screen thing."

"Yes, the laptop, and I showed you their evil e-pad and e-tablet devices too—their trinity of evil. Every person is assigned one at birth so the cybernetic bonding can start immediately, and so can the government's control. They just want to get their fingers in my wallet, my body parts, including my private ones…"

"Pagan Paul, stop that talk."

"And rip my brain open to access my mind. Not me! I wear an aluminum helmet!"

When Paul arrived in the Quarter he wore his aluminum helmet everywhere. Some of the Amish kids at the time even thought it was actually welded to his head. A few years ago, he stopped wearing it, and then the talk was of the wild hair on his head. He later started going to the Amish barbershop like a respectable person and getting a proper cut every two weeks.

"You don't wear the helmet anymore."

"Yes, but I have it. And they know I do. That's why I search for their wires in the ground and in the walls. That's how you can tell they are lurking. There are no towers here, so they need their physical wires. They can't spread their tek without the wires. Everything is wireless for them, with their invisible rays, but they need the wires still for back-up."

Kristiana shakes her head, still smiling. One of his daily idiosyncrasies: searching his house thoroughly for wires in the floor, in the walls, in the ground around his house. Paul had a genuine morbid fear of wires of any kind.

"Kristiana, you must never leave Amish Quarter and go near the Tek World. It seems wonderful and mesmerizing and exciting, but the Amish are right. English-world is the Devil's Playground. It's a bad, bad, bad place."

"God will protect me."

"I wish I could believe in God. I wish I knew there was a God with the certainty that you do. But the more I think about it, that's just too big for me. There's a God? There's some supreme being that created me and you and everything else and the universe. That's too big of an idea for me, too frightening of an idea to be allowed in my head. I'd hide under a rock someplace. I wish there is a God for your sake."

"Why?"

"If you go to the Devil's Playground, you'll die."

Kristiana looks at him. In all the many years she's known him, Pagan Paul has never tried to scare her. "I will not let you or Father or Mother change my mind. I'm going. I've been waiting ten years to get old enough, and then waited another year, and soon I'll be eighteen, so I'm leaving. You will not change my mind. I will come back, of course, but I have to explore it myself."

"Kristiana, do you think your father is a bad man?"

"No, of course not."

"He wants you to be safe and live a long life. Raise a family. Be a strong role model for your people."

"I will be fine."

"No you won't, Kristiana. I'm from English-world and even I wouldn't go there anymore. What chance do you think you'd have?"

"Pagan Paul, I'm going. It is my right to explore the English-world. Amish youth have been doing so for hundreds of years."

"This isn't hundreds of years ago. This the latter part of the twenty-first century, fast approaching the twenty-second century and the Amish live in the latter part of the nineteenth century. This ritual you all have…people call me crazy. This 'running around' will run you into the grave."

"I'm going."

Pagan Paul rises from the table. "Kristiana, I didn't want to do this, but you leave me no choice. I've saved this movie for you just in case we ever came to this point. I've shown it to several stubborn, hard-headed Amish youth like you who wouldn't listen to sanity."

The movie! Kristiana had heard all the rumors about it, and it did a lot more than dissuade other Amish youth from leaving the Quarter, it changed them. Her friend Ruth, two years her senior, had nightmares for months. Another friend changed from an outgoing, friendly girl to a paranoid wreck, only recently becoming more relaxed.

Kristiana dashes out of the shack and runs away as fast as she can. Pagan Paul won't make her watch the evil movie. She hears Pagan Paul yelling at her, but she ignores him. Her father and now Pagan Paul. The conspiracy to keep her from leaving the Quarter is growing.

She is back on the road to her home and passes by her father again.

"I finished talking to Pagan Paul. I'm going to do my chores now, Father," she says.

He continues his field work, visually spot-checking grapes, and pauses only for a moment to watch her walk to the main house. He stops his work and stares into space for a long while.

"Help me, God, save my daughter."

Kristiana enters the main house; her mother and sisters are busy at work themselves.

"Hello, Mother," she says as she walks into the kitchen. "What chores do you need me to do?"

"I had your sisters finish them," she says.

Her second-eldest sister glances at her disapprovingly and her two little sisters look at her and giggle.

"Go help your elder sister in the barn."

"Yes, Mother."

Her oldest sister Rebecca will be getting married soon so she will be with the family for only another few months. Kristiana finds her sister in the barn, sweeping. Rebecca is a slightly older version of Kristiana, only with darker-colored brown hair and brown eyes.

"Late again?" Rebecca doesn't even look up.

"No, doing twice the work you do, as usual."

"All the chores here are done. Why do you always play games?"

Kristiana is mad. "I'm not playing games. I did the family errands and just got home."

"You mean you needed another excuse to go into Town to talk to the English. You know Father and Mother will never let you leave to go into their English-world."

The Town is the commercial section of the Quarter, with all their stores and main market to sell their goods to the public.

Rather than going all the way to the main tek-city, buyers and other visitors just come to the Town to purchase Amish products.

"What are you talking about? I'm an adult, and I will be going for my rumspringa."

"Kristiana an adult? I'm the adult. Sarah is an adult. You are not an adult. You're a child, like Katie and Annie."

She is angry at the comparison. "I don't want to talk to you anymore. You are always so negative, and you're just jealous because I want to see the world. You're just getting married because you're too scared to leave the Quarter for yourself."

"Kristiana, do not talk bad about my upcoming marriage. You don't know anything about my husband-to-be or me."

"I know you don't love him. What else do I need to know?"

"You're excused from chores. Go away to your dream-land in your head. Go to the land of the English. No one can tell you anything, because Kristiana knows everything. And I don't want you to come to my wedding."

"Good! I don't want to go to your silly wedding."

Kristiana angrily turns and marches out of the barn and back into the main house. Her other sisters are gone, but her mother remains in the kitchen.

"Rebecca is already finished with all the chores, Mother."

"Why do you hate me, Kristiana?"

She stares at her stunned. "What? What do you mean Mother?"

"Your father told me. I want you to promise me right now, right here, that you will not leave the Quarter."

"No! *You* promised, Mother. I waited an extra year because you wanted me to stay."

"One more year."

"No, Mother."

"I'm begging you, Kristiana."

"No, Mother. I won't listen to you this time. You promised not to try to stop me again."

"Kristiana, if you leave...I don't know what I'll do." Her mother turns and sits slowly down in a chair in the dining room. She starts to cry. "You have to promise me you won't go. You can't imagine how terrible English-world is. I would never see you again."

Her mother continues to speak, but Kristiana is not listening; angry, she blocks out all her mother's words. The conspiracy now includes her Father, Pagan Paul, and her Mother. Who else have they enlisted? Her two youngest sisters enter the room and console their mother and look at Kristiana, wondering what she did to make her cry. Her older sisters enter and sit next their mother, giving Kristiana dirty looks. Both her elder sisters decided not to leave the Quarter when they came of age; they joined the church and were baptized. Everyone is talking. Then her father enters, and he walks to his crying wife. The conspiracy includes the entire family.

Kristiana turns and walks out of the dining room, as if to go to her room. When out of sight, she runs instead to the back door of the house. Once outside, she runs as fast as she can through the field. She runs to the trees just off their land and finds the one she wants. With a shovel hidden not too far under the dirt, she digs near it. With a few minutes of quick digging, she unearths a big, thick plastic bag. Inside are a knapsack and a small suitcase with wheels she can carry easily; she rips opens the plastic bag. After, she rolls it up, puts it back in the hole, shovels the dirt back over it, picks up her bags, and keeps moving.

This is not how she wanted to do it, but she can't stay another year, she can't. She knows her Father has something planned to keep her from leaving. She may not be able to figure out what it is, Father is very smart, but she'll outsmart him by not even being present for him to spring his trap. She'll hike to the General Store and call one of those taxis. She's saved enough money to hire the taxi to take her into the English city Philadelphia. Once she's there and gets settled, she'll contact her parents. She may be almost eighteen, but she might as well be five if she can't ever get her chance to be an adult. Philadelphia can't be all bad—it's called the City of Brotherly Love.

The only experience she has had with the English, aside from Pagan Paul, was when she was a child. A few Goths came into the Town, wearing their skin-tight black clothes, black makeup, and spiky black hair. Instead of buying things from the grocery store, they terrorized her and her younger sister, Katie; Annie wasn't born yet. The Goths picked on the girls, yelled at them and tried to pull their bonnets from their heads. As pacifists, she has always wondered what she would have done if not for the intervention of Pagan Paul, who appeared from nowhere, yelled at the Goths with a crazy intensity, and chased them on foot out of town. But now, she must venture into the English-world on her own.

It doesn't take her long to get to the General Store. But time isn't on her side. Maybe an hour or so for her family to figure out she is gone. Then her father will contact Pagan Paul. Between the two of them, they will most likely start looking for her right here in Town, and probably at the General Store.

But she'll be gone long before that. She has the store manager, an Amish boy from one of the other districts, call the taxi and ask to have it wait outside at the back of the store, so no one will see her with her knapsack and suitcase on wheels. As she stands there waiting, she can feel it growing, first as anticipation, then exhilaration, and now a bit of fear. But nothing will keep her from leaving this time. Her father went into English-world for his rumspringa, so did her mother, and now it's her turn.

"Are you some kind of fugitive, running from the police?"

The sound of the voice seems to make her heart stop a beat. She looks behind her, and there is her father, staring at her. She swallows hard and realizes that she's forgotten how to speak.

"How many times do I tell you and your sisters that I used to be your age? There is no thought that enters your head when it comes to mischief and recklessness that I haven't thought myself. Are your mother and I that scary that you need to secretly run away? Kristiana, I told you that no one would stop you this time. Didn't I?"

"Yes, Father," Kristiana answers slowly.

"Here." He hands her a piece of paper. "I know you are going to Philadelphia so take this with you."

She takes it. "What is it, Father?"

"Insurance. If you're right, then burn it. If I'm right, then you'll see."

"I don't know what you mean."

"You will."

She looks at the folded paper. She wants to read it when she hears the honk of a car horn from the front of the store.

"That must be your taxi. Don't keep them waiting."

She looks at him for a moment. She puts the paper in her skirt pocket and grabs her bags to walk around the store. Her father follows her to the bright yellow taxi waiting. The door opens, and a little man dressed in what seems to be a yellow jumpsuit exits the driver's side.

"Did you call for a taxi?" he asks.

"Yes. I did, sir," she says.

The man walks to her and takes her knapsack and suitcase and puts them in the trunk of the car. He closes it.

"You're one of those Jew Christians, aren't you?" he says.

"What is that?" she asks. "I'm Amish."

He smiles. "Okay. How do you plan to pay for the fare?"

"I have money, sir," she says.

"I don't mean to be rude, but I need to verify that before we go. I heard that Jew-Christians don't use digi-cards, so I'm not sure how you plan to pay."

Kristiana reaches into her skirt pocket and reveals a digi-card. "Do you mean this?"

The taxi man nods. "That's a digi-card. Philadelphia, here we come."

Her father holds the door open for her as Kristiana gets into the taxi. The man has already gotten into the driver's side and closes the door.

"I don't know what to say, Father."

"You'll think of something later. Kristiana, the reason that God made it so that adults are parents and not the children is that we've been every place you've been and many places you have never been. People are the only animals on the planet that need nurturing and guidance from their parents for fifteen to eighteen years of life. That's for a reason. So that we can go before you, tell you the paths that are good in life, and tell you to stay away from the paths that are not."

"I know, Father."

"It will be clear when you have children some day, as with all the things in time and space under God."

"Time and space" is an usual thing for an Amish person to say.

"Father, when you lived in the English-world, what did you do?"

He smiles. "I took classes at their local university."

She is intrigued and wonders why she never thought to ask before. "In what subject?"

"Theoretical physics. That was the temptation I had to deal with: pride. I had to show the English that this Amish boy was as smart as them. I did. For all their talk and bigotry against believers in God's Word, they have their own gods that they have such strong faith in. Their gods are the microscope, the electron-microscope, the world-wide connectivity of their machines. They believe in things that they will never see: dark matter, quasars, quarks, wormholes, things of their own mind."

At that very moment, her father looks different to her. She doesn't know what theoretical physics is exactly, but knows that it's something that only a person beyond smart would study.

"Kristiana, I see that you are becoming an adult now. You're starting to know that knowledge isn't simply knowing the answer. It starts by knowing the right questions to ask."

"I don't know what to say."

"Say nothing. Your mother and I will be praying for you all the time and we love you."

"I love you both too, Father."

He hugs his daughter and says nothing more. He closes the door and steps back as the taxi drives off.

Philadelphia, Pennsylvania
11:03 a.m., 14 September 2088

"Ever been to Philly?" the taxi man asks.

"No, sir."

He starts to cackle. "You're in for a big time then, Jew-Christian."

"What is a Jew-Christian?"

"You are. A religious person."

She ignores him; her eyes fix on the freeway as it speeds by, along with the many other cars. She now notices that the man is not even driving the car. "Your car is driving by itself!"

The taxi man starts to cackle again. "You're really in for a big time."

As the tek-metropolis of Philadelphia grows closer, she is starting to appreciate how massive the city really is. The sounds grow steadily louder and the lights grow steadily brighter and more frenetic as they approach. She has never seen anything like it, even on any of Pagan Paul's old movies.

"Still want me to drop you at the closest local bus depot?" he asks.

"Yes, I need a map."

He cackles again. "If you had a simple device, you could access a map."

"I can't buy a map?"

"Never heard of it, but I'm sure you can, or you can ask someone."

The taxi exits the freeway and after a few minutes arrives at one of the main transportation hubs of the city, where a person can get a taxi or catch a bus or the train. The taxi man takes her bags out of the trunk and extends his hand for the digi-card. She hands it to him, and he takes a palm-sized device from his pocket and swipes the card. The payment goes through.

"I don't imagine you have an email so I can send you the receipt."

"No sir, I don't. Can I have a paper receipt?"

"Christ! No one uses paper anymore. Hold on." He opens the driver side door and points the palm device at the dashboard. "I don't even know if this will work. Oh, it is." He grabs the plastic piece of paper that ejects slowly from the dashboard. "Here." He hands her the receipt. "Good luck, Jew-Christian."

With that, the taxi man gets in his car and drives away.

Kristiana watches the taxi disappear down the street. All her senses seem to turn on at once, and the reality begins to sink in that she is in a place that is nothing like the Quarter. She is in the Devil's Playground—the place she has dreamed about visiting for most of her life and thought of as just "the place where non-Amish live." But it must be called the Devil's Playground for a reason, and as she realizes that fact, she is practically frozen in place on the sidewalk, clutching her bags in each hand.

The first sensation is the atmosphere. Back home there was a slight chill in the air, but here the air seems artificially warmed somehow, not flowing and fresh. The second sensation is the slight tingling in her eyes and nose—there is something bad in the air, but she doesn't know what it is. She is now consciously blinking her eyes and now feels her throat start to tingle too from breathing the air. She takes a handkerchief from her skirt pocket to cover her nose and mouth.

"Yes! I exist!" The man's yelling startles her, but not as much as when she sees him. The Streaker, with his sun-burnt, naked skin, runs past her wearing only brown five-toed sandals. His head is a patch of bald spots and stringy clumps of hair. "Yes! Yes! The City of Brotherly Love! Full of love! Full of no love!"

It hits Kristiana all at once: the massive crowds of people, sounds and lights all around her. The lights actually hurt her eyes from the brightness and ever-flashing, ever-changing digital billboards on every place of business, on top of every building, everywhere. Images of people in flashy clothes or virtually no clothes; faces with multi-colored makeup and hair and tattoos; people singing, people dancing, people writhing on the floor or beds or outside; movies, clothes, cars; and images of strange things and unknown places. The rapid live-def static photos or full-fledged videos with the bold and vibrant colors, the loud and wild sounds, are physically giving her a headache; she closes her eyes for a moment.

She is startled again by some kind of flying globe high above in the air. The silver globe about twenty inches across hovers and then flies away. She sees another one further in the distance and flying much higher up in the sky.

Now she notices just how tall all the surrounding buildings are—they seem to go right into the clouds themselves. When she lowers her head from gaping at the buildings, she realizes that the tingling in her eyes is now a slight burning. *What is in the air?*

The hustle and bustle of the crowds is now starting to worry her. She's never seen so many people in one place. People in office-suits in a variety of colors from earth tones to rainbow colors to synthetic, techno colors and shiny silver, wearing all kinds of shoes, including ones that glow different colors. People in casual clothes, loose- or tight-fitting; a wide variety of glow clothes: shirts, boots, belts, bands, and hats. There are more naked and half naked people. People are zipping by, passing her on motorized bicycles or roller skates or skateboards or strange rolling pogo sticks.

Everyone has some type of portable device. The ones Pagan Paul is so scared of: e-pads, e-tablets, and their portable folding technology screens. The noise from the digital billboards and signs is only made worse by most of the people carrying on conversations with their machines—or are they just talking to themselves?

Some of the people have dogs. She sees some type of bird on a person's shoulder. Someone with a lizard. Someone with a snake! Someone with a humanoid robot following.

Kristiana has been fighting the feeling, but she is scared. This chaotic place is English-world? These are the people of the future?

"So who are you?" A man is standing next to her. If she weren't feeling poisoned by the air, she would have noticed him already. He stares at her with red pupils and a wide smile. "I can take your bags for you."

"Go away, predator!" She yells so loudly, dropping her handkerchief to the ground, that the man is genuinely shocked. His smile disappears and so does he, into the crowd.

A pack of kids runs by in the street, each one of them punching the other bloody while laughing hysterically. A drone flies by high in the air, tailing them.

The burning is now starting in her nose and throat. Her eyes are watering. *The air is poison!*

Kristiana grabs her bags and moves to the sidewalk to be closer to the building wall and away from the street. People push past her, let her pass or go around her. The smells! She starts to panic as her vision becomes blurry. She makes it to the wall and, with her back firmly pressed against it, drops her bags and uses her sleeves to wipe her eyes, but it is only a temporary remedy. She now feels her very skin start to tingle.

She remembers. She reaches into her pocket for her father's note. She can barely read it as her vision is not just blurry, but distorted.

"The fumes rock!" Two young men are standing next to her, grinning. One of them points to a large five foot tunnel rising from the ground. "You're sucking in the drugs good!"

Drugs? Kristiana immediately realizes what they are saying. She grabs her bags again and runs away, staying as close to the wall as she can.

She finds another spot and stands there. The sounds seem even louder now; the flashing lights seem brighter. Tears are streaming from her eyes, and her skin is starting to burn. The street seems to be more packed with people going every which way.

"Help!" Kristiana yells. "Can you help me?" She asks a young woman who passes. "Can you help me?" She asks an elderly woman with spiky red hair. "Does anyone know how to get to Providence? Can anyone help me get to Providence?"

She repeats the desperate request for more than an hour, then two, then longer. Her eyes have now swollen, and she has to fight to see though the slits. Her voice is hoarse and all of her skin is now crawling. She has no sense of time and is finding it hard to keep standing. She hears the chatter everywhere from people, the digital billboards, the machines—rolling, clicking, tapping. English-world is violence in all forms to her.

"What about Providence?" It is a woman's voice, but she is no longer able to see with her eyes nearly swollen shut and the bright, flashing multi-colored lights.

"Can you help me get there?"

"Why?"

"I need to get there, ma'am. That's where I'm supposed to go."

"Where are you from?"

"Amish Quarter in Lancaster."

There is a pause from the woman.

Kristiana can't see her to know what her expression is. "Can you help me get there? Or can you find someone who can help me?"

Another pause. "I'll be right back."

After a few minutes Kristiana has to sit on the ground. She clutches her bags tightly. None of the tek-city's noise or commotion ever stops. She can perceive the ever-flashing lights through her almost fully-closed eyelids. She is now exhausted by the lights and sounds.

"What is your name?" The woman is back.

"Kris..." She cannot talk properly. Her mouth is completely dry. "Kristiana."

"You're a Jew-Christian aren't you?"

Kristiana is now almost contorted into a ball, her skin crawling. "I am not that. I'm Amish. Please help me."

"I don't believe you."

"Please help me. I need to get to Providence."

"Who do you know there then?"

"My father told me to go there."

"Who is your father? I need to prove who you are."

"He is Elder Fisher of Amish Quarter."

"I'll be right back."

"No! Help me."

"I need to verify who you are."

"No. Help me. Verify later."

"I'll be right back."

The woman is gone and Kristiana just sits there in a huddled ball, still clutching her bags, for endless hours. She is now fighting to remain conscious. It is a battle she seems to be losing.

"I'm back. Can you hear me?"

Kristiana doesn't answer. The woman is *scamming* her, to use a word Pagan Paul taught her. She will not help her.

Suddenly she hears commotion around her. It sounds like people fighting. Then there is nothing. There is a loud yell that would have startled her before, but she cannot move anymore.

"Kristiana?" It is a new voice. "I heard you say your name before."

Kristiana cannot even answer anymore.

"You don't have to say anything. I'm going to flush your eyes out with water. I'm doing it now."

Kristiana feels water being poured over her eyes and a hand wiping both of them thoroughly with a cloth. They are still swollen, but she can see the face of the new woman. It is a woman with dark brown skin and gray eyes. She seems to be her eldest sister's age and she has a unique hairdo of large curls no longer than four inches; she is dressed in brown leather.

"Here, take the bottle and drink the water. You're very dehydrated. My name is Jo-Jo, and I'll take you to Providence."

Faith World!

"I'm not sure which is worse: Jews unilaterally disarming militarily in Israel or Christians unilaterally disarming politically and culturally in America. Look up the phrase 'stuck on stupid,' and you will see pictures of God's chosen people." – Reverend Dale, Resistance member, 2076

"Life's hard. It's even harder if you're stupid." – John Wayne, Old Hollywood icon

Lying on the ground is a motionless body. Kristiana wonders if this was the person talking to her before when she couldn't see. Jo-Jo walks her away from the crowds around the corner and waves her hands. A black car pulls up and stops; the front and back passenger doors open.

"Let me put your bags in the trunk," Jo-Jo says.

Kristiana realizes her fingers have almost locked in a death grip on her two bags. She manages to pry open her hands, and Jo-Jo takes the bags. Kristiana looks into the car and sees the figure of a large man in the driver's seat. She can't remember the term for it, but the sunlight is shielded from fully entering the car. However, there is one thing that shines bright: a gold cross hanging from the rear-view mirror on beads.

Jo-Jo sits in the passenger seat, half turned towards the driver, her back resting against the door. Kristiana has the rear seat all to herself. She feels disgusting. Her skin and hair seem to be caked with some kind of rancid chemical, her clean cotton clothes soaked with chemicals or her sweat from fear or both, but they feel like cardboard, and it seems like her bones—her whole body—have shrunken as she remains hunched over. Her hands are raw from clutching her bags so hard for so long. She notices that even her teeth feel strange in her mouth.

The drive seems smooth, but she can't see where she is going; the windows around her are darkened, and she is hunched so low that she can't see through the front window—tinted, that's the word, all the windows are tinted. She doesn't know how long the man has been driving, and he is driving not like the taxi driver man whose car was driving itself, but after a time the roads seems to change from smooth and artificial to bumpy and natural.

"Kristiana, do you have any type of mechanical body parts or organs?" Jo-Jo asks.

It is a very strange question. "No, but—I don't understand the question."

"Some people have mechanical arms or legs or eyes. Or they may have an artificial heart."

"No, I don't have any of that."

"We're almost there."

"What is Providence?"

"You don't know?"

"No, my father told me to go there, but I don't know about it."

"It's a Christian enclave."

"What is an enclave?"

"A secure gated community or, in our case, a city."

Suddenly the car seems to lose power and coast along the road, and then it seems to power on and drive normally again. This time, the man is not driving. The car drives maybe another five miles and then stops. The man exits from his side and Jo-Jo exits from hers. She opens the door for Kristiana.

She manages to drag herself out of the car. She looks all around and then up. The wall is massive and looks to be made of solid stone, all one piece, maybe ten feet tall, topped with the shiniest razor wire she's ever seen. They are at a gate, and she can see the man clearly now: a very large, bald, muscular man dressed in black, a long-sleeved top and pants, combat boots, a dark silver cross around his neck that looks more like a dagger than a cross.

Jo-Jo is holding her bags. "Follow me," she says but then stops to look at her. "Aren't the Amish pacifists?"

"We believe in non-resistance."

"We believe in big guns. Is that going to be a problem for you?"

"No. We don't tell non-Amish people how to live. We never do that."

Jo-Jo seems a bit annoyed. "We're more than non-Amish. We're Christians."

"Yes, of course."

Jo-Jo leads her into the enclave; the man doesn't follow, but watches them. When past the wall, she sees dozens of men in various military-type fatigues and combat boots. They are very heavily armed: guns, rifles, machine guns. There are some women too, equally well armed.

The civilian army people watch her. Kristiana isn't fearful at all. Most of the people have crosses around their necks on chains. Waiting is a golf cart, and Jo-Jo puts her bags in the back and gestures for Kristiana to sit in the passenger side. She hobbles to the other side of the cart and gets in.

"Kristiana, I'm going to have to blindfold you. It's not personal, but it is protocol for strangers. Until we can fully verify everything about you."

Kristiana nods quietly.

Jo-Jo blindfolds her with a thick black cloth cover around her eyes. "Is that too tight?"

Kristiana shakes her head.

The cart is off. It speeds up and down, turns sharply right and then left, does U-turns, and goes up and down inclines. The driving goes on for about an hour and at speeds Kristiana has never experienced before, but she savors the breeze around her face, refreshing as it seems to strip away some of the grime and chemicals from her skin.

Jo-Jo stops the cart. She hops out and instantly the blindfold is off. "Follow me." She grabs the two bags from the cart as Kristiana looks around again. The street is lined with beautiful uniform houses; some white, some gray, and some blue; all have well-kept lawns and white picket fences. She leads her up the walkway to the main porch, and Kristiana is so wrapped up admiring all the houses that she doesn't even notice that someone is already waiting for them.

Jo-Jo stops and rests the bags on the steps. Kristiana is startled a bit as she realizes another, older woman is standing on the porch at the open entrance of the main door. "So who might you be?" The woman is an older version of Jo-Jo, only she has green eyes too like Kristiana.

"My name is Kristiana Fisher, ma'am."

"I am Mother Moses. When I know you better, you can call me by my nickname."

"So, Kristiana, can you carry your own bags?"

"Yes, ma'am."

Mother Moses looks at Jo-Jo and nods. Kristiana quietly sighs in relief: she has passed the test. She can stay.

"Nice to meet you, Kristiana. I'll see you tomorrow," Jo-Jo says.

"Nice to meet you, too."

She walks back to the cart, hops in, and is gone like a jet. Kristiana turns back to the porch steps and grabs her bags and follows Mother Moses inside. Other than the light on in what looks to be the bathroom and some other room farther into the house, it is dark. She can only barely see the furniture.

"I know you've had a very long and trying day, so we'll talk tomorrow," the woman says as she leads Kristiana down a hallway. "You'll be able to stay in this room." She enters and turns on the light. A nice bedroom: a bed with thick pink covers, a dresser with many drawers, an empty case, and a small desk with a chair in the corner. "Oh, let me get that out of here." On the bed is a huge tan teddy bear. Mother Moses grabs it. "The children were playing and getting into the storage again. I'll take it out of here."

Kristiana can't stop staring at it. Strangely, it reminds her of a teddy bear she had when she was a small child. "Can…can I keep it here? It won't bother me."

"Are you sure?"

"Yes, it's okay. It can stay."

Mother Moses puts it back on the bed.

"Put your bags on the desk or dresser. I'll be right back. Let me get you a towel and night clothes."

Mother Moses leaves the room. Kristiana puts her knapsack on the desk and leans her small suitcase against the chair.

"Here you are." Mother Moses returns. "The room we passed is the bathroom. Here's a towel, night gown, and underclothes. Here is a bottle of liquid soap. First take a bath. Scrub and soak all those chemicals off of you. Then take a shower. Be very thorough, so take a long shower. Are you a shower person or bath person?"

"Bath person, ma'am. But I'll follow the rules of your house."

"Go take your bath and shower, and then go to bed and sleep. We'll talk in the morning. Good night, Kristiana."

"Good night, ma'am."

Mother Moses leaves again. Kristiana stands alone in the room. She walks over to the big teddy bear and touches its nose. She then grabs everything Mother Moses brought for her and walks quietly to the bathroom. The door clicks shuts.

Kristiana spends almost an hour soaking in the bath and then takes a fifteen-minute shower. When she gets back to the bedroom, she looks at her old clothes and wants to burn them, but for now balls them up and puts them into a pocket of her suitcase.

"Your name is Bo Bear from now on," she says as she situates the big teddy bear on one side of the bed. She looks around the room one last time, walks to the switch, and turns off the light. When she's under the covers, she realizes that she hasn't said her evening prayers. She decides to just close her eyes for a second and say them afterwards. She never does; she is fast asleep. It's been fourteen hours from the time her father closed the door of her taxi and waved good-bye.

Providence Enclave
After Midnight, 15 September 2088

Mother Moses walks across the street to one of the other houses. Even at this late hour, a man and a woman sit on rocking chairs on the porch, watching—they are both wearing dark sunglasses and say nothing. She enters the house.

The inside seems empty as she walks to one of the bedrooms, opens the large walk-in closet, and walks through the hanging clothes. In moments, a rear door opens, and she is walking down stairs into a massive underground room. There are dozens and dozens of people working at workstations, in cubicles, and at conference tables. Personnel in casual clothes, both male and female, are busy at work on laptops, reading text or watching vid-screens, typing communications or reports, listening on ear-sets.

At the bottom of the stairs, she walks under a silver arch which is spotted with all kinds of indicator lights; three heavily armed men stand nearby. She continues her walk into the hi-tek command center, past all of them to one of the secure conference rooms.

"I've been summoned," she says as she enters; the head of security sits at a conference table.

"I hear we have a new visitor to the enclave." His nickname is Sek, for "security." He is taller than average height with a very slim build, but this is deceiving—he's very muscular. He has brown eyes and close-cropped hair.

"Yes, an Amish young lady from Lancaster who had the brilliant idea to venture into Tek World for the first time by herself. She'll stay with me."

"M, that is very ill-advised. We can put her with a host family or in temp lodging."

She smiles. "Are you afraid President Galerius sent this little Amish girl to assassinate me?"

"With you as acting head of the enclave until General Moses returns, we need to keep a steady routine and not introduce any anomalies or distractions into your environment. Also, her full security check hasn't been completed."

"Sek, the girl stays with me. I already told her father that I would look after her."

He looks at her and shakes his head. "Is that why we sent our people out in the field to track down the girl's father in that Amish enclave? Why on earth would you do that? Make promises to strangers."

"Her father isn't a stranger. He's a parent like me. With a daughter like me. And this parent told that parent I would look after his daughter. When you have children one day, you'll understand. Do you have any other earth-shattering security concerns besides little Amish girls to bring to my attention?"

"Will you at least activate your home's proximity and internal surveillance systems while she's there?"

"Good night, Sek. See you tomorrow." Mother Moses waves and leaves the room.

Moses Home, Providence Enclave
6:00 a.m., 15 September 2088

For those Amish families whose lives center on farming, it is not unusual to wake up well before sunrise. Kristiana awakes from beneath the warm covers to peek out and notice the rising sun. The good night's sleep has almost made her nightmare maiden journey into English-world seem like a dream, but she knows it wasn't. Pagan Paul was almost right: she could have died if not for her rescue by these Christians. The house is very quiet, but her ears perceive that someone is moving about somewhere, probably in the kitchen. She sees Bo Bear lying next to her and touches his nose.

She gets a change of clothes and goes to the bathroom. After she returns her night clothes to her guest bedroom, she appears in the kitchen and sits down on a stool in the corner. She can smell breakfast cooking. Mother Moses moves pots and utensils around, making virtually no noise.

"Good morning, Kristiana," she says.

"Good morning, ma'am. Do you need me to help?"

"No thank you. Breakfast is done, and you're still a guest. I get up very early anyway, no matter how late I go to bed."

"Amish are early risers too. But we go to bed early."

"Do you have food restrictions? Anything you can't eat?"

"No, ma'am. I can eat anything."

"Even the things you hate?"

"Those too."

Mother Moses and Kristiana eat a quiet breakfast at the dining room table. The table can seat ten comfortably, but now it's only the two of them sitting at adjacent corners. The breakfast is pancakes served with maple syrup, honey, sausages, fruit, and juice.

"May I ask questions?" Kristiana says.

"You may ask anything you want."

"Does anyone else live in the house with you?"

"Yes, my husband and my youngest children. And we will be having other guests soon."

"Your husband isn't here?"

"No, he's on a trip now. He'll be back though. And my children will be back at lunch today. You already met one of them—Jo-Jo. I had them doing a special errand for me and they stayed overnight in another enclave."

"Enclaves are communities of Christians?"

"Yes, and there are enclaves of other religions."

"How big are enclaves? Jo-Jo said Providence isn't just a community, but a city."

"It's big. Thousands and thousands of people."

"All behind a wall with that sharp fencing and armed guards?"

"Yes, we chose to live separate from the outside world…like the Amish, I believe."

Kristiana smiles now for first time since her ordeal started.

"So Kristiana..."

"Yes, ma'am?"

"Explain to me why you did what you did. Leave your safe Amish community to go into Tek World, their city, all by yourself, not knowing anyone, not having a plan, not having anyone to protect you from physical harm, not wearing the proper clothes to protect you from the air and radiation."

Kristiana's eyes open wide. "Radiation?" Was Pagan Paul's brain-melting neurosis based on something real? "What do you mean? Invisible rays?"

"I didn't mean that, but yes, there are invisible rays everywhere to do all kinds of things in their tek-city: listen to everything you say and how you're saying it, watch every move you make, monitor your heart beat and read your brain waves to monitor your emotional state, watch your facial expressions and body language, monitor your perspiration rate and how fast you're walking and where you're walking to and from."

Kristiana sits there staring at her—the fear is back. "Why? Why would they do that?"

"Kristiana, why would you go into that place alone?"

Kristiana looks down and pauses for a moment. "I…I was stupid. I refused to listen to my family and others. They told me not to go. But…I was stupid. I have no one to blame but myself for what could have happened."

"Youth," Mother Moses says. "You always think you know more than us. Your father said you've always had a curiosity about life that could get you in serious trouble one day."

"Father?" Kristiana perks up. "You spoke with Father?"

"Yes, on the phone." Mother Moses stands up from the table and places a letter on it. "From your father."

As Mother Moses clears the table and begins to wash the dishes by hand, Kristiana reads the letter by her father; she recognizes his handwriting. She reads it once, then a second time, and then again. The very notion that her parents know where she is and that she is safe gives her a strong sense of comfort.

Mother Moses walks back to the dining room table as she wipes her hands on a towel. "What does your father say?"

"He says that as long as I'm here, I'm to listen to you and follow your rules. That Mother and my sisters are doing fine. That they'll pray for me every day. And that I'm never to go into the English-world again unless I get your permission."

"What do you think about what your father said?"

"I'll listen to him this time. I've been to English-world once and I will never go there again."

"Well, I know that's true today, but I don't know if I believe that will be true in the future for you. Kristiana, you can stay here in my house as my guest for as long as you want *but*—I am in charge. When my husband returns, who is in charge of the house then?"

"Your husband?"

"I am in charge! When Jesus returns, who is in charge of the house then?"

"Jesus."

"I am in charge!"

Kristiana bursts out laughing.

"You will have morning chores, chores after lunch and evening chores. As long as you do your chores, you can do as you please. Just be considerate of others and get permission when you need to. You can venture outside and explore the enclave to your heart's content whenever you like. Leaving the enclave is an entirely different matter that, as your father said, will require my permission."

"I'm going to stay inside the house for awhile. I'm not ready to go anywhere else."

"Okay. But the enclave is entirely safe. Questions on my rules?"

"No, ma'am."

"Questions on who's in charge?"

"No, ma'am." Kristiana smiles again.

"Now go get those bags of yours and bring them into the living room."

Kristiana leaves the kitchen and returns with them from her guest bedroom.

"What's in the bags?"

Kristiana opens her knapsack first and then her suitcase on wheels. Mother Moses looks through everything. "Do you have any weapons?"

She laughs again. "I'm Amish. We don't have weapons ever."

"You're Old Order Amish, right?"

"Yes."

"Isn't there a New Order Amish?"

"In the past, yes, but I don't think there are any left. They became part of the English-world."

"Tell me about that. The Amish make no other distinctions? It's either Amish or English?"

"Yes."

"What are we, then?"

"English."

"What are the people in the tek-city?"

"English."

"Are we the same as the people in the tek-city?"

Kristiana pauses for a moment. "No."

"The Amish may want to recognize a third category."

"What word do you think we should use?"

"Faithers. That's the term we use. Religious people are Faithers. And, specifically, you know we're Christians."

"Are all Faithers Christians?"

"No, it's just our term to distinguish ourselves from Pagans."

"What are other religious groups besides Christians?"

"You'll meet some of them here if you stay long enough: Jews, Mormons, Sikhs, Hindus. Faither is a political term, not a theological term. What we use instead of their offensive *Jew-Christian* term."

"Yes, I was called that."

"And we call where we live collectively Faith World. What are these books you have besides your Bible?"

"This is our book of hymns, the *Ausbund*. It is the oldest Protestant hymnbook in use and tells us about our people in the older times. *Marty's Mirror* is our book of Amish history. It honors the many Amish and Anabaptists who died for their faith. This is the *Ordung* for my district—our rules for our way of life, church, family, and community that every member has to follow. It can be different for each district and each community. This empty book is going to be my diary for my time here in English-world. I am going to write something every day."

"You'll have a lot to write."

Mother Moses is satisfied with her inspection of Kristiana's bags. The fact is that even before Kristiana entered Providence she and her bags were thoroughly scanned with the best See-Thru tek—first when she was in the car, before she entered the enclave, and finally at the Wall itself.

She creates a list for Kristiana of all her designated chores every week and starts her with thoroughly sweeping the entire house. When done, Kristiana spends the rest of the morning in the den, which is in fact an extensive library. She looks at all the books, mostly on the subjects of religion, history, culture, ethics, and government. There is also an extensive collection of different versions of the Bible and commentaries.

The house has been quiet all morning, even with Mother Moses preparing a huge family meal. By 11:00 a.m., people are starting to arrive.

"Kristiana!" Mother Moses calls out. The house is now alive with the new arrivals, and Kristiana appears in the dining room just as everyone is taking their seats. The multi-dish meals have already been placed on the table.

"I could have helped you set the table."

"I know you would have. Next time. Let me introduce you to everyone," Mother Moses says. "Everyone, this is Kristiana Fisher. She was born and raised in a place called Amish Quarter in Lancaster." To Kristiana, "You already know my youngest daughter Jo-Jo. She's with her fiancé, Micah. Next is my oldest daughter, Jada, with her husband, Omar. And the young man, he doesn't like to be called a boy anymore, is my son J.J."

Everyone cordially nods.

Mother Moses continues, "The tall gentleman at the end is known as Sek, a leader in the community too and a friend of the family. Now let's have lunch. Kristiana, do you want to say grace? Is there such thing as an Amish grace?"

Kristiana smiles. "Yes, I can say grace." Everyone bows their heads. "Our Father, thank you for this day, thank you for our friends, thank you for this food, we thank Thee. Amen," Kristiana says.

"Amen," everyone says.

The table is filled with a variety of food: mashed potatoes, black-eyed peas, cornbread, carrots, corn, a mixed salad, meats, and gravy. Serving trays are passed from person to person.

"What kind of food do the Amish eat?" Jo-Jo asks. "Are there common dishes?"

"No, we eat the same kinds of things, but we make everything from scratch, picked fresh from our own land, and the meat is from our community's livestock."

"Do you all live communally, or does everyone take care of their own food?" Jo-Jo asks.

"Everyone takes care of their own food except for the meat. We share that between families. Well, our district does. I'm not sure about others."

"Tell us about Amish Quarter," J.J. asks.

"Amish Quarter is grouped into independent church districts, each with about seventy-five baptized members, or twenty to forty families to form a congregation. Each district has a bishop, a few preachers, and an elder. The elder of our district is my father."

Jo-Jo takes another bite of her food. "Interesting. What type of Amish are you? Or is the proper word Anabaptist?"

Kristiana smiles. "You've been reading up on us."

"Just running around on the Net."

"The Net?" Kristiana asks, then remembers. "Oh, yes. Pagan Paul told us about that. You plug into it using a hand-held machine. Amish are one of the Anabaptist groups, and the other is Mennonite. There used to be a third, but they merged back with the Mennonites, so there are only two groups now."

"What's daily life like for Amish people?" Jada asks.

"It's different for different families and districts and communities. Farming families like mine, we get up before sunrise, feed the animals and milk the cows in the barn. The milk we process for delivery to Town. We pray as a family and have breakfast. Depending on the season, we'll work the fields—my family has a vineyard, the only one in the district—or we prepare the fields for planting in the winter time, plant crops in spring, and harvest crops in late summer and fall. We work sun-up to sundown, and in the evening we milk the cows again. That's what the men do.

"For the women, we help with the milking, prepare the meals, do laundry, work the garden—we have a big one actually—transport petrol to the home for our lanterns, other household chores like the sweeping and cleaning and sewing, other food work like making jams or canning the fruits and vegetables, and I like going into Town to sell our products or arrange for the deliveries and other family errands. Oh, and the men tend to the stables with the horses and maintain our buggies, too.

"Sundays we go to church service. When we aren't working in the fields or at home, we play all kinds of games in the field:

softball, volleyball, running and chasing, hacky sack—that's my favorite.

"People say Amish life is very slow-paced, but we say it's relaxed. When we work, we work and enjoy it. When we play, we enjoy it too."

"Nice," Jo-Jo says.

"How would you describe the Amish? I mean, Amish people overall," J.J. asks.

Kristiana pauses.

Mother Moses says, "Kristiana, eat your food or it'll get cold. You can chew between sentences."

"My mother says that to me all the time."

"Good, I take that as a compliment."

Kristiana quickly eats a few bites. "Amish people? We are plain people, simple people. That's the best way to describe us."

"Pacifistic people," Sek says, the head of all security for Providence. "You don't protect yourselves. You wait for others to do it."

Kristiana looks at him. "We simply believe in resistance through non-violence, that's all. It's our way. This is what works for us. We don't tell anyone else what way works best for them."

Sek is subdued, at least temporarily. "I didn't mean it as an attack. We are just very big about security here and everyone pulling their weight in maintaining that security."

"Oh, I will do my part while I stay here. There's a lot I can do."

Jo-Jo says, "I think what Sek is suggesting is that pacifism equals cowardice."

Sek says, "I'm not suggesting it, I'm stating it emphatically."

Jo-Jo looks at him, "Kristiana, you have to excuse him. Sek likes to fight, physically and verbally."

Sek says, "We're just having a cordial conversation. As for physical fights, I never throw the first punch, but I always throw the last."

Kristiana says to Jo-Jo, "It is okay. After four hundred years, the Amish have heard every argument against our beliefs and way of life, but we still have decided to stay with it." To Sek, she adds, "Pacifism doesn't mean cowardice. It can be, but that's not us. You have to remember the times we were in when the Amish

Mennonites formed in the late 1600s. Endless killing and wars—followers of Christ versus followers of Christ. We walked away from all that and separated our communities from the world."

"But you left that world," Sek says. "You left your peaceful world and ventured into the dangerous world, and if not for the warlike, non-Amish Christians, us, who knows what horrific fate would have befallen you."

Kristiana says, "You're right. My actions were foolish. I think maybe the rumspringa shouldn't be allowed anymore."

J.J. asks, "What's that?"

Kristiana says, "It means 'running around' in our original language. It's when young people—as early as sixteen but could be as late as twenty-one—can leave the community and go out and explore the English-world. The thinking is that one has to face the temptations of the world before one can reject them."

J.J. asks, "What temptations?"

"Everything: drugs, sex, drinking, immodest English clothes, make-up, jewelry for girls or flashy English cars for boys. Movies, music, vid-games. It could even be the modern-day conveniences of technology."

"No music or movies?" J.J. asks.

"We consider that to be *glassenheit*—worldly."

"And no tek? People don't say technology anymore. Unless you're a hundred years old like grandma," J.J. says, glancing at his mother.

"Stop talking about your father's mother like that. She isn't one hundred years old," Mother Moses says.

Jada leans over to him and whispers, "But she's close."

They start to laugh.

J.J. continues, "I read that the Amish hate tek. Why are you afraid of it?"

Kristiana laughs. "We don't hate it and we're not afraid of it. We just feel it is too disruptive to a God-centered church and family life."

"Amen," Mother Moses says. She turns to her son, "Hear that? I should take all your gadgets away and tell you we're going Amish."

"No, mom!"

"We use solar-powered machines for our fields and milking machines for our cows and we have a lot of windmill machines too, so we can use technology...tek. But we don't want it to control or distract our daily lives."

Kristiana eats more of her food. It is cold now, but as her father would often tell people, "Kristiana is always the center of entertainment at the dinner table."

"You have to understand that when Anabaptists came into the world, we were considered more dangerous than the Lutherans or Calvinists or other Protestants. They were part of the Reformation. We were part of the Radical Reformation—only no violence."

Sek smiles. "Ironic. Pacifist Christians part of the Radical Reformation. Martin Luther was definitely a radical revolutionary by our standards."

"He was only the regular Reformation. We went further than him. We rejected all church authority, we declared that a church can only be baptized members, and the main thing, we rejected the baptism of infants. Only an adult can choose whether to give their life to Christ, not their parents or the church. We take that most seriously of all. During your rumspringa, you have to make the most important decision in your life: remain in the English-world or return home to freely choose to be baptized, join the church, get married, have children and live as Amish for the rest of your life."

"Kristiana is a historian too. Mom has a great library in the house," Jo-Jo says.

Mother Moses nods. "She's already found it." To Kristiana, "What were you reading?"

"C.S. Lewis now."

"You pick one of the best right at the start." Mother Moses helps herself to more vegetables from the table.

Sek says, "The Protestant Reformation definitely was bloody. No argument there. Catholics and Protestants of the time definitely were more followers of Ezekiel 25:17, wrath and vengeance, than Matthew 5:39, turn the other cheek to your enemies."

"The Amish must have beautiful churches," J.J. says.

Kristiana smiles. "We do, but our churches are not like other Christians. We meet for Sunday service in a church member's home or their barn. That's why our communities are divided into small districts of about forty families or less. So we can meet mostly at homes. Or in barns. Everyone takes turns hosting services."

"Plain and simple," Mother Moses says.

"Yes," Kristiana says.

"Interesting," Jo-Jo says. "I like that there are so many different ways for Christ-followers to worship, pray, and live."

Sek says, "Admirable ritual, this rumspringa, but you admit that in today's world it's foolish."

Jada asks, "How many Amish youth choose to join your church after this rumspringa?"

"Almost all. I can only think of two people who didn't in the entire Quarter, out of hundreds." Kristiana says to Sek now, "Maybe it is foolish. I just don't know what the solution is. Allow the rumspringa, but provide safety."

Mother Moses says, "It seems to me that you already know the answer. Instead of going into Tek World, go to an enclave."

Kristiana perks up. "Yes, that's it. Go to Faith World instead of English-world."

Sek rolls his eyes. "M, that's all we need. Wayward Amish kids making pilgrimages to our enclaves to live like tourists. We'll have a regular nightmare on Elm Street."

Mother Moses says, smiling, "Imagine the chaos that Galerius could cause with that."

Kristiana looks at her, grinning.

"Why are you smiling at me, young lady?"

"I know your nickname now."

"But you didn't ask permission to use it, and I didn't offer it."

"Do I have permission to use your nickname, Mother Moses, ma'am?"

Mother Moses looks at Sek. "For a security chief, you really aren't good at keeping secrets at the dinner table." To Kristiana, "Are you going to cause me any problems while living in my house?"

"No, Mother Moses, ma'am."

"Stop with all that. Okay, you have permission."

"Thanks M."

"What's a 'nightmare on Elm Street'?" J.J. asks.

"It was bad enough that we had one biological entity in the enclave with the non-stop questions," Sek says.

"I am not a biological entity. I'm a Christian!" J.J. says.

"...now we got two," Sek continues. "It was something my grandfather used to say. I don't know where he got it from. It means a never-ending problem whether you're awake or asleep. Please don't ask me…"

Kristiana interjects, "What is Elm Street?"

"Yes, what's Elm Street, Sek?" J.J. asks.

Everyone laughs.

"And what is Galerius? Tell us, Sek," Kristiana adds, smiling.

A few days later, Kristiana feels comfortable enough to go outside—just for a few minutes, in the front and back yards behind the home's white picket fence, but she enjoys the sun, fresh air, and greenery.

A man and woman are led to the house by Sek. Two others follow—another man and woman. They all enter the house. After a few moments something tells Kristiana to go back inside.

Kristiana enters. The couple led by Sek are sitting on the couch, with Mother Moses in a chair facing them. Sek and the other two people stand near the door. The couple is crying.

"Kristiana, you can go to the den," Mother Moses says.

"Yes, M." Kristiana walks out of sight to the den. She grabs one of the books from the shelves to start reading and sits in a chair close to the open door. She is much more interested in the meeting outside.

"We beg you and the council to reconsider," the crying man says.

Mother Moses leans forward and looks at the couple directly. "In Tek World, they make no differentiation between a child and an adult, but we do. You are both adults. You know what the rules are. We believe in repentance. We're believers. We must. But we must maintain those rules or we're lost. I remember the coming of age ceremony for your teenage son."

"Yes, we appreciated that so much," the crying woman says. "He was so happy to have leadership attend his ceremony." Christian coming of age ceremonies, or Bar Barakahs, had become more frequent in the enclaves. They are family ceremonies, partly religious, for teenage boys and girls to give meaning to their transition from child to adult.

Mother Moses continues, "Maybe we also need classes for those who've lived so long out in the Pagan's tek-city wasteland. There are so many who come to us—parents, adults—who don't know what being an adult is."

"Please forgive us," the man begs again.

"If we have rules and they're allowed to be broken, then we have no rules. This is about consequences not forgiveness, which you already have. It's the third time, and now you both must leave the enclave."

The couple bows their heads. The man covers his closed eyes to hide the tears. The woman continues to cry.

Mother Moses continues, "We will not allow our enclave society to fragment and disintegrate. You both will be banished for a time not less than one year, after which time you may petition for re-entry."

The man stares at her, pausing. "We'll die out there."

"Then that should have been what you were thinking of when you decided to transgress the rules. We're not the bad guys here. It's no easy thing to get banished."

The couple says no more as they stand and are led out of the house by Sek, with the two others following.

Kristiana appears and looks out the window. The couple stops briefly to hug each other. They are led down the sidewalk. "Will they really die?"

Mother Moses stands. "Maybe." She walks into the kitchen.

Kristiana is somewhat surprised by her honest answer. "Our elders had to do this once. The man was shunned and had to leave Amish Quarter. We never saw him again. It's tough to be the leader."

"Yes, it is."

Almost three weeks later, Kristiana feels ready to explore the enclave. Most of her spare time is spent reading, voraciously so. She has learned so much. Mother Moses was right; she has also been doing a lot of writing in her diary and has already filled four notebooks.

"M, may I go exploring in the enclave?" Kristiana stands at the screen of the front door.

"I told you your very first day here you may explore anytime you want. As long as your chores are done," Mother Moses says.

"I'll go exploring, then."

Kristiana opens the door and walks onto the porch. The door closes, and she looks around to figure out her path. She looks across the street and can see the neighbors sitting on their rocking chairs on the porch, as they do every day except for Sundays. She looks to her right and then to her left. She decides to visit the next-door neighbor on the right first; she knows the family to the left isn't home—both are teachers at the enclave school.

"Good morning," Kristiana greets Mrs. Abigail working in her backyard garden at the white picket fence separating the properties. "I'm Kristiana, and I'm staying with Mother Moses as a guest."

"Yes, Kristiana. I know. I was wondering if you were some kind of barracks rat."

Kristiana starts laughing. "What is that?"

"Well, when I was in the military at your age it was the name for soldiers who just stayed in the barracks all the time and never went anywhere."

"Oh no, the Amish are not that. We like to be outside. I just needed to get comfortable first before doing so again. The last time I did, it was very bad for me."

"Yes, they told me that. Do you know my name already?"

"Yes, Mrs. Abigail."

"Nice to meet you, Kristiana." She shakes her hand. "Of the Old Amish Order. Old means you have a good, strong history to draw from."

"What Christian Order are you with?"

"I'm Abigail of the Ex-Baptist Order. That's the specific religious group that defines me."

"You said 'Ex.' The Baptist Order doesn't exist anymore?"

"It does, but I will no longer be a part of it. They joined the world. I'll stay with God." Abigail hands Kristiana one of her roses.

"Oh, thank you. How do you get them to be all these different colors?"

"Takes lots of patience. You have cross-breed different strains. It's part science, part art. I'll show you one day."

"Yes, I'd like that."

"So where are you going to go next?"

"I'm going to visit all the neighbors first and then take a walk. I used to walk at least a few miles every day when I was at my home in the Quarter."

"Good. Exercise keeps you young."

"Yes. Nice to meet you, Mrs. Abigail."

"Nice to meet you too, Kristiana. Enjoy your walk."

Kristiana looks across the street and notices that the 'rocking chair' couple is gone. She instead visits the house next to them. As soon as she approaches, the man sitting on the porch says, "You're the Amish girl." It seems everyone knows she is living in the enclave. She visits with him and his family for a few minutes. She then walks casually down the street and waves to everyone she sees: people walking, jogging, tending to their gardens or lawns, doing service on their golf-cart cars or washing them. The houses are constructed alike, but each has its own personality—different paint, different type of windows or doors, different type of gardens. But all are surrounded by the same white picket fences. All is very peaceful, and she notices how everyone in the community seems to watch out for everyone else.

She is about two miles away when a group of children, probably no older than five, playing kickball in the street, see her and run towards her.

"You're the Amish girl!" they say.

"Yes, I am. I'm visiting."

"What Order are you?" one of the little boys says.

"I'm Kristiana of the Old Amish Order."

The children seem to be amazed.

"I'm Elijah of the Ex-African Methodist Episcopal Order." He extends his hand.

She shakes his hand. "I'm sorry that it is Ex."

"One day we will have a new Order too so we can be an Old Order like you," he says.

"Yes. I believe it."

All the children introduce themselves and shake hands with her. They have all kinds of questions about her, her family, the Quarter, and the Amish people. Afterwards, she continues her walk and they continue their game.

The enclave is amazing to her. There is the residential area with these nice homes and white picket fences, then there is an area very much like the Town of her own home in Amish Quarter, but with a wider variety of shops: general stores, fruit and vegetable markets, fresh fish markets, barber shops, tailor and dry cleaners, ice cream stores, indoor and outdoor pools, indoor and outdoor tennis courts, racquet-ball courts, gymnasiums with indoor and outdoor running tracks.

There is Restaurant Row with restaurants of all kinds: West Indian, African, Indian, Mexican, Spanish American, Old Western European, and even Italian pizza places. Entertainment Row has large indoor-outdoor cafes, theaters, one large movie house which shows movies going back a hundred years, and retro video game parlors.

Education Square is even more impressive, with its single-gender elementary, middle, and high schools. The co-ed higher education and vocational campuses are even larger. There are even more quaint physical bookshops than the rest of the enclave. Someone told her that Tek World doesn't have physical books anymore; they're all on the Net or on their gadgets.

Kristiana continues her walk, past the large town hall buildings. Then there is the church. From outside it looks very un-church-like, almost like an abandoned warehouse, but the inside takes her breath away. There are a dozen different churches in the enclave.

Main Wall, Providence Enclave
10:46 a.m., 4 October 2088

"It's true," Armstrong says. "Pagans don't shake hands. That's another way you can pick them out. They share drugs and their bodies at a drop of a hat, but they consider a simple handshake greeting to be an old, archaic Jew-Christian custom."

"Do the English, I mean the Pagans, ever come to the wall?" Kristiana asks.

Armstrong answers, "No, the tek-jammers will get them."

"Tek-jammers?"

"Yes, they stay away because their tek, their devices, don't work. Pagans can't function without all their stupid devices. They can't go even five seconds without looking at their devices. They have nervous spasms, withdrawals if they do—it's call tek-tics. They're afraid they'll die if they're unconnected from their tek or the Net for even a brief moment."

"They must be connected to their technology all the time? That can't be true."

"Yes, their brains are addicted to it, and they even have laws that say they must be connected to it all the time. It's true. That's the main reason they stay away—not the wall, or the razor wire, or even that we'd shoot them. Tek-jammers is why."

"What do tek-jammers look like?"

"Are you an Amish spy?" Armstrong asks. He was the one driving the car when Jo-Jo rescued her from English-world.

Kristiana bursts out laughing. "Amish are not spies."

She has now made it to the Wall, with its armed men in military-type uniform.

One of them says, "Amish? You're like the Christian version of Hasidic Jews."

"Hasidic Jews? Who are they?" Kristiana asks.

"They're a specific Order of Jews," Armstrong says. "You may meet some one day."

Kristiana asks, "The Wall…is to keep out the Pagans?"

"And the storm troopers."

"What are storm troopers?"

"Blues, bobbies, feds, the police."

"You don't like police?" she asks.

Armstrong turns to one of the men: "Tobias what did you do before you came to Providence?"

"Buffalo, New York Police Force."

Armstrong turns to other men: "What about all of you?"

"Philadelphia Police Force, seven years."

"Trenton Police Force, twelve years."

"Jersey City Police Force, fourteen years."

Kristiana says, "You are all police."

Armstrong smiles and says, "Police, military, intelligence, all that."

"What are those other names? Blues, bobbies, feds?"

"Kristiana, you are a very inquisitive person. Those are nicknames. Different names for the same thing. Like in one region you say 'coke,' another coca-cola, another soda, another pop."

"I heard those before. I want to try coca-cola one day."

"That syrup water isn't kosher," Armstrong says.

"Kosher?"

"Please don't ask. Ask the Jews when you see them."

"But you're using the word and you're not Jewish."

"It means made by Faithers."

"Okay, but why the Wall?" Kristiana asks. "All you need is the tek-jammers."

"You were out there. What do you think? We need an anti-tek *and* physical wall. The Mexicans have a wall to keep out Americans; the Russian Bloc has one with their border with the Caliphate; the Chinese too. We're Christians and they're Pagans. We live here because they do bad things to us. Do you not know what's been going on in the world? Are the Amish that cut off from reality?"

"I don't think so. I'm sure the bishop and preachers know, and my father, other elders and other adults. But I've never been in the English-world before."

"It's Tek World. You have to call it by the right name. You really don't know what's been going on these past years, these past decades."

Kristiana shakes her head. "No."

Moses Home
11:28 a.m., 4 October 2088

Mother Moses is looking out the kitchen window when one of the city security guards drives up in his cart with a smiling Kristiana in the passenger seat. She thanks him and walks up the driveway. It looks like she has had a good first day of exploring.

Kristiana enters through the front door just as Jo-Jo is walking into the kitchen.

"You!" Kristiana yells out and points at her while laughing. "You tried to trick me."

Jo-Jo says, "What are you talking about?"

"When you brought me here the first day you were driving all over the place for hours fast, like a mad person. The main Wall entrance is just down the street!"

They both laugh.

Jo-Jo says, "You could have been a Pagan spy!"

Mother Moses calls from the kitchen. "Kristiana, where all did you go to?"

She runs into the kitchen and is almost unable to contain herself as she starts telling M and Jo-Jo about all the places she visited.

"Wow, you visited all that," Jo-Jo says.

"You had a productive day," Mother Moses says.

"I'll get to the other part of the city to see the Stadium and the farms tomorrow."

Mother Moses says, "Yes, the city has everything. We're totally self-sufficient."

"I like it here," Kristiana proclaims.

"I'm glad to hear that," Mother Moses responds.

"It's our own Faither paradise," Jo-Jo adds softly. "This side of Paradise."

Mother Moses says, "We've spent much hard work and time to create this sanctuary for ourselves over the years."

"Because of Galerius?" Kristiana asks.

Kristiana has found out who 'Galerius' is—the pejorative nickname for President T. Wilson. The Jews and Mormons have their own slurs for him, but Christians called him Galerius after the most vicious murderer of early Christians out of all the emperors of ancient Rome.

"Yes, President Galerius and his Grid government."

"And his chief opponent is General Moses?"

Mother Moses looks at her. "How do you know about my husband already?"

"I found out at the Wall when I was there," Kristiana says. "They were all talking about his mother."

"Mother Esther?" Mother Moses stops. "Today? She is there now?"

"Yes, they were talking about her. *They said she's in a body bag.* What's a body bag, M? Is that some type of clothing?"

Good Blood

"The sixties (1960s) were an era of extreme reality. I miss the smell of tear gas. I miss the fear of getting beaten."– Hunter S. Thompson, American author and gonzo journalist, 1997

"I do miss the '60s (2060s) actually. Even if it was the beginning of the end for religious majority America, we knew how to fight back then, how to take a punch and get up strong and throw a harder punch back. No fear—storm-troopers, drones, AI self-aware surveillance tracking systems—no matter. The lot we have now...it's like their blood's been drained from their souls. We're the walking dead waiting for the final death-blow from Tek World." –Elder Mother Esther, 2075

New Haven Colony, New Jersey
8:59 a.m., 1 October 2088

Esther Zipporah Moses (maiden name King) was born in 2000. She always liked that because, as she would often say, "I'll never forget my age because my age is the same as the year."

She always thought that Blue Eyes was the originator of her favorite saying of late. Paul Newman, "Blue Eyes" as she calls him, died at eighty-three when she was eight years old. He is still her favorite Old Hollywood movie icon. Her favorite movie of his is still the one where he and the "other guy" ran to the Spanish Americas to escape the Super Posse. Oh, and she likes the movie where he was that cool hand and the other one where he was that drunk lawyer making his comeback.

Her favorite saying of late was actually originated by another Old Hollywood icon: Bette Davis, known as an extremely difficult actress to work with and for her caustic insults. She was also known for her witty and sarcastic sayings; one of her best, after being diagnosed with cancer and suffering a stroke, was "Growing old is not for sissies."

"Growing old is not for sissies! Isn't that the truth." Esther has finally made it down the stairs from her upstairs bedroom, walking slowly with a cane in her left hand, which she hates with a passion.

George Jefferson is lying fast asleep on a cushion under the piano in her living room. All black, one of her four cats. Redd Foxx runs past her for another room, a blur of orange fur. She doesn't see Ella Fitz anywhere, she's an all-white Siamese, very adept at hiding. Archie Bunker is some kind of bastard, but still her favorite cat with his hyper-temperamental nature; he was a rescue and is the newest of her feline quartet. She sees him peeking out from the kitchen, with his motley, mixed patchwork of black, white, and brown fur, before scrabbling away.

At an age most people would be enjoying their golden years, she started her political activism in her sixties, a time she remembers fondly—though at the time it was anything but fun. She got involved almost by accident in what would later be called Religious Revivalism, a religious-based movement aggressively focused on the "rebirth" of what were then called poor urban communities. Inevitably they merged with the "end of vice" movements almost at the same time the nation was legalizing all narcotic drugs and prostitution and age-of-consent laws were being eliminated state by state. Her movement defined true feminism as anti-abortion, anti-infanticide, anti-prostitution, and anti-sex-slavery. Later they joined the international "the planet needs girls" movement in the Asian Consortium to end female-only abortions and infanticides.

When the bio-switch came and rendered abortion obsolete, she dreamed of the practice finally being eliminated across the entire world. "Since humans don't listen to religion or morals when it comes to valuing the pre-born, maybe science is the only god they will honor," she said in one of her many interviews, especially after she published *Dancing Babies of the Invisible Realm:*

the Triumphal End of Abortion in America in 2062. But as the adage says, "Be careful what you wish for. You may get it."

The Rebirth Movement won—Outland urban areas were transformed into safe, stable, productive communities, which had not been true for over a century. "The Unborn Are People Too" and 'The Planet Needs Girls" movements won—abortions and infanticides, 85 percent of which were girls, began to decline as worldwide attitudes in non-Islamic nations changed, even before the spread of advanced birth control and the bio-switch.

In the next decade, Esther became obsessed with the Pagans. "Their rise means our decline." She was convinced that American Christianity was dying, though most of her colleagues laughed at the notion. "The Pagans," she said, "were wild pit-bull puppies in the sixties, their viciousness not quite developed. The 2070s were quite different—they were full-grown, vicious beasts." The Separatist Movement was inevitable in her eyes and became the next chapter of her activism.

The 2080s would also be her time to make sure she passed the torch to worthy successors—her daughter-in-law and brilliant eldest son. There was just so much knowledge and experience to pass on.

"God better allow me to live long enough to do what I need to do." Elder Mother has slowly stepped through the living room towards the kitchen when she stops. *What is that noise outside?*

Esther lives in New Haven and not the tri-sister cities of Providence, Restoration, and Sanctuary that she founded decades ago, hiding from friend and enemy alike. Her enemies are few, but friends are too many for her liking—she is a living icon in the Faither community, a status she hates. Elder Mother Esther—the pioneer, leader, and trailblazer. With her youngest son and husband gone, she can't take the quasi-worship for her deeds or the pity over their murders that solidified the Separatist Movement.

There is a louder noise from the side gate to her house; it swings open, squeaking. She hobbles as quickly as she can to the side window of her living room. She gets there finally, climbing on the big couch against the wall and leaning her head forward while she pushes the dark drapes aside. *Standing only a few feet from the window is a red-eyed, white devil man looking dead at her with his fanged mouth hanging open.*

She is so startled that she falls straight back from the couch and crashes to the ground. She lies on her back, almost in tears. She looks at the window. The red-eyed, white devil peers into the window, his face pressed against the glass. His fangs scratch it, making a sickening noise like nails on a chalkboard.

Esther watches the devil man quietly from the floor, shaking. She is so angry that her body can't react like it used to be able to, even a decade ago—to defend herself, fight, run, something. Suddenly the devil man disappears from the window in a blur. Esther leans forward, but can't get up—something must be strained or broken. She struggles again to raise her front body, but she can't.

"Oh God, help me," she cries.

She has to know what the devil man is doing outside her house! She rolls over onto her stomach. Now she can get up; first onto one knee, slowly and using her right arm, she pushes with all her might to raise her body up. She manages to stand slowly despite the pain.

"This sucks! When I was young, I could jump down from a two story building!"

Where is that devil man?! She hobbles forward. When she reaches the kitchen, she is shocked at what she sees through the window.

The red-eyed devil man is spider-walking all over the ground, like a dog, with his palms and feet. He suddenly snaps up straight and spins around 180 degrees and locks eyes on her. Even his movements are evil!

He races to the doors and, with his fists, pounds the glass and wildly tries to open the door. He can't get in; the door is locked, so he throws his body against it. His fanged face is contorted in rage.

Esther shakes in fear. The devil man is trying to break into my house and I'm all alone! "Wait!" The idea flashes in her mind—but can she get to it in time?

The door may look like simple wood, but it is reinforced with solid-steel rods. The devil man realizes he can't get in that way. He dashes away, out of sight. She starts her slow walk away from the kitchen. She hears the devil trying to open the back door! How did he get there so fast?! She's out of the kitchen. It's quiet now. Where is the devil man? She is now in the living room. A noise comes from one of the rooms on the second floor! The devil man is there! She is out of the living room. She hears something breaking, the plant vases on the window sill of her bedroom. Then he screams, so loud, and she hears wild footsteps now. She reaches the closet. The devil man is in the house, running out of the second-floor bedroom.

"I know you're here bag of blood! I can smell your fear!" he yells.

She opens the closet.

"Come out now with your hands in the air!"

She gets into the closet.

"Resistance is futile you Jew-Christian terrorist. I don't see those hands in five seconds, I'm going to put you in a body bag!"

She closes the closet door.

"Did you hear me?!"

The devil man leaps down the stairs to the first floor. He knows exactly where she is; his bionic eyes are set to infrared, and he can see her frail body behind the closet door. He smiles as he approaches the door, gun drawn and trigger ready.

He grabs the door knob and throws the door open. "Say hello to the devil, Jew-Christian!"

Faithers don't believe in bionic body parts like Pagans. However, cybernetic exoskeletons are another matter. For the physically disabled, infirm, or paralyzed, exoskeleton tek was a godsend, allowing full mobility without the permanent merging of flesh and machine. Her godson, a doctor at New Sheba Hospital, had bought her the X-47 for her 80th birthday, straight from Jewish Israel itself before its fall. Who made better exos, the Jews or the Japanese? "I'll give my money to the Jews," she often said. "At least I know we're praying to the same God, still not sure about the Mormons. The Japs are Pagans."

She initially resisted the exo-suit: "That's for old people." But as her mobility continued to deteriorate, she soon grew very attached to her tek-toy. It fastened snugly to the body with a Velcro belt around the waist, and straps around the wrists. The smart-tek sensors molded the rest of it to the body along the spine, along the humerus to forearm radial of the arms, and along the gluteus maximus and femur to fibula radial of the outside legs. It didn't make one normal, it made one super-normal, and in her case due to modifications, though technically illegal, super-human.

Esther grabs the red-eyed devil man by the neck with both hands. He screams out as she, all of five feet, lifts his six foot frame off the ground.

Officer Red, the devil man, is violently thrown through the first floor ceiling. His body crashes through the second story ceiling and then the roof itself. His crushed and bloodied body sails through the air and then arcs down to land on the ground, dead.

Police cars roll up to the front of the house. A dozen policemen exit en masse and take positions behind their cars with rifles and guns drawn. From behind a bullet-proof shield, two policemen run to Officer Red's body.

A black SUV rolls up and the Vampire leader Bloodgood steps out of the vehicle. Other Vampires, all in black office-suits, exit from the other doors.

One of the policemen runs up to him. "They killed one of our men!" he yells.

Bloodgood says, "What's the intel?"

"There are at least seven Jew-Christian terrorists inside."

Bloodgood says to one of his Vampires, without taking his gaze off the house, "Call in the drone strike and level that house. Any that manage to get out, shoot 'em dead and zip 'em all up in the same body bag."

A "Free," "Safe," and "Civilized" Society

"Religion is comparable to a childhood neurosis." – Sigmund Freud, The Future of an Illusion (1927)

"Are you now or have you ever been a Jew-Christian?" – Anonymous

Washington DC
12:02 a.m., 11 August 2065

All throughout the District, e-pads, tablets, and devices are ringing in the homes of officials, staffers and aides—elected, security, state department, intelligence, military. The sheer number of people receiving calls suggests something terrible has happened.

His sleep is interrupted. He was up all night working on his memo to the new president and has just gotten to sleep when his e-pad loudly rings from his bedside table.

"T. Wilson here," he answers with eyes closed; the lights automatically turn on with any incoming call at night.

Homeland Defense and Intelligence Agency HQ, Elizabeth Center, Washington DC
2:16 a.m., 11 August 2065

It is complete chaos in the main Situation Room. Staffers, aides, aides to the aides, military run from one office to another, make frantic calls, receive frantic calls, scan the Net on their devices, and watch the vid-screens streaming different media channels.

Wilson arrives in the room. He has on the same clothes he

wore the previous day, which for him was just a couple of hours ago.

"What's going on?" he yells at one of the passing aides.

"The Muslims have taken over all of Western Europe."

"I know that! What's happening now?"

"It's terrible."

"What?"

"We think they're executing everyone in the secular governments; they're burning everything." The aide runs away to another office.

Wilson pauses: *Western Europe is Burning!*

He notices the Homeland director standing in the center of the room watching the vid-screens, all of which are blank except for the words in the top right of each screen: France, Germany, England, Belgium, the Netherlands, etcetera. Each screen represents the vid-link to the American embassy in each country; the broadcasts have *never* ceased before. The Homeland director's face is pale; he seems visibly overwhelmed by the events.

"They'll be writing about this for decades. Who lost Western Europe?" one of the aides standing next to him says. "What should we do? The Caliphate has seized all our embassies in all twenty countries. We've lost all communications. All we have is rumors. No way to confirm anything. We're hearing prime ministers and presidents are missing or dead. Scores of people are being killed. But all rumors. All we know for sure is that millions are fleeing the countries in cars, trucks, boats, on bicycles, helicopters, planes, by foot, swimming. They're escaping through Eastern Europe and Russia any way they can—those able to escape."

"Sir!" a military man runs up to the Homeland director. "People are taking to the streets here, and angry crowds are starting to form around all Muslim country embassies. We could have major riots."

The Homeland director seems paralyzed.

"What are we going to do?!" Wilson yells at the man.

Everyone freezes to watch this young man yell at the "boss of bosses". The Homeland director turns his head and gives him a dirty look.

"Are you going to do something or not?" Wilson yells again.

The Homeland director just stares at him.

"Shut your mouth!" the military man next to the Homeland director yells back.

Wilson storms out of the room and almost runs right smack into the vice president, surrounded by his Secret Service detail. The VP marches up to Homeland.

"What are we doing? The Muslims have seized Western Europe. We hear the Russians are preparing for war if they cross their borders. What are we doing?"

Again the Homeland director seems paralyzed.

The vice president yells at the top of his lungs, "Is someone going to take charge here?!!"

Wilson walks up him. "Mr. Vice President, sir, do I have your authorization to be appointed provisional Homeland director this instant to handle the crisis?"

People are shocked at his statement—the gall of this kid.

"He's just a junior analyst!" the military man yells.

"Mr. Vice President, I graduated from West Point and have a masters in economics and finance, game theory, foreign policy and international affairs, geopolitical strategy and chaos theory. Give me one hour before you fire me."

The vice president studies him.

"Would you describe yourself as a good person?" he asks.

"No, I'm a very bad person when it comes to keeping my country safe."

"Take charge then. You have your hour," the vice president says.

The Homeland director looks even paler than before and sits down in an empty chair. His civilian and military aides just stand there with their mouths open. Wilson walks up to them.

"If I give you an order regarding military troops, can you get it done?" Wilson asks.

The military man glares at him, but answers. "Yes."

"I want you to activate the military in all fifty states. Troops, tanks, and put our jets in the air. I want every embassy belonging to a Muslim country surrounded immediately. Make it look as if we are going there to protect them. Keep the civilian mobs from attacking."

The military man's expression changes; he's intrigued. "What are we really going to be there for?"

"To blow up every single one if the Caliphate doesn't release all our embassy personnel unharmed."

The military man nods. "I'll get it done in thirty minutes." He leaves the room.

Wilson now addresses the civilian aide. "I want you to call State and have them give us the name of the highest-ranking diplomat from the Muslim countries involved in this madness. I want you to get a meeting set up with him in the next fifteen minutes. Tell them we want them to negotiate the immediate release of our embassy personnel and that they will be our intermediaries. Tell them that they are to call their governments immediately to make sure no one is injured or killed. Tell them that the US will make very generous concessions to get our people released."

"Is that what we're going to do?"

"Of course not, we're buying time until we can get our military forces in place."

The civilian aide nods and walks out of the room.

Wilson looks at the vice president. Vice President Kanien nods in approval. Wilson looks at another aide and motions for her to approach. "I have a mission for you too. Someone who's secretly in America now. You'll find him at the Baron Trump Hotel."

Watergate Hotel
3:30 a.m., 11 August 2065

Wilson sits across from the man in the elegant conference room. His Excellency Prince Al-Abaza sits there with a smirk on his face in his outrageously expensive office-suit, solid gold Rolex studded with diamonds, and leather slip-on shoes. Wilson views these high-priced Muslim diplomats as the highest order of hypocrite—condemning Western capitalism and decadence at every chance, but engaged in every bit of vice and gross materialism they can manage.

Wilson has no guards. Al-Abaza has two hulking men standing behind him.

"I want you to contact the Caliphate," Wilson starts.

"The *Supreme Islamic* Caliphate," the man sneers.

Wilson continues, "All American embassy personnel and all American citizens are to be allowed to leave all former Western European countries unharmed immediately."

Al-Abaza smiles, "Soon the Supreme Islamic Caliphate will add countries twenty-one and twenty-two to our empire."

"What countries would that be?"

"Canada and America, of course."

Wilson leans back in his chair. "When will you release my people?"

"It is something we must carefully consider. It may take some time to negotiate. These are delicate matters and now that we have twenty new countries in the empire, other matters must take precedence. We will, however, thoroughly review your request as soon as we are able to give the time."

The door opens and a man enters. Though a small man of no more than five-foot-two, there is something scary about President Wen of the Chinese-Indian Alliance. He has one tall bodyguard with him. The Caliphate may now have a billion people in their empire, but the Chinese have had a billion plus in theirs for almost a century. Al-Abaza's smirk immediately disappears from his face, and even his two body guards seem nervous.

Wilson doesn't stand to address the man, one of the most powerful on the planet. "President Wen, so sorry to interrupt your trip to our country. Mr. Al-Abaza here of the Supreme Islamic Caliphate was telling me how they are not only going to refuse to release our people, but also all Chinese-Indian citizens."

Wen looks at Wilson, then at Al-Abaza. The two men stare at each other. Wilson stares at both and imagines that he can see right through them to their true forms. The Caliphate is a pack of noisy, clumsy, but ravenous jackals, ever prowling for their next victims—anyone not of the pack. The Chinese are massive black vultures hiding in the shadows, grinning, waiting to pounce on anything left behind by the jackals—but also, when the time is right, on the jackals themselves. America will have to deal with both these animals one day—decisively. Not today, not tomorrow, but one day, the day will arrive.

Wen looks back to Wilson. "They can keep them."

Al-Abaza seems genuinely surprised.

Wen continues, "I have already given the order to execute all Muslims within Chinese and Indian borders."

Al-Abaza is visibly shaken and stands. "You cannot do that! I will call my government now and we will start the deportations of all your citizens from our land immediately."

"Take as much time as you want," Wen says without emotion. "It takes a very long time for the trigger fingers of Chinese soldiers to get tired."

Al-Abaza rushes out of the room followed by his two men.

Wen looks at Wilson coldly. Wilson realizes that he truly is in the presence of an extremely dangerous man.

"One day the Muslims will come for you and they will destroy you," he says. "Then the next day, we will come and destroy them. And on the third day, all the world is China." The man smiles ever so slightly as he watches Wilson. He turns and leaves the room.

Secret Service men enter.

"How did you know the president of China was here in the country to secretly meet with the president? And how did you find him?" the lead agent asks.

"I know many things."

The lead agent seems angry. "That is not an answer to my question."

"When I become your employee and report to you, I will answer it. Until then, get out of this room and back to your post."

The agents hesitate, but exit the room.

Ten minutes later, Al-Abaza and his two guards return. He is still shaken, but tries to get back into character.

"When are my American citizens going to be released from Western Europe?" Wilson asks.

"Western Europe no longer exists. It is all the territory of the Supreme Islamic Caliphate. And I think we won't release any

Americans. Americans are not the Chinese. No one is scared of Americans."

Wilson takes his e-pad from his pocket and places it on the table. He touches the bottom of the e-pad. "General are you there?" he says into his ear-set. "Good. Initiate strike one."

An explosion shakes the building and the night sky lights up for an instant. They can hear commotion outside the doors—people in the hotel lobby panicking.

"What was that?!" Al-Abaza jumps from his chair.

"That was your Washington DC embassy. That's what one hundred and two dead Muslims, give or take a few dozen, sound like. We may not be Chinese, but we learn quickly. Let's move to strike number two."

"No!"

Wilson pauses. The men stare at each other. Al-Abaza's body shakes with rage.

Wilson glares at him. "People who like to blow people up shouldn't protest when their own people get blown up. Release my Americans!"

"They will be expelled with the Chinese and Indian pigs and monkeys."

"Thank you, Mr. Al-Abaza. This American pig-monkey thanks you. The president has already issued an executive order to grant immediate citizenship to any Western European who makes it to America. Be sure not to pursue anyone who escapes your borders, the old ones or the new ones. Sorry about the embassy."

"We won't forget this atrocity. We have very long memories."

"Go get my Americans on planes back here now. And then get yourself and your two girlfriends on the next plane to your empire of dirt."

Al-Abaza glares back. "We will not forget you, infidel," he says. "So that you know, we never did anything to your people—to any people. We will even allow the Vatican to keep Rome and show the great mercy of Allah and the Supreme Islamic Caliphate. We expelled your Americans from our new land hours ago. They are on planes coming here now. You might want to be careful.

We know how much you Americans like shooting planes out of the sky."

"We know how much you Muslims like flying planes into things, especially tall buildings," Wilson snaps.

"The Supreme Islamic Caliphate is a *civilized* society. We are going to submit a formal complaint to the United Nations World Court of your unprovoked war crime against us by killing our people and destroying our embassy—sovereign land of the Supreme Islamic Caliphate. America and Israel—the great criminal empires of the world. The Supreme Islamic Caliphate will have its revenge. Yes, we will not forget you, infidel." He walks to the door with his two guards and leave the room.

"And I won't forget you," Wilson says to himself.

The White House
4:55 a.m., 11 August 2065

Wilson walks into the White House itself, not Homeland HQ. In all the years he's been in the District, he has never set foot inside until now. People notice him immediately as he is led down the halls by Secret Service. Everyone knows what the "kid" has done. Everyone knows he's here to see the vice president. Everyone knows that they are looking at the man who will likely be running America's most powerful agency very soon.

He sits across from Vice President Kanien. They are in the VP's West Wing office.

"Am I in trouble, sir?"

"Why would you ask that?"

"I know you and the president don't get along, and you replaced his hand-picked Homeland director with me, and I made the Homeland director look bad. You made the president look bad."

"You let me worry about White House internal politics. What do you think I should do now?"

"Well, you haven't fired me, so I believe the next action is already indicated. The information you requested is already on your tablet. What my operational strategy will be as the nation's next Homeland director."

"How did you know the Chinese president was secretly in the country? With this crisis, he's en route back to China, but how did you know he was here? That was ultra-top secret. Literally only a few people in the entire District knew."

"He's a chess fanatic, as am I. The American Chess Masters are going on and he has secretly attended these tournaments all over the world. He's been doing so for years in disguise. And I know he and the president are…"

"It's okay if you say it. He and the president are too friendly for the comfort of the American people, and me. The president actually admires the maniac. He's into that whole Eastern, Oriental, Zen, tai-chi mystique crap. I'm surprised he hasn't mandated Mandarin Chinese as the national language."

"Yes. Unfortunately he has a nickname, too."

"Yes, the Manchurian. I call him that to his face."

"Sir, can I ask you why you became his VP, then? You obviously hate him."

Kanien smiles. "I'll tell you when I know you better."

"Yes, sir."

The vice president opens his tablet folder and touches the screen. "I glanced at your proposals. What would be the purpose of you gathering this information? What are we going to do with it?"

"Sir, we already gather this information. The government has been gathering this information on Americans for almost a century. This is nothing new. We still have public school and college teachers go through comprehensive in-service training programs on how to identify religious people, and especially those who disagree with government or its agendas. They've had the ability to designate anyone as an 'at risk individual' and refer anyone to counseling whose thoughts or actions don't conform to established cultural norms. All I'm suggesting is adding additional algorithms to create other categories. We need much more than just demographics; that to me is ultimately irrelevant. We need to expand what we know about the ideology of people. We need to strengthen our psychographic data: religious affiliation, religious ideology, religious tendencies, sexual orientation and tendencies—all which can be supplemental indicators. We need to use that segmentation data to figure out means to begin dividing the country based on ideology. Keep similar ideologies in the same geographical areas. Marginalize the undesired and dangerous ideologies. This war is about ideology. Western Europe has fallen and burns because of ideology."

"Muslim ideology."

"No, sir. Religious ideology."

"The Muslims are hell-bent on a one-world government and a one-world religion. Their sharia law becoming the law of the land in every nation on the planet."

"Sir, I believe in a one-world government and a one-world religion. That one government is America and that one religion is no religion. True religion is the problem. We have mild-mannered citizens transmuting into homicidal jihadis all the time and blowing people up. The largest act of infiltration into the American government in history was not the Old Soviet Union or the CHINs, but a group of religious fanatics over a century ago that included some five thousand saboteurs who infiltrated embassies all over the world. They called it Operation Snow White. Sir, we need this domestic strategy."

"Let me think about your plan for now."

Kanien doesn't get it. He makes a distinction between Muslims and other religions.

"Sir, a pacifist priest is the same as a bomb-happy Islamic jihadist. They are all from the same pool of religion. Religion is a dangerous, unhealthy, psychosis of the mind. Even our own American Psychological Association and all similar professional groups have declared that."

"Let me think about it."

Kanien is not only the number two most powerful person in America and one of the most powerful in the world, but also one of the most influential vice presidents in history. Wilson knows he has to make the man happy and remember always that it was him, Kanien, who has given him his chance at destiny.

"Sir, can I move forward with the program simply using the

algorithm for all Muslim factors?"

The vice president perks up. "You can do that?"

The bait has been taken. "Yes sir, I can."

"Do that now, then. We'll revisit your other suggestions at a later time. Do we need any new legislation on the books to deal with the Muslims?"

"No sir, we have all that we need. The Authorization of Uniform Military Force has been on the books for fifty years. Adjustments have been made over the decades. We can use whatever means to kill terrorism anywhere—even on American soil. We can classify anyone we want as a terrorist. We can implement enhanced sentences and detain anyone indefinitely. We don't need new laws; we just need to effectively use the ones we already have."

Kanien nods approvingly.

"I'll make it so then, sir. Because of your vision and your faith in my ability, no one will ever ask: Who lost America? We will create in America a truly *safe* society."

First A.M.E. Church of Atlanta, Georgia
10:30 a.m., 12 July 2065

The church's leadership council has voted and its chairman stands.

"Mrs. Esther, we are proud to bestow upon you the title of Elder Mother and welcome you to the leadership council. Your community work has been a blessing to all and you are exactly the example of a righteous sister in Christ," the chairman says.

Esther stands slowly, deeply moved. "I don't deserve such praise. I'm just an ordinary person doing ordinary work." Her husband, Pastor Atticus, smiles and hugs her.

"Then God needs to send us more ordinary people like you," the chairman says.

Atlanta, Georgia
7:59 a.m., 11 August 2065

Grady's is one of the largest bar and restaurants in this part of the city, known for its soul, Cajun, and Jamaican dishes; with live jazz music on the weekdays and gospel on the weekends. Today, however, it is the center of desperately sought-after knowledge. The building is packed with people flowing into the parking lot and sidewalks. Everyone has vid-screens in their own homes, but Grady's has hundred-inch vid-screens throughout the venue and access to off-Grid channels that only a handful of tek-heads have. Regular broadcasts out of Western Europe are non-existent, so people clamor for anyone who has any signals out of the area.

Each vid-screen has a different broadcast—all from civilians within the countries who have managed not to have their devices taken away or jammed. Western Europe is burning! The carnage is consuming: people running and screaming, gunfire, explosions, jets and helicopters flying above, missile strikes, bombed-out buildings, burning buildings, mobs everywhere, chaos.

The patrons of Grady's stand transfixed by the vid-screens, shocked, in disbelief and in distress. There is nothing they can do but watch.

Esther turns to her husband and says, "There may be one Satan, but he has plenty of devils in this world. Look what the Muslims have done today. I'm sure it'll inspire the Pagans to do the same to us here one day."

"Let's go," Atticus says. "There's nothing we can do, but pray for people to escape to safety."

Lewisburg, West Virginia
11:20 a.m., 17 October 2065

Their car drives up to a secluded house on the plains. Elder Mother Esther and Pastor Atticus have their twenty-something sons, Moses and Samson, stay with the car as they walk up to the house.

A man stands on the porch with his hands on his hips, watching them. He's dressed in blue overalls and a white shirt and wears a flat, tan cowboy hat. The screen door opens and two younger men, his sons, dressed similarly, but without hats, step onto the porch to join him.

"I hope you aren't salesmen, because we don't cozy to trespassers," the older man says.

"What about Christians?" Pastor Atticus asks, smiling.

"Well, that depends. 'Cause I'd trust a Pagan before I'd break bread with some of the so-called Christian denominations we got out there now. What did you think of the United Nations?"

"I prayed daily for an earthquake to open up and swallow it whole."

"Turn the other cheek or guns blazing?"

"Shoot first and aim for the cheek."

"That weird science bio-switch thing?"

"Keep your damn hands off my genitalia."

The man studies him and they all burst out laughing.

"You found me. They call me Mr. Wall-Builder."

Atticus shakes his hand. "Pastor Atticus, and this is my wife…"

"Elder Mother Esther." The man smiles and hugs her. "We own all your books."

Moments later, the man studies the map on a large worktable in the open garage adjoining the house. His two sons look on with Atticus as Esther continues pointing.

"Build it around this one, this one, and this one," she says. "The first town will be called Restoration, Sanctuary will be the second, and Providence the third."

"You want us to build large walls around entire civilian towns?"

"Like the Great Wall of China," she says.

"We're redefining the phrase *gated community*," Atticus says.

The man shakes his head. "We build walls around prisons, for the military, bridges, financial institutions; never for a place of people, families and children. The ancient Romans used to force us to do this in the past. Now we're going to do it to ourselves? What Christians will leave the cities to live in these self-segregated walled-in towns?"

Esther says, "Build them and they will come."

The main man smiles for a moment. "You've been leading the

way in righteous politics and transforming cities with openness and freedom, but this? You're going to get a lot of criticism and resistance on this. Most of it will be from Christians. The Pagans will probably be cheering."

"The Pagans will one day have police arresting you for having a Bible in your possession. I wouldn't put it past them," she says.

"I served in the US Navy and I saw it there every day," Atticus says. "Singling us out, trying to force-indoctrinate us with their re-education programs, believers kicked out of the service if we didn't submit. They claim to be tolerant, but we know that's code-speak for 'tolerate anything but us.'"

"I hear you; US Marines myself. I was done with all of them when they reinstituted the ban on family members bringing the Bible or any religious reading materials or items to wounded soldiers in the military hospital."

Atticus says, "Yes, and no prayers allowed at funerals for religious soldiers. No cross-shaped headstones for Christian soldiers or Stars of David ones for Jewish soldiers."

Mr. Wall-Builder sighs. "Don't we have to be the light of God in the world? When Christianity began, what so impressed outsiders with our faith was our community exhibiting God's love and grace. We reached out to them regardless of what they did to us. We reached out to the poor, the weak, the sick and disabled, the elderly. With this, you'd be withdrawing from the world. A just-hold-out-in-the-bunker-until-Jesus-comes-back mentality. You can't spread the Gospel from behind a ten-foot wall."

Esther responds, "You know why the Rebirth Movement succeeded? We created new communities of our own culture. It wasn't simply taking back our schools, but taking back the culture and our streets. We're not happy about this, but the world you and I grew up in is gone. It's all about survival now. As the saying goes: we will not allow ourselves to be thrown to the lions anymore."

"We must control our own communities, because it's impossible to live in peace with them anymore," Atticus says.

Esther says, "The world plays such an important role in shaping our children's views and values. It influences the character and future of our society. The social engineers know this. We can no longer afford to be at the mercy of that world. We have to be center. Our schools were the center of the Rebirth Movement. These new religious communities will be the center of this movement. The revival that our faith needs must be fundamental and profound.

"We know what the detractors will say, but it's not segregation. It's separatism. We must separate from the world to save our people. To save what's left of the faith. We can't lose anymore of our people. So we choose freedom over persecution."

Mr. Wall-Builder says, "We'll do it, of course, but it will be very expensive."

Esther smiles and says, "My husband and I have been very blessed from our world-wide advocacy work and my dabbling in real estate on the side. I believe the term is filthy rich."

Mr. Wall-Builder smiles. "Let's get started."

"Yes, let's build a *free* society for our people," Esther says. "Amen."

Locking the Gates

"Give me a child for the first five years of his life, and he will be mine forever." – Vladimir Lenin, Russian communist revolutionary and first premier of the Old Soviet Union (now Russian Bloc)

"Train up a child in the way he should go, and when he is old he will not depart from it." – Proverbs 22:6, Hebrew Bible (illegal in the United States, Supreme Islamic Caliphate territory, and Chinese-Indian Alliance territories)

The White House
9:05 a.m., 7 September 2088

The chief law enforcement advisor sits across from the president.
"Let the blues know that their loyal support to this administration, and more importantly, their stellar job in protecting this country has not gone unnoticed. Start spreading the word that I will be signing the Storm Trooper Bill in my next term," President Wilson says.
"Sir, I'm speechless. I thought Congress was adamantly opposed to it," the chief says. "How will you sell it? If I had a time machine, I'd go back in time and shoot dead all those film directors who made movies about evil, armored law enforcement of the future, especially their so-called prophet Lucas; he'd be at the top of my list, with their Jedi quasi-religions. They've kept us from using body-armor tek for decades when it could have saved, could be saving, countless law enforcement lives. People think that you armor up law enforcement and suddenly we're in

a fascist state."

"It's just like the public's irrational fear of AI when in fact they've been using machines running on AI for decades."

"Exactly, that's what smart-tek is. Mr. President, some people will have an aneurism if you say you'll sign this bill."

"Don't worry about any of that. I have a very good communications team. We'll get everyone in Congress aboard and then everyone else will follow. The first ninety days after my re-election we'll get it done," the president says. "I know they're still angry with me over the handling of the Kansas Event."

"Oh no, sir. You made the right call. I was wrong too. They know that now. They thank the Lord Charles Darwin every day that they weren't there, or what happened would have happened to them." He smiles. "Sir, transforming our street law enforcement to storm troopers makes me want to get back on a beat myself so I can kick some criminal and terrorist butt."

Providence Enclave
4:52 p.m., 7 January 2076

"The generations today are pathetically weak," Esther says. "Generations ago, women smoked non-drug cigarettes, drank alcohol, and still gave birth to healthy babies, people lived in lead-based-painted houses and didn't get cancer, people rode bikes without helmets and drove in cars without seatbelts or air bag tek and less people had accidents, people drank water straight from the house tap, children always played outside from sun-up to sundown, and they couldn't be reached all day by any device because they didn't have them and the kids were fine! Now look at the supposed, technologically advanced human. Ha! I laugh at the damn technologically advanced human! Weak! Unable to do a damn thing without their precious machines."

It is family time at the Moses home: Atticus, Moses, Samson, and the other men are in the den watching Japanese boxing on the vid-screen, but the younger ones are with the women.

"Mother Esther, watch the language," Mother Moses says.

Young Jada jumps on the couch to sit next to her. "Grandmama, what were you saying before?"

She looks at her, "You're not a body with a soul. You are a soul and you have a body. C.S. Lewis couldn't have said it better. The body will wither to dust at some point in the future, but your soul will endure forever." Back to the others, "And the worst of the bunch are my people. My Christians. The damn Pagans are evil sons-of-bitches…"

"Mother Esther, the language!" Mother Moses yells. Jada laughs.

"But it's nothing compared to my pathetic Christians. The *four horsemen have come: the end of the abortion wars*—we won, but now we see all it did was open a new evil door: genetics, cloning, soon the bastards will be able to create whole monsters from scratch. *The end of the marriage wars*—marriage modernization, their pan-sexual, alt lifestyle, ha! Their ruse to destroy our churches and wipe out Jews and Christians. *The death of the Constitution*—the nation's foundational document based on Judeo-Christian principles to protect all Americans, is their next goal! Now the final horseman is coming: *the final destruction of Christians here in the America.* I was here in my youth when they first tried to redefine us as terrorists. People who served in the military or quoted the Constitution or the Founding Fathers or anyone who owned or displayed the American flag or, the biggest offense—people who went to church or worshipped God! How many decades ago is that? They tried it back then! They've been trying to destroy Old Jerusalem too; though the damn Jewish politicians there seem to be hell-bent on unilaterally weakening themselves to point that they might as well stand up and surrender." She now looks at her son Moses, who has walked into the room. "The Pagans have been plotting our demise for centuries. We give them freedom in our country, and they repay us with persecution. I'm an old lady now, so I'm too set in my ways, but you young ones must lead! The Separatism Movement is our salvation. Separate from the Pagans and especially from the fake Christians, those collaborators that have infested the entire faith. Both of them. Imposing their immorality on us. I wouldn't put it past them to try to kill me one day."

Funeral Home, Providence Enclave
8:35 a.m., 9 October 2088

A silent and somber Moses stares at the coffin of his late mother. He fights an intense rage, barely kept contained.

"Mr. Moses," the undertaker standing next to him says, "please take as much time as you need. I'll be in the other room."

"No," he says. "I'm finished. Do we need to do anything else for the final preparations?"

"No, everything is complete and finalized. My staff and I are at your disposal, including on the day of the funeral itself."

"Thank you."

"Sir, I knew Elder Mother Esther since the fifties. She may have come to the fight later in life, but she was a fireball. People doubted her, but she always proved them wrong. And some of her biggest critics were other Christians. You can't save urban cities, they'd say. No one has in over a century of trying and spending trillions, they'd say. You can't get the world to stop killing the pre-born. You can't get the world to stop killing baby girls. You can't get Christian families to leave the tek-cities and create our own communities, like the Pilgrims and Puritans did almost half a millennium ago. She proved all of them wrong. I feel blessed to have been her friend. Never thought I'd outlive her. I thought she'd be fighting the fight well into the next century." The man is now crying.

"She was supposed to have outlived us all." Moses hugs the man. The embrace seems to steady the undertaker and he wipes the tears from his face.

"Please," the undertaker says. "Find the people who did this."

Moses looks dead at him. "However long, whatever is required. It will be done."

Elizabeth Center, Washington DC
1:38 p.m., 3 October 2088

A man in military dress greens lies dead in the center of the room. His throat ripped out and blood pools around the upper torso. Bloodgood sits casually at the conference table, smiling with fangs protruding, his chin dripping with blood.

Anita McDunn is rushed into the room, surrounded by homeland security guards, all with their guns drawn.

"What did you do?!" she yells.

Bloodgood says, "Did you know there was only an elderly Jew-Christian woman in there instead of the several highly trained, highly armed Jew-Christian terrorists I was told to expect?"

"I asked you, what did you do?!"

Bloodgood stands, smiling at the security personnel aiming their guns at him. "Do you know I was in this very place when Western Europe fell? That's when T. Wilson made his move and snatched the office of Homeland right out of the director's paws. Wilson was the best. You're just a sad substitute."

"That elderly Jew-Christian woman was a leading terrorist. She was a major leader herself and the mother of another leading terrorist leader," she says.

"You want to do bad things and not get your hands dirty? Well, I like to do bad things and get my hands very dirty. Your military slave and I were having difficulty communicating, so I terminated him from existence. Now let's try talking directly instead of through intermediaries. I will say to you what I said to him: You ever lie to me again, and I'll rip your throat right from your body and eat it whole. Do I make myself clear? You want to assassinate someone? Good. But you will give me *all* the facts right from the beginning, without fail, at all times. No exceptions. Are we communicating better now?"

"Yes, we are," says Homeland Director McDunn. "But if you ever kill one of my men again, I'll have you vaporized."

He smiles. "I am *your* man, boss. You're the one acting as if we're working separately."

"Understood."

"Good. You threatened me and I threatened you. I'm a Vampire and you're just a weak human, so we can safely assume which threat is better grounded."

"I'm the director of one of the most powerful agencies in the world. You're not even a registered voter."

"I'm the director of the president's black ops operations, with a license to kill and the extraordinary skill to do so often. If you'd like to end our relationship now, then pay me and my team for time served, and I'll be on my way. Find some other dupes."

A license to kill was a very serious matter in the black ops world. Many years ago, a kill-team was commissioned to assassinate a foreign terrorist, and though they eventually succeeded, the operation was a mess—dozens of innocents were also killed. The next presidential administration had them arrested and prosecuted. Their attorneys got them acquitted, but from then on no covert operative would work for America. It caused a severe crisis, as the CHINs, Russian Bloc, Spanish Americas and even the Caliphate were offering astronomical sums of money to hire away America's entire black ops community. The solution was what was commonly called—Ian Fleming would smile—the License to Kill Executive Order granting total and perpetual immunity to anyone granted such a license. It could be taken away at any time, but an operative could never be prosecuted for any crime while possessing it. Still controversial to this day, but subsequent presidents have universally felt it was essential to national security.

"That will not be necessary. The intel you got was faulty, but it won't happen again. And we still consider the op a success."

"The intel I was given was intentionally false. Please stop jerking me off, Director. I've been in this game a lot longer than you. Are we having communication problems again, like I did with your military slave?"

"No, we understand each other."

"I want to be read into the entire operation. Not what you have erroneously determined to be my 'need to know.'"

"I need to clear that with the president."

"Then do it."

"Mr. Bloodgood, you need to understand that we don't view any of this as a game. It is deadly serious to us, which is why we brought you and your team in. The domestic terrorist threat on our soil is real, whether the target is eight years old or eighty. You're worrying about yourself, we're worrying about millions.

We're preparing for a doomsday scenario when we could have both the Caliphate and the CHINs attack us. We must secure the Homeland, and these homegrown, domestic Jew-Christian terrorists must be neutralized. Old Western Europe failed to deal with their religious, and now there is no more Old Western Europe."

"I don't care about your political theories, so save the speeches. Just don't keep me in the dark ever again. Real Vampires prefer the bright, naked light at all times."

Secure Room, Providence Enclave
2:07 p.m., 9 October 2088

Inside the large, dimly lit meeting room, in one of the many secure houses in Providence, Moses addresses them. The room is packed with people sitting in orderly arranged chairs and standing to the sides and back. They are of different ages, backgrounds, dress, and ethnicities. They are the citizen network of the Faither covert intelligence community.

"My mother, Esther Zipporah Moses, was one of the greatest people I ever knew. I was blessed to have been brought into this world and raised by her. She was my mom. To the world she was an extraordinary political activist who started at the rambunctious young age of sixty. She was a leader in the Rebirth Movement to save our own communities, house-by-house, block-by-block, neighborhood-by-neighborhood, ending kids killing kids. She helped transform whole cities. She was a leader in the End of Vice Movement to get the drugs, prostitutes, and crime out of our communities. 'Let it be in the Pagan communities,' she'd say. She was a leader in 'the Unborn are People Too' and 'the Planet Needs Girls' movements, to ensure little babies were not killed before they even had a chance to have their first breath of life, especially our girls, still viewed as lesser humans in much of the world, even today. She did all that.

"In her seventies, she dedicated her time and energy to the Separatist Movement, highly controversial among Faithers at the time. She and my father founded our tri-sister cities of Providence, Restoration, and Sanctuary."

Moses stops suddenly, as if his rage or his tears is about to explode.

"The bastards killed my mother! Terrorist?! That's what they called her. An eighty-year old woman who never touched a weapon in her life. Even after they killed her husband and son, my father and brother!" He looks at all of them with red eyes. "I don't care how long it takes, what resources need to be used, or what methods. I want the names of *everyone* involved. Three questions: Who did it? Who sent them? Who informed on her?"

A few moments pass, as Moses composes himself. Almost on cue, people in the gathering rise and begin to file out of the room. The room is empty for him and Sek.

"They've already classified the entire incident to stop the information flow. It will take some time to get through it all," Sek says.

Moses looks up. "What unassigned tek-lords do we have on payroll?"

"None, all our tek-lords are working on the project."

"Do we have to contract this one out?"

"We have to. I recommend the Jews. They have the best ones."

"Better than ours?"

"I wouldn't want to have to live off the difference, but they have a lot more free agents right now."

"What about the Mormons?"

"They have something major going on internally and are even less accessible than normal. We're not sure what it is yet," Sek continues

"Let's not go with the Jews now. They're still piecing themselves back together after three civil wars and the Fall of Jewish Israel. They have too many internal things going on to deal with this. We need someone completely focused. Call the African Collective. Maybe they have some 'young lions' on the way up we can contract."

"I'll get it done," Sek says. "Are you staying?"

"No, I'll leave in the morning. The project has to remain on schedule."

Moses Home
5:00 p.m., 9 October 2088

Kristiana hugs Mother Moses. "I'm so sorry about your mother-in-law."

"Thank you, Kristiana."

Kristiana stills feel bad about how she so clumsily revealed this massive tragedy to the Moses family. But no one gives a second thought to her innocent naiveté.

It is the first quiet time the house has had. Visits from family and friends have been endless since yesterday. Between the shock of Elder Mother Esther's murder and the sheer volume of condolence wishers, everyone, even casual observers like Kristiana, is exhausted.

"Let me know how I can help," Kristiana says.

Mother Moses gives her a strong embrace. "Thank you."

8:05 p.m.

Moses has been extremely detached from everyone in the house, even his own wife. The emotions are too raw for him to function normally. He lies on the couch, his back facing out. Everyone knows to let him have his space. Kristiana, however, has heard so much about the "General" since she first arrived in Providence and can't stop herself from finding out if she can chat with him, even for a brief moment.

She quietly walks into the living room and looks at him. Is he sleeping?

"You must be our new house guest," he says without moving or turning.

"Yes, sir. My name is Kristiana Fisher of the Old Amish Order."

"How long have you been visiting with us for your rumspringa?"

He knows about Amish ways. "For over a month now, sir. I arrived in September."

"Good."

"Are you back for good, sir?"

"No, I'll be leaving again."

"I wanted to ask you all about the Resistance."

"I'm told you know a lot already, Kristiana Fisher. But I'll let others tell you more. I'm not good company now. When I return, I'll tell you about everything…and the future."

Kristiana smiles. "I'd like that a lot, sir."

"Have a good night then, Kristiana Fisher."

"Good night, sir, and God bless."

Kristiana awakes early as usual the next morning to start her day by poking the button nose of Bo Bear lying next to her. When she enters the living room, General Moses is already gone.

The killing of Elder Mother Esther has touched a sensitive nerve with many Faithers across the country. Even as far as Africa and the Asian Consortium, people are mourning her passing. After the final viewing of the coffin at one of the Providence underground churches, she is buried next to her husband Atticus and her youngest son Samson at an undisclosed location.

Washington Hilton Hotel Ballroom (Thirteen Years Earlier)
11:41 a.m., 7 April 2071

Rabbi Susan and Bishop Joe stand on the stage, each at a podium, looking out at the attending crowd of pastors, reverends, bishops and rabbis.

"Are there any questions?" Rabbi Susan asks.

The rabbis at the back of the auditorium immediately rise from their table and leave. At a nearby table, Moses sits with Senior Pastor Atticus and Assistant Pastor Samson, his father and younger brother.

"Those Orthodox Jews do in one minute what takes orthodox Christians a whole hour," Senior Pastor Atticus says, smiling.

"Then let's do like the Jews," Samson says.

"When in Rome," Atticus says, and they both rise from their chairs.

"Dad, I'll stick around awhile," Moses says.

Atticus says, "I thought you hated this religious political stuff."

"I do, but I want to make sure that's all it is. I'll blend in. Listen and learn."

"Son, don't worry. We're not going to follow any of their illegal laws. What are they going to do? Take our Bibles away at gunpoint? Shut down churches and synagogues? Once everyone reads the fine print of these Registration Initiatives, that will end it. Telling churches what to preach, what Bible they can have, must have members of 'alternative lifestyles' on their leadership boards. Never."

"I'm glad you have so much confidence. Looking around, half this bunch seems ready and willing to sign on the dotted line now."

Atticus makes a disapproving noise. "I wouldn't call half this bunch in here Christians, so that's not surprising. This Registration will go nowhere. See you at dinner tonight, son."

The two men leave, but Moses remains behind to observe. Reverend Benjamin and his delegation are now heading towards the exit. He notices that most of the people in the room are not leaving, and some are making their way to the stage to Rabbi Susan and Bishop Joe. They have an admiration society already.

Providence Enclave
1:45 p.m., 2 November 2088

Kristiana had walked to Education Square right after her morning chores. She has explored the Square many times, especially the book stores and libraries—she still can't believe that English-world doesn't have physical books anymore and hasn't for many decades—but this is the first time she's been in the main administrative headquarters.

She waits for her appointment in one of the small conference rooms closest to the main offices. She reads the plaque on the wall:

"It's time to admit that public education operates a planned economy, a bureaucratic system in which everybody's role is spelled out in advance and there are few incentives for innovation and productivity. It's no surprise that our school system doesn't improve: it more resembles the communist economy than our own

market economy." Albert Shanker, Former President of The American Federation of Teachers.

Mr. Super, the head of the Education Square, arrives. That's what everyone calls him, though his full name is Superian.

"Good afternoon, Miss Fisher."

"Good afternoon, sir. What is this organization mentioned in this plaque?" Kristiana asks.

"The organization has long been defunct, and the man's been dead for several decades. It was a secular organization of teachers. Back in the bad times."

"You mean before the Rebirth Movement."

"Yes, before we took back the education of our communities and moved from secular co-ed government schools to single-sex, private parochial ones. The devil goes after the young."

"I didn't know General Moses lost his father and brother too."

"Yes, there has been much tragedy in the Moses family," Mr. Super says. "Sadly it seems to be a common occurrence for those who do great things for humankind. So what can I do for you, Miss Fisher? Do you want take classes with us? Formal Amish primary education ends at age thirteen or fourteen, correct? Tell me more about that."

"Yes. All grades are in one big schoolhouse and we learn all subjects—reading, writing, mathematics, geography, all about Amish history; we learn farming and agriculture, animal care, carpentry, masonry, homemaking, and other skills for Amish life. After that, we begin our work life but we consider learning a life-time activity. But you know about us already." He smiles. "I'd like to have a special tutor, sir."

"Why a special tutor? You're an intelligent young Christian woman. You'd be able to hold your own in any of our classroom settings."

"I want to know about very specific things. I want to know all about the Resistance and the Separatist Movement, the Registrants and President Galerius and…"

"Okay, Miss Fisher. You want to know everything."

She laughs. "Well, not everything, just almost everything. I would read books, but there are no books on those subjects."

"Very true. It's too recent. There is only one I know of to date: *The Perpetual War to Destroy the Chosen People*."

"Really? Where can I get it, sir?"

"We can get you a copy. It's not in circulation yet in the libraries."

"Who's the author?"

"I am."

Secure House, Providence Enclave
3:00 p.m., 2 November 2088

Sek sits with Mother Moses as she reads his report on a tablet.

"Is this number correct?" she asks. "This is incredible. Where are they all coming from? A twenty percent increase in new applicant submissions?"

"It's getting worse out there. They don't want to live in tek-cities anymore."

"Why now?" Mother Moses asks.

"Tired of fighting, tired of hiding, tired of pretending, Elder Mother Esther's murder, and the re-election today," Sek says dryly. "It's wearing people down. And they're scared. They want to meet you."

"They'll undoubtedly want to tell us how they want us to run our enclaves."

"Undoubtedly."

Providence Enclave
4:45 p.m., 2 November 2088

Kristiana loves to walk, no matter the distance.

Mr. Super lent her the book, agreed to be her tutor on recent American Faither history, and with his staff sat with her for half an hour to give her a preview.

"Everyone has a boiling point. And even modern-day Christians, who are predisposed to be very, very slow to react, finally reacted," he said. "People wrongly say it was government persecution that brought about the Separatist Movement. No, that just hastened it. It was our children trapped in their mandatory

Pagan public schools that were the catalyst. They wanted to keep their claws on our children. Destroying our communities and the churches were just the fringe benefits."

Kristiana, with her new book tucked under her arm, has been walking for almost an hour. On her way, several residents, new acquaintances she's made in the neighborhood, offer to drive her to the Moses house, but she declines. The next-door neighbor called her a "sun worshipper." She's not a fan of the term, but she does love the outdoors, the sun, the breeze, the sky, all of it—just not in Tek World.

She stops suddenly. In the distance, she sees her: a Goth! The female with her black clothing and spiky black hair is walking up the street ahead of her in the same direction. How did she get in here? How? Sek and M must be told of the intruder! Goths would come into Amish Quarter when she was a child and beat the children up, until Pagan Paul arrived. How did this one breach the Wall? The Goth must be up to no good.

Kristiana suddenly has a singular purpose. She quickens her pace, then starts to jog. She reaches the Goth, who turns around. Kristiana slaps her face. The Goth is stunned and instinctively punches her in the center of her chest. Kristiana falls to the ground. The Goth touches her mouth and sees she's actually bleeding. Kristiana jumps back up, ready to slap her again, but the Goth is ready.

People come from everywhere and hold them back before the fight can start again.

"Why the hell did you hit me?!" the Goth yells. She curses at the Amish girl.

From within the crowd restraining them comes a voice: "Kristiana!" Kristiana snaps out of her rage and looks at the approaching Mother Moses. M points at the Goth. "You leave that Pagan-speak on the outside."

Among Faithers, all cursing is called Pagan-speak and is universally condemned.

"Sorry M. She attacked me for no reason."

Mother Moses walks to Kristiana and takes her hand. "I thought the Amish were pacifists?"

"She…she invaded the enclave," Kristiana manages to say, but even she isn't satisfied with her response and is now completely ashamed.

"Kristiana, this is Lila. She is with the Christian Goths. She is not a Pagan."

"A Christian? Dressed like that?"

Goth Lila is still mad, "Yes, little Amish girl, dressed like this."

Suddenly laughter erupts from the crowd. It is Sek. "Goth Lila got beat up by the pacifist Amish girl!"

Goth Lila turns red and other people in the crowd start to laugh.

5:30 p.m.

The vid-screen is set up in the Moses living room. Most Faither homes don't have them. Only for special occasions are they brought out to watch a broadcast or movie. This is a special occasion, a dark occasion.

A crowd is now assembled in the house to watch, some thirty-five people. Mother Moses, Jo-Jo and J.J. are on the main couch. Everyone else is seated on other chairs or on the floor, or standing. Sek stands at the door. Goth Lila is lying on her stomach; her head propped up on her elbows, and is one of the closest to the vid-screen.

Though polls have not closed on the West Coast yet, the media is already able to call the presidential election. "American President Torrey E.C. Wilson, known more commonly as President T. Wilson, has been re-elected to his third term in office in a landslide. Nothing surprising, he has been expected to win for over two years. Commentators are already saying that, with the new Rule of Law repealing presidential term limits, President T. Wilson could conceivably break the record of terms in office held by President F. Roosevelt some one hundred-thirty-nine years ago, who was elected four times by the American people."

Kristiana notices the heavy tension in the room. She has questions, but this is not the time.

"Ahhh!" Goth Lila screams. "Galerius is going to be elected a fourth, a fifth, a sixth time. How do we stop him?! Before he tries to wipe all Faithers off the planet?" Goth Lila buries her head in her arms on the floor.

"Okay everyone, the show is over," Mother Moses says in a low tone. People rise and start to file out of the house; some say brief words to her on the way out. "Miss Kristiana Fisher and Goth Lila will remain behind." People start to smile or chuckle.

When everyone is gone, all that remains is Mother Moses sitting on the couch with her youngest children. Goth Lila watches Kristiana. Sek still stands at the door.

M looks at Jo-Jo and J.J. "Go to your rooms, please."

"No, mom," J.J. says, smiling. "This is too good to miss."

"Mom, I'm a grown person with a husband-to-be." Jo-Jo too can barely keep from laughing.

Mother Moses says to J.J., "Off to your room now or the only thing you'll get for Gift Day next month is a bag of dirty rocks."

"No, Mother!" J.J. jumps off the couch and disappears down the hall. They hear the door of his bedroom slam shut.

Mother Moses says to Jo-Jo, "I am a grown person too, with a husband *now*, and the last time I looked, this house belongs to me. I follow your rules in your house. You follow mine here."

Jo-Jo reluctantly gets up and leaves too.

Kristiana stands up from the floor and walks over to Goth Lila who is still lying on the floor, but now is on her back.

"I'm so sorry," she says. "I don't know what came over me. I just had an uncontrollable urge to hit you. When I was a child, these Goths would come to Town in Amish Quarter and beat the Amish children up. I know that wasn't you. I'm so sorry. Please forgive me. I never did that before ever."

Goth Lila sits up. "I forgive you. But how am I going to get my reputation back? Everyone in Providence is going to laugh at me when they see me and say, 'oh you're the one the Amish girl beat up.' Goths don't get beat up by anyone. So what do I do about that?"

Kristiana thinks for a moment and then says, "Oh, I know. When I go for my walks, I'll tell everyone in the neighborhood the truth, and we'll get your violent reputation back." She smiles.

Mother Moses and Sek laugh.

"I believe you," Goth Lila says. "Okay, that works for me. Will you attack me again?"

Kristiana seems genuinely embarrassed. "Oh no, never again."

Goth Lila stands up and shakes her hand. "I'm Goth Lila of the Goth Christian Order."

"I'm Kristiana Fisher of the Old Amish Order."

Mother Moses says, "That's what I like. People solving problems on their own."

There are many kinds of Goths: Hedonists, Nihilists, Anarchists, Vampires, Wiccans, Witches, but there are also Goth Faithers. Goth Jews aren't really accepted by most Jewish Orders, so often they work with Christians; no one knows if there are any Goth Mormons; and Goth Christians are the main human intelligence gatherers in Tek World for Faithers. Gothism is more than black hair, black makeup, and black leather clothes; it is an attitude. However, for the non-Goth, what that means exactly is endlessly debated. A Goth Christian can instantly spot a Goth Hedonist and a Goth Anarchist could recognize a Goth Jew on sight. For those outside Gothism, all Goths look alike.

Mother Moses says, "So Lila, what brings you to Providence?"

Goth Lila hesitates for a moment.

"Kristiana, Lila and I need to speak privately," Mother Moses says.

"Yes, M," she says. "I have my new book from Mr. Super. I'll be in the library room."

Kristiana leaves the two women in the living room.

Providence Enclave, The Stadium
10:00 a.m., Saturday, 13 November 2088

The Stadium not only functions as the center of sports entertainment, but doubles as the place for serious city-wide town hall meetings.

The auditorium is packed with new potential Christian entrants to Providence. Many of them resisted the Separatist Movement, but now are here to embrace it. The silent controversy is over; there is only consensus now.

Mother Moses sits with the Providence Council, the seven men and seven women who review the applicants of those who wish to move to Providence. She remains quiet as the boisterous crowd asks a myriad of questions to the Council.

"Does the Council tell individuals and families how to live?" a man asks.

"No," the chairman answers. "But the city has rules and everyone follows them. You don't follow them and you have to leave. Very simple. We like simple."

"Are there any rules not listed?"

"No," he answers again. "Everything is written out in precise language."

"Is the Council a political body or a religious body?"

"Political only."

"So you've adopted the Pagan propaganda of *separation of church and state?*"

The chairman smiles—a universally reviled phrase among Faithers. "No, we've adopted the American Christian belief of being against theocracies. Theocracies almost destroyed Christianity in ancient history and look at the Caliphate if you need any further examples of why it must be avoided at all costs—until we get to Heaven of course. The Council runs the affairs of the city and our churches have their own leadership to run their own affairs. We're all of the same faith, so there is overlap of course, but there is a clear distinction of duties."

"If this really is a self-sustaining city, then what government services do you provide? Such as for the unemployed," a woman asks.

Mother Moses stands. "Everyone is obligated to work in Providence. If you don't have a job, then you are obligated to volunteer wherever the city places you until you find one."

The crowd seems surprised by her answer.

"Your city doesn't provide assistance to the sick, needy, or unemployed?"

"You're changing the question. What do you want me to answer? The sick, the needy or the unemployed?"

"All of them."

"I answered about unemployment already. Everyone works here, but no one cares as long as you pay your bills and handle your own life."

"But what about the homeless?"

"We have no homeless. Everyone owns their homes here, and we even have bare-hands people who build their own homes from scratch after they buy the land."

"What if someone doesn't have a job and can't buy food?"

"Then they go to their church for hot meals as long as needed until they get a new job."

"That seems very undignified for an adult or family to have to go to church to get a hot meal, as you say. That's public humiliation. They should get the money to buy what they want in privacy."

"Why?"

"People, even the unemployed, should be allowed to live with dignity."

"Who cares about dignity? Do you want food, or do you want to starve? And when would this person, living in dignity, be required to get a job? It sounds to me that in your system there would be no such requirement."

"Your system is crazy. I can't support that. Do you have any notion what unemployment is for Christians out there?"

Mother Moses walks to the center of the stage. "The woman just said to me that our system is crazy and she can't support it. I'm very glad to hear that. Then leave." Mother Moses pauses and looks out at the entire crowd. "No one asked you to come here. My mother-in-law, with my father-in-law, didn't start this community in '76, as many believe. She started it in '66. She started the Separatist Movement before the movement had a name, before the movement was even known as a movement. When we started we had just a handful of homes and stores. Now we have over two hundred and fifty thousand people and it's a thriving city. You all come here and ask us not about the great community we have here—our church life, the rich education community, the vibrant culture, how we protect our people from the Pagans and other enemies. What do you ask about? *Government* assistance. An evil euphemism if I ever heard one. Government entrapment of our people is what it is. I'm actually old enough to remember what it was like back in the bad times, whole neighborhoods, whole cities with able-bodied men and women on government assistance for years, for decades—a permanent, not temporary, way of life for generations of our people. Satan's greatest invention. Permanent dependence rather than noble self-reliance. There is another word for it: slavery! Weakening our people down to their very souls. The emptiness, the drugs and every other known vice, the street killings, grown adults reduced to children and children reduced to animals. Yes, that worked out so well for us.

"The answer to the question is we take care of all our people. If someone doesn't have food, then the community pitches in and makes sure they have three hot meals a day for themselves and for their families. If they are sick or injured, our doctors provide services without question. We have no homeless, because everyone owns their own homes that they bought or built with their own hands. This community takes care of its people in keeping with our long Christian heritage. Christians were taking care of the sick, poor, elderly, needy, and diseased before there was a United States of Pagan America. We invented caring for the sick, poor, and disabled. We invented hospitals. Are you suggesting we allow Galerius to take care of our people? That's so smart. That's as smart as a fool volunteering to be the dentist for a great white shark. 'Oh kind sir, please step into my mouth and clean my razor sharp teeth. I promise not to eat you.' We escaped from the bad times, but now you want to return to them. The Pagans have trained you well. If that's what you care about, then go back and live in that great society of Pagans and leave us alone. You stay in your community and live the way you want. We'll live in our communities and live the way we want. Please use the rear exits on your way out back to Tek World. Good day." She walks off the stage. There is no reaction, no applause, and no sounds of any kind. She tries to show no emotion, but she is mad. Her husband has a gift for insulting people with a smile. She, however, is not interested in the niceties, even for fellow Christians. Guess I'm becoming more like Elder Mother Esther.

The other members of the council remain behind, quietly, in their chairs.

5:20 p.m.

Mother Moses is in her kitchen teaching Kristiana how to make empanadas. The council chairman knocks on the door and announces himself as he enters the house.

"In here," Mother Moses says.

The chairman enters the kitchen. "There's no food under God's sun that the Moses family doesn't know how to make."

Kristiana smiles and says, "Do you need to talk with M privately?"

"Oh no, this isn't top secret. Besides, everyone in Providence knows you aren't an Amish spy."

She laughs.

"Did you come here to scold me for not being friendlier to our visitors?" Mother Moses asks.

The chairman smiles. "No, I came to tell you that we will be greatly expanding the Providence population."

"How many want to join?"

"We accepted all who submitted applications. *All* of them submitted applications."

Mother Moses stops and looks at him. "All?"

The chairman smiles again. "M, it's something your mother-in-law realized a long time ago. People crave strong leaders. They want strong leaders who are decisive, firm, and not afraid to make the big but fair decisions. Leaders who will look them in the eye and call them out when they're doing the wrong thing. They didn't like your bitter medicine speech, but they respected it and felt that if that's how you talk to them, Providence will definitely say and do what needs to be done to protect them and their families."

Mother Moses shakes her head. "Every time I want to give up

on the human race, they turn around and surprise me."

The chairman says, smiling, "It's funny how that works. Our total population will be growing again. Largest single-year increase since '76."

"Seems like the enclaves grow in size every time someone in the Moses family dies," Mother Moses says quietly.

"Don't think of it like that," he says.

"I'm sorry." She turns to Kristiana. "Let's finish up all our Argentinean dishes and then go down to the main library to watch some old interviews of my mother-in-law on the vid. She had a mouth on her."

Kristiana smiles. "Yes, let's go."

Southern Africa
9:02 a.m., 8 August 2088

The man walks through the hot sun and blowing sand, dressed in casual clothes: a white t-shirt with an unbuttoned short-sleeved shirt over it, dark khaki pants and a white *keffiyeh*, the traditional long cloth headdress of desert-dwelling Arabs. He watches through his circular eye-glasses that seem to glow neon blue. Three seven-foot-tall men wait by an all-terrain SUV.

"ID?" one of the giants asks.

The man in the keffiyeh smiles as he holds up his right palm for a scan. His forearm is covered by some type of wide bracelet that crackles with electric charges.

Private Restaurant, Providence Enclave
1:30 p.m., 11 August 2088

General Moses sits quietly as he eats his food, all seafood dishes. Across from him is the American with the circular eye-glasses that glow neon blue intermittently. In the corner, a large man sits on a tall stool holding a gun, resting on his lap.

"I'm the best tek-lord on the continent," the bespectacled man says.

General Moses looks at him as he takes a sip from his glass.

"This isn't Africa. We need someone whose ability exceeds their hubris, Mr. NIS."

"Only the Magi are better than me," he says. "They're far beyond tek-lords. We haven't yet invented the lingo to describe what they are. But as far as Christians go, I'm the best. I can't alter reality, consciousness and perception like the Magi, but I manipulate electricity. The building blocks of all that is Tek World." While he is talking, his glasses turn pitch black, and there now seems to be a faint yellow glow behind them. He wiggles his fingers, and streams of yellow electricity emit from his fingertips.

"NIS? Does your name mean something?" Moses asks.

He smiles. "Notoriously invasive species."

Moses smiles. "There are a lot of tek-heads out there passing themselves off as tek-lords."

NIS sighs. "I can assure you that I'm one of the best, whether it's Africa or here in America. I think there are only about ten people walking around who are of my caliber. You have my references. My sources say you have six of those ten already on your payroll."

"Your sources?"

"My fellow tek-lords."

"I don't know why someone would tell you that."

NIS smiles. "I'm sorry. Did I reveal a secret no one is supposed to know?"

"Who are the other three, since you claim to be in the top ten?"

"One of them is Jewish, all the chatter says he's *real* good, one of the best. The other two are a problem: two Pagans, one is some Anarchist, and the other works for the Grid as a tek-lord bounty hunter for the government."

Being a tek-lord as a profession is illegal, and a whole division of Homeland is dedicated to their identification, capture, and imprisonment. The integrity and stability of the Grid, the Net, and the Data Stream are the fundamental mandates of the government. Nothing and no one can be allowed to undermine Tek World.

"Yes, we know of them. Why were you in Africa?"

"I was fighting in the Christo-Islamic War against the Muslims. Not as a soldier, of course, but as a tek. I was very…disturbed by the Fall of Western Europe as a kid, even though I felt they deserved it and brought it on themselves. I felt my talents would be of greater use there than here. I didn't want to see the Fall of Africa. Not if I had anything to do with it. Now, things are reversed. America needs my talents more. Africa is okay now. The Muslims were winning before. Now they aren't. Our side has a Catholic general who is the most extraordinary leader I've ever seen." He smiles. "I haven't seen you yet." He continues. "The African Collective will either drive them out or make sure they go no further. The Caliphate will not have Africa."

"Who's in the African Collective these days?"

"Catholics, Christians, Coptics, Armenians, Ethiopian Jews; various deists and agnostics."

"Why would you leave such excitement?"

"I am and always will be American. I was always going to come back eventually. Like I said, I did my part for their war, now I need to do my part for the war effort here."

"What Order are you?"

"That, sadly, is a complicated situation currently. Was Catholic in my adolescence, I probably identified with them the most because they were the most persecuted of all Christians. Then I was spiritual. Now I believe I'm ready to come back to God as a Protestant, but which group I have no idea. They're a lot of Christians-in-Name-Only running around in Protestantism."

"We have designed a battery of tests for you."

"Naturally."

"To see what your tek ability is."

"The project must be big if you want to hire and dedicate a tek-lord from outside your known circles to work on it."

Moses smiles. These tek-lords are very good at figuring things out, piecing things together with just a few strands of data here and there.

"We'll contact you after you finish the tests."

He nods. "I'm going to ace all your tests. I was expecting you to grill me for a few hours or put me in front of a mind-bender."

The common slang for a psychiatrist-interrogator-profiler.

"We have all we need."

He stands. "I thought you were more paranoid than that, General."

"We are very paranoid people, Mr. NIS. We don't talk to anyone or let anyone near us unless they have been thoroughly investigated. And we don't fly them all the way from Africa, all expenses paid. We have been watching you for some time. We also know your boss, Archbishop Masai of the African Catholic Order. He told us that you were much more than the average tek-lord. You come highly recommended by the African Collective."

"Good. You know my rep. Do I still need to take the tests?"

"Yes, it includes some very unique problems. We need to know if you can solve them."

"As I said, I'll ace everything. What's the job?"

"We'll talk after your tests."

"In addition to my compensation, I have other items that must be included in my payment. I'm a major gamer—addiction to vid-games is my only vice, but it's for work reasons. I also play a lot of tri-dimensional chess. I need to keep my brain pathways always active and stretching."

"We can accommodate all that. Providence is self-sufficient and we grow all our own food."

"Good. You know I'm a vegan already. I consume lots of the natural stuff. My favorite is on-the-spot-made fruit juices and veggie juices. I take my commercial juicer and two-liter glass bottle with me wherever I go. I don't really do too much eating, but lots of drinking."

"We prefer to eat our food rather than drink it, but there's nothing in the scripture against it."

"And I keep my wristbands and special glasses."

"Why do you need those?"

"I like to play with the electricity discharges when I work. It keeps me focused."

"You have some very strange needs."

"I'm a tek-lord. We're all a bit strange in our own ways."

"I believe that."

"Sir, I just need to say that my condolences go to you and your family for the loss of your mother. You should have seen the virtual funeral they had for her in Christian Africa."

"Thank you."

"Also, I've always wanted to work with you—ever since the Kansas Event. The Magi stood as close to you as I am to you now. They spoke to you. That means something, sir."

General Moses smiles.

"On a critical side-note, how good is your security here in the tri-cities?" NIS asks.

"The best. You should know. You've tried for years to hack in."

NIS smiles. "A good tek-lord always tries to anticipate the needs of a potential client. Give them a little taste of what they can do. Tease them a bit to get the job or get a bigger pay-day. I won't tell you what I did to get the Archbishop to hire me, but I had to stand out from at least a hundred other teks."

"And?"

"You're in serious danger, sir."

"We're always in danger. That's nothing new."

"Have you ever heard of a Pagan, Vampire, same difference, named Bloodgood?"

"No." Moses drinks from his glass.

"You need to know this one. He's been hunting Faithers for awhile. He's effective, and he has his own personal army paid for at taxpayer's expense. All the chatter says something is going to happen. If I were you, I would build bigger walls and start locking the gates."

"We're already doing that. We know about the chatter."

"I know you have a lot of resources on the streets gathering data—the Goths especially. They'll find out for you soon enough, but I can give you one piece of the puzzle now. This Bloodgood was the one who killed your mother."

The Last Christians

"The policeman said we were not allowed to pray or even have our Bibles in public." – Mrs. Abigail as a young woman, first trip to Washington DC

"If Christ were here, there is one thing he would not be—a Christian." – Mark Twain, iconic American author and humorist

Jerusalem, Israel
11:05 a.m., 29 June 2059

The Church of the Holy Sepulchre is a church within the Christian Quarter of Old Jerusalem and one of the two sites venerated as *Golgotha*, the Hill of Calvary where Jesus Christ was crucified and buried. It is also claimed to be the resurrection site of Jesus and Christians from around the world flock here.

It will be many years until he is known as General Moses; everyone just calls him Mo for short. He sits with his fiancée Emma—whom everyone just calls "M"—and his brother Sam. The Holy Land Tour was put together by one of the many interfaith groups in the United States viewed as more religiously traditional and pro-Israel. On the bus are not only Christians, but Jews, Mormons, and people of other faiths—none of whom have ever been to Israel before. Mo and M have befriended a number of people: the Tovas, American Conservative Jews who actually served in the Israeli Defense Force, but surprisingly never toured Old Jerusalem—all the other Jews are Conservative or Reform; Vincent, a Mormon, is some kind of oceanographer-marine biologist and the only one of his group of fellow Mormons who doesn't just keep to himself; and Sikh Bob, the only Sikh on the bus. There are some forty people on the trip; the oldest is not more than twenty-four years old.

The Church of the Holy Sepulchre is also known as the Church of the Resurrection. Six Christian denominations oversee the church with primary custodianship shared among the Greek Orthodox, Armenian Apostolic, and Roman Catholic, with lesser duties shared by Coptic, Ethiopian and Syriac Orthodox churches. These denominations control the church in a bizarre arrangement unchanged for centuries—this area belongs to this denomination, this corner to another, this section of the roof to another, and of course….the Immovable Ladder, the ultimate symbol of Christian division. The fight for dominance of the church by these denominations has been bad enough, but their tactics in trying to best one another have included bribery, blackmail, and physical force. Someone in the first half of the nineteenth century placed the Ladder up against the upper level of the church. No one could touch it, or move it as none of the denominations could agree on whom the Ladder belonged. Therefore, it has remained in the same spot ever since, lest a violent outbreak erupt amongst the denominations. Everyone on to the tour laughs, as frankly, no one believes the story; it is too ridiculous.

The tour guide remarks how the site of the church had actually been a Pagan temple to the Goddess of Venus in the second century. It was the Roman Emperor Constantine who had that temple destroyed and the soil removed to build the current holy church. In 614 AD, it survived attacks from the Persians, who burned the building when they invaded and captured the site; early Muslim rulers did protect all Christian sites in the city, but the building was damaged again by fire in a riot in 966 AD; and then the Muslim Fatimid Caliph Al-Hakim bi-Amr Allah launched the complete destruction of the church in 1009, except for the massive pillars that were too hard to destroy. This Muslim act so shocked European Christians that it provided a catalyst for the Crusades.

The historical account of the church only made the tour

group more eager to see inside—even those who don't consider Jesus the Messiah. Mo and M are the first from the group to get in through the crowds. They are struck by how dim it is, but immediately make their way to the Altar of the Crucifixion and its likeness of Jesus on the cross, the place where Jesus is purported to have been crucified; then the group views the Stone of Anointing, which tradition says is the exact spot where Joseph of Arimathea prepared the body of Jesus for burial. They take millions of photos with e-pads, as any good tour group does, as they move between sites of interest. The Rock of the Calvary (beneath which is said to be the hole where the cross with the crucified Jesus was raised), the Chapel of the Nailing Cross, the Chapel of Adam, the Greek Chapel of St. Longinus (dedicated to the Roman soldier who pierced Jesus with a spear), the Chapel of the Invention of the Holy Cross, the Franciscan Chapel of St. Mary Magdalene (the place where she met Jesus after the Resurrection), the Franciscan Chapel of the Blessed Sacrament, the Catholicon, and the Prison of Christ. Everywhere there are ceremonies from the different Christian denominations. There are people with candles everywhere too. Beautiful paintings adorn different parts of the walls and the floors.

The climax of the visit is the Tomb of Christ, the Edicule of the Holy Sepulchre, with its beautiful, gold-decorated exterior. The group has to line up along a rope, as if they are awaiting entry to a nightclub. The Tomb is a small space, and they must duck down to get into the first room, which contains the Angel's Stone, a fragment of the stone believed to have sealed the tomb Jesus was buried in. However, it also contains a very surly priest standing in the corner, waiting. As the previous group of four people exit the altar, the priest yells: "Go, go, go!"

Mo and M with the Tovas and Sikh Bob enter the inner room. The space is very cramped, but before they can visually absorb the artifact, they hear:

"Get out! Go! Get out now!" the priest yells.

The five of them look at each other, but they back out slowly. The priest doesn't even look at them as he gestures for them to leave the Edicule; he is already glaring at the next group of visitors.

They are not happy as they exit.

"One of the holiest sites in Christianity, and we're able to see it for all of a half second," Moses says. "So much for our pilgrimage."

"Don't feel bad, Mo. Christians are only one percent of the population in Israel. These Christians are trying very hard to get it down to half that," Sikh Bob says. "No other religion rushes you out of a sacred holy site: Jews, Muslims, our Sikh temples, none."

"Don't tell your mother about this," M says. "That's all we need is her coming down here and causing an international incident."

As they walk out of the church, none of them can help looking up at the Immovable Ladder. So the story is true after all.

Later, their tour group goes to the Garden Tomb, the other site in Old Jerusalem also believed to be the true place of the crucifixion and resurrection of Jesus. It is the more popular pilgrimage site for Protestant denominations, as opposed to Catholics and East Orthodox. Vincent tells them that this is the site Mormons recognize as the true location of the tomb of Jesus.

Moses doesn't know why his experience at the Holy Sepulchre bothers him so much, but it does.

Moses House, Providence Enclave
8:00 a.m., 3 January 2089

"Father!" Kristiana shouts, smiling. She just happens to be on the porch when a golf cart rolls up, driven by Armstrong. In the passenger seat sits the Amish Quarter elder in typical Amish attire: dark denim pants with suspenders, light blue shirt, and a wide-brim straw hat.

He gets out and says a few words of thanks to his driver and shakes his hand. By the time he turns around, Kristiana has already reached him and grabbed him. He hugs his daughter.

Mother Moses exits the house onto the porch, drying her hands with a hand towel.

"You came all this way alone, Father? No one else came with you?"Kristiana asks.

"Just me. I couldn't drag your mother away, but…"

Kristiana looks up at him.

"I have a very long letter from her." He reaches into his vest pocket and hands her the letter. She takes it and looks at him, smiling.

Kristiana takes his hand and leads him up the walkway to the house. "M, this is my father."

"Good afternoon, Mr. Fisher."

"Thank you. Good afternoon. I'm sure your name isn't M."

She smiles, "No, just a nickname. Mrs. Moses. I'm an elder of the community so formally I'm known as Mother Moses."

"Very nice to meet you in person, Mother Moses." He shakes her hand and turns to Kristiana. "You go read your mother's letter. There's even a couple from your little sisters. We'll talk afterwards, after I speak with your host."

"Yes, Father." Kristiana runs inside, holding the letters with both hands as if she has received a perishable, precious gift.

"Come inside, Mr. Fisher. We can talk privately in the sitting room."

She leads him into the house and past the living room to largest room in the house. Kristiana has practically made the library room her own, but the sitting room is kept closed except for special meetings. The room is very large room, but there are three couches arranged in a squared U-shape in the center on a thick patterned rug, the floors are hardwood, and along the walls are shelves, mostly covered with various plants. There are also two plush leather chairs pointed towards the room's large windows. They sit facing each other.

"How was your trip, Mr. Fisher?"

"My arrival in Philadelphia was good. Thanks for having your people meet me."

"Our pleasure. Call on Providence anytime you wish to visit. Have you ever been to Philadelphia before?"

"Last time I was here was…twelve years ago. Kristiana doesn't know that. Last time I lived out in English-world was when I was Kristiana's age, some twenty-five years ago."

"Do you ever miss it?"

"Men miss the vehicles. Women miss the clothes…and the shoes."

They laugh.

He continues, "Things have dramatically changed."

"Yes, they have. Some of us would say for the worst. But we keep all of that ugliness outside our walls."

"Yes, Kristiana is quite detailed in her letters to us."

"Is Amish Quarter a long-established Amish community?"

"My uncle, who has passed, was one of its founders some thirty years ago."

"Who is this Pagan Paul who lives in Amish Quarter? The one delivering her letters to you."

Mr. Fisher smiles. "He's a guest of the Quarter. He's been with us almost twenty years."

"A long time."

"He contributes in many ways to the Quarter. He also works the machines."

"Mr. Fisher, I must say that I very much enjoy having your daughter as a houseguest, and the community speaks very highly of her. You and Mrs. Fisher did an outstanding job raising that young lady. Her only possible weakness, also one of her greatest strengths, is her incredible curiosity for things. But if that's the only thing about your child that you can even try to say is a vice, then God has surely blessed you indeed."

He smiles again. "Yes, Curious Kristiana. I need to express the deep gratitude of my wife and me for watching over her. Kristiana understands her good God's fortune in having your people find her and bring her to safety."

"It was my youngest daughter who happened to find her when she did."

"Yes."

"What would you like to speak about, Mr. Fisher?"

The man hesitates. "Is there a time limit on how long my daughter can stay in Providence?"

"As long as it's less than twenty years, she can stay as long as she wants."

He smiles. "What is your policy on accepting guests to your

community?"

"Mr. Fisher, my late mother-in-law used to tell me, when you want something, just come out in a straightforward manner and ask. The worst thing they can do is say 'no,' but you're often surprised how many times a person will say 'yes.'"

He smiles, "Amish people are not aggressive people. We place a very high value in our lives on *demut* and *gelassenheit*. Being humble and being calm and composed in all that we do. I would like to ask if other Amish can temporarily stay as guests in Providence."

"Of course. How many people? What ages?"

"The oldest would be twenty-one, my oldest daughter, and three others."

"We have plenty of room to accommodate four guests. And it would be an easy matter to create a program for Amish to visit in any of our tri-cities."

"Thank you. My daughter aside, most Amish youth do in fact stay in their communities and join the church without ever leaving for rumspringa."

"Mr. Fisher, are these four all your daughters?"

"Yes."

"Isn't your eldest one getting married?"

"Yes, but it may be a little while before her husband-to-be can join her."

"Mr. Fisher, what's going on? Why are you moving all your daughters out of Amish Quarter?"

"There is a dispute that the elders and I have to sort through. English men came to the Quarter with these documents saying that they have discovered precious minerals on our land and that we must sell to them and the Pennsylvanian government will relocate us. We hired lawyers and they assure us that these claims are baseless, but we do need to protect ourselves."

"How will you protect yourselves if you're pacifists?"

"We believe in non-resistance, yes, but that doesn't mean we must stand there to take any kind of trouble. We will simply stay in each other's homes together while the lawyers do their work. My property is large and is the center of the dispute, so we have decided to have the girls stay here, and my wife and I will stay with the bishop and his family."

"Mr. Fisher, do you need us to help you resolve this matter?"

He smiles, "Somehow, I suspect our definition of the word *resolve* is different than yours. Thank you, but no. We'll let the lawyers do the fighting. There was a time when the Keystone State felt the Amish complemented their communities."

"May I ask a personal question, Mr. Fisher?"

"Yes, of course."

"Why would you allow your daughter to leave your home and go by herself into that evil tek-city? The Amish rightly call it the Devil's Playground. She could have been killed, or worse."

"We have faith in *Gotte's will*. God's will. God saves what is worth saving."

Mother Moses doesn't like his answer. "Mr. Fisher, there may come a time in the near future when the Amish will have to make some very hard decisions."

"Yes." He looks sadly at her. "We know. Our people have been here before."

"What did you do then?"

"We left Europe and came to America and Canada to escape the religious persecution."

Mother Moses leans forward. "If you ever wish to leave your lands again, then call us. We can find you land next to our enclaves or others in the country where you can live in peace. We are already doing so for others. We may be different Orders, but we read the same Bible."

"Yes, you have decided to do as we do. Stay separate from the world to support your way of life."

"Actually, the world decided to separate from us."

"Thank you for the offer, but my current request is sufficient for now. However, may I ask that we keep the door open on your offers?"

"Of course."

"Thank you. And please don't tell Kristiana any of this now."

"I won't. This was a good talk. Let's get you settled in with lodgings for the night, and then I leave you to have your daughter talk your ears off," she says, smiling.

The Christianity of the Constantine era was far different from the humble beginnings of Apostles Peter and Paul. Churches were massive and named after great saints, worship services began with elaborate proceedings, priests and bishops became exalted dignitaries. The ancient Rome that reveled in throwing early Christians to lions and tigers or crucifying them to die horribly on the side of the road had now totally adopted that same religion, made it the only religion of the state, and converted the entire population to it.

The Middle Ages, often called the Dark Ages, in Western Europe included the bloody Crusades (1095-1291), which were not one war but nine different Crusades and several subsequent minor Crusades adding up to eight generations of fighting to take back the Holy Land of Jerusalem from the Muslims.

The time was also known for its "convert or die" brand of Christianity, rapid anti-Semitism and pogroms, violent riots against Jews condoned by law. Jews were killed by Christian mobs for "killing Christ" and even blamed for such things as bringing the Black Death, the plague that killed some thirty to sixty percent of the world's population in only three years, starting in 1348. There was much death in this time, but there was something else happening as well.

Monasteries became the center of civic power and commerce, Christian monks saved the historical and cultural literature by copying works by hand, which otherwise would have been lost forever. Christianity became the order in a world of chaos.

Even the violence and corruption of the Christian Church led to profound things in the world: the Dark Ages was followed by the Renaissance and the Protestant Reformation. It also led to the fleeing of the Puritans and Pilgrims to the New World. These new Christian Protestant pioneers would not only invent representative republic government and the Judeo-Christian ethic, but create of one of the greatest empires in human history—the United States of America.

But that was then. The Pagans rule now.

Moses House, Providence Enclave
5:22 p.m., 4 January 2089

Kristiana has been a bit sad since her father left to go back to the Quarter. She wrote a special letter for her mother and she got up extra early to say goodbye. "God bless and goodbye Kristiana and Bo Bear," were his last words before Jo-Jo sped him off in the cart. Her father seemed to be very amused with her large stuffed teddy bear.

But today is special and she can barely contain her anticipation for the meeting Mother Moses has put together. She still doesn't know the purpose of the meeting; all she knows is that there will be a lot of new people arriving from all across the nation.

"My name is Kristiana of the Old Amish Order."

Kristiana has volunteered to be the main greeter at the door. The first couple arrives, chauffeured to the house by carts driven by security personnel.

"My name is Dalmatia, and this is my husband, Thaddeus. Well, that's a conundrum for us. Sadly, we're ex-Southern Baptists. But nice to meet you, Kristiana of the Old Amish Order."

Dalmatia is an African woman, her name meaning "priestly robe," and she does look like royalty, refined and poised. Her husband Thaddeus is Caucasian, tall and well built with a tan complexion.

"I wish our Orders were as unified as the Amish," Dalmatia says.

"Oh, don't feel bad. The Amish are human too. We actually split from the Mennonites in 1693, led by our founder, Jakob Amman. In the 1850s, we split again into the Old and the New Amish Orders. We wanted to maintain our traditional Amish ways. Those were the major ones, but there have been others."

"You're a history expert," Thaddeus says.

"All the Amish know Amish history."

"What happened to the New Amish Order?" Dalmatia asks.

"They went English. Oh, sorry. It's an Amish expression. They became part of the outside world."

"So Kristiana, what's your favorite Bible verse?" Thaddeus asks.

Kristiana smiles, "Are you testing me?"

Thaddeus smiles too. "Kinda."

"Let me think of a good verse. I know. 1 John 2:17. 'The world and its desires pass away, but whoever does the will of God lives forever.'"

"Good one," Thaddeus says.

"But you Faithers sure do have a lot of different translations of the Bible. You have almost twenty different Bibles. The Amish only have one, but the different versions are interesting."

Dalmatia says, "You should learn Hebrew then and read that version too."

"Really? Hebrew?"

Thaddeus says, "The original version of the text. English and German were not even languages yet when the Bible was written and no one speaks Aramaic. The early text was translated from Hebrew to ancient Greek."

"I'll ask about Hebrew language classes at Education Square."

"Providence has classes, but if I were you I'd go straight to the source. Go to one of the Jewish enclaves for a semester. One where Hebrew is spoken daily," Dalmatia says.

"Most of their Hebrew classes are filled with Christians anyway. And I'd say ten percent of the students are Mormons. And their Torah classes always have some percentage of Christians. They're used to it," Thaddeus says.

Kristiana smiles at the new knowledge. "I didn't know that. Are you both pastors?"

Thaddeus says, "For eighteen years."

"Oh, I was born eighteen years ago."

"Now Kristiana, we were having such a nice conversation, and now you want to start calling us old."

Kristiana laughs. "I'm eighteen. Anything older than me is old."

Everyone that arrives is extremely friendly and gracious. Some are very curious about the Amish and ask Kristiana all kinds of questions. Sister Madalene, known as Maggie, gives her such a great hug, and Pastor Joshua prays over her. Sapphire is named after her birthstone and wears matching shimmering blue sapphire ear rings. She tells her that sapphires come in other colors: pink, purples, green, orange, yellow, and a ruby is the red version of the stone.

Kristiana leads all the arrivals to the sitting room. Jo-Jo and J.J. are on food duty, and the buffet table in the room is well stocked with finger foods, beverages, and water.

Kristiana listens to the pre-meeting conversations of the assembled group.

"You still can't find the Bible anywhere on the Net; not even in Freespace. Not an authentic one. Only their devil bible, the Good Bible. God's Word is obscenity, but all manner of filth and violence flows all throughout the Net."

"Well, they banned all public religious holidays. All they have now is a mishmash of celebrity and political days, and anniversaries for legalization of prostitution, euthanasia, alt-marriages and all their other immoralities."

"They even banned National Days of Prayer, which had always been a long tradition in our major cities with mayors. My late father was a mayor."

"Their Brave Tek World."

"We lost America."

"No, we gave it away."

"We didn't. The progenitors did. Churches back then, all the people did was sit there, listen, and then walk out and forget everything. They'd proclaim it but do nothing. They'd preach it but not do it. Faith requires action."

Mother Moses lets the group talk, vent, and reminisce. It takes nearly forty minutes for the greetings, small talk, additional consolations to Mother Moses over the death of Elder Mother Moses, and the initial eating to run its course, but that's why people came early. The meeting is officially kicked off by a five-minute inspiring group prayer.

Kristiana has noticed that all of them refer to themselves as "ex," "used-to-be," or "former." Thaddeus and Dalmatia are ex-Southern Baptist. Both were pastors in the denomination most of their lives separately, and when they married, pastored various churches jointly. The denomination had divided many times in the past and they were active in the movement to merge the factions together again, but the Registrant-Resister conflict fractured the Order beyond repair. No one trusted anyone outside their own church.

Andrew and Faith, ex-Episcopalians; Peter and Zoe, ex-Lutherans; and Dale and Cordelia, ex-Presbyterians, were the three couples who were members of once the largest Orders in Protestantism, and as with all its members, tried mightily to save their churches. Episcopalians, Lutherans, and Presbyterians were blamed, fairly or unfairly, by all Faithers for causing American Christianity to lose the marriage wars.

Father Daniel and Sister Madalene, were loyal Catholics from birth though the largest Christian Order in the world has dwindled down to nothing in America. American Catholicism still suffers from the sex scandals of a century ago, even though the Vatican created a global division known commonly as the "sex police" who do what the Church had never effectively done in the past: aggressively deal with not only charges of sexual misconduct, but rumors of such. But the rampant twentieth-century Catholic clergy pedophilia scandals didn't destroy the American Catholic Church—it was the twenty-first-century accelerated secularization of the Church, culminating in the leadership's quick embracing of the Registration Initiatives that did. People like Father Daniel and Sister Maggie warned the Vatican what would happen but were ignored. American Catholicism followed the same path of Western European Catholicism outside Italy: dwindling congregations, severe priest and nun shortages, and empty churches.

Father Daniel, a licensed psychologist himself, has the further distinction of being a frequent target of the American Psychological Association (APA)—the larger International Psychological Association disappeared with the fall of Western Europe. The APA is the organization he spent the better part of two decades trying to destroy by protest campaigns, rallies, letter-writing campaigns and other legal harassment efforts. The group was one of the leading organizations giving cover to banning the psychological/therapist community from counseling individuals in favor of heterosexuality, and violators of the ban could lose their licenses for life. He also fought against the movement to end all age-of-consent and anti-pedophilia laws in the fifty-three states. The Father had been the APA's main opponent in trying to reverse federal anti-child-pornography laws. To fight these cases in court, both the Father and Sister Maggie had to register, making them the only Registrants in the Resistance.

Cyrus and Phoebe, ex-Anglicans, are in the enviable position of not having experienced any major schism within their own Order. Their church attracts disillusioned Catholics especially and also more traditional members of other Orders. However, the spiritual fortress of their unified resolve against secularism was not crumbling due to the Pagans, but due to Christians who viewed the Bible as a "living, breathing text" that could be "modified" to conform to the greater secular majority.

Seth and Cressa, ex-Baptists, were not even born yet when the Baptist church split into different groups: the National Baptist Convention, the National Baptist Convention of America, the Progressive National Convention, and the Full Gospel Baptist Church Fellowship. Each group has grown weaker and weaker as the Pagans have grown stronger.

Jason and Sapphire, ex-Pentecostal, are very charismatic, always with a Bible verse at the tip of the tongue. They feel Christians must live with boldness and heads held high, even with their own Order collapsing as well.

In the time of and after skin-color segregation in America, when the concept of race existed, the seven major Black churches in the nation were the National Baptist Convention, the National Baptist Convention of America, the Progressive National Convention, the African Methodist Episcopal Church, the African Methodist Episcopal Zion Church, the Christian Methodist Episcopal Church, and the Church of God in Christ. Joshua and Charity are ex-Church in God in Christ. Today most of these churches are no longer majority Black.

Lucius and Ruth are ex-United Methodist and readily joked that they are proud members of the Order that began to implode and diminish before all others.

Mother Moses used to be of the African Methodist Episcopal Zion (AME Zion) Church, and her husband General Moses used to be of the African Methodist Episcopal (AME) Church.

Kristiana is very impressed by the gathering, but senses an underlying collective weariness, despite their victory over the Registrants several years ago. Their enclave communities are so stable and full of life, and the people are happy and productive, but she knows that the leaders always know more of the true dangers lurking in the shadows for their people. The battle between the Resisters and the Registrants nearly destroyed all remnants of the largest Christian and Jewish Orders in the country and fractured all others.

They all take seats around long tables connected to form a square.

"Master Pastor is back and is organizing again," Dalmatia says.

The revelation catches most of the group off guard.

"Rumor or verified?" Mother Moses asks.

Dalmatia says, "At this point, I'd say it's a fact that needs to be verified."

"Let him organize," Joshua says. "There's nothing for him to organize."

"With Galerius re-elected again," Cyrus says. "I imagine he feels comfortable that he will be in office forever and has started dusting off his Project Purify plans."

"If he couldn't get it done then, how could he now?" Sister Maggie says.

"Yeah, how could he?" Dale says sarcastically. "Especially with all of us in such large, easy targets called enclaves, instead of scattered, hidden, and difficult to track."

"It was our strength and unity in our enclaves that allowed us to win," Sister Maggie says.

"Agreed, but let's not fool ourselves. They might not have their Bishop Joe and Rabbi Susan puppet show anymore, but I'm sure they have new ones. Maybe they promoted Master Pastor?"

"Let's find out for sure," Mother Moses says.

"I know you didn't call this meeting for this, but shouldn't we discuss it?" Charity asks. "Is this madness going to start all over again? They put me in jail."

"Yes, I hear you found a husband in there," Zoe says.

Charity looks at her husband Joshua, smiling.

"We'll find out what's going on. A lot seems to have been triggered now that the elections are over," Mother Moses says.

"Why won't they just leave us alone? We live far from their tek-cities, beyond their Outlands, past their Trog-land, and still..." Ruth says, shaking her head.

"Where's the General?" Cyrus asks.

Mother Moses looks at him. "He'll return soon. He's finishing important work for the enclaves." She can tell he isn't satisfied with the response. "We called this special meeting tonight, ahead of time from our normal annual meetings, because of all the things that have happened recently. Have any of your enclaves heard of any other rumors, heard of anything strange, seen anything strange?"

"What strange things have you seen?" Cyrus asks. "So that we know what we're talking about. Has something else occurred besides Esther's murder? Do you know who did it yet?"

"Not yet. We're still gathering all the facts. I'm not trying to be intentionally mysterious, but the Goth Christians—I think most of you know Goth Lila—informed us that her sources say that something major is being planned, and yes, we can infer that it has to do with the elections being over. And now this apparent return of Master Pastor. I don't believe in coincidences—except when it comes to God of course, but this isn't God."

"Basically, you're suggesting it's all going to start again," Cordelia says.

Mother Moses says, "Christians have been in much darker places than this. We're still here. Our enemies are not."

"But the ancient Romans didn't have kill drones or federal storm trooper armies," Dale says. "Our enemies today don't need lions or crucifixions anymore. We've lost the war, no matter how many battles we manage to win. They can wipe us out with the touch of a button."

"No, they can't. God will help us stop them." Kristiana realizes that she has just spoken up in the meeting. Everyone looks to the back where she sits in a chair close to the door. "I'm sorry."

"No, it's okay for you to speak, Kristiana," Mother Moses says.

"She's right, of course," Dale says. "I'm just…so tired of the fighting. I signed on to be a spiritual soldier, not a physical one."

His wife hugs him. Dale bows his head, and his eyes tear up.

Mother Moses says, "Let's take a break."

Joshua says, "Brother Dale, let me pray for you." He and his wife Charity lead Dale and his wife Cordelia out of the room. Others follow.

More stay behind and Mother Moses knows they want to speak with her privately.

Cyrus says, "When they come at us again, I sincerely doubt that we'll be as successful as we were last time. Our victory was an illusion. The only real fight we had was in Kansas and the Magi saved our skin. We won the battle because we left Tek World, created our own enclaves and walled ourselves in. Seems they plan to confront us right in our own front yards, despite our defenses."

"Let them come then!" Thaddeus says. "It will be a righteous kill if they attack us in our own communities and homes with our families."

Cyrus says, "Who's fooling who? They have armies."

Dalmatia quips, "We have God."

Cyrus looks at her. "Yes, we have God. I feel perfectly secure and indestructible all of a sudden. We have nothing to worry about anymore. Let's go home and be happy."

Thaddeus says, "No need to be sarcastic."

Cyrus says, "I'm sorry, but I feel very much like Reverend Dale. An ever-present bull's eye on our backs." He says to Mother Moses, "Where is the General? Since no one will tell you, I will. The rumor out there is that your great secret project is to evacuate Providence, Restoration, and Sanctuary to a secret hidden location. Do like the Mormons. Disappear into secret enclaves hidden from the world. Evacuate your three cities and leave the rest of us to fend for ourselves."

Mother Moses says, "I'm not sure if I should be offended by such a baseless rumor."

Cyrus says, "I'm just telling you that the rumor is out there. Now word will spread of the return of the so-called Master Pastor. The other rumor is that the General is secretly in negotiations with the government so that Galerius will leave us alone."

"Equally offensive and disgusting," Mother Moses says.

"I'm only the messenger."

"M, you obviously know more than what you've been telling us over the past several months, so what do you expect?" Cressa asks.

"I expect you to trust me and be patient. Trust my husband, who's risking his life to protect all of us and fighting his own intense grief over the murder of his mother."

"The mind creates all kinds of things to fill the darkness when darkness is all there is," Seth says. "You know that. Uninformed people are scared people."

Mother Moses shakes her head. "We handled this whole thing badly. It's not your fault. I take the blame. Let's bring everyone back in."

The group is back in their seats to start again. Everyone is surprised to see General Moses walk into the room. He is flanked by Sek, who waits at the doorway. The general is dressed in black and looks tired, as if he's been up for days, but he also has a determined look. He personally greets everyone before walking to the front of the gathering.

"It's so good to be with everyone. I promise we will have more time together. My wife had the foresight to have me flown in last night, in case I was needed. And here I am.

"Throughout human history there have been apocalyptic, end-of-the-world groups. They were never of any significant number. I always thought them crazy. My mother would say: 'God didn't put you on this earth for you to then go and kill yourself.' Back in ancient Roman times, there were two kinds of Christians: those that allowed themselves to be thrown to the lions—devoured by whatever beasts the Romans had in their gladiator pits for their sick, personal amusement—and those that didn't. We are all descendants of the latter. There are no descendants of the other. There seem to be a lot of descendants, however, of those apocalyptic groups. They may not be as fanatical, but they are very much of the same mind—waiting for the end. I'm of course talking about us. What sits here tonight in this room is not merely our key enclave leadership in America—we are what could well be called the *Last Christians*." The gravity of his words weighs heavily on everyone as he continues. "The world's end, as the Bible says, may be at any time and will come like a thief in the night; no one will ever know when. What I can say, using the little prophetic instincts passed to me by my mother, is that *this* is clearly *not* the last stand of the Christians. Our destiny has always been in our own hands—with God's guidance, but we must always do our part. He will open the door. He will guide us through, but if we refuse to get up and walk forward, then that is on us, not Him.

"My wife and I have felt for the last couple of years there's been a smell of death from the leadership of our Christian enclaves. While our people, communities, families, and enclaves grow stronger and happier and prosper, the very burden of leadership and the second-by-second knowledge of the dangers we face has been slowly suffocating our enclave leadership. The Jews may not make it—Jewish Israel has fallen just like Western Europe at the hands of the Muslims, supported by the Pagans, and Jews have had three violent civil wars on American soil. The Mormons are also going through some major internal schism. I am not interested in seeing the Christians of America collapse to nothingness, especially after the victories we've won against our enemies, and yes, they were victories, and the great communities we've created for our people. We will win the ultimate battle. As we all will one day be beyond the very grasp of Galerius and all our enemies."

Everyone now looks at him with puzzlement. *What does that mean?*

"As far as the issue of fighting, we are always supposed to be fighting. There is never a time when we're not supposed to be fighting. It's called living. Give yourself credit for your strength, wisdom, accomplishments. The Serenity Prayer: 'God grant me the serenity to accept the things I cannot change; courage to change the things I can; and wisdom to know the difference.' We are leaders because we were meant to be in the roles we have taken. And we're more than just the religious leadership, or a civilian quasi-military force to protect our people; we're a nation unto ourselves—great and noble, righteous and just. We don't seek evil, we defend against it. We're not armed with sticks, stones and slingshots here. We are very good at what we do, and I'd put our tek up against Galerius himself.

"You wanted to see me. Now you've seen me. I'm going to go back to work…on *Project Noah*. Galerius has his projects, so do we. Have a good night everyone, and God bless."

The name of the secret project seems to hang in the air. General Moses leaves the room with Sek. Project Noah? Such a code-name for a project makes the mind of a Faither conjure up so many things.

Moses leaves, with Sek following.

In an instant, the group's defeatism is gone.

Resistance Rising

"The time is fast approaching, when Christianity will be almost as openly disavowed in the language, as in fact, it is already supposed to have disappeared from the conduct of men; when infidelity will be held to be the necessary appendage of a man of fashion; and to believe will be deemed the indication of a feeble mind..." – William Wilberforce, Old England politician, philanthropist and the leader of the slave trade abolishment movement (1759-1833)

"Of all the tyrannies, a tyranny exercised for the good of its victims may be the most oppressive. It may be better to live under robber barons than under omnipotent moral busybodies. The robber baron's cruelty may sometimes sleep, his cupidity may at some point be satiated; but those who torment us for our own good will torment us without end for they do so with the approval of their own conscience. They may be more likely to go to Heaven yet at the same time likelier to make a Hell of earth." – C. S. Lewis, Old English writer, intellectual (1898-1963)

The White House
7:55 a.m., 5 January 2089

"Chess Master is moving," the Secret Service agent says into his ear-set, standing at his hallway post.

The president walks briskly to his first meeting of the day. His senior advisor knows that if he wants to talk with him without being officially scheduled, this will be his only chance.

"Mr. President, we promised the governors that we wouldn't do this," he says.

"No," the president says. "We said, to ensure my election win, we wouldn't move at that time. It was always the intent to deal with this at a later date. Now is that later date. We wanted to make sure I won my first election. I just won my third in a walk, and we'll win the fourth, fifth, and sixth in a walk. There is nothing to stop me from dealing with them now."

"So the project will be activated, sir?"

"Project Purify has *already* been activated. Since the Supreme Senate saw fit to expand rather than repeal the Posse Comitatus Act in the Rule of Law, keeping me from using our standing military army against them, we'll soon have a new army to deal with them."

President Wilson and his executive staff arrive to meet with senior law enforcement leaders from around the country in the Oval Office.

The senior law enforcement advisor says, "The passing of the Storm Trooper Bill will put the latest body-armor tek on the back of every police person in the nation. Virtually bullet proof, explosion resistant, fully linked to the Net for enhanced power, equipped with internal surveillance using all optics and audios, complete interface with the Grid to coordinate tactical operations, internal climate control, GPS link is a given, and it even has exo-skeleton strength enhancements."

"Thank you, Mr. President, for this," the chief of police says. "This will do for police what auto-drive tek did for vehicle transportation—virtually eliminate all deaths. You got our support, and my vote for life, Mr. President."

"I appreciate it, Chief," President Wilson says. "More proof of the dangers of religion. To think that the *Star Wars* religion has been costing police lives all these many years and decades—it's reprehensible. But it ends on my watch. We'll have our Storm Trooper army."

Theodore Roosevelt Statute at Presidential Row, Washington DC
10:00 a.m., 5 January 2089

Dozens of uniformed police officers stand behind a podium

with the large statue of President Theodore Roosevelt, the nation's 26th president, as their backdrop. The statue is a larger replica of the one on Theodore Roosevelt Island located on the District's Potomac River. This site is a frequent place for press conferences about legislation and announcements related to law enforcement issues. A crowd of reporters face them, filming and taking photos.

The Washington DC chief of police continues, "Law enforcement all across this nation, from the uniformed beat cop to office-suit brass, unanimously applaud the decision of the president to adopt the long-overdue Storm Trooper Bill. Our men, women, transgender, bi-gender, and neuter-asexual officers in law enforcement that protect the people of America will now have the latest tek to save their own lives. To think that juvenile fears from fantasy movies have kept this from use these many decades is a mark of shame upon the politicians and activists behind it. We have always felt body-armor tek to be a civil right for our officers, and now that right is attained. Every police officer in the nation will be replaced by a friendly neighborhood storm trooper."

Off to the side, Bloodgood stands, wearing dark-red glasses, smiling.

The Stadium, Providence Enclave
10 a.m., 5 January 2089

The dapper, authoritative Mr. Super stands before the crowd on the stage.

"The New England Primer was the first reading book in the original thirteen colonies. It became the most successful educational textbook published in eighteenth-century America, and it became the foundation of most schooling before the 1790s. Often said about it: 'taught millions to read and not one to sin.'

"It is ironic that it was Christians who set up the nation's public schools and college and university systems, only to have them taken over by Pagans over a century ago. Then the purging began—our history first, then our values, and finally religious people themselves.

"Christian religious instruction was the primary purpose of public education when the Old US Constitution was written, but we went from teaching essential core subjects to indoctrination. Educational excellence was replaced by ideological propaganda and political and religious bigotry. They created not merely dumb kids, but dumb, hate-filled kids. The latter being the only thing scarier for a society than the former.

"My parents were obsessed with quality education. They would curse government schools and wouldn't even allow my brothers, sisters, and me to look at them, let alone go to one. There was this old, tiny Catholic school five miles away, run by a strong Catholic nun, but she died, and the Catholics never did replace her, and the school closed. My parents then sent us to a Jewish day school. They worked out an arrangement with the community for us to go there. My mother said, 'This is pathetic! All these Christians in this country, and they don't have one Christian parochial school for our children to go to. The Jews are smarter than us; they have non-government Jewish schools for all their children. We have none!'

"Well, we have our own schools here, and my parents were able to see them with their own eyes as you see them now. My name is Mr. Super, and you can also address me as Super or Mr. Super, sir. Super is not short for Superman—I have never and will never wear tights or a cape—but I am faster than a speeding bullet, more powerful than a locomotive, that's a fast-track for those of you not up on your ancient history, and able to leap tall buildings in a single bound when it comes to education.

"We all know why you are here. The Pagans did a whole mess of evil to our schools, and you finally woke up from your mentally drunken stupor to save your children and grandchildren. They banned all public prayer, even moments of silence. They banned the Pledge of Allegiance, first with the word God, then the entire thing. They banned hanging up the Ten Commandments. They instituted their so-called comprehensive sex ed—all about mechanics and alternate sexualities, but never morality, responsibility or even basic meaningful relationships. They forced their politics. They forced their bigotry.

"Here in Providence, as in our sister cities of Sanctuary and Restoration, excellence is the driver and education-hungry students are the passengers. Our Education Ten Commandments are as follows: Since boys play the fool when girls are around and girls play the fool when boys are around, thou shall have single-sex schools only from kindergarten to high school. Your dress code is well groomed and in school uniforms; you can wear your Pagan clothes on the weekends when I can't see you. Your parents work, your grandparents worked, school is your work; thou shall work hard five days a week to be the best student you can be, do all your classwork, do all your homework, and master and excel at your own education. Unlike in Tek World, students are not graded simply on sitting in their chairs and looking cute. Grades are based on mastery of the work, achievement through competition. No absenteeism or low standards here. And respect is essential. Students will respect their principals and teachers at all times and listen to their instructions. Teachers and principals will respect their students at all times and challenge them in the classroom. Parents will also fulfill their schooling responsibility. Parents, your responsibility is to make sure your children arrive at school on time, well-fed, properly dressed, homework done, and ready for a full day of schoolwork. Profanity of any kind will not be tolerated by anyone, anywhere on school property or in Providence. That includes 'bitch,' 'bastard,' calling someone by the name of feminine products, and trying to be clever by using new words such as 'frack,' 'fock,' 'shat,' or 'motherfacker.' Paganspeak is an indication of an empty head, because with almost a million words in the English language to choose from, if all you can say is the same ten curse words, you are a moron and need to live with the Pagans where you belong. The only Pagan rule we have here is no crosses around the neck—that's jewelry, and we know students will try to see who can have the biggest cross or the one with the most precious stones. Kids are kids.

"We also are not interested in self-pity of any kind, no whining, no crying; life is not fair, Adam and Eve could have told you that. A commonly read Faither author, whom I don't care for, blames the fall of Faithers on Pagans and homosexuals. I tell you, that is a bunch of rubbish. We were a majority before we were a minority, so that means we had a whole lot of Christians cross over to the dark side for them to get a majority. Whose fault is that? And homosexuals? They've been one to five percent of the general population forever. One to five percent of the population can't get ninety-five to ninety-nine percent of the population to do anything. 'Poly-marriage,' 'pedi-marriage,' 'incesters,' and 'beasties.' Again, your fault. Marriage going from one man and one woman to marriage between anything other than one heterosexual human male above the age of eighteen and one heterosexual human female above the age of eighteen within fifteen years of each other. Destroying the five-thousand-year-old institution of marriage didn't happen all in one day, so if you didn't like it, you could have stopped it at any time. Moreover, it took them less than one hundred years to destroy this country and its God-given freedoms. We—with our pervasive ignorance and inaction—were the co-conspirators, and specifically our Christian population, not knowing our own history, our own values, why we believe what we believe. You can't fight for your faith or your country if you don't even know who you are. The enemy surely does.

"Now, self-esteem here is achieved through hard work and not good feelings. Every year there will be a list of the best academic achievers in the school, and there will be only one grade valedictorian, not fifty. Each day of school starts out with invocation, that's a fancy word for prayer, and then the Pledge of Allegiance, the version with 'under God.' Yes, we hate the governmental regime, but as long as we breathe we will honor the country's existence, because we live in it. So unlike in the Pagan's world, prayer is encouraged and Bibles are plentiful. You'll see mine on my desk always and there is no dust on it. The Ten Commandments are posted on the wall at the main entrance, and you'll even see some crosses on the wall. During our Christian High Holy Days, you'll see the Nativity scene, so we hope you don't suffer 'irreparable harm.' If you say Jesus or God, no storm trooper will arrest you as in Tek World, and no judge will put you in jail. So if you're a Christian offended by any of that, please see me so I can hit you up the side of your head with my Bible. Providence schools are parochial, not secular.

"The goal of Providence education is your mastery of reading, writing, mathematics, history, and current events. We believe the banishment of God from the classroom means exclusion of much of the most important aspects of Western civilization, the American Founding Fathers, the first civil rights movement, the second civil rights movement, the abolitionist movement, and the women's suffrage movement. We also teach theological studies, Christian history, and morality—yes, there is absolute truth and no, everything isn't relative. Albert Einstein, when he found out that his theory of relativity was being smeared over into all kinds of other disciplines, said, 'Relativity applies to physics, not ethics.' We teach economics, finance, government, and tek sciences. We teach ethics, logic, problem solving and critical thinking, responsibility, character, and social etiquette. Our philosophy is abstinence-only; that on-the-circuit, sluts-are-us is good for Pagans, but not us. And unlike Pagan schools, we won't be telling you: 'Your parents don't have to know' or 'If you have trouble with your parents, tell us and we'll handle them.' There will be no daylight between us and your parents. We are following our mandate. Deuteronomy 6:7: And thou shall teach them diligently.

"Students: If after all this learning, you wish to become a lazy bum, then fine. You will be the brightest, most gifted, most tek-savvy, well-bred, classy bum around. Education is exercise for the mind, and a great education helps create great minds. That's it; I'm done. Period. End quotation marks. You can applaud now."

Sitting Room, Moses House
6:00 p.m., 6 January 2089

The new painting hangs in the Sitting Room. The almost three-feet-by-five-feet picture is *The Christian Martyrs' Last Prayer* by the artist Jean-Léon Gérôme, 1883. A majestic painting of Christians; men, woman and children, huddled together praying in a packed Roman coliseum as a lion prepares to pounce and kill them.

Early Christians were greatly persecuted under ancient Rome, first by Emperor Nero in 64 AD (the Apostles Peter and Paul were both killed) and ending after the reign of Emperors Diocletian and finally Galerius with the Edict of Milan in 313 AD by Christian convert Emperor Constantine. Christians had endured some one hundred twenty-nine years of persecution. However, more Christians were killed in the last fifty years of the Roman Empire than in the previous three hundred years.

When General Moses left two nights ago, Mother Moses purposely ended the meeting so that they could go home and reflect on her husband's words. Kristiana had never been interested in district politics and governance in Amish Quarter, but this is altogether different, and the stakes are very high.

Mother Moses has been called away to the secure house for a private call. Everyone sits, waiting, all the visiting religious leaders. Jo-Jo and J.J. are joined by several new young people, the oldest children of these religious leaders. They all sit quietly in the back with Kristiana, obviously as eager to hear the discussion as she is.

Peter and Zoe, the ex-Lutherans, are actually the oldest in the group, but look much, much younger, except for their gray hair. Kristiana has learned that, of all things, these sixty-somethings are "dancing fools," but the phrase is every bit the compliment. They had been dancing champions in tango, salsa, rumba, and ballroom-dancing. Kristiana, of course, has no idea what any of these styles of dance are, since the Amish don't allow dancing in their communities.

"Joshua, do you still have those musical instruments on your e-pad?" Zoe asks.

"Yes, always," Joshua, the ex-Church-of-God-in-Christer says.

"Play us a tune then while we wait," Zoe says as she rises from her chair and grabs the hand of her dozing husband. "Dancing time," she says to him, pulling him up.

Joshua takes out his e-pad and within seconds it is blaring dancing music.

The room is so big that there is plenty of room around the set-up chairs. Zoe and Peter definitely can dance; she does most of the leading at first until Peter wakes up fully.

Dalmatia grabs Thaddeus next. Cyrus leads Phoebe. Within minutes everyone is dancing to the 'Joshua and Charity double e-pad musical extravaganza' before they too join the impromptu dance floor. The kids join in, and Kristiana says "why not" and joins the group to have both Jo-Jo and J.J. show her some moves.

Mother Moses has returned, but no one has seen her. She stands just beyond the threshold of the main door in the very dim light with her arms folded, smiling. No need to interrupt the festivities. Oh, and she'll film Kristiana's first dancing effort for Goth Lila who undoubtedly won't be able to stop laughing.

Secure House, Providence Enclave
11:12 p.m., 6 January 2089

Sek sits in a secure booth with a tiny desk in front of him. The face of General Moses looks up at him from the e-pad screen on the desk.

Sek says, "We confirmed Q1 and Q2."

"All I care about is Q3."

"The reason I broke protocol is that V wants to take care of Q1 for us."

"Why?"

"He said it's a personal matter, but he would owe us if we agreed."

"BG is off-limits, but all other action is approved."

Sek nods. "Out."

The secure sat-link disconnects.

Question 1 (Q1): who killed Elder Mother Esther? Q2: who sent them? Q3: who informed on her and told the killers where to find her? Vincent wants to deal with Q1 personally. The Christians don't know why, but the Vampires are involved in some kind of major schism within the Mormon Order. Bloodgood, however, will be left for the Christians to deal with.

Sitting Room, Moses House
7:15 p.m., 6 January 2089

Mother Moses has started the meeting. The religious leaders are all seated and serious, despite the fun they were having just moments ago.

"We used to call them that name for spite, but now there will be real storm troopers in this country. And Project Purity has been renewed," Mother Moses says. "For the public, they're calling it the Religious Homeland Initiative."

The room is quiet.

"Master Pastor has re-emerged on the public scene. He's organizing Faithers into a new coalition and claims to have signed an iron-clad agreement with Galerius for the safety and amnesty of all Faithers. Amnesty for all crimes. All Faithers will be relocated to the former and expanded Navajo Indian Reservation, covering parts of Arizona, Utah, and New Mexico. The native population of ten thousand will be relocated elsewhere. Faithers will be given full control of the territory and it will be recognized by the government as a sovereign US commonwealth. According to the White House, it will be similar to the creation of Pakistan out of the nation of India or the original two-state divisional plan for a Muslim Palestine and Jewish Israel."

The group starts to laugh from the absurdity of the last sentence.

"The Palestinian Muslims killed Jews and invaded Jewish Israel!"

"Renamed it Palestine Israel and then destroyed it—turned a beautiful country into a barren wasteland."

"If I thought I could learn Spanish at my age, I would go live in Mexico. I think I would rather tolerate the cartels there than this. Their nation is at least majority Christian Catholic."

"I'm sure the fine print of this Religious Homeland deal is that anyone not agreeing will continue to be designated as a terrorist."

"There you have it. This is the something big they've been planning. Jews have called emergency meetings of their enclaves. Hindus and Sikhs, the ones remaining, are mass-exiting to India and the Asian Consortium. Who knows where the Mormon enclaves are located, but they are not even responding. There are no others. The bottom line is it will be just Christians and Jews to bear the brunt of this 'relocation' effort," Mother Moses concludes.

The leaders shake their heads, look at each other, and look at Mother Moses.

Mother Moses says, "We all knew this day would come. It's time to rebuild the Resistance."

The White House
6:30 a.m., 7 January 2089

"At 10:56 p.m. last night, President Fu Wen died of natural causes in the presidential residence of Zhongnanhai. His son Ri Wen succeeded him at a ceremony as of 6 a.m. our time today," the secretary of state says.

President Wilson listens with the joint chiefs assembled around him in the Situation Room.

"As you know, former President Wen had allowed the formation of opposition parties. Never any real power or any real threat to the government, just official gadflies of the government, within the government. The new President Wen gathered them all for the funeral ceremony and had all them executed on the grounds. Over four hundred people."

Everyone looks at each other. President Wilson doesn't take his eyes off the secretary.

The chairman of the joint chiefs of staff says, "Mr. President, as of thirty minutes ago, CHIN troops began massing along their border with the Russian Bloc."

Everyone is concerned.

"It's a ruse," President Wilson says calmly.

"Excuse me, sir?" a general says.

"It's a ruse. He allowed these opposition parties to exist and grow a bit so that his son could do this very thing when it was time to succeed him. This military move against the Russian Bloc—there will be no invasion. With Wen, it was always a game of chess and diversion. Make your opponent look to the left as you do something on the right. This is not the move. They are doing something else that they don't want us to know about. Elevate the threat level immediately."

"Yes, sir," the general says.

President Wilson turns to the secretary of state. "Has the Russian Bloc asked for assistance?"

"No sir."

"Then get on the line and offer it. Even if we don't mean it, we have to play the game like the good superpower we are." To an aide, he says, "Is everyone assembled?"

"Yes, sir," the aide says. "They are all in the Oval Office."

The president returns to the Oval Office. They are already waiting: the homeland director, his presidential advisor, the senior advisor, chief law enforcement advisor, and military leaders.

"Deploy the storm troopers," President Wilson says.

"Is deadly force authorized against any violent resistance?" a general asks.

"I expect it to be avoided. But, yes. Authorized," President Wilson says.

Australia
2:12 p.m., 10 January 2089

Edison Blair races frantically across the open plain. He looks back, then starts to sprint again, almost tripping and falling. He is starting to pick up his stride when he is hit by a projectile. The boomerang knocks him off his feet. The Aborigine approaches him, another boomerang in his left hand ready to be thrown. Edison, a man of high tek, is caught by a group of primitives.

Edison is tied up with rope and a jeep is used to drive him back to town. His three captors take him to one of the shacks. A group of men are talking, with American accents, clustered around vehicles.

He is sat down in a chair, where he waits. It feels like a dream, and he's shocked by how fearful he is. Anything could happen. He imagines how his friends and family must have felt at the time of the Fall of Western Europe, those not killed immediately. This can't be happening. This is the latter part of the twenty-first century, damnit! It's the civilized world.

"Good morning, Mr. Edison," the voice says. Edison doesn't answer. "I don't know why you were running from my Aborigine colleagues. If they wanted to kill you, you wouldn't have even seen them coming. And they've already saved your life once before."

"What do you mean?" Edison asks.

"The rendition team that was sent to capture and transport you back to America for secret trial, conviction and life imprisonment for the attempted leaking of classified national security material on the Net. They killed the team to protect you."

Edison looks at him. "Who are you?"

"I believe you Pagans call us Jew-Christians," the man says.

Edison perks up. "I'm on your side then. They killed my friend because of the story he was going to break on the American president. I data-dumped it, but it was blocked somehow. I realized I was being hunted almost as soon as I arrived. I didn't think they could get to me here."

"Everyone has covert operatives in every territory on the planet. Everyone," he says. "We did manage, however, to get the full Data Stream that you attempted to upload."

"How?"

"We have tek-lords too, Mr. Edison. The tek-lord who gave it to your man Logan, also gave it to us."

"Good, then you have to use it! Dump it on the Net! Stab that bloody bastard T. Wilson. We may not be able to topple his administration, but you can cause such chaos that it will take him years to recover, if ever."

"Such anti-Wilson sentiments from a Pagan."

"He killed my friend. Frankly, I want him dead, but I'll settle for this."

"We need your help then."

Edison looks at him. "Me? You have all the dynamite you need in the story."

"One must know *where* to place the dynamite to have the most explosive impact. My people tell me you are the best journalistic dynamite expert in the world."

Edison smiles. "In exchange for what?"

"In exchange for transport to a place where no one can ever find you again."

"Where on earth would that be?"

"Among your most favorite people in the world."

Edison looks at him for a moment as he's thinking. "A ridiculous notion just popped into my mind, but it couldn't be what you are suggesting. If those people start with the letter 'm,' then this conversation is over."

"Mr. Edison, they have your psychological profile. They know how much you hate Muslims. Caliphate territory is the one place they would never look for you. Russian Bloc, Asian Consortium, and CHIN, but not there."

"But the Muslims are killing your people now in Africa. Look what they did in Jewish Israel. I would expect you to hate them as much as I."

"We do, Mr. Edison, but not all of them. The Muslims are more…diverse than you imagine. There are anti-Caliphate groups in existence."

"Impossible."

"It's true, but obviously the Caliphate doesn't want anyone to know about it," the man says. "We'll get you to a secure location in Caliphate territory. As I said, everyone has covert operatives in every territory on the planet. New flat—I believe that's the word you English use—new identity, and you'd be able to even secretly run your media empire from there."

Edison says, "They killed my friend over this story."

"No, they put out the kill-order *before* he finished the story. It was something else he stumbled on."

"What? No, it was the story. Even if they wanted him dead before the story was done, they knew he was going to finish it."

"We feel there's much more to it. We need his full itinerary and a list of everyone he talked to so we can be thorough. It was something else they were scared of. Many, many people knew of Project Purify. We all already know about it, for years in fact. Only the general public didn't know."

Edison shakes his head. "You knew already? Something else? What could it be? Okay, I'll get you the list and tell you what to do with the story. This is a superpower, not an individual or group. Only a superpower can destroy a superpower."

"Or themselves," the man interjects.

"All we can really do is hurt them. Nothing more. What's your name, anyway?"

"People call me General Moses."

"Let's do some plotting then and blow him a kiss to show how much we love the maggot."

Hotel Residences, Neo-Orleans, Louisiana
7:07 p.m., 15 January 2089

A Vampire walks down the hallway carrying a bottle-bag of blood-juice. He hears the beep of the elevator opening, but doesn't look back as he turns the corner. He's hungry and tired.

The elevator opens and three people step out—the first is a man dressed in a tan office-suit, but on his head is an astronaut's helmet with a large mirrored front; with him on either side are two men dressed in black, wearing white masks.

The Vampire is standing in the kitchenette of his hotel room pouring the blood-juice into a large glass, when the fire alarms sound.

"Fire alarm has been activated! Please evacuate your room immediately and proceed down the nearest staircase to the lobby for safety!" the computer voice says. The message repeats.

This is a common trick that even he has used in the past to get someone out of a room. He grabs his gun from his shoulder holster, slowly walks to his door, and touches the small vid-screen on the door to activate the vid-cam view. People are moving quickly through the halls to the elevators. Maybe it is a legitimate fire alarm, but he is still suspicious.

The sounds of people have faded to silence. He opens the door slowly and peeks his head out and looks both ways—no one to be seen. The message is repeating outside too, and the hallway lights are still flashing. He aims his gun as he walks to the elevator and touches the button. If the elevator doesn't take him down to the lobby, then the fire alarm is real.

The elevator opens, and he walks in and turns as the doors close. But there is no motion downward. The alarm is real. The door opens again. *The astronaut runs in and immediately shoots him with a wireless taser.* The Vampire's body starts to convulse violently.

The astronaut grabs his shoulders and head-butts him. But the helmet doesn't bang the Vampire's head and the mirrored face plate doesn't shatter; the Vampire screams as it envelops his entire head. The elevator doors close again. The Vampire lies on the floor, shaking, and the astronaut is revealed to be Vincent of the Mormon Order. The elevator doors open again, and the two other masked men appear and grab the Vampire, whose entire head is encased in a silver cocoon. They drag him away along the floor. Vincent exits the elevator too, and they disappear as it closes again.

Hotel Residence, Alexandria, Virginia
11:05 a.m., 27 January 2089

Bloodgood yells in his ear-set, "My men are disappearing! We've been compromised! I don't need you to investigate to tell me what's going on! I know what's going on! We've been compromised and they're knocking off all my men, one by one! Shut up, you useless bag of blood, and get people over here now!"

The Vampire special ops leader stands in the empty public bathroom of his hotel residence. The door opens and a man starts to enter, but stops in his tracks shocked to see Bloodgood pointing a large gun at him.

"Get out of here now! Go use the tree outside!"

The man runs out of the bathroom. Bloodgood knows that this is probably not the best place to have a stand-off; there are no good exits. He heads for the door and peeks out slowly.

Bloodgood walks through the main lobby towards the underground parking lot. He hears screams and ducks without thinking. Bullets hit the door as he opens it. He runs down the stairs to the underground parking—his attackers are already here! He jumps over the rail and down to the next landing. Staying low, he scrambles out the door to the P-1 level of the underground parking, only to dodge the bullets of another gunman. He dives to the ground and rolls under a vehicle. The shots stop, but he hears the door he just passed through open, and he sees three sets of feet run out.

At least here he will be have plenty of places for a secure shooting site with multiple exit points until back-up arrives, but how long will that be?

He rolls out and fires rapidly at the three gunman; they fall, dead. Another gunman begins firing again, and the shots are getting closer. Bloodgood rolls under the car again as more shots ring out and then more. There must be at least two other gunmen—and then there is such a flurry of gunfire at the very car he's hiding under that he thinks there may be no fewer than six.

He hears gunshots from a whole new location, and suddenly the shots that were aimed at his hiding spot are being directed elsewhere. He hears voices cry out, people obviously shot. Then it all stops.

"Bloodgood!" a man's voice yells. "Are you there? We're your back-up detail. Contact HQ for confirmation."

Bloodgood is already reaching for his e-pad when a call comes in. He touches his ear-set and the same idiot he was yelling at before is on the line again.

"Mr. Bloodgood, we've sent two agents to your site, and they are there now. Confirmation pics attached."

Bloodgood doesn't answer him. He looks at his e-pad to see the pictures of the two agents: Agent Lariat and Agent Runningstar. He disconnects the line as he rolls out from the car. His bionic eyes can see no one else, and he calls out: "I'm here!"

Agent Lariat appears first and runs to him. Agent Runningstar follows, aiming her gun in the opposite direction to cover the rear.

"Are you okay, sir?" Agent Lariat asks.

"Are you all that they sent?"

"Sir, we have twelve storm troopers outside securing the entire perimeter. Effective as of now, we are your personal detail."

"I don't need bodyguards, I need men. Have any of my team

survived?"

"No, they're all lying in the morgue. No pulse or brainwave patterns, but you Vampires can do that," Agent Runningstar says, half-laughing.

"I'm not amused by your joking."

"Then get up off the ground and let's get you to a secure location," Agent Runningstar says.

"Get Homeland on the line now! How did the Jew-Christians identify my men and our locations? We have a damn leak!"

"Sir, understand that wherever you go, we go," Agent Lariat says. "This situation is a lot more serious than Jew-Christian terrorists neutralizing your current team. They've leaked a story into the Vampire community about something called Project Purify."

"What about it?"

"That the government plans to round up all Jew-Christians in the country—and all Vampires," Agent Lariat says.

"Vampires won't be touched!"

"And that a Vampire named Bloodgood, you, will be the appointed overseer of this new Vampire ghetto."

Bloodgood laughs. "The Jew-Christians are trying to get my own people to hurt me."

Agent Runningstar walks up to him and looks him in the eyes. "What kind of brain damage do you have? Look around, idiot. *The gunmen who just tried to kill you are all Vampires!*"

The Oval Office, The White House
9:55 a.m., 7 January 2089

President Wilson sits watching the broadcasts on the vidscreen with his staff. The media frenzy says that a war looms between the CHIN under its new leader and the Russian Bloc.

"Mr. President, the forces sent into action reached their targets an hour ago. They're encircling the Jew-Christian ghettoes. As you know, sir, they have all kinds of tek jammers, so it's hard to get real-time vid links, but we'll have audio confirmation soon," the chief law enforcement advisor says.

They hear a commotion outside. A female aide is let in by

Secret Service.

"Mr. President!" The woman seems frantic.

President Wilson rises from his chair. "What's wrong?"

"Our forces killed his son! At one of those Jew-Christian ghettoes."

"What? Who's son?"

"Governor Chauncey's son!" she says.

New Hampshire Governor's Mansion
10:00 a.m., 10 January 2089

Storm trooper forces arrived at the Christian enclave of Purity in New Jersey at 9:00 a.m. and were immediately met by gunfire. After twenty minutes of gunfire exchange, the enclave stopped to say that one person had been killed. The person was identified as twenty-two year-old Jorgen Chauncey, the youngest son of New Hampshire Governor Chauncey—not only the most influential governor in the nation, but the most vocal antagonist of the president since Wilson was first elected nine years ago.

Governor Chauncey faces the reporters at the hastily set-up press conference in front of the New Hampshire Governor State Building. His eyes and face are red with anger.

"Yes, my youngest son was a Jew-Christian, but *that* didn't give forces of the President of the United States the right to murder him! And he was murdered!"

The press conference goes on for some forty minutes. The governor yells, cries, and makes charges of conspiracies against him and his family. Every question from a reporter starts a new line of rants from him.

The president watches the press conference on the vid-screen with his senior advisors in the Oval Office.

"What's the fall-out from this?" President Wilson asks.

"We should have told him about re-activating Project Purify," the senior advisor says.

"What can he do?"

"Mr. President, he's already done it."

"What are you talking about?"

"He's split the Supreme Senate and is taking Vermont, Maine, Rhode Island, Connecticut, Minnesota, and Wisconsin to join New Hampshire to form what they're calling the new Northern Confederacy. Those states control key military bases and installations and our North American Grid control hubs."

Wilson seethes with anger. He looks to his communications director.

"I want a list on my desk at close of business of everyone working in this administration who has biological, adopted, or conjugal family or relatives who are confirmed Jew-Christians."

"Mr. President?" Communications Director Frinos asks.

"You heard me."

Frinos is somewhat stunned by the request. "Mr. President, we shouldn't go down that path. We have a lot of loyal people on the team. They shouldn't be tarnished because of parents, offspring or relatives."

"'The unfettered ability of the state to manage its people requires the purging of the Jew-Christians, as they represent the largest bloc of voters and netizens unsupportive of the state.' 'We can make a more perfect union by this purge of religiosity and its adherents, resulting in an ordered nation which will be a nation-state that as closely resembles paradise as humanly possible.' Who said that, Mr. Frinos?"

Frinos swallows hard. "I did."

"Then go do what I told you to do."

The White House
1 February 2089

At 6:00 a.m. EST, news breaks out from the Supreme Islamic Caliphate that President Wilson had his own staffer Lucifer Mestopheles killed back in January of 2089, mere months after being re-elected for a third term. On every media channel in the Caliphate are the audio tapes of Lucifer speaking and the vid of the two assassins. The Islamic press states Wilson killed the man because Mestopheles wanted to normalize friendly relations with the Caliphate and that Wilson went mad, hateful of anything Islam. The reasons are a lie, but the data files broadcasting everywhere are authentic—files that were supposed to have been permanently deleted.

President Wilson sits behind his desk, shaking his head. All of his senior advisors stand in front of him.

"You all are killing me," Wilson says. "I have a man, a sitting governor, who's telling everyone who'll listen that the president of the United States, me, killed his son. This man is going to be an enemy of this administration for life. The man has gotten a handful of governors, but key to the nation, to join him in breaking away from the Supreme Senate, claiming that the fourth branch of government is run by my personal puppets, which means the Supreme Senate is now going to do everything the opposite of what I want just to prove him wrong. I have one of this nation's greatest enemies, the Caliphate, having a field day with charges that I killed my own national campaign manager, senior advisor, and friend, and they're using our own secret, classified data files. Now I have to face his parents. They may be in their nineties, but they could still sink this entire administration. On the foreign political front, we have a new Chinese president and a possible CHIN-Russian Bloc war. Even if it isn't war, we could still have a lot of people dead. I still feel the CHINs are up to something else against us, but now I have to deal with all this." The president shakes his head again. "I need a team that protects this office and I don't feel it's this team."

"Mr. President," the chief law enforcement advisor says, "the governor's son was the only one who was killed at the incident, no one else. Our men on the field feel that it could have been purposely staged so he could be killed."

"Is that what I'm supposed to tell the governor? Tell the media? His son jumped in front of a bullet—our bullet—on purpose? He's saying that we picked this one Jew-Christian ghetto out of the hundreds and hundreds in the country because it happened to have his son. You want me to say back to him that his son killed himself and not us?"

The chief says nothing more.

"And now I find out that our great Vampire black ops team has been virtually wiped out."

Homeland Director McDunn says, "We've already put together a new team. The leader is housed at a secure location with two personal bodyguards and an army of security."

"Weren't they at secure locations before?"

"Yes, sir," she says with hesitation. "We must have a leak."

Wilson says, "A leak. In the most powerful office in the land."

Homeland says, "Mr. President, it couldn't possibly be anyone here. Someone on a lower level. We'll find them."

"I want Governor Chauncey and this new Northern Confederacy monitored around the clock."

"Yes, sir," Homeland answers.

"What's the situation on the CHIN's war action with the Russian Bloc?"

The secretary of state says, "Mr. President, they have tanks stationed on the borders and jets in the air. War is a fifty-fifty prospect at this point. I also had a call from the Russian Bloc consulate asking us to publicly condemn the action. That's a big step, sir. They would only do that if they were sure of an attack."

"Then tell them I will make a public statement against the CHINs. Get it set up for the next thirty minutes. Do it now."

"Yes, sir." The secretary leaves the Oval Office.

"Do you have that list for me?" the president asks Frinos.

"Yes, sir."

"Who in this room is on that list?"

Frinos's face turns red. "Just one."

The president looks at him. "We'll talk tomorrow morning. You can go now."

Frinos turns and leaves the Office.

"What's that about?" the senior advisor asks.

"Nothing," the president says. "Everyone please leave, except you two." He points to the senior advisor and his presidential advisor.

Everyone else leaves the room.

"Did we kill Lucifer?" the senior advisor asks when the door closes.

"Lucifer was attempting to sell classified material to foreign agents," the president's advisor answers.

"Why would he do that? It makes no sense."

"That's what happened," President Wilson says. "I feel right now that a giant game of chess is being played with me and I'm on the losing side." He stares at him for a moment. "Tell me as soon as you come up with something on the CHINs."

"Yes, sir." The senior advisor pauses on his way out. He knows that the president has already decided to fire him. He closes the door.

The president says, "Tell me about these traitor reporters again."

"The surviving one was in Australia, sir, but has disappeared completely. We sent two teams there, but both have also disappeared."

Wilson angrily shakes his head. "Who killed the original reporter?"

"We did, sir," the president's advisor says. "Action was pre-approved because he stumbled onto Project New People."

The president looks at him. "Is there any way possible that those files can be accessed?"

"None. They are housed in a secret underground server that must be manually connected to the Net for access, and even then it has our most advanced firewall and log-on security protocols. No one can access it unless you personally authorize it."

"People keep telling me that this isn't possible and that isn't possible, but somehow it always manages to be possible."

"No, sir. Not this time. It has to be physically connected to access."

"Are there any other ways?"

"No sir. Unless they walk into one of our body farms and just happen to poke around in the right place. But they could only do that with the proper authorizations. Sir, it's all very secure. No one will go looking for it, because no one knows it exists."

"They learned about Project Purify somehow when no one knew about it. Our other black box projects must not be compromised. I'm only in my third term and it's all unraveling. The

Caliphate has our top-secret American data files. Our top secret black ops team has been all but neutralized. We have a high-level leak in the center of my administration. We killed a sitting governor's son, my chief political rival. The CHINs are plotting against us. I need to start firing people, too much sloppiness and incompetence."

"Mr. President, I know you don't want to hear this because you think it will mean surrendering, but you have to shelve the Purify Project again until this settles down. Keep the smaller ops going, but the big, public displays…you can't politically afford this now. Also, you need to publicly distance yourself from all this. You're the president, not Homeland anymore. You need to be president, not micro-managing black ops. When you went from the Office of Finance to Homeland, you didn't keep showing up there to crunch numbers. You left that behind. You understood it. You knew the questions to ask, but that wasn't your role anymore. Let your staff do their work. That's what we're here for, what I'm here for. You need to stay above it all, in case things go wrong."

"Nothing should go wrong," President Wilson says.

"Sir, this is the real world. You were the one who told me that things always go wrong in this office."

"Make sure the black ops team has what it needs."

"Sir, let me deal with the team with Homeland. We'll handle everything. Stay above it all."

The president considers his words. "I don't believe in coincidences," he says. "I know they are behind all of this."

"Sir, we'll handle the Jew-Christians."

"I expect you to do a lot more than handle them."

"Of course, sir."

Guess Who's Coming to Passover Seder Dinner

"The ignorance of one voter in a democracy impairs the security of all." – John F. Kennedy, 35th President of the United States

"Freedom is never more than one generation away from extinction." – Ronald W. Reagan, 40th President of the United States

Jewish Israel
9:47 a.m., 3 July 2059

The tour group switched from their bright, cheery white bus to an armored, dark-gray bus in Old Jerusalem and was off to Bethlehem. Whether it was spontaneous silliness or drinking too much the night before, the group has decided to create their own travel songs. Both their Jewish tour guide and Muslim bus driver also can't stop laughing.

"We're going to Bethlehem in a bullet-proof bus! That's right, that's right!"

The trip to the birth city of Jesus goes by fast. Especially popular is Sikh Bob teaching everyone to sing the same song in Hindi after the Tovas' funny attempts to teach everyone to sing it in Hebrew.

When they do arrive, it is jarring to have read about this holy city for so long and to finally see it as it is now, with high, graffiti-painted steel walls, armed checkpoints and a scarce, poor Muslim population—all remaining Christians left decades ago.

It is on this trip the Moseses and Tovas began their friendship.

Tek World did away with Christmas a long time ago—banning the word Christmas and anything associated with it: nativity scenes, red poinsettias, Christmas trees, and parades; then incredibly (or ridiculously), Santa Claus, Frosty the Snowman, and Rudolph the Red-nosed Reindeer; then the holiday itself; and finally even the word "holiday" (which means "holy day") because it was religious and therefore unconstitutional. Any religiosity is unconstitutional, which became the legal grounds to find even the US Constitution unconstitutional. This included any displays of Judaism, including saying "happy Hanukah" and lighting menorahs. But for Jews, their holidays are primarily a private family and community affair, so the Pagan purging of their holiday was not hard felt. The later weeks of the year are now considered Solstice time by the Pagans, the last public display of unbridled consumerism before the New Year.

Among Christians, Christmas, the birth of Jesus Christ, had been as controversial from its beginnings as it was in its final abandonment in America. Jesus was not born on December 25th, though both Catholics and Protestants celebrated that date for centuries. That can be inferred by date calculations from the reading of the Bible and the fact that the story of the birth suggests a time of season other than winter—the arduous journey from Nazareth to Bethlehem, shepherds with flocks in the open field; the Eastern Orthodox celebrated January 6th as the holy day, which was not much better.

Early Christians were unconcerned by the birth of Christ because they felt He would soon return. Early Christian leaders chose December 25th to lure new followers to Christianity from the Pagan multi-day holiday of Saturnalia, December 17th to December 23rd, the festival in honor of their god Saturn, where slaves were masters and masters were slaves for a day. It also overlapped with their winter solstice holiday of December 21st celebrating their sun god being reborn as the days began to get longer.

Christmas was hated by the early Protestant Reformers: Martin Luther hated saints and holidays, not because they were

Catholic, but because they were not specifically in the text of the Bible. English Puritans went so far as to make the holiday illegal and viewed it as Pagan and unchristian. American Puritans felt it dishonored Christ and said the Bible stated no such holiday besides the Sabbath, and the festival associated with the holiday was more of hell than the Son of God.

After the American Civil War, with the large Catholic immigration that followed, Christmas began to find universal favor, becoming a federal holiday in 1870 and the perennial staple of American life. The final war against Christmas came again not from Christians, as in the past, but from the new Pagans of America leading to its legal abolishment.

The debate among Christian historians never ended as to the true day of the birth of Jesus. If not December 25th when? September 29th, May 20th, May 28th, April, October, March? The Rebirth Movement settled the argument. As one historian said, "American Protestants went from being more Catholic to being more Jewish."

Moses Home, Providence
2:35 p.m., Saturday, 26 March 2089

"First Sunday in March?" Kristiana says with a perplexed look.

The house is a beehive of coordinated chaos, with Mother Moses, her daughters, their husbands, her son, and Kristiana getting everything ready for their guests.

"That seems strange," she says. "Then what is December 25th?"

"Gift Day," J.J. says. "My favorite."

Mother Moses shoots him a disapproving look as he smiles back at her.

"Jesus is the reason for the season," Mother Moses says.

"Do all Protestants do the same?" Kristiana asks.

"Now, yes," Mother Moses says. "I'm surprised the Amish celebrate Christmas on that day coming out of the Radical Reformation."

"Why did you pick March?" she asks.

"For the same reason early Christians picked December 25th—political. Since we don't know the exact day, we chose a date before Easter. First Sunday of March to kick off our Christian High Holy Days, which end with Easter—the first Sunday of April, this year," Mother Moses says. "The Pagans legally destroyed the day for us, but long before that Santa Claus and Christmas toys hijacked the day from Jesus." She looks at J.J. "We needed a month where we can focus on God, worship, prayer, biblical study, and reflection without any worldly distractions."

"Mom, I like gifts *and* Jesus!" he says.

She looks at him and stops.

"I mean Jesus and gifts."

She takes her hands off her hips and starts working again.

"What is tonight's dinner all about? I don't think I've ever met Jews," Kristiana says.

"They're good friends from before my kids were born. We met on an inter-faith tour trip to Jewish Israel. I wasn't even married to Moses yet."

Jada says, "Now that's a long time ago."

"It's a Jewish and Christian tradition. Passover Seder dinner," M continues.

Passover celebrates the liberation of the Israelites from slavery in Egypt. Jews celebrate liberation from slavery; Christians celebrate liberation from the slavery of sin at Communion, the meaning of the Lord's Supper. The Seder, pronounced say-der, is a holiday of tradition and ritual to teach the joint history of Jews and Christians by eating special foods.

Christians of the past viewed Passover as an outdated Jewish holiday that was replaced by Easter, but modern Christians view it as a Bible-commanded holiday and a memorial day to celebrate God's ongoing work of deliverance. To many, the message of the historic deliverance from slavery is as powerful as the daily deliverance from sin.

For Jews, it is one of the most powerful of the traditional holidays, with the Seder being made up of fifteen specific steps which are each followed to completion. The Passover Seder is not a meaningless annual ritual, but calls for the Jewish People to become free people, defeat evil and enslavement, build a more perfect world, and become closer to God.

"You know what I think, M?" Kristiana says. "I think this Passover dinner is actually a ruse to talk about secret things so that none of us are aware of it."

Mother Moses smiles. "Kristiana, soon you'll be so wise that a person will have to start a whole year in advance to be able to fool you. And then only for a second or two."

The High Holy Days for Christians also included Palm Sunday, the Sunday before Easter, recognizing the entry of Christ into Jerusalem, and Good Friday, the Friday before Easter, recognizing the Passion (suffering) and crucifixion of Christ on the cross. Some also recognize Ash Wednesday in February, forty days prior to Easter, a day of fasting, self-examination, and preparation for Easter, and New Advent, a two-week spiritual preparation for the arrival of Christmas. For Jews, their High Holy Days begin with Rosh Hashanah, the Jewish New Year, which includes special prayers and Psalm 27 added to the morning and evening prayers; the Ten Days of Repentance to follow; and finally Yom Kippur, the Day of Atonement, which is a devoted to prayer, repentance, and fasting.

The Tovas and their family arrived after 5:00 p.m. Tova Ben-Hurin is in her forties, her honey-brown hair pulled back in a ponytail. Her brown eyes match her simple but elegant tan-brown dress suit. Mr. Tova (no one calls him Mr. Ben-Hurin) is the same age, brown eyes, balding, tan skin, and very muscular, strong, confident. He wears a light tan suit. With them are their children: their eldest son with his wife and three small children, their second-eldest son with his pregnant wife, their daughter with her fiancé, and their two youngest sons.

Both families graciously greet each other and afterwards naturally drift into smaller groups, spread out, standing in the living room and kitchen. The Tovas and Mother Moses, the two elder Tova sons and their wives with Jada and her husband, the middle Tova daughter and Jo-Jo with their fiancés, the next youngest Tova son and J.J., and the small children take to running around the house. They are all so loud—talking and laughing.

"Kristiana," Mother Moses calls.

"These are my good friends, Mr. and Mrs. Tova."

"You are Jews?" Kristiana asks.

"Yes," Tova says.

"My Amish community hasn't been in contact with Jews for a long time," Kristiana says. "What do Jews and Christians have in common again?"

"That Jewish guy Jesus," Mr. Tova says. They laugh.

Kristiana spends time mostly with Mother Moses and the Tovas, but manages to drift into other groups to get the full flavor of the different conversations.

"How can you have that many?" Kristiana asks.

"It's the Torah. Your Old Testament. Jews have six-hundred and thirteen laws or commandments."

"Are all Jews the same?"

The Tovas laugh. "Absolutely not," Tova says. "We have different groups just like Christians, just not as many."

"There are Jews who can't stand Jewish religiosity and are very uncomfortable with it. There are some who don't think Tova and I are religious enough," Mr. Tova says.

"What does that small, flat hat that some Jews wear mean?" Kristiana asks.

Mr. Tova says, "It's called a kippah or yarmulke. Non-orthodox Jewish men wear it only at synagogue. Orthodox Jewish men wear it always. It is to remind us simply that God is above."

Other members of the Tova family ask Kristiana about the Amish, her people and her community. She learns as much as she can about the different Orders in Judaism.

Mr. Tova at one point comes out of the bathroom and says, "God, thank you for putting the holes in our bodies or we'd be in big trouble!"

Kristiana bursts out laughing.

"Let's eat," Mr. Tova says.

"Did you bring it this time?" J.J. asks.

"Oh yes," he says. "I hid it on the porch." Mr. Tova steps out on the front porch and comes back in with something wrapped in a blanket. He opens it to reveal a two-foot ivory ram's horn.

"What is that?" Kristiana asks.

"This, Kristiana the Amish gentlelady, is a *shofar*," Mr. Tova says. "It is used in the Jewish High Holy tradition of Rosh Hashanah, the Jewish New Year. We blow it at the end of morning and evening prayers during the weekday, except for the evening of first day. And when we come to visit J.J. at our annual Passover Seder dinner get-togethers."

He puts the ram's horn to his lips and blows—the thunderous sound ripples throughout the house, bringing all the little children running to him, smiling. Kristiana laughs.

"I like that," she says.

Two hours go by quickly with the many conversations in the house. By 7:00 p.m., the group is in the dining room as Mother Moses and her daughters start bringing the various dishes to the table from the kitchen.

"The agreements go back awhile," Tova says.

Kristiana asks, "What things were agreed upon?"

"Well, I have a good friend and rabbi who got two groups called Jews for Jesus and Messianic Jews to stop calling themselves that and call themselves, big drum roll please, Christians." Kristiana smiles. "Jews as whole stopped with the obsolete distinctions of religious Jew and secular Jew—you're either a Jew, which itself means religious, or a Pagan, non-religious. The Mormons only refer to themselves as Mormons, not Christians. The whole Faither conversations were just to get everyone on the same page. Address those little annoyances. The Christian word 'crusade' is not a positive word in Judaism. All Christians are not Catholics, as many Jews believed for a long time, not that there's anything wrong with Catholics. It was just a group inter-faith dialog that became something more."

"Do you all live in enclaves too?" Kristiana asks.

"Let's all sit down," Tova says. Kristiana realizes that she has asked something of a more sensitive nature. "Kristiana, what holidays do the Amish celebrate?"

"We celebrate Holy Communion twice a year. Christmas, Easter, Good Friday and some Amish, like mine, Old Christmas on January 6th, which is also called the Epiphany, when the wise men brought gifts to Jesus."

Everyone is now seated.

Mother Moses says, "We are all very thankful to have our good friends here for our annual special time. The Tovas with their children and grandchildren. The day that both Jews and Christians consider part of their High Holy Days. Last year they hosted us in their wonderful *shtetal* in Alabama. This year we host, and we've been alternating for the last twelve years.

"Thirty-three hundred years ago was the Exodus of the Israelites from Egypt led by the original Moses, a transformation of God's Chosen People from slavery to the nation-state of Israel. God helped His people escape slavery in Egypt by inflicting ten plagues upon the Egyptians, forcing Pharaoh to release the Israelites. The Exodus was the first massive Jewish immigration to Israel.

"Passover is the holiday that commemorates the Jewish People who were 'passed over' by the Angel of Death. It is celebrated on the 15th of the Jewish month of Nissan, the month of miracles like the parting of the Red Sea, Jacob wrestling the Angel, Daniel in the lion's den. Monotheism, the Sabbath, the Ten Commandments, repentance, and Passover are all Jewish gifts to humanity. Jews have been rightly perceived as the messengers of liberty as a God-given, natural right and equality before the law.

"Passover inspired no lesser people than the Pilgrims, the Puritans and the Founding Fathers of this nation. Those Founding Americans viewed themselves as the modern day People of the Covenant, King George III was the modern Pharaoh, the Atlantic Ocean was the modern-day Red Sea, and America was the modern-day Promised Land.

"It is said that when Pharaoh freed the Israelites, they left in such a hurry that they did not wait for their bread dough to rise. In commemoration, for the duration of Passover, no leavened bread is eaten, which is why the holiday is also called the Festival of the Unleavened Bread, and matzah—flat, unleavened bread—is a symbol of the holiday.

"Let's pray."

Mother Moses turns it over to Mr. Tova, who says a prayer in

Hebrew. Kristiana doesn't know what he's saying, but she realizes everyone else does and that the prayer is a good one. He looks at Mother Moses and she ends:

"In Psalm 33:12 it says, blessed is the nation whose God is Lord," she says.

"Amen," everyone says.

Time to eat! The Passover Seder plate, Kristiana learns, has a special traditional meaning: three pieces of matzah; a shank bone, a piece of roasted meat, or bone of a lamb representing the special sacrifice on the eve of the Exodus from Egypt; a hard-boiled egg representing the holiday offering in the days of the Holy Temple; *maror* or bitter herbs, often horseradish, commemorating the bitterness of the slavery of their forefathers; the *haroset* paste, a mixture of apples, cinnamon, sugar, and nuts resembling the mortar and brick made by the Jews when they worked for Pharaoh; the *karpas*—a vegetable such as parsley, celery, or potato dipped in saltwater—to commemorate the grueling work of the Jews as slaves; and lettuce representing their bitter enslavement. Wine is also consumed during the course of the meal.

Candles are lit by Mother Moses and the rest of the dinner ritual proceeds. Prayers are recited and Bible verses are read before each item of food on the plate is eaten and everyone drinks from their glass of wine—the children's favorite since they are forbidden to drink wine most days of the year.

Mr. Tova and his first grandchild continue with the ritual.

"Why do we eat unleavened bread at this special meal?" the grandson asks.

"It is written in Exodus 12:17 that we celebrate the Feast of the Unleavened Bread because it was on this very day that God brought our people out of Egypt. We celebrate this day as a lasting ordinance for the generations to come," Mr. Tova recites. "When Pharaoh let us go from Egypt, we ran so quickly that there was not enough time to let the bread rise and bake it."

The Tovas enact the rest of ritual. Tova then says: "We lived, our enemies tried to kill us, God killed them, and we lived. Let's eat."

Kristiana laughs. She learns there are all-Jewish Seders dinners and all-Christian Seders, but quite common now were the joint Jewish and Christian ones. She finds the entire dinner fascinating and more like a play with different members of the Tova and Moses families playing their parts in the ritual.

The ritual may be over, but the night is far from it.

"What is a shtetal?" Kristiana asks.

Tova smiles. "One of our Jewish enclaves. It actually means little Jewish town in Yiddish, a tight knit community. Most Jewish enclaves are cities too, but not walled up like Christian ones. Though that will change very soon."

"Why haven't you done the same thing?"

"It's a historic thing. In ancient Europe, Jews were put in walled ghettoes, segregated away from everyone. By the Catholics of the time, or dark Christians as both Jews and Christians call them now. By the Muslims who had us in their version of ghettoes called *mellahs* in Northern Africa for four hundred years. By the Nazis.

"Many Jewish Orders have resisted walling up our enclaves too because some have seen it as a return to the mellahs or skin-color segregation times. But the fact is we've had our own Jewish communities for centuries in America, most of that by choice. We left the public schools behind decades before Christians. We left the public colleges and universities for different reasons: their bigoted BDS to BAJ campaigns by Pagans and Muslims."

Mr. Tova answers before Kristiana can ask the question. "BDS were boycott-divestment-sanction campaigns that colleges and universities had against what they called evil countries, but the only country in the world that they used them against was Jewish Israel. So it really was a BAJ campaign: Boycott All Jews."

Kristiana shakes her head. "There's so much I don't know about the world."

He smiles. "I've been on the planet a lot longer, and I still don't know anything."

"Well, that's what the pre-New-America Catholics and Muslims did," Tova continues.

"Why did the Catholics do that to Jews? I know about the others," Kristiana says.

"Simple. We weren't Christians."

Mother Moses says, "Christians at that time were very different from early Christians and modern-day ones. They saw the Crucifixion as tragedy rather than triumph. Obviously, they never actually read the Bible."

"So you call them dark Christians?" Kristiana asks.

"Yes, the Christians who did bad things to Jews," Tova says. "And bad things to Christians."

"They led to the Reformation and the Radical Reformation and us—Mennonites and the Amish," Kristiana says.

"Yes, they did," Tova says.

"What do you think, M?" Kristiana asks.

"They were very bad. Everyone universally agrees—Protestant, Catholic, all. That's why the land they occupied is cursed and gave us two world wars and will most likely give us a third," Mother Moses says.

Kristiana asks the Tovas, "Do you have a term for Jews who did bad things to Jews?"

"Yes," Mr. Tova says. "Jew bastards."

They laugh.

"You don't want to wall up your shtetals?" Kristiana asks.

"No, but we have to deal with reality. The safety of our community and families is our top concern. That's what all Faithers share in common—physical freedom and religious freedom. We will never stop fighting for either." Tova takes another sip of wine.

Mr. Tova says, "One of our American presidents said almost a century ago: 'Freedom is never more than one generation away from extinction. We didn't pass it to our children in the bloodstream. It must be fought for, promoted, and handed on for them to do the same, or one day we will spend our sunset years telling our children and our children's children what it was once like in the United States where men were free.'"

Mother Moses says, "The only way evil wins, is if we give up."

"So true," Tova says. "We're very unhappy about walling up our cities, but we'll be copying the Christians."

"You copy them and they copy you," Kristiana says.

"Our joint enemies copy each other too," Mr. Tova says.

"Hitler once said, 'Who today remembers the extermination of the Armenians?' Turkish Muslims killed almost two million Armenian Christians and that inspired a Pagan madman to kill six million European Jews."

Kristiana says, "They were evil people, Nazis."

"Kristiana, the most important lesson is not that it happened there in Europe, in Old Germany. Germans were well-educated and sophisticated. The true lesson of the *Shoah*—the Holocaust—is that if it could happen there, it could happen anywhere," Tova says.

"Speaking of mass murderers," Mother Moses says to the Tovas.

They speak just a few sentences to each other, but Kristiana doesn't know what they mean.

Mother Moses says, "Time to say good night to our guests, Kristiana."

Saying the good-nights and good-byes takes over thirty minutes itself.

"How do you say good-bye in Hebrew?" Kristiana asks.

"There's no such word in Hebrew," Tova says. "So we use the same word for hello: *shalom*."

"Shalom, Mr. and Mrs. Tova."

Kristiana knows she will have plenty to write in her diary and in her next letter to her parents. Later that night she can't sleep because her mind is racing thinking about her new Jewish friends, the holy dinner she shared, but more so, going over in her mind that short, cryptic conversation that M and the Tovas had before everyone started saying their goodnights and good byes.

"*The plagues are upon Galerius even now,*" Mother Moses says.

"*A plague of death for Haman is beyond us though; desired but not advisable,*" Tova says.

"*But plagues of disorder and distrust within and diminution of his clan are not. Galerius will be reduced to a prison of his own making when the 'finger of God' touches him,*" Mother Moses says.

The two Faither Orders had their secret meeting in plain view and in less than a minute. While Christians called him Galerius, the Jews called him Haman after the fifth-century BC noble of the Persian Empire who instigated a plot to kill all of the Jews of ancient Persia, but was foiled by Queen Esther.

Kristiana knows that they have planned something bad for President T. Wilson.

Objects Are Closer Than They Appear

"The storm is already here." – General Moses, leader in the Resistance

The White House
12 noon, 2 February, 2089

President Wilson listens to his communications team presenting their strategy, but his mind is disengaged.

The easy days seem to be over. He is now in the midst of a real political crisis. He managed to avoid any scandal from the Kansas Event to get elected the first time by classifying the whole thing as top secret, which prevented media scrutiny. Now, in his third term, his domestic troubles have eclipsed all his foreign policy concerns; it is all damage control now. He wouldn't be surprised if his entire term is consumed with political survival.

"The Islamic Caliphate has been broadcasting throughout their empire that the American president killed his own staffer," says a White House communications aide.

Fortunately, the story is unremarkable, even to the Muslim populations of the Caliphate. Islamic media has been accusing America and its presidents of every foul deed and conspiracy imaginable on a daily basis for many decades, doubly so now that there is no Jewish Israel. Now it's true, and their population ignores it.

The domestic front is another matter. "Governor Chauncey has gone mad with revenge for the death of his son and is using the new Northern Confederacy to be a permanent dagger in the eye of the administration," says another aide. The story is being broadcasted non-stop in much of the world, but in America he has managed to make the story disappear by again simply classifying the entire matter as a national security issue; preventing any of the media from reporting it or risk federal prosecution and imprisonment. But the District elite already know. He has to face the Lucifers and see if he can get clear of these ninety-somethings of the District uber-elite—the parents of Lucifer Mestopheles, the man he had killed.

Bethesda, Maryland
9:30 a.m., 3 February 2089

Mrs. Lucifer tends to the multi-colored orchids in her indoor garden. Dressed in a blood-red dress and white pearls, she leans over to snip leaves from various flowers to keep them in visual balance. Her husband sits nearby like a mute sentinel, in his blood-red suit, with his snow-white hair and mustache, watching everything.

The president walks into the nursery at 9:45 a.m. Mr. Lucifer sees the most powerful man in America approach without a Secret Service agent anywhere in view, but he knows an army of them must be right outside the doors. Mr. Lucifer smiles as he imagines himself assassinating the murderer of his bio-son with the small revolver hidden in the small of his back—maybe next time.

Mrs. Lucifer sees him and stands up. President Wilson walks up to her and stops. He looks at her hands. She looks down too and notices that she is holding the shears in her pasty-white, bony hand in a somewhat menacing fashion.

"Oh, sorry," she says and places the shears on a nearby table and walks back to him. She leads him to a set of twin chairs facing at opposite angles in the center of the indoor garden. Mr. Lucifer swivels on his stool to watch them. Wilson notices that the man's lower body seems unconnected to his upper half—his legs are crossed ninety degrees behind him, his upper body faces them.

She motions to Wilson to sit, and they do so at the same time. President Wilson sits quietly, crossing his legs and clasping his hands comfortably. Mrs. Lucifer straightens her clothes and sits with her legs and hands in similar fashion.

They stare at each other for a moment.

"You are a very brave man to come here. Politicians are rarely so bold these days," she says.

"I felt I owed it to you for your support over the years. I'm president today because of that support."

"But my offspring lies dead despite it," she says contemptuously.

Wilson pauses. "Your son was killed because he was passing highly classified information to enemies of this country."

"Oh yes. Your slaves briefed my husband and me very thoroughly."

Wilson sits quietly as she watches him.

"Why would he do that, Mr. President—my son? Loyal to this nation for over fifty years, helping those who defend it get elected to the highest offices, ensuring those against it get defeated. All of a sudden, he becomes a traitor. Or so you say."

"That's what happened."

"Where are the….two people you sent to *neutralize* my son? I believe that's the national security term for murder."

"Why?"

"My husband and I would like to talk to them."

"I don't think that would be wise under the current circumstances."

"Of course," she says. "Did you neutralize them too?"

Wilson looks at her with a smirk. "I came out of respect, but if you feel I'm being disrespectful, please tell me and I'll go."

"Oh no, we appreciate the gesture. After all, you're the president of the United States. You still haven't answered our question. Why our son would turn traitor?"

"I don't know. Why does anyone turn traitor?"

"I heard that you and my son were doing something you weren't supposed to be doing, and you had a falling out. He sought to destroy you, and you sought the same for him. We know who triumphed in the end. Anything to that rumor, Mr. President?"

"You were briefed thoroughly as to what happen."

"You seem to have a lot of people accusing you of killing their sons," she says with a slight smile. "My husband and I were thinking of moving to New Hampshire."

"I hear the weather is nice up there—except for the fall, spring, winter, and summer."

"I think we could get used to it up there."

He nods.

"How are you liking your gilded cage, Mr. President? I've always felt that anyone who seeks the office of the presidency must be mentally unbalanced in some way. An inmate in a super-max prison has more freedom. Soon you'll be sitting in your presidential chair staring out your presidential window reminiscing of the early days before your imprisonment and torment."

"A prisoner of a super-max facility isn't one of the most powerful people in the world."

"True." She looks at her fingernails and then at her palms. "I have a new associate who was sitting right where you are now. She told me that you'd come down here and lie to my face about murdering our son. And here you are."

"I'm not concerned about what you believe or don't believe about what happened. You're in your nineties. You won't have to endure the grief for too much longer."

She grins. "My mother lived until a hundred and ten and she wasn't in even half as healthy as I am in. I expect to live until a hundred and twenty, maybe a hundred and fifty with how biotek is advancing. We may even live long enough to see you buried. Maybe right next to our son."

Wilson uncrosses his legs and leans forward. "The reason you live so well is because you and your husband can do the things you want, eat the things you want, and pump all those fluids in and out of your bodies. But if I were to deem you both a threat to national security and lock you up in a super-max facility, without those creature comforts and foods and sex-mates and fluid-pumping devices and those sickly flowers you tend for hours on end, I doubt you'd make it to your next birthday. Do I need to demonstrate that power to you?"

She stares at him a moment. "No."

He rises from the chair. "Let it go. Let it go." He stares at her a moment. "I'm going to have you and your husband monitored to make sure you don't fall into any illegalities or anything that could become an illegality. I'm not just the president of the United States, I'm your friend, and friends look out for each other. I wouldn't want you to end up in a small gray box for the rest of your life. I'll show myself out."

Wilson walks out of the indoor garden. Mrs. Lucifer sits there, seething with anger. She stands and walks to the table where she placed the shears and looks at a small blue business card.

One Month Earlier

Mrs. Lucifer sits across from a petite woman dressed in a white dress office-suit and a frilly white hat and a white veil to obscure the face.

"I'll leave my card for you and your partner," she says. "I suspect that sometime in the near future your interests and ours will briefly coalesce. Feel free to call then."

"I doubt that I'll ever have cause to call upon a Jew-Christian slag terrorist like you or your kind."

The woman in white smiles. "We'll see how you feel after the inevitable visit of your *good friend* and murderer of your bio-son, President T. Wilson." She stands and says, smiling, "I hope you and your partner burn in hell in the next life. Oh, you hedonist disciples of Satan actually believe that to be a good thing and desire it. We'll talk again soon. Have a bad day." She leaves their indoor garden and walks out the same doors President Wilson will exit one month later.

10:16 a.m., 3 February 2089

Her husband, adjusting his lower mechanical body, joins her at the table. She hands him the blue card. They still look at the door that Wilson just exited. "We're going to pray every day to the dark lord himself for your horrible end," she whispers.

Her husband taps her and then raises a finger to his lips—shhh. She nods and looks around the garden. Wilson probably has them under surveillance even now.

Moses House, Providence
9:25 a.m., 5 April 2089

"Kristiana, you have visitors." Armstrong has sent one of his men to deliver the message to her and drive her to the Wall.

Kristiana hops out the cart and walks to the Wall. About ten feet away, she stops, noticing the people standing next to a waiting Sek—her sisters! She runs to them, and her little sisters jump on her. Her second oldest sister gives her a hug and her oldest sister, always cold to her, embraces her too. The little sisters are smiling from ear to ear; her older sisters are only marginally expressive.

"From Father." Her eldest sister Rebecca hands her a letter.

"How long are you visiting?" Kristiana asks.

"We're going to be staying here for awhile."

Kristiana immediately opens the letter and begins reading. Her father is often a man of few words, but this letter is five pages long. When she's finished, she folds it up and puts it in her skirt pocket. She has them remain where they are while she walks over to Sek.

He speaks before she can say anything. "We have lodging already set aside for them."

"How long have you known about this?"

"M told me after your father's visit, but also not to tell you until he was able to."

Kristiana nods. "What part of the city is it in? I want to be close to here."

Sek smiles. "You want to be close to the action. It's close. You can take them there. You know how to drive a cart, or are you going to tell me that it's forbidden for you to drive?"

"Do you have bicycles?"

Sek sighs—out-smarted. "Yes, we'll find some for all of you."

"Thanks, Sek. My little sisters especially, love bicycles."

Kristiana walks back to her sisters. Rebecca steps forward.

"I know what Father said in the letter, but I'm the oldest," she says. "I'm in charge as long as I'm here."

"Father said I'm in charge of all of you, so that's how it's going to be."

"I'm in charge. I'm the oldest. Soon I'll be married."

"You've been saying that for the last two years."

"Say what you want, but I'm in charge. I want that agreed to right now."

Kristiana looks at her for a moment. She walks away from them and they see her talking to Sek again. She walks back to them.

"Follow me."

They all follow her back to the Wall and then, strangely, out one of the main entrances. There is a black bus parked outside. Buses like these are used by the Faithers to transport goods, large groups, or both between the enclaves, often as part of convoys. She opens the door and sits in the first seat behind the driver's seat. Her sisters get on and they each take a seat. Kristiana then gets up and sits in the driver's seat of the bus and closes the door. In a second, she has started the vehicle and is driving the bus, turning it onto the road.

"What are you doing, Kristiana? Where are we going?" her second eldest sister Sarah asks.

Kristiana ignores her. The bus is now barreling down the road away from the enclave and towards the tek-city Philadelphia.

"What are you doing?!" Sarah yells. "Where are we going?!"

"I'm in charge because I went to the tek-city by myself and survived. So whoever is in charge of me has to have done at least that. Father has, Mother has, and I have. None of you have. So I'm going to drive to the Devil's Playground and dump you there. You get back on your own, and then you will have the authority to be in charge."

"No!" Katie yells. "Make her stop, Rebecca!"

"You don't scare me!" Rebecca snarls. "You don't know how to drive a vehicle!"

"Yes, I do," Kristiana says to Rebecca. "And I know red means stop, green means go, and yellow means speed up and drive faster!"

"Stop it, Kristiana," Katie, the youngest sister, says. "We're scared."

Rebecca sits there quietly, fighting her growing panic. Katie and Annie are now crying. Sarah has run to Kristiana and is pleading with her, also crying. Sarah turns to Rebecca. "Please, Rebecca, tell her that she's in charge."

Annie and Katie join her: "Please, Rebecca. Kristiana is in charge. Please!"

Tears flow down Rebecca's face, and she stands and walks to Kristiana. "You're in charge."

The bus stops and Kristiana turns to look at her. Rebecca sits back down and doesn't look at her anymore.

It takes Kristiana only moments to drive back to Providence, park, and lead her sisters back in. Her sisters are visibly shaken and everyone can see they have been crying. Sek waits, watches Kristiana with a disapproving look, but says nothing. Five bicycles are waiting. They all follow Kristiana's actions; she gets on one and they ride away.

The house where her sisters will stay is ten minutes away by bicycle. It's a one-level white house, with a white picket fence. Kristiana walks through the entire residence to inspect each room. It is furnished, and the kitchen is stocked with some basic food.

She walks back to the main door where her sisters wait, watching her.

"This is where you'll be. Did you bring suitcases or things?" Kristiana asks.

Rebecca says. "They're at the walled entrance."

"I'll have them brought here for you. You get settled in, and I'll be back tomorrow morning."

"Where are you going?" Katie asks.

"I have a room already."

"But there are rooms here."

"I'll be back. I'm not far away at all." Kristiana leaves and closes the door behind her.

When she arrives back at Mother Moses's house, she is so

happy to walk through the front door. She is doing her normal chores, dusting the house, when M appears.

"What are you doing, Kristiana?"

Kristiana looks up, confused. "My chores."

"Aren't your sisters here?"

"Yes, I got them all settled into their new guest house."

"*Their* guest house?"

Kristiana is still confused.

"You mean *your* guest house. Kristiana Fisher, do you mean to tell me that you are going to leave your family all alone while you stand in my house dusting? I have children to do that."

"But my oldest sister is in charge of them so I don't need to be there."

"Kristiana, pack your things and go take care of your family."

"But they are fine."

"Kristiana, in all the time I've known you this is the first time you have ever acted like a child. You should be ashamed of yourself. You treat that teddy bear of yours better than how you're acting with your own family. Are you behaving like a Christian or a Pagan?"

Kristiana's face turns sad. She puts the feather duster away and walks to her guest bedroom. It takes only a few minutes to pack her two bags. She sits on the bed, looking at the packed bags and then at Bo Bear.

Mother Moses stands at the door. "Kristiana, you haven't been exiled. Why have you gotten it into your head that you can't do what you need to do *and* take care of your family?"

She perks up now and declares, "I can do both." She smiles, stands up, and hugs Mother Moses. "M, you're the best."

M sends a happy Kristiana off on her way with her two bags, some food for her sisters, and Bo Bear.

Secure House, Providence Enclave
8:05 a.m., 11 April 2089

They all sit in a secure conference room: Sek, Mother Moses, and the Providence chairman, with security, intelligence, and council members.

"It's a go," Sek says.

"When does the team leave?" the chairman asks.

"Within the week," Sek says. "We want everything ready when they return."

"We'll be ready," the chairman says.

"I want you to take her with you," Mother Moses says.

Sek looks at her. "This is a para-military operation, M. She would be of no use."

"It's her home, her people. Take her. She'll do fine."

Sek sighs.

Kristiana is no longer the only Amish in Providence. On her daily walks, she is now accompanied by the entire Fisher sister clan. She arrives at the Moses house around 3:00 p.m. with her sisters. As soon as she enters the house she laughs, seeing Goth Lila.

"If you say anything to embarrass me, I'll show your pathetic dancing pictures to your sisters," Goth Lila says.

"That's okay. I never danced before."

Kristiana introduces everyone to her sisters: Goth Lila, Sek, Armstrong, Mother Moses, Jo-Jo, Jada, the Providence Council chairman and other security personnel whom she knows personally from her frequent walks to the Wall.

Mother Moses says, "If you want your older sisters to stay that's fine, but have your younger sisters go and play outside."

Sarah says, "I'll take them outside and mind them. You can stay," she says to Rebecca. Sarah takes Katie and Annie outside.

"What's wrong, M?" Kristiana asks.

Mother Moses leads the group to the sitting room where the tables and chairs have all been arranged like a conference board room. Everyone takes their seats.

Mother Moses says, "Sek will be leading a team to Amish Quarter, and we're going to relocate the entire population to Providence."

Kristiana looks at Rebecca; they are stunned. Then she asks, "What has happened?"

"This is to keep things from happening," Sek says.

"Is it Galerius?" Kristiana asks. Rebecca looks at her, confused—unaware of the reference.

"It's always Galerius," Sek says.

"What do you need me to do?"

Mother Moses says, "I want you to go with the team, but only if you want to. I don't want you to be nervous or scared, but it could be dangerous."

"Who's going on the team?"

"Sek, Armstrong, Lila, Jo-Jo, and armed security."

"Guns?" Rebecca asks nervously.

"Guns don't bother me," Kristiana says. "But danger does." She thinks for a moment. "Okay. I'll go. When do we leave?"

"Right now?" Sek says.

The chairman laughs. "You said your team would be leaving within the week."

"We are leaving within the week," Sek says. "Right now is within the week."

Rebecca is worried. "Maybe you should stay. If it's dangerous, you shouldn't be there."

"I have to go. They don't know Amish Quarter or the people. I have to make sure everyone gets back here safe."

Sek looks at M and smiles.

"Great," Goth Lila says. "It'll be like a road trip."

Later at the Wall, Kristiana is becoming nervous at the prospect of actually going near a tek-city again. But this time she won't be alone. She sits in the waiting room of one of the shacks next to the Wall, looking out the window as the team gets the convoy ready. Goth Lila walks in carrying a bundle of clothes.

"Come here for a minute," she says. "Try these on."

"Those are combat boots."

"Yes, put them on and make sure they fit."

"Amish don't wear combat boots."

"You do. You're going on a secret mission."

Kristiana takes off her shoes to put them on. "Why do I need these? Are we going to be tip-toeing through a mine field?" She looks up with a smile.

"You're a real comedienne, Kristiana. Now stand up. Here, put on this jacket I got you."

"This is a very thick gray jacket."

"Yes, I know, very un-Amish. Put it on. You're going back into Tek World. You remember what happened the last time you were there unprotected. You had to burn your clothes because of the filth and chemicals."

"And it got into my hair and skin too."

The gray jacket covers Kristiana completely down to her calves and the combat boots go up to her knees.

"Three more things: a gray leather bonnet."

Kristiana laughs. "That's not a bonnet."

"Well just pretend it is. It's made of leather. And here's your face mask so you'll always have fresh air to breathe. It will filter all those drugs out of the air."

"That poison," Kristiana says and puts the mask up to cover her nose and mouth to test the fit. Lila then puts a pair of clear goggle-glasses over Kristiana's eyes.

"You now have the whole gray outfit. You'll be the first Amish of the New Gray Order."

"Gray Amish? I like that. It'll be s.m.i.c."

They laugh. "How do you know s.m.i.c.?"

Stupendously, magnificent, incredibly cool. Every decade seems to come up with its own word for cool: groovy, fly, tight, awesome, hot, smic.

Pennsylvania
5:44 p.m., 11 April 2089

The caravan is on the road. The first RV has Sek at the wheel; Armstrong sits next to him; and behind his passenger seat sits Jo-Jo. In the third set of seats are Goth Lila and Kristiana. The second vehicle is another RV filled with security people, and the last vehicle is a large black SUV.

Sek hasn't given any more details about the trip. All Kristiana knows is that they are not heading toward Amish Quarter, but in the opposite direction. She wonders when they will double back.

"How long will it take to get there?" Kristiana asks.

"We'll be gone for at least a week," Sek responds, not really answering.

"Just enjoy the scenery," Goth Lila says.

Sek is like some kind of machine, driving now for four hours straight, never using the auto-drive. Everyone else has been snacking on all kinds of food in the back kitchenette of the RV. All Sek has had is a couple of small bottles of juice. It's dark out, and for the first time, he takes an off-ramp. The area has a lot of greenery. It turns out to be a resort area near a lake.

"We'll make camp here for the night," Sek says.

The main RV is transformed into a sleeping area with two sets of bunk beds for the women including one for a female member of the security detail. A few tents are set up on the perimeter for the night guards, the black SUV is parked between the RVs, and the other RV will be both a sleeping area and a command center.

Everyone is so busy with work, but Kristiana is not on the work roster at all. She fortunately has brought a bag full of books to occupy her time.

At 11:30 p.m., Kristiana is summoned from her seat in the RV, where she has been reading. She follows Jo-Jo and Goth Lila to the road, where a different caravan of two RVs and an SUV is waiting. They all get into the new SUV, and this time Armstrong is the driver. Sek watches from the seat behind him. For the rest of them in the RV, it's time for sleep in the fold-down beds that are already set up. Jo-Jo closes the partition, and the women go to sleep as the caravan drives. Kristiana now realizes that the road trip will be non-stop, with them changing caravan vehicles all along the way. This is like a secret mission.

The next day, the RV rolls down the road with Sek as the driver again. They have all had breakfast; Sek had his at the wheel. Goth Lila is taking a nap, Jo-Jo is reading her book, and Kristiana was reading, but is now watching the road from the window. She doesn't know where they are.

"Oh, look at that," she says.

"What?" Jo-Jo says, opening her eyes.

"Sek, you have to stop there," Kristiana says.

"Why would I want to do that?" he asks.

"That store has Coca-Cola," she says. Jo-Jo laughs.

"You must be joking," Sek says.

"It's on the way. Just stop for a second. I have Pagan money on me."

"You're serious?"

"Yes, I always wanted to get one of them."

"It could be poisoned," Sek says.

Kristiana laughs. "They didn't poison it. They had no idea we would be here today at this spot. Just one second, Sek. Besides, it will give you a chance to see if we're being followed, which is why you're doing all this long driving. You and Jo-Jo like to do the long driving."

Jo-Jo smiles. "Sek, let's make a pit stop. Two minutes isn't going to upset your carefully laid plans."

Sek thinks and then relents. He touches the dashboard and connects to the other vehicles. "Team, we're making a quick stop at one of the local stores. Stay in formation." He disconnects and looks at Armstrong. "Check it out."

The caravan turns into the mini shopping center near the red and white store with the bright Coca-Cola digital signs. They pull into the back of the store. Armstrong exits the vehicle and disappears. When he returns, he gestures to Kristiana. She smiles and puts on her leather jacket, facemask and leather bonnet and gets out of the RV. She is still not used to walking in combat boots, but she strolls around the back and into the store with Armstrong following. Inside the store the lights are dim, but she can see the thin cloud of smoke throughout. Drug vapor!

Kristiana makes sure her face mask is fastened properly and walks up to the main counter, where a tiny man with pale porcelain skin and a bald head except for a blond Mohawk stands. He has no top on and she can't tell if he even has pants on, but at least that's behind the counter.

"I want to buy a bottle or can of Coca-Cola, sir," she says.

The man grins. "Are you one of those Asian Consortium tourists?"

"Not at all, sir. Just a buyer of Coca-Cola."

The man points to the side of the store. She turns and walks to the wall with freezers. Behind the glass she sees it, and she opens the freezer door.

"What kind of store is this?" Kristiana says. "You don't have any kind of tek."

The man grins. "Yes, this is a retro store. No mechanization at all. These kinds of stores are making a come-back. People are wanting the personal touch again. They want to be able to walk in and walk to their product and pick it up themselves. No touching screens from a device and having it shipped to you from far away. Our chain of stores is no-tek retro. This is how they did it in the stone ages."

"Like Jew-Christians," Kristiana says.

The man laughs. "Oh yeah, Jew-Christians. The original stone-age people."

"How much, sir?"

"Well, for you, I think I'll give half off the price."

"Thank you then."

She hands her the digi-card. He swipes it with a wand and hands it back.

"Anything else you need?"

"I don't think so, sir."

"This store has all kinds of retro. Do you know back in the stone ages they had another kind of coca-cola. It was called cocaine. We got that too. I'll give you half off."

Armstrong clears his throat, signaling that it's time to go.

"Thank you, but no. I got my Coca-Cola, so I got all the retro I need for the day. Next time I'll try another retro, but thank you."

"Well, look me up. I'll be your steady counter slave."

"Thanks, sir. Now what's this nonsense I hear about all these Jew-Christians in this area? That's why I'm going back to Asian Consortium."

"No, not PA. We don't have any kind of problems at all. The new governor and the Congress, I mean the legislator, passed new laws and they're taking all their land and moving all of them out of state. They'll have their forty acres and a cow someplace else."

"Seriously?"

"Oh yeah, this is a very progressive state. We don't tolerate Jew-Christians at all. I can't wait until they start getting rid of the Vampires and the Jedis too."

"I read about this group of Jew-Christians who've been in the state for centuries."

"Yeah, the Amish. Them too. The governor is sending storm troopers after them. They have those horses and buggies. Have you seen how much crap comes out of the butt of a horse? It's mega-huge! PA is a very clean state, we like nature. All that horse crap pollutes the environment."

"Where are they putting those Jew-Christians?"

"Somewhere not PA! I think Kansas."

"Thanks, sir. That is so good to hear. America has such good governors and a great president."

"The president? I hate that bastard. I didn't vote for him at all. He's too soft on crime for me. Don't like him at all."

"Thanks for the Coca-Cola, sir!"

"Come back soon!"

Everyone sits in the RV, waiting, when the door opens and Kristiana pulls her face mask off and sternly looks at them. "Sek, stop this long driving nonsense and get me to Amish Quarter now!"

Pennsylvania, One Hour From Amish Quarter

Very impressive how she got intelligence out of the Pagan, Armstrong thinks to himself. The caravan is on the move again, and he turns to glance at her with her Coca-Cola bottle.

"Do you know they could have poisoned that?" he says.

She looks at him while drinking. "No, you can't have any." She drinks another sip.

He laughs. "No one here wants any of that."

"Want some?" She says playfully, first holding it out and then quickly pulling the bottle back.

"That crap isn't kosher," he says.

"Coca-Cola. Yummy." She drinks the rest of the bottle, sticks a napkin in the top of it, and places it in her knapsack. "Sek, are we there yet?"

Everyone is amused. Sek looks in the rear-view mirror to glance at her.

"I see why Faithers are so paranoid," she says. "America isn't one nation, it's two."

"Paranoia makes for a long life," Sek says.

"That's what Pagan Paul says."

"What would the Amish response be to this forced relocation evil since you're pacifists?" Sek asks.

"We resist. We won't comply."

"What if it's comply or jail?"

"Then we go to jail."

"Comply or get killed?"

"Then die. Amish people have been through this before in history. We'll never comply. Are there Faithers who actually follow Galerius?"

Sek says, "Well you know the answer to that."

"Yes, fake Christians and Jew bastards."

Jo-Jo and Goth Lila burst out laughing. Jo-Jo says, "Where did you learn that phrase?"

"The Jews."

Jo-Jo says, "Be careful who you say that around."

The caravan is stopped in a secluded wooded area—they have arrived. They can see no one. Sek and Armstrong scan the entire countryside with devices. Everyone else waits in the RV.

"I'll go," Kristiana says. She puts on her leather bonnet and starts to fasten her face mask.

Sek says, "This place has not been secured. We have to do that first."

"Do your machines see anything dangerous?"

"That's not the point. We have to send in a team to recon the area first."

"Sek, this is my home. I've walked this entire area for fifteen years straight. You wouldn't even know if something was not right. You've never been here before. I'll go and recon. This is Amish territory, so now I'm in charge. Outside Amish territory, you're in charge."

Sek grins. He knows better than to argue. "Put a tracker on her."

Goth Lila takes a small, round, silver object and clips it to her collar.

"What is that?"

"We'll be able to hear you when you talk, and we will also know your exact location at all times," Goth Lila answers.

"Okay, time for my recon."

They smile as Kristiana walks off.

The first place she comes across is Pagan Paul's shack, but the entire house is obliterated. She stares at it in shock. Did he finally blow it up looking for his wires or did something else happen more terrible?

When she gets into Town, she is struck by the emptiness, not a person around. Every store is empty. It's a ghost town. It doesn't take her long to get to the residential area, again no one, every home is empty. Could the government already have come for them? No, if that were the case there would be something left behind, the livestock would definitely be left behind, some of the pets would be around. There is nothing. No, everyone has packed up everything and left. But gone where?

She has an idea and walks past the residences and fields into the "wild country"—dense brush, trees, mountainous area. To an outsider it would seem impossible, but there is actually an invisible path that all the children know of and most of the adults. Using that path, she passes through the dense part and back into the open field area. She can see the small mountains nearby. She walks to the left to go around them.

"I don't believe in imaginary notions of God! I believe in my 357 magnum, Pagan! You came for the Jew-Christians, and now I bring down my wrath of God upon you!" Pagan Paul stands there pointing his large gun at her.

She pulls off her face mask. "Pagan Paul, stop that dirty-harry nonsense!"

"Kristiana?!"

"Of course. Where is everyone? And put away that weapon."

Pagan Paul lowers the gun and starts to laugh. "What are you supposed to be?"

"I am the Amish of the New Gray Order!"

He starts to laugh even louder and practically falls down. She is now laughing too.

"Okay, where is everyone? We have to find them now. The government is coming for us."

He looks up at her and starts to calm down. "The storm troopers are here?"

"Not yet, but we have to hurry."

Pagan Paul has been keeping daily guard from one of the caves in the mountain. He saw Kristiana as soon as she came out of the forest. He leads her around the mountain and there everyone is. All of Amish Quarter is in a tent city—hundreds and hundreds of tents. The horses and livestock are kept in a makeshift fenced-in area to the back.

"Father! Mother!" She runs to her parents and hugs them both. Other adults start to congregate around her. She looks up and notices that there are a lot of new faces.

"Who are all these new people, Father?" She notices another group approaching. "Mennonites." The Mennonite men have blue denim overalls over their dark-colored shirts and wear black fedoras; the women dress similar to Amish, but wear wide-brimmed hats.

"Other Amish communities from Ohio, the West and Canada. The Mennonites are from Canada," her father answers. "Almost eight thousand of us."

Kristiana is surprised. "That's a lot of Anabaptists in one place."

"Yes, but we have our very own Amish super-heroine to protect us." He smiles.

"How are your sisters?" her mother asks.

"They're fine, Mother."

Her father asks, "Where are the Providence Christians?"

They have even managed to create a large work table for meeting. The Amish and Mennonite leaders—bishops, priests, and elders—are all gathered around the table. Sek has them looking at a large map of tri-city enclaves.

"We were expecting only a thousand people," he says.

"Are we going to be a burden for your community?" one of the bishops asks.

"No, we can split up the populations between all three enclaves. The Amish Quarter population we can move to the lands outside Providence as planned, the Ohio and Washington and Mennonites to Sanctuary, the Canadians to Restoration. What about your other Amish and Mennonites communities?"

"We won't be able to convince them until we're all settled."

"There are many Christian enclaves throughout the country, and I'd recommend the Jewish enclaves too as options. What is your plan to get to the enclaves?"

"We've built large wagons that can accommodate everyone," one of them says.

Sek is annoyed. "We can't have eight thousand people in wagons, horse-drawn buggies, or on horseback on the open road. It's dangerous on so many different fronts. We're vulnerable from the ground and the air. Besides, it's illegal to have your horse-and-buggy vehicles or any animals on the freeways and it would take forever, even if it weren't illegal. No wagons or any animal-pulled vehicles. Everyone will be loaded onto buses, animals on trucks, and we get to our destinations as quickly as possible with armed vehicle escorts."

The Amish and Mennonites look at each other.

"We can't have the horses on trucks. They'll get hurt. And the cows and larger animals."

"Then we'll get animal transports for them, but the primary concern is to get all of you, the people, out of here now. The horses and livestock will have to wait."

"We'll stay behind then and mind them," one of the Mennonites says.

"No one is staying behind," Sek says.

"We can't leave our animals. Don't your enclaves have animals?" the Mennonite man asks.

"Yes, we do, and we take care of them very well, but people and children come first."

"We're not leaving our animals. People must protect them."

Sek sighs. "You're willing to die over these animals because we don't have the vehicles now to transport them? It will take only a day or two for us to get back here for them."

"We've been out here for weeks. Two days is no problem for us. We can hide until then."

Sek says, "Let me ask you, so that I know what kind of people I'm dealing with, your own dog and a person, someone you don't know, are drowning in a river, and you can only save one. Which do you save?"

"The person of course," the Mennonite man says.

"Let's say it's Hitler and a dog. Which do you save?"

The Mennonite smiles and says, "Hitler and a rat? The rat, of course."

Everyone laughs and Sek smiles. "Okay. You're okay. As long as you're not moral relativists, pacifism I can deal with. Let's get everyone ready for transport."

The Amish and Mennonites pack up all their things. They wait in groups, families with their children and districts with their communities. Sek leads the entire group back through the forest, but instead of going to Amish Quarter, he takes them over a new path. They emerge and there waits seemingly an army of buses on the road.

Goth Lila has decided to put a cap over her spiky hair and to don a big jacket. If Kristiana's initial reaction to her many months back was any indication, the sight of a Goth might not be well received, even if the Goth is a Christian. She stands with Jo-Jo near the middle of the bus caravan. Security personnel are evenly spaced at the entrance of each bus.

Sek designates a leader for each bus whose responsibility is to count each person on their bus and keep them together until arrival at their enclave. He stresses that no one else will be allowed onto a bus once its leader has a final count.

Jo-Jo and Goth Lila notice Kristiana talking to one of the

Amish boys. After a few minutes of conversation, he joins his group heading to their bus. Kristiana seems very comfortable in her gray leather outfit and combat boots. She walks to each bus and helps people board.

"Who was that you were talking to?" Jo-Jo asks. She and Goth Lila stand smiling near one of the buses.

Kristiana smiles. "He's the Canadian."

"And?"

"And what?"

"Who's the Canadian?"

"He's probably going to be my husband when I get baptized and officially join the church."

"I see." Jo-Jo smiles and nods. "We have a saying."

"What saying?"

"You two are a smart match."

Kristiana smiles. "Yes, I know that one. Yes, we are."

Pagan Paul sits on the ground right behind the last bus. Sek walks to him.

"You must be the Pagan Paul that I've heard so much about. The Pagan who lives with Christians. But why?"

He smiles. "I believe man spontaneously popped out of nothing. You believe man was created and put down naked in some Garden with free food. I think your belief in some fantasy called God is stupid. You think I'm stupid believing man evolved from monkeys and protoplasm." He smiles again. "We're all stupid. That's why we get along so well."

"Why aren't you getting on one of the buses? You had it with living with Christians?" Sek asks.

"It does me no injury for my neighbor to say there are twenty gods or no god. It neither picks my pocket nor breaks my leg." Pagan Paul says. "That's from Thomas Jefferson, the author of the Declaration of Independence, and that's what I believe. They call me a Pagan, but today's Pagan is a fascist. I don't believe in anything. I don't know and I really don't care, but these Pagans actually do believe in something, and they are very certain about it. They're slaves to the Grid." He smiles. "See, I know my factoids too."

"Get on the bus," Sek commands.

He lowers his head and starts to cry. "I can't!"

"Pagan Paul what are you doing?" a voice calls out. Kristiana walks to them. "Why are you sitting there? Did you really blow up your house with dynamite?"

"No, I did that to trick the fascists. If I left the house intact, they would have saturated it with wires."

"Why are you sitting there? It's time to go to our new home," Kristiana says.

"I can't go!" He's crying again. "I can never go back to the city. The invisible rays will hurt my brain again. I probably have no resistance anymore. They'll melt holes right through my brain. There will be nothing to stop them from getting right into my mind-universe. I can't go. I can't take the pain, the biological devastation."

"You have your aluminum helmet," Kristiana says.

"No, it won't work. It's too old. I have no resistance anymore and their invisible rays are much, much more powerful."

Sek kneels down next to him. He's heard of people with it before, but never actually met someone in person. Whether the affliction is real or imagined, it has a name: electromagnetic hypersensitivity syndrome. Even if it is as small as one-half of one percent of the population, that's still three million people. Their lives in Tek World would be virtually unlivable.

"None of the invisible rays can reach you where we live," Sek says.

Pagan Paul looks up at him, his eyes filled with hope.

"Enclaves have tek-jammers. It's like a force bubble around our entire city. We call it null-tek. No rays get in. Their machines stop working if they get close to us. It can even stop a mechanical heart from beating or keep bionic eyes from seeing," Sek says.

"There you are, Pagan Paul. You can go after all," Kristiana says.

He jumps up with a smile. "I can go! We can be free!"

The buses are packed and ready to go. A group of Amish and Mennonites will stay behind with the animals until proper transport arrives. Kristiana takes her mother to join her in the lead RV. She notices that her father still hasn't gotten on the bus and is standing with a group of bishops and elders. She gets off the RV.

"Father, why aren't you on the bus?"

"I won't be coming just yet."

"What do you mean? Why not?"

"I have another mission."

"I don't understand."

"You will take your mother with you and watch over the family."

"But I'm going to be joining the church, Father."

"Then I promise to be back before your baptism."

"Where will you be?"

"I need to begin the conversations with all our Old Order Amish across the country. Get them prepared."

She looks at him with worry.

"But Galerius is dangerous."

He laughs. "You're starting to talk like them now. No, he won't get me, Kristiana. My work now is to see that all our people get to safety. The Old Amish Order will become simply the Amish Order with you and young people like you. This is the new chapter in history for all us...Faithers."

Teeth

"You can get the entire world to believe in anything without God. But you need to purge those who believe in God." – S. Frinos, White House communications director

"We don't merely seek tolerance of all that we say and do. We demand acceptance and celebration of all that we say and do—forcibly, if necessary." – Lucifer Mestopheles, White House chief senior advisor, former national campaign manager to the president

"America isn't one nation, it's two." – Kristiana Fisher, future elder of the Amish Order

Officer Red starts his day as he always does by polishing his fangs in the mirror—incisors, fanged canines, premolars, molars. He smiles a big smile at himself.

New Haven Colony, New Jersey
8:59 a.m., 1 October 2088

He arrives at the suspects' house before everyone else. He has been told to wait in his car, but playing it safe is not the path for rapid promotions up the ranks. If he can subdue the terrorists before the main assault force arrives, it will look very good in his file. After all, he's a Vampire, and the terrorists are puny Jew-Christian humans.

He gets out of his car and focuses his bionic eyes on the surroundings; it's all clear.

What is that noise outside?

He swings open the side gate. *Squeeeaak!* If he wanted the

element of surprise, that is now gone. Angry, he slams the gate shut. He runs to the house and notices the draped window. He peers right into it, his bionic red eyes switching from visual to infrared; maybe he can adjust the depth to see through them. Suddenly he sees the drapes move a bit to the side—someone is in there! One of the terrorists! He's about to move when he hears a thunderous sound inside. He ducks as he runs to the window. They must have dropped something. He rests his face on the glass and accidentally scratches it with his fangs. He hears another sound to the side of the house and instinctively ducks down again; he bolts to it.

He looks around carefully and starts to run forward. *Meow!* An evil cat comes out of nowhere with the word "Elle" on its name-tag collar and trips him. He falls forward and catches himself with his palms on the ground; he has to spider-walk rapidly forward to keep from falling flat. To slow his momentum, he snaps up straight and spins around 180 degrees. He now notices someone staring at him from inside the house. The figure disappears.

He runs to the side door and pounds the glass with his fists, then wildly tries to open the door, but it's locked. There is only one terrorist inside! If he can subdue that one, he can wait until the other terrorists show up and surprise them all. He throws his body against the door, and again, and again. The wooden door is obviously reinforced with steel rods of some kind or he would have been able to rip it open with his strength.

He runs to the back of the house and tries to open or rip open the back door. He realizes he can't get in this way either after a few solid attempts. He stops and walks back a few feet, then looks up to the second floor. One of the windows looks to be slightly open. Aha!

He runs back to the end of the yard, then runs forward with all his speed and jumps up to the second floor. He grabs the window sill and kicks through the glass. Pots or vases crash to the ground. He dives through the window and then picks himself up off the floor. He sees no one and runs out of the bedroom.

He smiles as he can now see the single person in the house on the first floor with his bionic eyes.

"I know you're here, bag of blood! I can smell your fear!" he yells. "Come out now with your hands in the air! Resistance is futile, you Jew-Christian terrorist. I don't see those hands in five seconds, I'm going to put you in a body bag! Did you hear me?!"

He leaps down the stairs to the ground floor. He knows exactly where she is; his bionic eyes are set to infrared, and he can see her frail body behind the closet door. He smiles as he approaches the door, gun drawn and hairpin trigger ready.

He grabs the door knob and throws the door open. "Say hello to the devil, Jew-Christian!"

The terrorist is just a short elderly woman. He screams out as she lifts his six-foot frame off the ground.

It all seems to occur in slow motion as his body flies away from her and he feels unimaginable pain and it seems the ceilings and walls are breaking apart around him. He realizes that he is crashing upwards through the house. He feels light-headed and sees red fluid spilling from him. It's his blood, and he sails through the house, into the air, into the sunlight. His crushed and bloodied body sails through the air and then arcs down to land on the ground. Blackness.

The policemen, rifles and guns drawn, take positions behind their police cars. Bloodgood emerges from his black SUV with his Vampire special ops team, all in black office-suits.

Outside Amish Quarter
11:44 a.m., 13 April 2089

All the intelligence they have given him about the Jew-Christians is that they are unsophisticated, of low intelligence, anarchistic, paranoid, techno-phobic, and violent. He can definitely attest to the last point, but Bloodgood has never believed any of the rest. In his field, you find out about the real enemy you're fighting yourself, not what your government bosses say. If your enemy is five feet tall, they will say he's ten feet. If he's missing one arm, they will say he has four arms. If he has only one gun, they will say he has two machine guns. He doesn't care why the government has designated them enemies of the state, but what he does care about is that they have destroyed his life.

In the world of espionage and counter-terrorism, it's called psyops—psychological operations. Harass or damage the enemy by using psychological warfare tactics against them: plant a story in the media that they're actually double agents, tell their partner that they're sleeping with two other bed-mates, spread rumors that they've contracted a communicable disease, have someone accuse them of venal crimes with the local police. The list of possibilities is endless.

What the Jew-Christians did to him was beyond that. They were actually trying to kill him with his own people. Vampirism has turned into a worldwide religion, but there are also the mentally unbalanced who *really* believe they are vampires: needing to drink human blood, believing they can turn into a bat or a wolf, believing that any exposure to daylight will kill them. The Jew-Christians seem to have somehow found every one of these crazy people with vampire-syndrome, and set seemingly *all* of them after him—to kill him on sight.

And there is another group of delusional people out there—those who believe themselves to be some variation of Van Helsing from the book and movies. These Vampire hunters are also after him and they enjoy staking Vampires.

Bloodgood has been in special ops for decades, so these nutcases hardly worry him. He has to be careful, but he is always careful. He can kill any of these deranged people with his bare hands if needed. What does concern him is how skillfully the Jew-Christians have spread these rumors in the general Vampire community—lies of his complicity in Project Purify, which now allege that the Project is a government plot to round up all Vampires and exterminate them in fire chambers. If he ever leaves the service of government employment, he will have no place in his own community ever again.

Life in the black ops world isn't for the timid. His old Vampire team of over fifty men was killed but he has a new team now: Agent Lariat and Agent Runningstar as his personal special op bodyguards, and his own personal army of storm troopers. The

White House wanted to add teeth to its counter-Jew-Christian campaign, and so they have—Vampires *and* storm troopers.

Bloodgood aims his weapon at the road. He doesn't know why President Wilson is scared of the Jew-Christians. It was hatred before, but now it seems to be more about fear. What did they do at the Kansas Event? No matter, it will all be over soon.

He pushes the button on his rocket launcher, and the missile hits dead center in the middle of the road. It explodes, leaving a massive crater. *The lead vehicle, the RV driven by Sek with the others—Armstrong, Jo-Jo, Goth Lila, Kristiana, and her mother—drives off the edge and drops into the chasm's darkness.*

The Magi

"May the forces of evil become confused on the way to your house." – George Carlin, 21st century Pagan comedian, satirist and writer-actor

The event that took place in Kansas City, Kansas, between 8:37 a.m. and 9:00 a.m., 17 May 2076 has been classified as top secret by the American government. The official position of the government is that the Event never took place. The victims of the Event are unable to say with certainty that the Event took place, even though many were injured, and many seriously. The Jew-Christians present at the Event are also unable to say with certainty that what they experienced was real. What is certain is that Kansas Governor Turgood was killed in unusual and still unexplained circumstances; a new Jew-Christian group called the Magi (pronounced *may-jie*) was revealed; and immediately following the Event, the president of the United States shelved Project Purify for over a decade.

Location Unknown
10:12 a.m., 25 December 2080

President-Elect Wilson begins, "What are we to do about religion as a society?—the bizarre beliefs, the delusion, the illogic, the violence. The future must be allowed to progress completely; Tek World must be allowed to grow perfectly. No religious, cultural or terroristic forces will stand in our way. America will not be denied.

"I know that my executive order is somewhat controversial among some of you, but I tell you, this is being done not out of malice, but out of compassion. If Jew-Christians will not obey the laws of the land, will not accept our engineered society free of hatred and intolerance, then I say we separate them from the tek-society. This will be a symbol of how America is creative enough and sophisticated enough to deal with its sub-classes without going to war with them. We never take that option off the table, but we show our ultimate wisdom and maturity as a nation when we show that violence is not our solution to every problem."

Governor's Mansion, Kansas City, Kansas
11:00 p.m., 16 May 2076

Governor Turgood says sternly, "*The entire city is at war with us.* We need military troops now! I got governors all over the damn country scared to death that the same could happen in their states. If military boots are not on the ground fast, Director, you *will* have a second American Civil War on your hands."

He stands in the Governor's Mansion situation room with all his department heads, senior advisors, and staff. They watch President Wilson and his staff on the large vid-screen.

President Wilson pauses in thought. "Governor let me confer with my advisors. We'll call you back immediately."

The screen goes black.

"What a bastard!" the governor yells. "He's going to tell us to pull back. I just know it. He's one of those who loves to push the button to send kill drones after people, but has no stomach for the up-close-and-personal killing that sometimes is necessary." He looks at one of his men. "Chief, prepare to get *everything* in the air."

"Shouldn't we wait until the president gets back to us?" the chief asks.

"I don't know. Should we? It's only our people dying in the street while he and his people are a thousand miles away in a cozy office surrounded by thousands of agents. So should we wait?"

"No, governor, I'll get all forces ready."

The chief and his men leave the state situation room. On all the other vid-screens are various sections of Kansas—the cities, the state is burning! Law enforcement is losing the battle with civilian mobs.

"How did this happen again?" the governor asks, staring at the vid-screens.

"The rumor is that our policemen went in there and starting killing people in possession of their holy books and killing their religious leaders," an aide says. "Governor, all lies."

They watch the violence of the city streets on the vid-screens. One of the aides jumps up from the table listening through his ear-set. "Governor, the president is ordering you to stand down. He wants you to pull Kansas forces out of the hot spots and stand down."

The governor shakes his head. "The bastard! I'll be damned if I let him into the White House unchallenged this election."

5:00 a.m.

"What are your orders, Governor?" an advisor asks.

"Are all the forces in the air?"

"Yes, Governor."

"Give them my authorization to attack. We'll put down this insurrection ourselves. Tell them to attack with extreme prejudice."

The aide moves to a corner of the room to make the call.

The Governor looks to his men. "Warm up Kansas One. I'm going to the front line myself. And get some of those reporters. Get them on the bird too."

"Governor, you can't fly your helicopter *into* an insurrection."

"I can and I will." The governor marches out of the situation room and down the hall.

"Governor, I'm going to insist you take a complete military attack squad with you on Kansas One."

"Major, you can put whatever you want on the bird as long as I can sit comfortable and we can get a few of those reporters on there. I'm going to my office to get my gun and we're going."

The officer takes his e-pad from his pocket and starts yelling orders to someone on the other end.

Governor Turgood takes the stairs up one level followed by scores of people, all his staff and security. More staffers are waiting for him in the hallway immediately outside his office.

"Governor, the White House is demanding we confirm the presidential stand-down order," one of them says.

"I'm giving you the order not to respond in any way." He walks past them into the office and around to his desk. He sits down in the chair and opens a concealed door in the right side of the desk, a biometric safe. He takes out his foldable rifle. "Now let's go do some hunting." He stands and moves one end of the rifle, locking it open. He puts the magazine in and touches a button to activate all its features. "I'll be damned if these Jew-Christians destroy my state with me as governor. We are going to kill them all! All of them!"

One of his aides screams at something behind him. Governor Turgood turns around to face the large open bay windows. Seven drones crash through the windows, showering the room with shattered glass. The globe-drones move as a unit, lifting the governor off the ground like a giant hand as he drops his weapon in panic. The drones fly him out of the office.

His security detail draws their weapons, but they are helpless to do anything, fearing hitting the governor. Everyone watches in horror as the drones fly the screaming governor miles into the sky. They are a dot away and then are gone.

Holy Redeemer Church, Kansas City, Kansas
5:00 a.m., 16 May 2076

The insurrection prepares to make its last stand in a three-block-by-three-block area of the city. Using vehicles, furniture, and whatever they can find they have created a barricade wall around themselves. It is now morning, and with the sun up, they know the final attack is near.

First come the endless police-cars taking up positions and encircling them, then more police with guns and rifles drawn. Then come more state troops in their armored vehicles, taking positions behind the police and aiming their weapon systems at the insurrection members within the massive barricade. They know the air forces will arrive any minute.

"We're all going to die," says one of women.

"No one is going to die but them," says a man.

"I'm not afraid to die," another man says. "Let's take as many of them with us."

"Stop talking like that. We're going to beat them. All we have to do is pray."

"Have you ever been in any kind of military action like this?" another man asks. "What do you do for a living?"

"I'm a bartender," the man says.

"Does anyone here have any military training at all? Maybe someone with that kind of training should lead this."

"I do," a man steps forward from the crowd.

"What training to do you have?"

"My father was Navy. I was Army—Army Corps of Engineers, actually. After that I was a transporter for a number of years."

"Transporter?"

"Helping Christians and Jews escape from Muslim and CHIN territory and also the Russian Bloc. I ran mass people relocation actions: American Ethiopian Christians and Jews to Africa, Coptic Christians out of Muslim territories to Africa, Sikhs into their new homeland in India, others."

"What's your name?"

"Moses."

"What was your highest rank when you left the Army?"

"Sergeant First Class."

"I say we all vote you in to take control of this civilian mess of ours. Can you handle being a general? There's a nice ring to it, almost biblical. General Moses."

He smiles. "Yes, I can handle that."

General Moses quickly moves among the civilian resistance fighters and organizes them as best he can.

"You have to see things as they really are. Not just the forest but you have to see each tree. Look at their forces, each person. They're normed," Moses says.

"Normed?" a man asks.

"The Achilles heel of the modern-day police and military—group-norming. There is no objective or high standard when it comes to their training; all must be the same—from the strong to the pathetic. They judge themselves by the random standards set by the weakest one."

They now study the army of law enforcement waiting outside the barricades.

Moses continues, "When I look at the police and state troops out there, I don't see two hundred in front of us. I see maybe fifty for us to deal with. The rest are men and women who scarcely weigh a hundred pounds and can barely hold their own weapons. We target the fifty first. The others will hide behind cover or be very timid in their assault. Those that do attack, we'll deal with in the second volley. What we do now is organize quickly, because when they come, it will be from everywhere at once."

General Moses takes what he believes will be the best fighters to the point with the toughest police and state troopers and gets them ready for the attack.

Moses says, "Here they come."

Everyone sees them. The air gun-ships arrive like a swarm of giant mechanical bees, so many helicopters and drones in the sky. The Resisters all expect to die.

Moses talks into his mic with his voice echoing throughout their barricaded area. "I'm not going to lie to any of you. A lot of us are probably going to die today—they're already killed dozens of us, but just do what I told you and stick to the plan, and not all of us will—and we will stop as many of them as possible. Any moment now, they will use their bullhorns to tell us to surrender. Then they will demand that we do. Then will come the threats. Some of you know that the two pastors they killed yesterday were my father and younger brother. No one will fault you for wanting to give up, but I will never give up. Whatever you decide, this is the time to pray and fight for the lives of our people."

The police chief's voice booms through the bullhorn of every police car. He asks everyone to drop their weapons, leave the barricades and surrender. No one does. After ten minutes, he demands that they do. Everyone stands their ground. Then after ten more minutes, he tells them that if they don't, not one of them will be left alive.

The couple was described as a young man with dark tan skin, short, curly black hair, and dressed in a white office-suit and white leather slip-on shoes. People said wings were painted on the back of his white jacket. The young woman had a fair complexion, blond hair tied in a ponytail, and was dressed in a black office-suit, black heeled boots, and wore a black top hat.

At 8:37 a.m., the couple was standing next to General Moses and his main fighters at the northeastern part of the barricade. But at 8:36 a.m., people said the couple was actually helping move children into one of the churches at the southern part of the barricade for safety. But at 8:37 a.m., people said the couple was helping fighters strengthen the barricade on the western side. Other people said they saw the couple at the same time at many different sites: walking to another area, passing out water, joining in group prayers, or actually posted on the barricade, armed and ready to fight. No one knew who they were and no one had ever seen them before.

"We're going to launch our attack first," Moses says. "Pass the word."

"Wait," the young man in white says. The young woman in the top hat stands next to him.

"Why?" Moses asks.

"It's not time yet. No more of you can die today. An alternate probability must be allowed to play out."

"Who are you?" Moses asks.

"The question of importance is who you'll be. We'll deal with the dark humans." He points up.

Everyone sees a dot appear from far up in the air and descend rapidly towards them. No one can quite make it out at first. Is it a missile?

As it gets closer, they can hear the sound of a man screaming. The dot comes into focus as a man being carried down by drones. The drones suddenly seem to disintegrate from the descent. Governor Turgood plummets through the air and smashes to the ground a mere ten feet from the chief of police and his police commander. The two men, along with every policeman, guardsman, and soldier within a twenty-foot radius, are covered in blood and bio-matter. The commander screams in horror. The chief runs hysterically back into his car.

The sky seems to be getting darker somehow and the air feels strange, as if a storm is coming in, but there are no clouds. The cars and armored vehicles start to roll backwards, slowly, by themselves. The police and military drivers run to get control of their vehicles, but they speed away backwards like rockets. The drivers have never seen a vehicle move so fast.

The chief is careening backwards at incredible speed in his car. He looks at the odometer—the numbers are beyond belief. It says 150 mph, 210 mph, 340 mph, 510 mph, then 560, then 749. He passes out.

The police and soldiers left behind watch the vehicles disappear into the distance. They look around, at each other, and back at the barricade, stunned. They no longer have their vehicles for cover or the benefit of the military ground weapon systems. Their guns and rifles then come *alive* and jump from their hands, dropping to the ground, turning and shooting at them; the policemen and soldiers scramble away in shock.

The wind howls and seems to turn black. A dark cyclone appears and grabs every helicopter and drone in the air. In moments, all these objects of metal are spinning in a massive funnel around the barricade of Resisters. Moses and every one of them watch in disbelief as the cyclone also sucks up all the police and soldiers from the ground. The funnel rises higher in the air, the speed of its spinning grows, and the sky all around them gets darker.

In an instant it is all gone.

Moses looks to the side, and the couple is gone. Everyone looks out past the barricade and nothing is there—not a policeman, state trooper, vehicle, weapon, helicopter, or drone. There are no tracks or footprints of any kind on the ground. In fact, there is no evidence that the attacking government forces were ever there.

The chief sits in the police car in a near catatonic state. The vehicle is stopped, but his body is shaking in some type of mild spasm, and he can't move or talk. Awareness returns slowly: there is water in the car, up to his chest—fishes swimming in the water. The vehicle is in some type of lake. His eyes notices signs in the distance: Welcome to Hell!

He would later learn that he is in Hell, California, some 1,300 miles away from Kansas City. His boss was the man who crashed to the earth in front of him and whose blood and bio-matter covered him. Every person from the law enforcement and state trooper attack force was in the lake around him, along with all their vehicles and helicopters.

But up until today, there never has been a lake in Hell, California. No one knows how it got there.

At the barricades, the Resisters stand in a daze. "Are we dreaming?" "Did what I just saw happen, happen?" "I'm still not sure." "What did just happen?"

"The Magi just happened," Moses says.

"Who are they?"

"Exactly."

"That couple was the Magi? They're on our side?"

"Yes. You've heard of the group of Christians called the Amish who reject most tek and live as they did two hundred years ago," Moses says. "The Magi are a group of Christians who are on the other far end of the spectrum. Yes, they're on our side. I learned about them when I was in Africa."

"Thank God for the Magi, then."

"Yes, thank God. But we're never going to allow ourselves to be in a position where we need them to save us again," Moses declares.

Slow Boil

"If the watchman sees the sword coming and does not blow the trumpet to warn the people and the sword comes and takes the life of one of them, that man will be taken away because of his sin, but I will hold the watchman accountable for his blood." – Ezekiel 33:6

"Insanity will be normal and logic will be outlawed. You'll wake up one day and wonder how you ever got to this point. Just like the frog that knowingly hopped into the pot on the stove and then sat there moronically as it slowly boiled to death." – Mr. Super, education chief, Providence enclave

Outside Amish Quarter, Pennsylvania
11:44 a.m., 13 April 2089

The Amish/Mennonite caravan buses screech to a stop.
Bloodgood is very satisfied with himself. He turns to members of his own storm trooper army. "Take everyone from the vehicles into custody."

Other storm troopers start coming down from the hills on either side of the road. There are dozens of them, and a group of attack vehicles rolls down, following.

"Sir, the new Pennsylvanian governor is in one of the armored vehicles," a soldier says.

Bloodgood looks up at them and sees someone wave to him from the passenger side.

"He says he owes you for saving him the time and expense of doing this."

Bloodgood focuses back on his soldiers. "Make sure all possible escape routes are secure."

"None of them can escape, sir, but none of them have even attempted to leave their vehicles or drive away."

"Good. They know when they are beat."

The storm troopers are approaching the vehicles filled with Amish, Mennonites, and Providence Christians from all sides when the ground starts to shake.

From within the chasm, the RV that Bloodgood thought destroyed rises. It's a hovercraft, and it hangs in the air level to them. It spins around, and the front of the vehicle points directly at Bloodgood.

Squads of storm troopers have weapons drawn and take positions in front of Bloodgood to shield him. They hear the explosions—all around them. The noises start out as pops and then get louder and louder. Projectiles rise into the air in the distance and arc towards the ground, encircling them all, and explode upon impact. Another wave arcs up and flies to them, exploding on ground impact with even greater intensity; then another wave and another, making a circle of complete destruction.

"Call in back-up, now!" Bloodgood yells.

The lead storm trooper has begun to talk into his shoulder-comm when his face contorts and his whole body starts to shake. The words seem to be pulled violently from his mouth. *They are using a silencer on them!*—he is unable to speak. Others try to talk or yell out, but are also disturbingly affected by the weapon.

Bloodgood hears a click and looks at the hovering RV. The hover-vehicle now has gun turrets visible and Bloodgood dives away just as it starts firing. Storm troopers are hit, and others run or dive for cover.

The entire ground beneath their feet falls. Bloodgood leaps for the hillside. They created a crater to swallow up the lead RV, but this crater so large it could swallow up an entire New York City block. All of them—storm troopers, soldiers, and vehicles—disappear as the ground collapses. The explosions stop and the massive dust cloud billows higher and higher into the air until the wind starts to dissipate it.

Bloodgood hangs off the hillside with his clawed hands, his

feet dangling into the emptiness. He looks up, and not only is the RV hovering in the air, but so is every other bus and vehicle. His eyes fixate on the gun turrets of the lead hover-vehicle as his breathing gets louder; he braces for the end.

The RV turns and flies away. The hover-buses follow, and as they turn, he can see the faces of the Jew-Christians staring at him, men with straw hats or black fedoras, women with bonnets or straw hats. The remaining RV and SUV hover-vehicles take up the rear. The flying convoy moves away, and he watches them become specks in the distance. He looks around at the devastation.

Bloodgood claws his way up and jumps onto the ground. He sees another SUV racing to him, and it stops. Agent Lariat and Agent Runningstar exit and run to him.

He yells, "What took you two so long? Get on the line and tell them we need sat-tracking and air support now. Damn! I could be calling in now myself. They took their silencer weapon with them." He immediately takes out his e-pad.

Bloodgood suddenly yells out as a metal stake pierces through his body and breaks through his chest! He realizes that he is being held up on his feet as he is turned around by two pairs of hands. Agent Lariat looks at him with a completely emotionless face; there is a cross on a chain around his neck. Agent Runningstar smiles; she is wearing a necklace with a Star of David.

Agent Lariat says, "You should never have killed that eighty-year-old woman."

The two double-agents lift Bloodgood up and throw him off the edge into the massive chasm.

Supreme Senate Assembly Headquarters, Colorado Springs, Colorado
9:00 a.m., 14 April 2089

It doesn't take long for the Supreme Senate of Governors to find out that another governor has been killed in an action against the Jew-Christians. There is pandemonium as governors yell for answers, demand explanations, and call for hearings and investigations.

At the back of the chambers, Governor Chauncey of New

Hampshire stands with the governors of Vermont, Maine, Rhode Island, Connecticut, Wisconsin, and Minnesota—the new Northern Confederacy.

Governor Chauncey shakes his head. "Another dead governor. Wilson will get us all killed. Maybe…if he were…killed first…"

The female governor of Vermont grabs him by the arm. "You will not get *us* killed. You know that kind of talk will get you thrown in prison. What's wrong with you? You want to end the Confederacy before it even gets started."

"Chauncey, this is not the time to lose it. We have other states quietly asking about joining us," the Maine governor says. "But we have to hold it together—and ourselves too."

"Chauncey," the Vermont governor says, "I'm not going to say I understand what you're going through, because I don't. But revenge in this case will end us all, even thinking about it. Wilson is untouchable. We have to accept that. Our only way is to defeat him in an election."

"He shot my son in the head! He wasn't even armed!"

"Chauncey, this pain is going to destroy you, and that will destroy us. I beg you to seek help. Whatever psych-therapy you need to control your rage, you have to do it. If not for your sake, for the sake of the Confederacy," the Vermont governor says.

"Wilson has all of us under surveillance," the Wisconsin governor says. "He's not going to allow a viable power-base to grow that can oppose him. We have to be clever, cautious. It's going to take us a time, working quietly, behind the scenes. None of us can do anything to attract attention."

Chauncey looks at all of them. "You're right. I'm a liability to the Confederacy." He motions to one of the security agents standing on the side. "Give me your e-pad."

The agent hands him his device. Chauncey quickly types something on the screen.

"I want you to go right now and bring this back to me."

The agent looks at it and his face is shocked. "Governor, why do you want this?"

"That's my business. Go get it."

"Governor…"

"I just want to do a simple demonstration. It will be okay. You know me."

The agent looks at him, thinking. He turns and leaves the chambers.

"Chauncey, what are you about to do?" the Vermont governor asks.

"I want you all to build the Confederacy into one of the most powerful forces in the nation," Governor Chauncey says. "Under our control, not Wilson's."

"Wilson isn't stupid, Chauncey. If we do anything against his presidency, he will use it as an excuse to dissolve the Supreme Senate or even impose martial law. That's what he'll do. We have to be very careful. He got one Constitution abolished. Why not the new one for his purposes?" the Rhode Island governor says.

"I want you to be his friend. Volunteer to help him in every way possible. Take the lead in his initiatives. We won't be able to destroy him by acting against him. You're right. He'd have us imprisoned or worse. We will destroy him by *not* acting at the right time. That time will come, tomorrow, next year, a decade from now. It will come, and then the Confederacy will be ready."

"Chauncey, you're not planning suicide, are you?" the Vermont governor asks.

"No, I plan to live a long life to see the Confederacy destroy the man who killed my son."

The agent reappears with a bag and hands it to Governor Chauncey. He motions to his lieutenant governor, who is seated nearby.

"Cain, I want you to get to know my friends here very well. After today, the seven of you will be the only people in this entire nation who can avenge my son and save America from Wilson."

"Chauncey, do not do whatever you are about to do," the Vermont governor pleads.

Governor Chauncey reaches into the bag and takes out the machine gun. They all freeze. He casually walks away from them and across the back of the chamber. He is so calm that none of the security agents even notice what he's carrying in his hand.

It is common for the Supreme Senate to invite guests for special recognition during the proceedings: community activists, celebrities, other politicians, people in the news. They sit in the front row of the chamber and wait until that part of the program begins, always near the beginning, as Supreme Senate proceedings can last many hours.

Governor Chauncey walks up a center aisle to one of the people in the special recognition row—a muscular man with a crew cut. He walks up to him and shots him with machine-gun fire. The chamber erupts in panic as everyone runs to the exits as Governor Chauncey casually puts the weapon on the ground and raises his hands in the air. Security agents surround him, guns pointing.

The White House
1:02 p.m., 14 April 2089

"He was taken into custody and will be convicted on first-degree murder," Homeland Director McDunn says.

"No special circumstances?" President Wilson asks.

"No, sir. It was part of his plea deal to avoid a trial. He was deemed insane. The victim was the officer who killed his son at the Pennsylvania incident."

Wilson yells, "How did he find that out? Wasn't everything classified pending investigation?"

"Yes, sir. It was. But Governor Chauncey has a lot of friends in the District. Any one of them could have leaked him the name."

The presidential advisor says, "Sir, the Confederacy held a press conference strongly condemning Governor Chauncey's actions, and his lieutenant governor who will be replacing him said the state of New Hampshire will make full restitution to the man's family. Sir, they are distancing themselves from Chauncey as fast and as far as they can. The Confederacy said that Chauncey's views were his own."

The Homeland director says, "Also, sir, they are taking lead roles in our new Atlantic Seaboard Defense. Their states will be taking primary lead roles in protecting not just their northeastern states, but New York and the District as well."

"Sir, Chauncey has effectively neutralized himself. He might not be executed, but he will be in prison long into the distant future. No elective office or appointed office will ever see him again. One of your major problems removed from the domestic board, sir." The president's advisor is smiling.

"True," President Wilson says. "But the Lucifers are out there. They can say what they want, but they will try to hurt me somehow."

The president's advisor says, smiling. "Sir, Mrs. Lucifer had a stroke yesterday. She's in a coma and not expected to survive."

Location Unknown
5:30 a.m., 15 April 2089

Sek has flown into the undisclosed location and the meeting is starting on time.

"Everyone has been settled in nicely. We split up the Amish populations between Providence and Restoration. The Mennonites are at Sanctuary. They're not in our enclaves, but on connecting adjacent land. They don't have physical walls or fencing around their territory, but with our tek they will be as protected as if they had solid twenty-foot walls."

"Good," Moses says. "And?"

NIS types away, working on two e-pads at the same time, sitting next to him.

"Everyone involved directly in her murder has been dealt with permanently," Sek says. "As for our…contractor—the Goths say with the drugs, she'll be under for a few months," Sek says.

Moses now looks to NIS.

NIS says, "My turn, boss. You wanted three things: who killed her, who sent them, and who informed on her location. We've dealt with the first and are about to deal with the second." He pushes one of his e-pads to Moses. "The name of the informant who got Elder Mother Esther killed."

Moses looks at it and then looks up at him.

NIS says, "You don't have to say it. It's been triple checked and quadruple checked backwards and forwards and sideways. Every bit of proof is attached."

Moses says, "I need to see that proof, and I can't be the one to authorize the contract. Sek, you'll need to have leadership evaluate it."

NIS says, "We've also identified every government collaborator they have working within the Christian community. You never found them before because they weren't directly in the Resistance itself. They even have agents in the Jewish enclaves. Should we inform them?"

Moses reflects on the information. "No. Let them find them on their own. Their intelligence is supposed to be as good as ours. When they do, we'll know they've put themselves back together."

Sek says, "I'll have a team ready when it's approved."

"No," Moses says. "I didn't deal with that Vampire directly because all he did was call in the drone strike. The collaborator is the one who made it all happen. I'll handle him personally."

The White House
10:00 a.m., 18 April 2089

President Wilson feels a heavy weight has lifted from his shoulders with Governor Chauncey sent to prison for the next thirty years and Mrs. Lucifer lying in a coma not expected to revive, her cyborg partner never leaving her side. The two people in the nation who could conceivably hurt him politically are no longer a threat to him and will never be again. Now he can refocus on the domestic threat that he's wanted to deal with decisively for over a decade.

Eighteen years ago, it started out so promisingly, but his Jew-Christian useful idiots failed. He had high hopes for Rabbi Susan, who once said in a speech: "The problem with Jew-Christians is that they have this dual persecution-superiority complex. They have this perpetual fixation on being the victims of a genocide, and another is always around the corner. They have this perpetual attitude that they are 'the Chosen People' as if their existence is special. We cannot cater to group delusions of any kind. Religiosity has no place in the public square or as a shield to the law of the land. To this end, the Good Bible must replace all Torahs and Bibles in the nation. No American citizen, religious or secular, is above the Rule of Law, and that includes my fellow Jews." But in the end, her Jew-Christians ostracized her completely and her own deputy director got himself killed; Wilson didn't hesitate to fire her. The Vampires also failed miserably. However, he still has double-agents in the Jew-Christian community.

President Wilson says to the gathering of reporters and staff, "We can never stop in our resolve. We're America. There is nothing we can't do. Look how long it took for us to end slavery, get women the right to vote, end child labor exploitation, end skin-color segregation, get universal healthcare, legalize all pan-sexual unions, get the new constitution—our Rule of Law—enacted.

"We will relocate Jew-Christians from their ghettoes around the nation into the new Lebanon Reservation. One hundred square miles of federally acquired land and will be located at co-ordinates thirty-nine degrees fifty minutes latitude, ninety-eight degrees thirty-five minutes longitude—the geographical center of the nation. The Lebanon Reservation in Lebanon, Kansas will be the new sanctuary for Jew-Christians in America."

No more governors could be allowed to get themselves killed; the Supreme Senate could grow into a serious threat if that happened again. He sought out their guidance in the implementation of Project Purify. He would do what was necessary to placate them and get the Project done.

Then Master Pastor reappeared on the scene, eager to help the government enact the Project, as long as he would be the appointed governor of the new Lebanon Reservation, which he unilaterally renamed *Promise-Land*.

The Coliseum, Sanctuary Enclave
10 a.m., 22 April 2089

Master Pastor is coming to town!
The largest meeting place of the three sister enclaves in Pennsylvania is in Sanctuary. The Coliseum can accommodate twenty

thousand people, and in attendance are people from Providence sitting in the first third of the seating, Sanctuary in the middle, and Restoration in the last third.

Master Pastor's Greatest Church in the World mega-church no longer exists. Many of his congregation abandoned him, and then the city council re-zoned the entire tek-city, banning any religious organization or institution from the area.

The chairman of the Sanctuary enclave introduces him. He is back with a new church, a new leadership board, new members, and a new favored relationship with the government. The meeting is supposed to be secular, but Master Pastor has organized it to be a pseudo-service, and he smiles wide as he stands on the stage to address the crowds, the massive vid-screens hanging down from the ceilings making his likeness visible to the furthest corners of the Coliseum. He even has a new dancing and singing chorus, which opens the meeting with uplifting gospel numbers. When they're done, Master Pastor spends almost ten minutes greeting each member of his gospel chorus and engaging in jokes and horseplay.

"Dear good people of Sanctuary, Restoration, and Providence, I thank you and your leadership for allowing me to address this body today, and I thank you for attending this important meeting for us, followers of Christ in a world of darkness. We may have been on opposite sides in the past, but as it says in Psalm 133:1, 'How good and pleasant it is when brothers live together in unity!' I am here to talk to you about Promise-Land. Not a sanctuary enclave, but a sanctuary multi-state for all our people, our families, our children. It's time to end our self-imprisonment, the fear, the running, the hiding, the violence. We're tired, overwhelmed, and battle-weary."

"Yes, we need to end many things," a voice booms.

General Moses walks down the main aisle of the Coliseum, a mic fastened to his lapel.

Moses continues, "The largest church in America, the first mega-church, for the first one hundred and sixty years of America, was the US Capitol building itself. Two thousand could attend service. In regular attendance were all the Founding Fathers and the Congress. But from that foundational history the Pagans and their religious collaborators have spread such convincing propaganda to deny what was. They argued that religiosity in the public square was not permissible, when the very people who founded the nation, wrote the original Constitution that governed the nation in its beginning did such now-illegal things as pray on government property, carry around a Bible, and hang the Ten Commandments up on the wall. Many different Orders met in the Capitol building. Even Mr. Thomas Jefferson, not popular among Faithers of this generation, attended those services regularly, a member of the Anglican and Episcopalian churches.

"And here we are to behold the one who so humbly calls himself Master Pastor, the *President's Pastor*. The flamboyant one who had a dog with solid gold food and water dishes, a cat with a solid gold litter box, in a ten-thousand-square-foot house."

Master Pastor counters, "God doesn't want his people to be poor and destitute. We must be of means so that we can help the poor and spread the Word. Do not judge me, Moses. You are not worthy to do so. I am doing what's in my heart. Now I am being guided by God to save our people. Not to watch them slaughtered or carried off to jail. Do not judge me."

"Those who say 'who are we to judge' can cite a verse out of context, but nothing more. There's a whole book in the Bible titled Judges, so the Bible does call on us to make judgments, or how would you live in faith rather than sin? Yes, Jesus says we shouldn't be finding fault with people, but again He says there are times when we *must* make righteous judgments. I judge you, sir. I judge you to be an evil man with nothing but blackness in your heart and a forked serpent's tongue."

Master Pastor is now angry. "I came here as a guest of the Sanctuary Enclave Council. I do not have to hear your words!"

Moses says, "Proverbs 6:16-19 speaks of the seven things that are detestable to the Lord. We will never submit to false prophets who try to take our Bibles, our churches, our lives. We will never submit to you."

"Good people of Sanctuary, Restoration and Providence. I came here in good faith to speak with you. Not to be harassed by this man who has always harbored hate in his heart for me because a long, long time ago I was chosen for the leadership of an old organization, the United National Baptist Convention, over his father. This is the source of his hatred, this pettiness. I want to speak with you honestly and directly, without his harassment," Master Pastor calls out to the audience.

Moses ignores the lie and continues, "Throughout the New Testament, there are warnings of both false prophets and false Messiahs, and believers are called upon to be vigilant. From Jesus's own Sermon on the Mount in Matthew 7:15–23: 'Watch out for false prophets. They come to you in sheep's clothing, but inwardly they are ferocious wolves. By their fruit you will recognize them. Do people pick grapes from thorn bushes, or figs from thistles? Likewise every good tree bears good fruit, but a bad tree bears bad fruit. A good tree cannot bear bad fruit, and a bad tree cannot bear good fruit. Every tree that does not bear good fruit is cut down and thrown into the fire. Thus, by their fruit you will recognize them.'

"Yes, a false prophet on the payroll of Galerius, bought with promises of power and grandeur, secret Russian Bloc bank accounts, and access to a steady supply of sex slaves, his favorites being twin eleven-year-old girls with his name tattooed on their breasts."

"F--- you!" Master Pastor yells.

Cursing of any kind—Pagan-speak—in an enclave is forbidden. But the notion of a clergyman yelling such an expletive in a house of worship is not only beyond the pale in Faither society, it is near blasphemy. There is deafening silence in the grand Coliseum.

Moses says softly, "The false prophet, a Judas most vile, who told Galerius the location of my mother, Elder Mother Esther, where he immediately sent Pagan assassins to kill her."

The color from Master Pastor's face seems to disappear. He now realizes from the expressions of the faces in the crowd that everyone already knows. *They have invited him here to kill him.*

He is somewhat light-headed now and walks away from the center of the stage, then steps slowly down the steps. His chorus stands to the side and looks away from him in utter terror, internally praying for him not to acknowledge them in any way. He walks slowly to the main aisle.

Mother Moses rises to her feet from the center of the first row. "All salute Master Pastor, the Great and Powerful!"

Everyone in the Coliseum stands. In a deafening thunder of unison: "Hail Master Pastor, the Great and Powerful!"

He starts to walk up the aisle to the exit as people start to file out from the rows towards him. Each one salutes him by touching their right temple with their hand and saying "Hail Master Pastor, the Great and Powerful." As he continues to walk up the aisle, tears start to roll down the side of his face. The crowds of people walk up to him, but never obstructing his path, with the same chant from everyone from the youngest child to the oldest person, "Hail Master Pastor, the Great and Powerful." He can see the exit doors open in the back and the light shining in. He cries even more knowing that, despite the daylight, this is the end.

Arlington, Virginia
22 April 2089

President Wilson did it. He fired nearly everyone from his inner circle of advisors, who had served him loyally for eight years, but he would ensure all of them got powerful jobs in the private sector. Only the Homeland director and chief presidential advisor are retained. Wilson even got his Vice President to step down so he could get a new one.

Wilson quickly appointed his new team of staffers.

At 8:37 p.m., Ms. Gee, his new flamboyant, ever-visible White House press secretary, comes home with her partners. They are commonly known as "big-bedders," slang for people in communal or group marriages. The reality today is that though marriage is legal for any lifestyle, only Jew-Christians get married. It is rare for Pagans to engage in the practice.

After dinner, they all go to bed. She and all twelve of her partners go to the giant mattress in the bedroom where they all sleep together. She often says that's just how animals sleep in the wild.

At 5:05 a.m., she awakens to some noise and walks out into the kitchen. She screams out and faints.

The body of Master Pastor is slumped dead in a chair at their dinner table. In other chairs around him, six on each side, are the dead bodies of all the moles within the Christian community.

Homeland personnel can't explain how the Jew-Christians were able to identify every agent in the country, including those that had been in deep cover for close to fifteen years.

There are no wounds or marks of any kind and no traces of poison among any of the thirteen Christian collaborators. Unlike the others, the face of Master Pastor is anything but emotionless—crushing, bottomless despair and horror.

The Continuum

"Any kingdom divided against itself will be ruined, and a house divided against itself will fall." – Jesus of Nazareth, Luke 11:17, New Testament

"It is dangerous to be right when the government is wrong." – Voltaire, 18th century writer, historian, philosopher of the Enlightenment

Providence Enclave
9:36 a.m., 2 May 2089

With the nearly eight thousand members of the Anabaptist Orders, mostly Amish with a minority population of Mennonites, someone had to be appointed as the chief liaison between the Anabaptists and Protestants. That person could be no other.

"What did you do to that boy?" Mrs. Abigail scolds the new Anabaptist liaison ambassador.

"Which boy?" Kristiana asks.

"That Canadian Amish boy."

"Oh, him."

"Yes, him. What did you do to him? I thought you were going to marry that boy."

"The Canadian? I'm not sure. Maybe I should 'buy American' only."

"Stop fooling around."

"He did a horrible thing and I don't think I can forgive him for it."

"Don't you Amish forgive everyone for anything?"

"Not this."

"What did he do?"

"He was visiting and he was inside the house and I caught him in my bedroom."

"Is this going to be a G-rated story?"

"He was trying to rip apart Bo Bear! I practically had a heart attack. I don't think I could marry someone with such violence in his heart. It's a slippery slope. Beat up a helpless teddy bear one day, who knows what's next."

"Stop fooling around. What did he say?"

"Nothing, I threw him out of the house. I've shunned him!"

"Go talk to that boy and get control of this situation. You have that boy walking around the entire town with a big teddy bear, publicly humiliating himself, apologizing to you."

"Yes, the Bo Bear imposter!"

"Aren't you some kind of new, big leader for your Amish? You are not allowed to act childish anymore."

"Yes, I can. I'm not married yet."

"Go talk to that boy! Your eldest sisters are married now, right?"

"Yes."

"You're number three. Get your mind right and your life right and talk to that boy. Believe me, if the worst your husband-to-be has done is beat up a teddy bear, then snatch him up. Husbands are known for doing dumb things. It's called being a male."

"Okay, I'll talk to the Canadian."

"Good!"

"Fine!"

Kristiana storms off. As she approaches the Moses house, she almost forgets why she has come. She walks up the walkway and knocks on the door before opening and entering. Mother Moses is in the kitchen cooking something new.

"Hi, M," Kristiana says in a huff.

"Well, you're in a bad mood. What happened?"

"Nothing important."

Mother Moses smiles. "I have a job for you."

"A job?"

"Since your leaders don't want to participate on our leadership council."

"We don't join any political groups of any kind. Just tell us what you need us to do."

"How about we pick some Amish person to attend our meetings so that we have Amish representation in the room? An observer."

"Oh, yes. We can do that. What will this group be called?"

"The Continuum."

Moses House
5:00 p.m., 3 May 2089

"Okay Moses. Spill the secrets," Thaddeus says.

The Resistance leadership meets in the sitting room of the Moses house again. Assembled are the same leaders from around the nation as before: Dalmatia and Thaddeus (ex-Southern Baptist), Andrew and Faith (ex-Episcopalian), Peter and Zoe (ex-Lutheran), Dale and Cordelia (ex-Presbyterian), Father Daniel and Sister Maggie (ex-Catholic), Seth and Cressa (ex-American Baptist), Bishop Cyrus and Phoebe (ex-Anglican), Jason and Sapphire (ex-Pentecostal), Joshua and Charity (ex-Church of God in Christ), Lucius and Ruth (ex-Methodist).

"The year 732 AD," Moses says.

"The Battle of Tours," Dale responds.

"Thirteen hundred and fifty-seven years ago, Muslim armies were advancing throughout the entire known world to conquer and convert all to Islam. At that time, Egypt, Jordan, and Syria were the center of Christendom. The Battle of Tours was fought on the tenth of October, 732 AD, and if the Christian leader Charles Martel had not been victorious against the Muslims, there would have been no Christian Western Europe and no America later. Martel defeated far superior forces. It was a miracle. So was the fledgling America defeating the British Empire to form the United States of America. So was Moses and the Israelites being freed from the ancient Egyptian empire to form Jewish Israel. We Christians have faced supposedly superior forces throughout our entire existence, and we're still here. Most of our enemies are not. So for me, it's never been about whether we'd survive Galerius. I've never doubted that. My fear has always been elsewhere.

"I was talking to my son one day. Must have been about two years ago now. He said to me, 'Father, you don't have to deal with the Pagans too much longer, because once I get big, I'll make it so they can never touch, harm, or kill another Faither again.' At first, I was proud of his resolve. But the more I thought of it, I was actually…scared.

"There was Charles Martel the First, Charles the Hammer, who saved Christendom. But we also had his grandson, Charlemagne, who was involved in war every year of his fifty-year reign. He was big on the masses learning to read and write, but took our noble, historical Christian practice of evangelizing into the realm of evil with vicious conversion campaigns and massacres—'Become a Christian or die.'"

"Moses, you don't think we're going to regress into the dark Christians?"

"Us, no. But can we be so sure about our children, or our children's children?"

"Well, that's absolutely unfair. We have to deal with the mess of a country the progenitors left to us. Now you want us to worry ourselves with what our offspring may or may not do in the future when none of us are here. Why should we have a double burden?"

"Because we're the only ones who can handle such a double burden. We are where we are supposed to be." Moses says. "We see the Amish, for instance, and reject their pacifism, but we understand how they came to that path out of the extremely violent world they lived in. But what path will we choose in our battle with the Pagans, one of greater violence? We'll win this second civil war, but at what cost? We know there is no limit to the depth of the world's violence, depravity, and immorality. Will we sink to even lower depths to defeat our enemies? Because I fear it may come to that. Self-defense is forever. Pre-emptive actions will always remain on the table. But it's not about the violence. It never has been. It is about preserving our God-centered communities and way of life, protecting our families and homes, not just for our sake, but for our children's sake."

"What are you saying, Moses? We don't want to misinterpret. You're not talking about surrender are you?"

"Never. The story of Noah is not one of surrender or retreat. I'm talking about *transcending*. Let your enemies fight with sticks and stones on the ground, while you walk far above all of them in the clouds with your laser pistol in your pocket. You don't mind them, because they no longer matter."

"The secretive Project Noah?"

"Yes."

"You're still talking in riddles, Moses."

"Ladies and gentleman, I formally present to you a proposal for the Continuum. An Order is a specific group or movement within a religion, replacing the old words 'denomination' or 'sect'. A Continuum is the alliance of all the Orders within a faith, with the dual and separate duties of both religious and secular leadership. The religious side will deal with our biblical doctrine, philosophies, and teaching; the historical preservation of our religious texts and artifacts; and our churches. The secular will be our own standing government, including security, defense, intelligence, and overall tek supremacy. This new Continuum will ally with both the African Collective and the Magi, among others. Project Noah will be the largest endeavor in the history of mankind. I'll tell you what the project is at a later date, as its scope is so incredible that you would not believe it even if I did tell you. We've gotten the secular part down magnificently: we've stopped Galerius's Project Purify again; neutralized his collaborators, kill-teams and storm trooper attacks; and we're not done with him yet. We may not be powerful enough to make him disappear. But we can hurt him—badly—until we are. And when we are able, we won't even care about him anymore. We'll be beyond his reach.

"The religious element for us is quite another matter. We have great leaders in faith and churches, but that is on the micro level. We still have not resolved the issue of the collapse of our Orders as a result of the Registrant-Resister wars. We can't be 'former' this and 'ex' that forever.

"In the past, all Christians were Catholics. Then came the Protestant Reformation. Then we had new splits: Lutherans, Calvinists, and Methodists. And we're not even talking about the split of the Eastern Orthodox from Catholicism before the Reformation. In our pre-modern times, we had some fifty thousand different Christian denominations in the world at our peak. Almost a million Protestants and over one billion Catholics. The Catholics, only because of Africa and the Spanish Americas, have retained most of their numbers. We, however, with the secularization and end of Western Europe and the rise of Pagans in America—we have been slowly declining. The Eastern Orthodox are trapped in the Russian Bloc.

"Protestantism is in shambles. And it happened long before our Registrant-Resister civil war. Religiously, we lost our way a long time ago," Moses says. "We have excelled at the secular, now we must get our Faith house in order. I formally propose to move our own Orders from religious disorder to a new structure of order. *Re-unification.*"

Quiet.

"You can't be serious."

"It's a radical idea, but the emergence of Protestantism was radical. The emergence of America in the eighteenth century was radical. As Christ said, and as was reiterated by Abraham Lincoln: united we stand, divided we fall. Fundamentally, how do our Orders differ anymore? In the 1700s, yes. The 1800s, yes. The 1900s, maybe. Now?"

"Moses, each of our Orders has a unique history."

"1521, Lutheranism. 1534, Episcopalianism. 1607, the Baptist Church. 1739, the Methodist Church. Three hundred and fifty years, endless division and revisions, forty thousand other different Protestant Orders later. What does any of it have to do with our relationship with God through Jesus Christ? I submit to you that no lay member of any of our Orders could tell you what makes their Order different from all the others. Maybe a little variety in terms of length of church service, type of worship, type of music, or the loudness of said worship. The unique doctrines are gone. All that remains are…the names. I propose re-unification into the *New Protestant Order*."

Zoe breaks the silence. "I'll be first, then: I like it. Lutherans now have such a foul reputation among Faithers. Ironic, considering we were the first Protestants. Let's be first again. I like it, and I think our group will as well." Her husband Peter smiles at her.

Moses looks to the ex-Anglicans and ex-Catholics. "I do respect your unique position in all of this. The Anglican Order has been taking in former Catholics for decades. I could understand if you wanted to maintain something different—a renewed Order of some kind. And Father Daniel and Sister Maggie, it would be real hard for you to give up your forty-six books in the Old Testament for us thirty-nine-book Old Testament Protestant minimalists."

People smile.

All the branches of Christianity had twenty-seven books in the New Testament, but for Protestants there were thirty-nine books in the Old Testament. The Old Testament of Catholics and Eastern Orthodox contained additional deuterocanonical books—forty-six books for Catholicism and fifty-one books for Eastern Christianity.

Cyrus smiles. "We can speak with Father Daniel and Sister Maggie privately. Yes, we've been taking in former Catholics, but we've also lost a lot more Anglicans."

Father Daniel says, "Sadly, the American Catholic Order is no more. Most of our churches are gone, condemned and sold away all over the country. Pedophile psychiatrist organizations and the growing secularization of the church destroyed what was left even before the Registrants came around. Many of us are very tempted to move to Africa, where Catholicism has been reborn. None of us will set foot on European soil, even to live in Vatican Italy, with the Caliphate surrounding them. None of us believes that truce will last, regardless of what the Pope says. I wish the Spanish Americas weren't dominated by so many narco-Catholic priests on the payroll of the cartels there. They need a savior." He looks at Cyrus. "Our groups can talk privately. We are not opposed to converting to Protestantism. I never thought I would ever think such a thing, let alone say it aloud, but we're open."

Cyrus says, "Don't let our groups' particular issues influence what everyone here has to decide."

Moses continues, "All of us really are so alike theologically that we would be hard-pressed to lay out real present-day differences, the history aside. One: the Godhead—the Father, the Son, the Holy spirit. Two: Jesus is the Son of God. Three: Salvation through Him. Four: The soul is immortal. Five: The Bible is divinely inspired. Six: The second coming of Christ. Seven: The Final Judgment, though we all believe the end of the world started the second Adam and Eve were expelled from Eden, but we live and act as if the End Times will be sometime in year 56,541 AD. Our focus is not the Apocalypse, but living the role God set out for us. Eight: Belief in a heaven and hell. Nine: The power of prayer. We pray every day; some of us even face Old Jerusalem when we do. Ten: obeying the commandment of tithing to our church. Eleven: Observing the Sabbath, or day of rest, no work, no tek, every week. Again, in truth, we no longer are different Orders. Our Registrant-Resister war, the Separatist movement, our creation of the Resistance, the excommunication of collaborators, the neutralization of spies, the continued persecution by the Pagans have created the perfect storm for, I believe, an inevitable re-unification for us."

Kristiana, though invited, is not in the meeting. She stands on the porch of the Moses house watching the home of Mrs. Abigail, next door. The front door opens, and one of the female guards exits and walks to her.

"Are you not going to be attending the meeting?" she asks. She has a black tear tattooed under her eye and fiddles with her wedding ring as she talks.

Kristiana notices. "Are you newly married?"

"Yes, I am. To a great and decent man."

"Congratulations. Both my older sisters got married recently. Their husbands are from Ohio Amish communities."

"Congratulations to you, then. You're next in line."

Kristiana makes a disapproving sound. "My mind is still not

settled on that yet."

"Well, I don't mean to interrupt you, but I need to keep the porch clear. At least until the meeting is over."

"Is Sek in the meeting too?"

"Yes, he is."

"I need to talk to Sek, right now."

Dyna, the security guard, looks at her. "I can't disturb the meeting. It'll have to wait until it's over."

"No, right now. Immediately," Kristiana insists.

Inside, Moses is speaking: "I see no reason to re-invent the wheel. We can adopt portions of the old Declaration of Independence."

The door of the sitting room opens slowly. Sek immediately notices the security man motioning for him to come outside.

Sek appears outside the room and closes the door. The male and female security duo waits for him.

"This better be important," Sek says.

"The Amish girl insisted she see you," Dyna says.

He walks to her. "Kristiana, this is a very important meeting. In fact, why aren't you inside? We invited you."

"Where's Mrs. Abigail?" Kristiana asks.

"The next-door neighbor?"

"Yes."

"She's visiting family in Sanctuary. Kristiana, we check all those things before we have a high-level meeting with our leaders."

"When did she leave?"

"Why are you asking me these questions? She left two days ago."

"No, she didn't. I was talking to her yesterday. I came by to talk to M. That's when M invited me. Mrs. Abigail was here yesterday."

Sek is now suspicious. "Okay, so she left yesterday and not two days ago."

"Mrs. Abigail follows the exact same routine every morning. She opens all the windows on the first floor, and you can always smell the breakfast she is cooking. And she sings too when she makes her breakfast. At noon she comes outside to tend to her garden. She spends at least an hour outside while she does that, and she always drinks at least one glass of juice. In the mid-afternoon, she goes on her power-walk. For that she's gone at least two hours, sometimes three hours, because she doesn't just walk but she visits with all her friends. She's back by five o'clock and she waters the lawn. She always sits on the porch and drinks her tea. She loves her mahogany rocking chair, a gift from her late husband. She closes all the windows shut and locks them before she goes to bed, which is always no later than nine p.m. When she does take trips out of the enclave, she always sets her machines to automatically water the lawn at five a.m., and she always puts those mini plant robots, the ones that clip onto the pot and look like upside-down water bottles with tentacles to water all the plants at the same time. She also leaves all the first-floor windows open."

Sek asks, "What about the next-door neighbors on the other side?"

"The Huxtables have no routine. They have three small children. The only routine for them is Mr. Huxtable gets up at five a.m. to jog in the morning. But they're all in Sanctuary for the next two months helping my people and the Mennonites get settled in. They're teachers. Their house is empty."

"The neighbors across the street?"

"The Fergusons on the left are retired too, and all they do is sit on their porch and watch the street. I'm still not sure if you pay them to do that, and they go inside whenever I come by. And the Mellneys on the other side always have their children visiting and they are always playing with the grandchildren. You hardly ever see them, but you can sure hear the grandkids. Sek, I know everyone on this block and all the blocks around us."

Sek and the other security personnel stare at her. He walks to the window of the house and can see Mrs. Abigail's house clearly. No sprinklers, no plant robots on the pots, all the windows are closed. He looks at his watch: 5:10 p.m.

He turns around and marches to the sitting room and opens the door.

"Ladies and gentlemen, we have a code red," Sek says. Everyone stands up from their chairs. "Everyone into the panic room now."

Mother Moses runs to the far wall and taps it, and a hidden door pops open. Everyone files down a long set of stairs to the underground.

"Stick to Moses as if you're his second skin," Sek says to the security team and they disappear down the stairs too. He takes Kristiana by the arm. "Follow them."

"What's happening?"

"Follow them down into the panic room."

"What is that?"

"Go downstairs and ask someone when you see them."

Kristiana quickly runs down the stairs. Sek follows as several heavily armed men in military fatigues enter the house from a secret door and they all go down the stairs. The solid steel door to the stairs closes automatically and clicks. The wall door closes automatically.

Storm troopers pour out of the Abigail house and race into the Moses house. As soon as the first few enter, they begin rapidly firing stun grenades and tear gas pellets; they explode all throughout the house in blinding light flashes and clouds of yellow gas. Within moments there are at least fifty of them inside the house, moving from room to room.

Outside, there are now so many of them that the front, side, and back yards are packed with them, facing the house, encircling the property, aiming their weapons.

"We're inside," the storm trooper assault commander says into his ear-set. "But it looks like we just missed them. We'll find them, sir. We're in their perimeter, so if they disengage their tek-jammers, our jets are standing by for air assault."

On the porch of the secure house, the Fergusons, wearing their dark sunglasses, rise from their rocking chairs. Suddenly, they run to the army of storm troopers and are immediately shot by stun grenade fire and tear gas. Through the thick yellow smoke, the Fergusons continue towards the troopers, but their arms have now become gun-turrets. Other Fergusons appear—the androids approach the storm troopers from everywhere, alternatively firing heavy rounds and pulse blasts.

"We're under heavy fire! I have men down!" the storm trooper commander yells. His men dive for cover, others try to run into the house but the gun-fire is too intense, other troopers return fire from the house, but more attacking androids keep appearing. The gun battle is massive. Troopers and androids fall.

The storm trooper commander lies flat on the ground pinned by android gunfire. He hears a noise in the air and looks up. Missiles rise from the enclave wall towards them.

"Retreat! Retreat! They *can* use their own tek with their tek-jammers engaged!" The troopers dive for cover in futility—the mini-missiles rain down on them.

In the secure Providence situation room, the Resistance leaders sit at a conference table. Security stays close, and all of them watch the vid-link of the siege above.

Sek looks at his e-pad and says, "Almost two hundred troops. They tunneled right up and through the Abigail house." He shakes his head. "They got past our seismic sensors somehow."

Moses gestures Sek to the side. Mother Moses joins them.

"They've got jets and drones in the air, but our Iron Dome is activated," Sck says. He is deeply distressed. "I'm sorry, boss."

"Let's worry about that later," Moses says. "Get NIS on the line."

"If it weren't for Kristiana, we all could be dead now," Sek says.

"Yes. We saved them. They saved us. Exactly how it's supposed to be," Mother Moses says.

Sek steps away to talk on his secure e-pad.

Moses looks at his wife. They seem to be speaking without words. They walk back to the conference table.

"Ladies and gentlemen, we have our new ambassador of the Amish Order to thank for making sure the new Continuum didn't end on the very day it was about to begin."

Everyone looks at her with smiles and thank yous.

Moses says, "Providence security forces are doing their work so we will transport everyone safely to our air-evac points to your enclaves. And the Resistance will let Galerius know how much we appreciate that he still wants to play with us."

The White House Situation Room
7:10 p.m., 3 May 2089

The Homeland director is being briefed.

The general is angry. "I was told that we had officially stood down from any further actions against these people. We've lost an entire force again. And now two state-of-the-art, space-capable jets!"

"I thought they had auto-self-destruct," Homeland says. "How is this even possible?"

"Ma'am, you're not listening. It is possible because they did it. They blew all the drones out of the air and remoted into the two space-capable jets. The jets are gone! Do you have any idea what this means?"

"How is that possible?" Homeland says again. "We have GPS, sat-tracking, fail-safes, all-encrypted systems. It's not possible."

"There is chatter on the Net that our two jets are for sale! Do you have any idea of the damage to national security if the Caliphate or the CHINs get their hands on our jets? The CHINs have been stealing military secrets from us forever, but to get their hands on the actual hardware. These governments will pay *anything* to acquire them."

"What about the attack force?"

"What about them, ma'am? They're done—half dead, half incapacitated. I guess our intel that their own tek won't work within in their ghettoes with their tek-jammers engaged is false."

None one speaks for a few moments.

"I heard these tek-jammers are so strong that they can make a person's heart stop," an aide says. "Don't we have tek to neutralize their tek-jammers?"

"That's an urban myth," one of the general's aides says. "They can't make your heart stop. They're just powerful enough to keep most devices from working, and we have the tek too, but we've never developed it because we must have our tek operational at all times. Tek-cities must function at all times, so unfortunately they're ahead of us on that front. But it's all confined to their ghettoes, far from our tek-cities."

"Can we get the conversation back to the matter at hand?!" the general yells. To Homeland, he says, "Does the president have any idea of the disaster this is? Why does he keep doing it? We have Muslims and Anarchists to deal with. We have the CHINs and the Caliphate, and he's obsessed with backwards Jew-Christians walled up in their own self-segregated ghettoes. Why? The man gets elected to a third term and he seems determined to crash and burn his entire administration over this. Dead men, dead governors. Tell me, ma'am, does any of this make us look strong to our enemies?"

Secure Situation Room, Moses Home
9:31 p.m., 3 May 2089

The Resistance leaders continue with the meeting as they watch the vid-screens and get live text messages from their respective enclaves.

"How did they find out about our meeting? The exact location? Know we'd be here? Collaborators we missed?" Moses asks.

"Everyone is on this," Sek says. "No one sleeps until we have answers. But I have to say my incompetence on this incident is unforgiveable. We all could have been killed. There is no excuse for this lapse in security. I need to put myself on leave."

"And who's going to find out how this breach happened if you are on leave? No, I need you here. We have to figure this out. Do they have some kind of new tek that can beat our tek-jammers? New sat-recon that can see through our electro-mag shield?"

"We're looking at everything."

"How did they do it, Sek? Think it through step by step, just like you taught me. You've done it before a million times. How did they breach our security?"

Sek bows his head with his eyes closed. "What is different in Providence? Something new. An anomaly." He opens his eyes and suddenly realizes it. In his mind's eye, he sees all the many

Amish taking walks in the street at all times of day—men and women, young and old. He looks at Kristiana.

She looks back at him and realizes it too.

Washington Hilton Hotel Ballroom, Washington DC
6:30 p.m., 4 June 2089

President Wilson has not been seen in public for many months. The event is a special fundraiser of his major donors in the District. It is a tuxedo affair for the men and little black dress affair for the women.

Mrs. Lucifer is rolled into the banquet room by her cyborg husband. She may be in a wheelchair, but she is stunningly dressed.

"Hades, my God, you look amazing. And you just came out of a coma. How do you do it?" one the women says; everyone is noticing her.

She smiles and says, "Don't you know ninety is the new fifty?"

President Wilson gives a good speech. He smiles and waves as the attendees applaud.

The Supreme Senate has enacted law banning any presidential action against any Jew-Christian ghetto without the explicit approval from a majority of the nation's governors. They would only allow action against a Jew-Christian enclave in the nation if the administration could prove that that the enclave was behind a specific act of terrorism. Congress supported the law.

The National Police Chiefs Association has also banned the use of storm troopers for any federal action not approved by the Supreme Senate. The president of the NPCA said, "I have enough funerals to attend to carry me well into the next decade."

The entire intelligence community had been consumed with locating the missing American jets. The Northern Confederacy floated the idea of intervening on behalf of the White House and opened a dialogue with the Jew-Christians. Later, the jets were "found"—delivered, disassembled, to the Asian Consortium.

Wilson uses the return of the jets to overshadow his defeats to the Supreme Senate and the NPCA—and it has worked.

"Mr. President. It looks like we both seem to have come back from the dead," Mrs. Lucifer says, smiling. The president has moved from the stage to meet the attending donors at the event.

"Thank you, Mrs. Lucifer. Yes, we are both survivors."

"Yes, we are."

He continues to mingle in the crowd with his Secret Service detail close. They move him from the VIP section of the banquet, with its one hundred major donors, to the general area, where thousands of people wait behind a partition—smiling, cheering, reaching out their hands to greet him. He immediately walks to them. Such events with a celebrity of some sort greeting a crowd are the only times Pagans do shake hands. Wilson does so with a large smile on his face. He has managed to survive another crisis.

The man in the red fedora extends his hand towards the president. The man is smiling, unthreatening, but instead of shaking the president's hand, he reaches in and pokes him in the center of his chest with his index finger.

"The finger of God," he says and starts to walk backwards.

President Wilson is unnerved and his Secret Service detail is already calling in on their ear-sets to apprehend the man. The man seems to be enveloped by the crowd. Plainclothes Secret Servicemen rush into the crowd from three different sides. The man ducks down into the mass of people. They can't see him. The three Secret Servicemen reach the spot and all there is, lying on the ground, is the red fedora. The man is gone.

The lead Secret Service agent takes no chances. They surround the president and whisk him out of a side door to the secure parking lot and into the presidential limousine. Agents swarm into the banquet hall to detain the entire body of attendees.

Mrs. Lucifer starts to laugh. "Let's get out of here, husband. We've done our evil deed. Our little temporary alliance with the Jew-Christians is over. Let's disappear into the night before our good and dear friend the president sends a kill-team after us too like he did to our son."

Providence Enclave
8:05 a.m., 4 May 2089

Mr. Fisher walks through New Amish Quarter, a virtual replica of the old Amish Quarter only this one is right outside Providence enclave. Amish are busy at work everywhere, building their new community. He reaches a group of men putting up a new barn.

"Good afternoon, brother," he says to one of the men. "Which community are you with?"

The man stops hammering some nails and looks at him with a smile. "I'm from the Ohio community."

"Two of my daughters have married men from there. Good people there. But no one knows who you are, none of the Amish communities. Why are you pretending to be an Amish man?"

"I am from there, brother."

The other men stop their work and look at him.

"Speak to me in German then," Mr. Fisher says in Pennsylvania Dutch.

The man just looks at him. He picks up his hammer and holds it firmly.

"You're not thinking to harm me with that hammer. I'll take it from you."

The man suddenly throws the hammer at him. Mr. Fisher catches it in his hand effortlessly. The man runs away like a rabbit. No one chases him, but everyone watches him run out of New Amish Quarter.

Location Unknown
11:00 p.m., 4 May 2089

Sek says, "A good thing about the Amish and Mennonites is that they know everyone in their community. When no one was looking for you, you were safe. But the second we asked which Amish man or woman isn't accounted for, they picked you out in five seconds."

The Amish spy is handcuffed and his legs are shackled. Two large Providence security guards stand on either side of him.

"You are hereby convicted by the Continuum for espionage, attempted murder, attempted kidnapping, attempted false imprisonment, and conspiracy. You will be immediately transported to Africa for full interrogation by the best mind-benders on the planet. You will never return to America in your lifetime."

The man's face is angry, but he says nothing. The two large security men pull him off his feet and drag him from the room.

"We found his device and his cache of weapons buried in the woods," Sek says. Moses stands in the corner.

"How did he know about the meeting?—to tip off Galerius, tunnel up through the Abigail house," Moses asks.

"The late Master Pastor and the other recently deceased collaborators. They knew about the meeting and which Resistance members would be attending. The government simply tracked them here."

"How? We're so careful to avoid their facial-recog drones, Eyes, satellite scans. All enclaves are protected by tek-jammers, electro-mag shields."

"Yes, but the government has new tek—new bio-trackers. Binds with metal, polymer, cloth objects; can be injected into flesh. Special scanners are needed to detect them. They're quite good. We've already notified all Faithers about them. They told their Amish spy which house to watch, not the other way around. He simply provided them the precise intel that they needed to plan the strike."

Moses nods, then says, "Please tell me Mrs. Abigail is okay."

"We know where she is."

Pennsylvania, State Prison Facility
7:05 a.m., 5 May 2089

Agent Lariat and Agent Runningstar run to the prison bus and knock on the door before it can drive away. The bus driver opens the door.

"What is it?"

"I have orders here to relieve you," Agent Lariat says.

"What? I have no authorization for that."

"We have intel that this bus may be hit by terrorists," Agent Runningstar says. "We were sent to drive the bus in, but if you want to do it yourself, that's fine. We can say we missed you before you left."

The bus driver jumps up from his seat. "I don't get paid enough to take on terrorists. The bus is yours."

He gets off the bus and the agents get on. They look back at all their prisoners behind the glass partition separating the front seats from the rest of the bus. Mrs. Abigail sits sadly in a bright orange jumpsuit shackled to a seat; she has been crying. She stares aimlessly out the window.

The bus drives off.

Location Unknown
6:30 p.m., 4 June 2089

The secret underground data-bank looks very sci-fi. The tower servers are fifteen feet tall, encased in a blue reflective covering, each on wheels to be manually rolled and connected to the wall for access. Guards are on duty at all times, and patrolling the facility on foot.

Two guards stop at one of the rooms behind closed glass doors. They notice that the servers are all connected to the wall.

"How did the data-banks get connected?!" one of them yells.

They immediately call Central to have the doors opened. They slide open, and the two guards rush in and immediately roll the servers away from the wall.

Restoration Enclave
9:00 a.m., 4 July 2089

They gather in the massive underground auditorium. The meeting includes all the Resistance leaders from across the country. It is the new governing body of all thirty states for the Continuum—no Faithers live in the other American states.

The speakers address the crowd of some 571 leaders, one at a time:

"When this country was founded in 1776, ninety-eight percent was Protestant, less than two percent Catholic, and less than two-tenths of a percent was Jewish. Now less than ten percent are Jewish and two are Catholic." They laugh at Father Daniel's joke. He is good natured about a very sensitive issue for him and Sister Maggie. "But seriously, we have a momentous and historic decision to make here tonight. The debate between traditional versus non-traditional ended a long time ago. What we're fighting for now is even more fundamental than that—biblical versus non-biblical. Leaders going by scripture versus those making up things as they go to fit in with the Pagan world."

"The moral life of a nation is the foundation of its culture," Bishop Cyrus proclaims. "America may be lost, but the descendants of its Judeo-Christian people are still here. I know many of us still harbor contempt for our recent ancestors, the progenitors as we call them, who lost America. They publicly shied away from defending our faith, supported Pagan moral and cultural authority without question or opposition, loving the world's way rather than the Lord's, until they became nothing more than Pagans in Christian clothing, weakening the body of Christ. Our religious leaders cursed the darkness rather than being the light against it, their sermons became more secular, their understanding of biblical principles became more removed from the Bible, and others incredibly said there was no threat at all, until their very religious freedoms were taken from them."

"American values and religious values used to be the same thing. But now they are two radically different and separate things. We will always be the Resistance, but now we will be so much more. The Continuum will be a new chapter for us. Not just to move from defense to offense, but to transcend the very battle that rages," a West Coast reverend expresses.

"America's greatness was always three-fold: democracy, capitalism, and religion," Sapphire remarks. "But it devolved into a three-headed monster: no one votes, money without morals, and religion persecuted out of the public square. Religious liberty may be gone, but not us—freedom's greatest champions."

"The final battle of Registrants and Resisters actually did the separating for us by creating the sharpest contrast of differences between our people," Thaddeus notes. "Even more so than two hundred thirty-eight years ago when Christians divided over the issue of slavery in America. In our modern battle, the Registrants worshiped the political manipulation of the church, ignored biblical doctrines that defined our Orders and our faith; biblical theology became so watered down it could no longer be called Christianity. They embraced every fad and immorality of the world, pan-sexuality and entertainment celebrities became their religion, 'spiritual not religious' their chant, churches desperate to mean more in politics actually had the perverse opposite effect. They stood still when the Bible itself was ruled illegal hate-language and erased from society."

"All the labels of the past are gone: mainline, evangelical, leftist, rightist, traditional, modern. In the end it has come down to two camps: one for God and one for Galerius. The America we knew may be gone, but the American Experiment will live on through us," a reverend from the South professes. "E Pluribus Unum. It used to be the motto of America. It remains ours. From many, come one!"

"Our people made crucial mistakes. We put everything in one basket believing that defending the Constitution in our ineffective way would keep us a free, self-governing nation. We learned the hard way that it never was the Constitution that made us free; we make us free. It was a brilliant document, but still a piece of paper. We are the flesh-and-blood reality that makes it all real. Even the crafters of the original Constitution, the Founding Fathers, realized it was always up to us to keep the republic," Moses speaks. "We got caught up in the weeds with the pan-sexuality movement and political tribes. It never was about that, but we didn't see it. It was always about two words: religious freedom. It was always about the basic civil right—with our Holy Book, from Genesis 1:1 to Revelation 22:21, in hand—to have the fundamental religious freedom to say 'no' to their secular, immoral dictates and retain our citizenship for life, liberty, and the pursuit of happiness."

The gathering votes on the new proposals: the old Orders merge into the New Protestant Order, with a dozen different *styles* of churches based on types of worship and service. The structure of the new Continuum is adopted by all.

Several Continuum members create a new document to specifically lay out the religious-cultural-political positions of the Continuum. The document is called the *Manhattan Doctrine*. The preamble to the new document is the opening of the Old Declaration of Independence.

Kristiana, newly baptized and officially a member of the Amish Order, is a signer on behalf of the Anabaptists as an appointed elder one month before her marriage to the Canadian.

The Secure House, Providence Enclave
10:05 a.m., 5 June 2089

NIS sits with Moses in one of the small conference rooms.

"That reporter Logan was not killed over Project Purify," NIS says. "It was over this *Project New People*. They remoted into his device and accessed the entire text-recorded conversation he had with this District lobbyist from Old Greece. We don't know all the details yet, but it is just one of many black box government projects that Galerius has in place, each one of a higher top secret SCI clearance than the other. They seem to involve quite a number of scientists and involvement in other countries such as Canada, Mexico, and Brazil," NIS says. "The reporter was killed because he stumbled onto this project, or they thought he did. It wasn't about Project Purify or even the Lucifer murder."

"Project New People? What devilish things are they plotting now?" Moses asks.

"Not just Galerius, all of them. The CHINs are secretly in the American real estate market. The Caliphate has been sending agents to various states, especially Michigan. The state is sixty percent Muslim now."

"So everyone is plotting things in the darkness," Moses says. "Then we need to make sure we're done with our secret projects before they're done with theirs."

"That would be very advisable."

The White House Doctor's Office

7:35 a.m., 5 June 2089

The doctor sits back down as the president buttons his shirt.

"Mr. President, you are in perfect health. There's nothing on the bio-scans or blood work. Everything is in order."

The president looks at him and gives him a very forced smile. "Thank you, doctor."

**The Oval Office
2:35 p.m., 5 June 2089**

"We spent so much time cultivating our own informants within their ranks, and not only do they find all of them in a day, it seems they have their own in the government," Wilson says, staring out the window in his chair.

"Sir, we'll find them all," Homeland says.

Wilson swivels around to face them. "Chauncey's Northern Confederacy grows. The Lucifers are out there who knows where, plotting who knows what. Project Purify is shelved again. Why do I feel we lost this battle?"

"We'll get back on track, sir," Homeland says. "You're the president."

President Wilson leans back and says, "I remember all us economists around the table back when I was at the Office of Finance in the '60s. They saw deficits, debt, and decline. I saw, like a shining beacon on a hill, the path to America's rise. You could watch the municipalities all across the nation fall like dominoes, mayors unable to fund their own police forces and begging the District to save them. Someone else got the credit, but I was the one who drafted the whole plan to allow us to federalize all the police in the nation. I realized that any setback or crisis on the local or state level always meant an opportunity for the District, and specifically for the White House. This office is always the center of it all, the heart of the nation. Fiscal irresponsibility allowed us to do what we could never do before: consolidate our national power and shred the old Constitution, long before we were able to do so legally. No one talks about supposed freedoms when you can't eat or you're afraid because you have no police."

"Sir," his advisor starts, "maybe the problem isn't our attempts, but our target. We've been focused all these years on the largest group of the Jew-Christians, thinking that once the largest collapses, all the smaller ones will follow. Let's reverse it. Deal with the smallest ones first. The larger ones may have found all our informants, but the smaller ones haven't."

President Wilson seems distracted. "Who would we task with the mission? The Registrants are gone. The Vampires failed too."

"*Werewolves,*" the president's advisor says.

Wilson looks at him. "Please. There's a Werewolf fake religion too?"

The advisor smiles. "No, sir. They are a platoon of super soldiers we have on the black ops payroll. We've had them in other parts of the world on continuous duty. They're called the Werewolf S.S. The good thing about them is none of them are Jew-Christians—all Pagans."

"Good. Bring them back to the States and get them to work."

Homeland adds, "And sir, we've created a new division—Special Services—to act as the military branch of this office, since the Supreme Senate has taken away your direct control authority over any storm troopers without their consent. The Werewolves will operate under this new division. We will have sole authority."

"Good."

"Also, sir, have you decided to take a more behind-the-scenes role now? It's the best way. It's why you have us. So we can protect you," the advisor says.

President Wilson touches his chest. "Yes, I've decided. You're right. I'll remain in the shadows from now on and focus on resurrecting the administration after all these setbacks."

"Guarantee your fourth presidential term, and beyond," the advisor says.

"The Wilson American Dynasty, sir," Homeland says with a smile.

"Yes, an American empire that lasts forever. No jackals, no vultures, no one will interfere in the vision and resolve of this office to make this entire world our own, keep every American safe. But we must be free of distractions." He looks at them coldly. "I want a *solution of finality* to these Jew-Christians," President Wilson says. "What's that word they have?—Amen."

The Continuum grows in power. The Conspiracy grows in treachery. Thirty-six years until the first attack of World War III.

The AFTER EDEN saga continues in Book Two:

STARS & SCORPIONS

www.afteredenbooks.com